Land and Water Rats

Barbados, with a cry, sprang backward, and the señorita slumped to the deck at the foot of the mast. And Zorro realized in that instant that he had stepped forward too far and had been seen. Sanchez gave a cry and started toward him. The pirates whirled from the rail to look. Barbados saw him.

"'Tis Zorro!" Barbados shrieked. "After him! Fetch him to me alive! An extra share of loot to the man who gets him!"

It was the promise of loot that drove them on. They shrieked and rushed forward. Zorro put the blade of his sword between his teeth and darted up into the rigging. And then began a fight the like of which the pirates never had seen before. Zorro seemed scarcely human. Up the rigging he went like a monkey. He sprang from spar to spar.

Down the ratlines he rushed, down the ropes he slid.

Now and then he clashed with one of the pirates, and always the sword of Zorro darted in and out, and a wounded man was left behind.

"Seize him!" Barbados shrieked. "After him, dogs! Is one man to hold you off forever? Do not slay him! An extra share of loot —"

*Under one cover — **The Further Adventures of Zorro** and two additional adventures by Johnston McCulley, featuring the legendary fighting hidalgo!*

Zorro: The Complete Pulp Adventures *is a six-volume series reprinting Johnston McCulley's original Zorro stories for the first time!*

Zorro®

THE COMPLETE PULP ADVENTURES™ VOL. 2

Johnston McCulley

Featuring

The Further Adventures of Zorro

Illustrated by Ed Coutts

Rich Harvey
Editor & Designer

Ed Coutts, Illustrations
Pages 47, 81, 119, 153

Thanks

Anthony Tollin

Richard P. Hall

Sai Shanker

ISBN-13: 978-1534602007
Retail cover price $19.95

Printed and bound in the United States.
10 9 8 7 6 5 4 3 2 1

Published by Bold Venture Press
www.boldventurepress.com

Contents

ARGOSY ALL-STORY WEEKLY

Johnston McCulley's

Further Adventures of Zoro

In which Douglas Fairbanks will again play the Hero

10¢ PER COPY   MAY 6   BY THE YEAR $4.00

The legend continues — *The Further Adventures of Zorro* was 10,000 words shorter than the original Zorro novel, but it was serialized in *six* issues of *Argosy All-Story Weekly*.   Cover painting by P.J. Monahan.

Alias, Johnston McCulley

by Seth Bailey

I F YOU have ever read stories written by Harrington Strong, John Mack Stone, Walter Pierson or Camden Stuart, you have read works by the author about whom this article is written — Johnston McCulley.

But few authors boast as many as four *nom de plumes*, and few with as many as Johnston McCulley. Some of his best known stories and books are *Broadway Babs*, *The Mark of Zorro*, *The Masked Woman* and *The Black Star*. His most interesting creations were "Thubway Tham" and "Zorro," who have left more laughs and tears in their wake than any other creation by this star of fiction.

"Thubway Tham" was created quite by accident. McCulley was in New York and not getting on any too well when he received a hurry-up call from one of the magazine editors he knew, asking for a story to fill a certain portion of a magazine in a few days. McCulley sat down at his typewriter and whistled. He had everything with which to produce what the magazine editor wanted except the story itself. He had imagination, courage and the willingness to work. So at random he banged at the typewriter keys, grinding out something that had come into his mind

Originally published in the Oakland Tribune, May 20, 1923

only that morning. It was but an incident that had occurred on the subway — a mere nothing at all to anyone else. But it had left a suggestion in McCulley's mind, and his imagination had pounced on it and seized it by the throat. It had been so recent that his mind had not ample time to treat it justly. The seed had been sown but the proper time had not elapsed to allow it to spring into life.

As the typewriter keys recorded the grain of thoughts, pinning them together in a ripping story, there came into the scene from out of nowhere the character of Thubway Tham. There was a strong appeal for more of him, and the next week saw Johnston McCulley wrestling with his latest character. He has since written more than one hundred tales, using the same character, all of which have appeared in magazines.

McCulley created the character of Zorro in *The Curse of Capistrano*. He studied the old Californian mission empire for years, and has written several stories dealing with mission times. Zorro was intended to reflect the spirit of the caballero of the times, and to everyone's satisfaction he did. Douglas Fairbanks made his greatest screen success with Zorro.

One of the interesting things about Johnston McCulley is his source of plots. Most writers have a particular source for their plots, usually from association with the things about which they like best to write. But not so with McCulley. Everything and everywhere is his source. He looks for plots while fishing or motoring, or while digging in the garden. There is nothing prosaic or commonplace in all the world [or a working author]. There's a plot in the peculiar facial expression of the man he meets on the street, or [the lyrics of a] song. Love, hate, greed, revenge, self-sacrifice have a million angles each. "Combine two or three, mix with a few characters, and you have a plot," he says.

McCulley is very successfully married, so successfully married that he calls himself the one-half-of-one-percenter. His other ninety-nine and one-half per cent is also constantly on the alert for suggestions (one-half-of-one-percenter will help the one-half-of-one-percenter in his daily task of writing successfully). His only children are brain children, but they cause him as much combined worry and joy as real ones, he asserts.

Calling at his home, 1939 ½ Argyle Avenue, one might find

Johnston McCulley's novels frequently became the cover stories in popular pulp magazines of the day.

McCulley pounding away at the typewriter, or on the same day a week later he might be working in his garden back of the house, out fishing or motoring. He has not set a schedule for work. In writing long stories, he usually begins work soon after breakfast and works until late at night, with time off for meals. He will often, after finishing one story, putter around in the garden, or do some repair work on his car until 10 o'clock in the morning, or three or four in the afternoon, then sit down and write a new tale, writing until he is tired. Some days he works all day, other days but half a day, and some days not at all. He is subject to loafing spells of several days at a stretch, and sometimes weeks. He dignifies these spells with the title of "slump." Whenever he gets into a "slump," he usually goes fishing till he finds the "slump" wearing off.

Most of his plots are thought out at bedtime, generally just after retiring. He carries the plot over until morning and if it then appears to be as good as he believed it to be the night before, he gets up [and prepares to work].

"What kind of a story is easiest for you to write?" I asked him.

"That in which I am interested myself," he replied, "rather than the one written to fill some editorial request. Swift-moving romance is the easiest, particularly of olden times. Detective and mystery tales are the hardest, though I have written hundreds of them. They are more like work than anything else."

[Writing consumes much of his] time, as possible, when he is not subject to a "slump," at work in his studio, but he does not forget that he owes some of his time to his wife and home. He aims to spend as much time with the other half of the family as he does in his studio.

Fishing is his middle name, be it trout or sea fishing. He has plotted many a tale whipping a stream. Of this recreation, he says:

"If mentally tired, I can get more rest and real pleasure out of fishing than anything else I might do. I don't care much for hunting. I don't get half the kick from firing a gun at a running deer as I get when a trout strikes my fly. Man! That's sport. It takes greater skill to fish than to hunt. Here is a statement that I suppose would cause an argument most anywhere, but that's my way of looking at it."

He is what you might call an auto fiend. Nothing suits him better, and nothing will lure him away from his work quicker, than a long auto trip across the country. When he breaks camp in the morning, he looks at his speedometer, and when he reaches camp at night, his first act is to record the day's mileage. He prides himself in covering a greater distance quicker than someone else can cover it.

If you were to ask him why he doesn't play golf he would give you several legitimate reasons.

"I'm not old enough for golf yet. When I'm eighty perhaps I'll fall for it."

McCulley spent much of his early life in newspaper work — fourteen years, to be exact, in Chicago, Peoria, Columbus, Kansas City, Portland, Seattle, San Diego, Los Angeles and Denver. He travelled the road that many others have travelled, restless, looking for some new environment; then he began to write successfully.

"Do you attribute your success to newspaper training?" I asked him.

"Absolutely," he replied promptly, as though he had reached the

The Blue Streak was a featured novel in *Detective Story Magazine*; *The Curse of Capistrano* was retitled *The Mark of Zorro* in subsequent reprints.

conclusion some time ago. "The newspaper man, if he be a live one, meets all sorts and conditions of persons and learns to analyze men and motives. Thus he learns to create characters and [situations]. He mixes with the saintly and sinful, priest and [prostitute], sees virtue and vice in equal portion. In after years as he writes fiction, he is pretty liable to know what he's talking about. He will make a cop talk a police argot and he won't have a society leader drinking tea out of a saucer. If more motion picture people had been newspaper men we wouldn't see so many laughable breaks in the films."

McCulley was born in Ottawa, Illinois, February 2, 1883, according to his pedigree in *Who's Who*. He sold his first story while a cub reporter. It was a Goldfield yarn, written during the rush there. He sent it to Karl Edward Harriman of the *Red Book*, who immediately bought it. It was not the first one he had written. The first one eventually went into a sewer after it had been returned four times. The Goldfield story was his second. Possessed with new vigor, he wrote six more, and fizzled on all of them. Then he settled down to business. He watched carefully and learned his own faults. He never met an editor personally until he had sold two million words of fiction. This should smash the popular idea that a new writer must have a pull to get into print.

He reads about a dozen books a month by other authors and glances through all the magazines to watch the work of others and to keep tab on the ever changing market, noting changes in policy as indicated to him, changes in the style of stories that are popular, changes regarding length, and so on.

McCulley's advice to aspiring authors is briefly as follows:

"Have a story to write, and be sure you have a story before you commence to write one. That is where the average beginner falls down. The beginner often is inclined to start too slow and never wants to quit when the story is done. You can have a snappy ending and be true to life at the same time."

"Why seek to depress folks who have enough depression in the ordinary routine of their lives? Express contentment and happiness and the might of right without going to extremes and writing stuff of the silly happy life."

"Give the public action. That's what it wants — lots of it. Give them romance, the downfall of ulterior motives and the triumph of right. This can just as easily be done in a murder mystery tale the same as in a story of Biblical times, and in an entertaining manner instead of like a sermon."

"The novice can gain much by reading much. He must get some idea of how others do it — don't copy them, but get into the swing of telling stories the way the public. This swing can best be understood from reading popular stories or books, that have met with instant favor by the public. The [plot and story] is the big feature, but the way it is told is ninety percent of the success of the writer."

"The beginner is going to have many of his manuscripts returned, but that is no reason why he should quit. When a manuscript comes back, it is a sure shot that something is wrong with it. There is some fault in it that caused it to be rejected. He may have written his story properly, or told it properly [or submitted it to] the wrong magazine. But a story properly written and told properly usually draws more consideration than a printed rejection slip. So it pays to dig into it and discover for one's self wherein the trouble lies. After this discovery is made, it is quite an easy matter to correct one's faults."

McCulley was asked who, in his opinion, were the three leading authors of America, to which he replied:

"Booth Tarkington, who mingles realism and romance as none other; Joseph Hergesheimer, the best living imitator of dead and gone Europeans, Joseph C. Lincoln, who digs down to bedrock and comes up with the genuine roots of humor."

Every author whom I've asked that question, to date, has added just one other to the list, and McCulley did not fail in keeping up to standard.

"Those, of course, in addition to myself," he ended.

Certain portions of this article were illegible — usually no more than two or three words in a given section. The editor has inserted words in brackets to attempt short narrative bridges.

*This article was reprinted on **PulpFlakes**, a website/blog devoted to documenting pulp magazines, authors and their stories. Thanks to Sai Shanker for his help.*

The Further Adventures of Zorro

California

When the Spanish Empire encompassed the globe, and young blades were taught the fine and fashionable art of killing ...

CHAPTER 1
Land Rats and Water Rats

THROUGHOUT a long summer day of more than a hundred years ago the high fog had obscured the flaming ball of sun, and the coast of Southern California had been bathed in a haze.

Then came the night, with indication of a drizzle that did not materialize. For the bank of fog suddenly was split as though with a sword, and the brilliant moon poured down, and the riven mist floated away to let the land be blessed with brilliance and the tossing sea dance in the silvery moonbeams.

Approaching the shore came a sinister vessel, craft of ill omen. She sailed slowly under a spare spread of canvas, as though fearing to reach her destination too soon, and her lights were not burning. The hiss of the waters from her bows was a lazy sort of hiss, but the more suggestive because of that. It was the playful hiss of a serpent always ready to become enraged. Her appearance betokened stealth and crime.

She was low, rakish, swift. No proper seaman commanded her, since her decks were foul and her sides badly in need of protecting paint. But her sailing gear was in perfect condition, and the man at her helm could have told that she answered to her rudder like a love-sick maiden to her swain.

Amidships stood her commander, one Barbados, a monstrous giant of a man with repugnant visage. Gigantic brass rings were in his mutilated ears. His eyes were pig-like — tiny, glittering, wholly evil. His great gnarled hands continually were forming themselves into brutish fists. He wore no shirt, no shoes. His chest and back were covered with thick, black, matted hair.

"By the saints!" he swore in a voice that drowned the slush of the waters against the vessel's sides. "Sanchez! Fools and devils! Is it necessary to shout to the world our villainy? Look at that flag flapping against the mast! Three hours after set of sun, and the flag of the devil still flies! Discipline! Ha!"

"The flag!" Sanchez bellowed. There was no definite order given, but the man nearest the mast was quick to lower the flag. Sanchez looked back toward Barbados, and Barbados grunted and turned away to look toward the distant land.

Sanchez was a smaller edition of Barbados, the evil lieutenant of an evil chief. He was short and thick, and many a man had misjudged the strength of his shoulders and arms and had discovered his sorry error too late. The eyes of Sanchez glittered also, first as he looked at Barbados, and then turned, as the chief had, to glance toward the distant land.

A fair land it was, bathed in the mellow light of the moon. Along the shore uncertain shadows played, like shapeless fairies at a game. And here was a darker streak, where a cañon (*archaic spelling of canyon) ran down to the sea — a cañon with black depths caused by the rank undergrowth and stubby trees.

"There!" Barbados bellowed. He pointed toward the mouth of the cañon, where the water hissed white against a jumble of rocks. "We go ashore there, against the cliffs!"

Again there was no regular command, but the course of the pirate craft was changed a little, and she sailed slowly toward the spot Barbados had indicated. The chief grunted once more, and Sanchez hurried quickly to his side.

"We land twoscore men!" Barbados commanded. "Twoscore will be enough. I lead them, and you are to go with me. The others will remain aboard and take the ship off shore again, and return tomorrow night two hours before the dawn."

"Si!" Sanchez said.

"'Tis to be a pretty party, by the saints! Rich loot, food and wines, honey and olives, gold and jewels and precious stones! Bronze native wenches for such as like them! And time enough for it, eh? Ha! For some four months we have sailed up and down the coast, now and then landing and raiding to get a few pigs and cows. 'Tis time for a bold stroke! And this — "

"It is arranged?" Sanchez questioned.

"Am I in the habit of rushing in where things are not arranged?" Barbados demanded. "Señor Pirate, do you take me to be a weak and silly fool?"

"If I did," Sanchez replied, "I would have more wit than to say so to your face!"

"Ha! Is it arranged? When the Governor's own man arranges it? There is, a precious pair, the Governor and his man!" said Barbados, laughing raucously. "Pirates and rogues we may be, but we can take lessons in villainy from some of the gentry who bear the names of caballeros, but have foul blood in their veins!"

"The thing has an evil look," Sanchez was bold enough to assert. "I like not a task too easy. By my naked blade, that which looks easy often is not! If this should prove to be a trap—"

Barbados gave a cry of rage and whirled toward him suddenly, and Sanchez retreated a single step, and his hand dropped to the naked cutlass in his belt of tanned human skin.

"Try to draw it, fool!" Barbados cried. "I'll have you choked black in the face and hurled overboard for shark meat before your hand reaches the blade!"

"I made no move to draw," Sanchez wailed.

"There are times when I wonder why I allow you to remain at my side," Barbados told him, folding his gigantic arms across his hairy chest. "And there are times when I wonder whether your heart is not turning to that of a woman and your blood to water or swill. A trap, you fool! Am I the man to walk into traps? Kindly allow me to attend to the finer details of this business. And a pretty business it is!"

"The village of Reina de Los Angeles is miles in the interior," Sanchez wailed. "I do not like to get out of sight of the sea. With the pitching planks of a deck beneath my bare feet — ”

“Beware lest you have beneath your feet the plank that is walked until a man reaches its end and drops to watery death!” Barbados warned him. “Enough of this! Pick the men who are to land, and get ready the boats!”

An hour later the anchor had been dropped, and the pirate craft had swung with the tide and was tugging at her chains like — a puppy at a leash. Over the sides went the boats, Barbados growling soft curses at the noise his men made.

“We have nothing to fear, fools and devils!” he said. “But there will be no surprise if some converted native sees us and carries to Reina de Los Angeles word of our arrival. There is many a hacienda in these parts where pirates are detested. Silence, rogues! You’ll have your fill of noise tomorrow night!”

Without knowing it, Barbados practiced a deal of psychology. These wild men of the sea had before them a journey of some miles inland, and they knew it and hated it, but the pirate chief continually hinted to them of the rich loot at the end of the present trip, and his hints served their purpose well.

Toward the shore they rowed, tossing on the breakers, making for the dark spot where the cañon ran down into the sea. There a cliff some twelve feet high circled back into the land, forming a natural shelter against the land breeze at times and the sea winds at other times.

Through the surf they splashed, half naked, carrying naught except their weapons, and no weapons save their cutlasses. They gathered on the beach and watched the boats return to the ship, shrieking coarse jests at the men compelled to remain behind.

Barbaros took from his belt a tiny scrap of parchment and looked at it closely. With him this passed for a map He called Sanchez to his side, turned his back to the sea, and looked along the dark reaches of the cañon.

“Forward!” Barbados said. “And let there be little noise about it! If we stumble across one of the accursed natives, slit his throat and so silence it.”

“And if we meet a wandering fray of the missions, slit him into ribbons," Sanchez added, chuckling.

To his wonder, Barbados grasped his arm so that Sanchez thought the bone must break.

"Enough of that" Barbados cried. "Touch no fray in violence except I give the word!"

"You love the robes and gowns?" Sanchez asked, in wonder.

"I love to protect myself," Barbados replied. "It is an ill thing to assault a fray if it can be avoided." He stopped speaking for a moment, and seemed to shiver throughout the length and breadth of his gigantic frame. "I had a friend once who struck a fray," he added in a whisper. "I do not like to remember what happened to him. Forward!"

Inland they tramped, mile after mile, keeping to the cañons, following an arroyo now and then, dodging from dark spot to dark spot, while Barbados growled curses at the bright moon and Sanchez continually admonished the men behind to keep silent.

It was a journey they disliked, but they liked to think of the loot they would find at the end of it. On they went, toward the sleeping town of Reina de Los Angeles. Besides Barbados and Sanchez, few of them had seen the town. Pirates had been treated harshly there when they had wandered inland. But now something had happened, it appeared, that made a raid on the town a comparatively safe enterprise.

An hour before dawn they stumbled across a native, caught him as he started to flee, and left his lifeless body behind. Then came the day, and they went into hiding in a jumble of hills, within easy striking distance of the town. They had covered ground well.

Sprawled on the sward they slept. Barbados, a little way aside, consulted his poor map once more, and then called Sanchez to his side.

"Since we may have to split our force, it were well that you knew more of this business," he said.

"I am listening, Barbados."

"This man who is to meet us tomorrow night at the edge of the town is a high official,"

"I have heard you call him the Governor's man."

"Even so. He is to have matters arranged so that the town will be at our mercy. It never has been raided properly. It will be necessary, perhaps, to steal horses, and possibly a carreta or two in which to carry the loot. The town will be wide open for us, my friend."

"There is a presidio in Reina de Los Angeles, and where there is a presidio there are soldiers," Sanchez reminded him.

"And where there are soldiers there are fools," Barbados added. He stopped speaking long enough to chuckle. "I am not afraid of the soldiers. This man with whom we are to deal will care for the troops."

"I fail to understand it," Sanchez said, shaking his head. "Why should such things be? Do we split the loot with this high official?"

"Dream of innocence, listen!" Barbados hissed. "Listen, and comprehend, else I choke you to death! An emissary came to me in the south from this high official, and through him arrangements were made. Things have happened since last we were in the vicinity of Reina de Los Angeles. The Governor, I know, left San Francisco de Asis and journeyed south with his gallant company. And while he was at Reina de Los Angeles something happened that caused him to hate the town. There even was talk for a time of him being forced to abdicate his high station."

"Ha! More mystery!" Sanchez growled.

"It seems that in the southland there was a pest of a highwayman known as Señor Zorro, and whom men called the Curse of Capistrano. A land pirate, spit upon him! How can a man be a pirate on the land? However, this Señor Zoro did several things worthy of note. From what I have heard, I would we had a dozen of him in the ship's company. We could raid the whole of Mexico, capture the Spanish fleets and attack Europe."

"This Señor Zorro must be quite some man," Sanchez observed.

"I have heard but little, but enough to convince me that I would have him for a friend rather than an enemy. He is a sort of devil. Now he is here and now he is gone. Like a ghost he comes and like a specter he disappears. Ha! You, a pirate, cross yourself!"

"I am afraid of no live man who lives, save perhaps yourself," Sanchez observed. "But I like not this talk of ghosts."

"Here is the jest, fool and friend! It develops after a time that this terrible Señor Zorro is nothing but a caballero out to have a bit of fun

and protect the weak. There is a waste of time for you — protecting the weak. And other sundry caballeros joined hands with him and punished minor officials who sought to steal and deal crookedly. That is right and proper. If a thief, be a thief! If a pirate, be a pirate! But do not play at being an honest man and try to be thief and pirate at the same time.'"

"Ha!" Sanchez grunted, meaning that he wished the sermon to end and the tale to continue.

"This Señor Zorro, whose real name I have forgotten if ever I knew it, carved his initial with his sword into the cheeks and foreheads of many men. They call it the Mark of Zorro. And when his identity was disclosed his friends stood by him and told the Governor that it were best if he return to San Francisco de Asis and grace Reina de Los Angeles with his continual absence."

"And did he?"

"He did," Barbados replied, "with hatred in his heart for this same Reina de Los Angeles. He did not abdicate, of course. And he craves revenge."

"Ha! Here is where we enter?"

"It is," Barbados replied. "'We raid the town and take what we will, and the Governor hears of it, sends soldiers running wildly up and down the coast, and winks at himself in his looking-glass. For the information and protection we get, we hand to the governor's man at a certain time and place a certain share of the loot. Which we well can afford, since we are to get it so easily."

"If we forget to hand it — " Sanchez began.

"Friend and fool! By the saints! Are you an honest pirate or no? We shall deal fairly. Think of the future. It is not only Reina de Los Angeles. There is San Juan Capistrano, and rich San Diego de Alcala to come after. By that time we have this pretty Governor and certain of his officials in our mesh, and do as we will. Ha! What knaves! I would rather be an honest pirate — than a politician any day!"

The day passed and the dusk came. And once yet again Barbados indulged in curses. For it was a beautiful moonlight night, half as light as the day that had just died, and a man could be seen afar. But Barbados led his wretched company on toward the town, and after a time they came to the crest of a slope and saw lights twinkling in the distance.

Stretched on the ground so as not to form a silhouette against the sky, Barbados looked over the scene. He could see the plaza, tires burning before the huts of the natives, twinkling lights in the windows of the pretentious houses where lived the men of wealth and blood and rank. To one side was the presidio, and to the other the church.

Barbados grunted an order to Sanchez and crept forward alone. He approached the end of the village, reached a spot where the shadows were deep, and crouched to wait.

For half an hour he waited, grumbling his impatience. Then there came to him a figure. muffled in a long cloak. Barbados hissed a word that had been agreed upon. The figure stepped quickly to his side.

"You are ready?"

"Ready, señor," Barbados replied.

"Where are your men?"

"In hiding three hundred yards away, señor."

"It were best to strike in about an hour. The soldiers will be sent toward the south on a wild goose chase."

"I understand, señor."

"I ride back toward the hills to a hacienda to pay a social call. It would not do for me to be here, of course."

"Certainly not, señor."

"The way will be open to you. Take your will with the town, but do not use the torch, except it be on the hut of some native. As soon as you have your loot, make for the sea again. The soldiers will be sent on a useless trail."

"It is well arranged, señor. We'll strike as soon as the troopers are at a sufficient distance."

"There is something else. You must send a few men of your force to the hacienda of Don Carlos Pulido, three miles to the north."

"What is this, señor?" Barbados asked.

"A little matter of abducting a woman for me."

"Ha!"

"The Señorita Lolita Pulido, understand. She is to be seized and conducted to the coast and taken aboard ship. She is not to be harmed, but treated with every respect. In four or five days I shall meet you at the rendezvous on the southern coast, and claim her as my share of the loot. Do this well, and that is all the share of loot I ask this time."

"A mere detail," Barbados said.

"If the hacienda is disturbed a bit during the abduction, it will not cause the heartbreak of the Governor. This Don Carlos Pulido is no friend of His Excellency."

"I understand, señor."

"The señorita expects to become the bride tomorrow of Don Diego Vega — curse him! That large house at the side of the plaza is his. When you are raiding the town, Barbados, pay special attention to that house. And should he get a knifesd between his ribs there will be no sorrow on my part."

"I begin to comprehend," Barbados replied.

"I may depend upon you?"

"Si, señor! We attend to the house of this Don Diego Vega and to the don personally. I shall send a small force to abduct the girl and take her to the shore. She will be waiting for you at the rendezvous to the south."

"Good! Watch when the soldiers ride away, and strike an hour later. Adios!"

The cloak dropped for a moment as the man from the village straightened himself. Barbados got a good look at his face as the moonlight struck it. He gasped.

"Your forehead!" he said.

"It is nothing. That cursed beast of a Zorro put it there!"

Barbados looked again. On the man's forehead was a ragged Z, put there in a manner that it would remain forever. There was a moment of silence, and then Barbados found himself alone. The other had slipped away through the shadows.

Barbados grinned. "Here is a double deal of some sort, but it need bring me no fear," he mused. "Here would be startling news for all men to know. Wants to steal a girl now, does he? For his share of proper loot I'd steal him half a score of girls!"

He grinned again and started back toward his men. Barbados did not fear the soldiers, and he knew they would be sent away. He could be sure of that. For the conspirator who had come to him out of the dark was none other than Captain Ramón, commandante of the presidio at Reina de Los Angeles.

CHAPTER 2
Pedro the Boaster

SERGEANT PEDRO GONZALES, a giant of a wine-guzzling soldier whose heart was as large as his capacity for liquor, was known as "Pedro the Boaster." When there were military duties to be done he was to be found at his post in the presidio, but at other times one found him at the village posada, sitting before the big fireplace and remaking the world with words.

On this moonlight night, Sergeant Pedro Gonzales crossed the plaza with a corporal and a couple of soldier, entered the inn, and called in a loud voice for the landlord to fetch wine and be quick about it. The sergeant had learned long since that the fat landlord held him in terror, and did he but act surly and displeased he received excellent service.

"Landlord, you are as fat as your wine is thin!" Sergeant Pedro declared, sprawling at one of the tables. "I have a suspicion now and then that you keep a special wineskin for me, and mix water with my drink."

"Señor!" the landlord protested.

"We honest soldiers are stationed here to protect you from liars and thieves and dishonest travelers up and down El Camino Real, and you treat us like the dirt beneath your boots."

"Señor! I have the greatest respect — "

"One of these fine days," Gonzales interrupted, "there will be trouble. Some gentleman of the highway will approach you with an idea of robbery, and you'll shriek for the soldiery. And then, fat one, I may remember the watered wine, and be busy elsewhere!"

"But I protest — " the landlord began.

"More wine!" the sergeant shouted. "Must I get out my blade and carve your wineskins — or your own skin? More wine of the best, and you'll get your pay when I get mine, if it is an honest score you keep. If my friend, Don Diego Vega, was here — !"

"That same friend of yours makes merry a little later in the evening," the landlord said, as he went to fill the wine cups. "Tomorrow he is to take a bride."

"Pig, do you suppose I do not know it?" Gonzales screeched. "Think you that I have been asleep these past few months? Was I not in the thick of it when Don Diego Vega played at being Señor Zorro?"

"You were in the thick of it," the corporal admitted, with a touch of sarcasm in his voice.

"Ha!" cried the sergeant. "There was a turbulent time for you! Here in this very room I fought him, blade to blade, thinking that he was some stinking highwayman. And just as I was getting the better of it — "

"How is this?" the corporal shrieked.

"Just as I was getting the better of the blade match," Gonzales reaffirmed, glaring at the corporal, "back he went and dashed through the door! And thereafter he set the town about its own ears for some time to come."

"It occurs to me that I saw that fight," the corporal declared. "If you were getting the best of it at any stage, then were mine eyes at fault."

"I know a man," said the sergeant, darkly, "who will do extra guard duty for a score of days."

"Ha!" the corporal grunted. "You do not like plain speech!"

"I do not like a soldier to make mock of his superiors," the sergeant replied. "It were unseemly for me to make remarks, for instance, concerning our commandante, Captain Ramón, but let it be said that he fought this Señor Zorro, too. And Captain Ramón wears on his forehead Zorro's mark. You will notice that there is no carved Z on my face!"

"Ha!' the corporal grunted again. "It were best, sergeant, to voice such remarks inwardly. The commandante is not proud of the mark he wears."

Gonzales changed the subject. "The wine!" he thundered. "It goes well on a moonlight night, the same as on a stormy one. But moonlight is a poor business save for lovesick swains. 'Tis no night for a soldier. Would one expect thieves to descend through the moonlight?"

"There be pirates," the corporal said.

"Pirates!" Gonzales's great fist descended and met the table with a crash, sending the wine cups bouncing. "Pirates! You have noticed no pirates in Reina de Los Angeles, have you? They have not been playing around the presidio, have they? I am not saying that they know I am stationed here, however — Meal mush and goat's milk! Pirates is my dish!"

"The town grows wealthy, and they may come," the corporal said.

"You fear? You tremble?" Gonzales tried. "Are you soldier or fray? Pirates! By the saints, I would that they came! My sword arm grows fat from little use."

"Talk not of pirates!" the landlord begged. "Suppose they did come?"

"And what if they did?" Gonzales demanded. "Am I not here, dolt? Are there not soldiers? Pirates? Ha!"

He sprang to his feet, those same feet spread wide apart. His hand darted down, and he whipped out his blade.

"That for a pirate!" he shouted, and made a mighty thrust at the wall. "This for a pirate!" And he slashed through the air, his blade whistling so that the corporal and soldiers sprang backward, and the four or five natives who happened to be in the inn cringed in a corner. "Pirates!" cried Gonzales. "I would I could meet one this very night! We grow stale from inaction. There is too much peace in the world! Meal mush and goat's milk!"

The door opened suddenly. Sergeant Gonzales stopped in the middle of a sentence, and his blade stopped in the middle of an arc. And then the sergeant and the other soldiers snapped to attention, for the commandant was before them.

"Sergeant Gonzales!" Captain Ramón commanded.

"Si!"

"I could hear you shouting half way across the plaza. If you wish to meet a pirate, perhaps you may have your wish. Rumors have been brought by natives. Mount your men and proceed along El Camino Real toward the south. Search the country well, once you are four or five miles from the town. It is a bright moonlight night, and men may be seen at a great distance."

"It is an order!" the sergeant admitted.

"Leave but one man at the presidio as guard. Return before dawn. Have my best horse made ready, as I ride out to a hacienda for a visit. Go!"

"Si!" Sergeant Gonzales grunted. He motioned to the soldiers, and they hurried through the door. He sheathed his sword, and when the back of Captain Ramón was turned for an instant he tossed off the wine that had been before him, and hurried after his men. The commandante drew off his gloves and sat at one of the tables.

Gonzales led the way across the plaza and toward the presidio. He was growling low down in his throat.

"This is a fine state of affairs!" he said. "Ride all night and kick up the dust! Back before, dawn with nothing done!"

"But you wanted pirates," the corporal protested.

"Think you they will stand in the middle of El Camino Real and await our pleasure?" Gonzales growled. "What pirate would be abroad a night like this? Could we but meet some — ha! There is a special reward for pirates!"

Even before they had reached the entrance of the presidio, he began shouting his orders. Torches flared, and men ran to prepare the horses. Fifteen minutes later, with Gonzales at their head, they rode across the plaza and out upon El Camino Real, their mounts snorting, their sabers rattling.

From the crest of a slope a few hundred yards away, Barbados and his evil crew watched them depart upon their mounts.

CHAPTER 3
Sudden Turmoil

WHILE the blushes played across her cheeks, Señorita Lolita Pulido sat at one end of the big table in the great living-room of her father's house and watched the final preparations for her wedding.

Don Carlos, her gray-haired father, watched proudly from the foot of the table. Doña Catalina, her mother, walked majestically around the room and gave soft commands. Native servants scurried like rats in and out of the great room, carrying bundles of silks and satins, gowns, intimate garments.

"Tomorrow!" Don Carlos sighed, and in the sign was that which spoke of cruelties bravely borne. "Tomorrow, señorita, you become the bride of Don Diego Vega, and the first lady of Reina de Los Angeles. And my troubles, let us hope, are at an end."

"Let us hope so," said Doña Catalina.

"The Governor himself dare not raise his hand against the father-in-law of Don Diego Vega. My fortunes will increase again. And you, daughter of my heart, will be a great lady, with wealth at your command."

"And love also," the little señorita said, bowing her head.

"Love, also!" said Doña Catalina.

"Ha!" Don Carlos cried, with a gale of laughter. "It is love now, is it? And when first Don Diego came wooing, the girl would have none of him, even to better the family fortunes. He was dull, he yawned, and she wanted a man of hot blood and romantic. But when it was learned that he was Señor Zorro — that made a difference! Love, also! It is well!"

Señorita Lolita blushed again, and fumbled at a soft garment upon her lap. There came a pounding at the door, and one of the servants opened it. Don Carlos glanced up to find a man of the village there.

"It is a message, señor," he said.

"From whom?" Don Carlos asked.

"From Don Diego Vega, to the little señorita."

Señorita Lolita dimpled, and her black eyes flashed as she bent over the heap of garments again. Don Carlos stood up and stalked majestically toward the door.

"I take the message," he said, and he took it, and handed it to Doña Catalina, that she might read it first. "Don Diego Vega is not wed to my daughter as yet. It is not proper that he send her sealed messages."

His eyes were twinkling as he turned away. Señorita Lolita pouted and pretended indifference, and Doña Catalina, her mother, unfolded the message, and read it with a smile upon her lips.

"It is harmless," she announced.

Señorita Lolita looked up, and took the message from her mother's hand. Don Diego Vega, it appeared, wasted no words. His message was read swiftly:

This man has orders to make a record carrying this greeting of love to you and fetching yours in return.

Thine, Diego.

"Ha!" Don Carlos shouted. "Economy is a great thing, but not in words when there is love to be spoken. You should have seen the messages I sent to Catalina in the old days!"

"Carlos!" Doña Catalina warned.

"And paid a native wench royally to slip them to her," Don Carlos continued, shamelessly. "Behind the back of her duenna! Page after page, and every, word a labor! I could fight better than I could write!"

"Perhaps so can Don Diego," the little señorita said.

"Staunch and loyal to him, are you?" Don Carlos roared. "That is proper. Pen your reply, my daughter, and let this man establish his record for the return trip to Reina de Los Angeles. Do not keep Don Diego waiting."

The señorita blushed yet again, got up, and swept into a room adjoining.

Don Carlos addressed the messenger: "How are things in the town?"

"Don Diego entertains his caballero friends at a last bachelor supper, señor," the man replied.

"Ha! Young men only, I suppose?" Si, señor!"

"Wine flows, I take it, and the table is piled high with rich food?"

"Si, señor!"

"Ah, well! I shall have my turn tomorrow at the marriage feast," Don Carlos said. "My regards to Don Diego Vega!"

"They shall be given him, señor."

The señorita returned and handed what she had written to her mother, who perused it and sealed it, and handed it to the messenger in turn. The man bobbed his head in respectful salute, and hurried out. A native servant closed the door behind him — but neglected to drop the heavy bar in place. Because of the unusual excitement, none noticed.

Don Carlos resumed his position at the foot of the table. This was a great night for him, and tomorrow would be a great day. He was happy because his fortunes were on the mend, because the Governor had been forced to cease his persecutions. But he was happy also because his daughter was to have happiness.

Don Carlos and his wife had lavished upon this, their only child, love enough for a dozen. And now both glanced at her as she fumbled at a silken shawl. Her black eyes were sparkling again, though dreams were glistening in them. Her cheeks were delicately flushed. Her dainty hands played with the silks. One tiny tip of a boot peeped from beneath her voluminous skirts. A bride of whom any man could honestly be proud, Don Carlos thought, and with proper blood in her veins and proper thoughts in her head.

"So Don Diego makes merry tonight with his young friends!" Don Carlos said. "I would like to peer in upon him now."

Could he have done so, he would have seen a merry gathering. In the big living room of Don Diego's town casa a huge table had been spread. Don Diego sat at the head, of it, dressed in fastidious garments, and caballeros were grouped around it. Richly dressed they were, with blades at their sides, blades with jeweled hilts, but serviceable weapons for all that. Wine cups and dishes were before them. They feasted, and they drank. They toasted Don Diego, and the Señorita Lolita, Don Diego's father, and the señorita's father, and one another.

"Another good man gone wrong!" cried Don Audre Ruiz. He sat at Don Diego's right hand, because he was Don Diego's closest friend. "Here is our comrade Don Diego, about to turn into a family man!" he continued. "This scion of Old Spain, this delicate morsel of caballero blood to be gobbled up by the monster of matrimony! It is time to weep!"

"Into your wine cup" Don Diego added.

"Ha!" Don Audre Ruiz cried. "But a few days ago, it seems, we rode after him as though he had been the devil, rode hard upon his heels, thinking that we were following some sort of renegade caballero playing at highwayman. Señor Zorro, by the. saints! We shouted praises of him because for a time he took us out of our monotony. Then came the unmasking, and we found that Don Diego and Señor Zorro were one and the same!"

He ceased speaking long enough to empty his wine cup and make certain that a servant refilled it.

"Señor Zorro!" he continued. "Those were happy moments! And now he is to turn husband, and no more riding abroad with sword in hand. We shall die of monotony, Diego, my friend!"

"Of fat!" Don Diego corrected.

"What has become of the wild blood that coursed your veins for a few moons?" Don Audre Ruiz, demanded. "Where are those precious, turbulent drops that were in Zorro!"

"They linger," Don Diego declared.

It needs but the cause to churn them into active being."

"Ha! A cause! Caballeros, let us find him a cause, that this good friend of ours will be too busy to get married."

"One moment!" Don Diego cried. He stood up and smiled at them, gave a little twitch to his shoulders, and then turned his back upon the brilliant company and hurried from the room. They drank again and waited. And after a time, back he came, a silk-draped bundle beneath one arm.

"What mystery is this?" Don Audre demanded. He sprawled back in his chair and prepared to laugh. It was said of Don Audre that he always was prepared to laugh. He laughed when he made love, when he fought, as he ate and drank, his bubbling spirit always upon his lips.

"Here is no mystery," Don Diego Vega declared. He smiled at them again, unwrapped what he held, and suddenly exhibited a sword. "The blade of Zorro!" he cried.

There was an instant of silence, and then every caballero sprang to his feet. Their own swords came flashing from their scabbards, flashed on high, reflected in a million rays the glowing lights of the candelabra.

"Zorro" they shouted. "Zorro!"

"Good old blade!" Don Diego said, a whimsical smile playing about his lips.

"Good old point!" exclaimed Don Audre Ruiz. "With it you marked many a scoundrel with your mark, notably and especially one Captain Ramón. Why do we endure his presence here in Reina de Los Angeles? Why not force the Governor to send him north?"

"Let us not mar a perfect evening with thoughts of him," Don Diego begged. "Caballeros, I have brought this blade before you for a purpose. We have drunk toasts to everything of which we could think, and there still remains an abundance of rare wine that has not been guzzled. A toast to the sword of Zorro!"

"Ha! A happy thought! " Don Audre Ruiz cried. "Caballeros, a toast to the sword of Zorro!"

They drank it, put down their golden. goblets, and sighed. They glanced at one another, each thinking of the days when Señor Zorro had ruled El Camino Real for a time. And then they dropped into their chairs once more, and Don Diego Vega sat down also, the sword on the table before him.

"It was a great game," he said, and sighed himself. "But it is in the past. Now I shall be a man of peace and quiet."

"That remains to be seen," Don Audre declared. "There may be domestic warfare, you know. A man takes a terrible chance when he weds."

"Nothing but peace and quiet," Don Diego responded. "The sword of Zorro is but a relic. Years from now I may look upon it and smile. It has served its purpose."

He yawned.

"By the saints!" Don Audre Ruiz breathed. "Did you see him? He yawned! While yet the word 'Zorro' was upon his lips, he yawned. And this is the man who defended persecuted priests and natives, defied the soldiery and made the Governor do a dance! 'Tis a cause he wants and needs, something to change him into Zorro again!"

"Tomorrow I become a husband," Don Diego answered him, yawning yet once more and fumbling with a handkerchief. "By the way, señores, have you ever seen this one?"

He spread the handkerchief over the wine goblet before him, and as the caballeros bent forward to watch, smiles upon their faces, he passed one hand rapidly back and forth across the covered goblet with such rapidity that it was hidden almost all the time, and with the other hand he reached beneath the edge of the handkerchief and jerked the goblet away, letting it drop to the floor. The handkerchief collapsed on the table. Don Diego waved a hand languidly.

"See? It is gone!" he breathed.

"Bah!" Don Audre cried as the others laughed. "At your boy's tricks, again, are you? Where is your wild blood now?"

"I am done with roistering and adventure."

"A man never knows when his words may be hurled back at him and cause him to look foolish," said Don Andre. "It is foolish to take everything for granted. For instance — "

He stopped. The sounds of a tumult had reached their ears. For a moment they, were silent, listening. Shouts, oaths, the sounds of blows, the clashing of blades.

"What in the name of the saints is that?" Don Diego asked.

A trembling servant answered him.

"There are men fighting over by the inn, señor," he said. "I heard someone shout of pirates!"

Chapter 4
Fray Felipe Makes a Vow

BARBADOS continued to mutter curses as he watched the sky. Not a cloud marred its face, and the moon was at the full. But here was an enterprise where there was small risk, so he could discount the bright night.

He grunted his pleasure as he saw Sergeant Gonzales and the troopers ride away from the presidio, cross the plaza, and continue toward the south. He called Sanchez to him and explained what was to be done at the hacienda of Don Carlos Pulido.

You will take half a dozen men," Barbados commanded. "Do as you please at the place, but capture the señorita by all means, and go quickly back over the hills to the mouth of the cañon. Steal horses, and ride. Get there before the break of day! We shall do the same. The ship will be putting in at dawn or before."

"Si!" Sanchez replied. "And do you care for my share of the loot here. There may be small profit at the hacienda!"

Sanchez selected his ruffians and led them away around a hill and toward the north, where the hacienda of Don Carlos Pulido rested. Barbados whispered instructions to the remainder of the crew. And then they waited, for Barbados wished to make sure that the soldiers did not return.

For more than an hour longer he waited, and then gave the word.

Down from the crest of the slope they slipped, breathing heavily, lusting for illegal gain, holding their cutlasses in readiness for instant use. They kept in the scant shadows as much as possible — scattered as they crossed the wider light spaces, made their way slowly to the edge of the town.

There, in the shadows cast by an empty adobe building, they separated, and Barbados whispered his final instructions. They were to look for rich loot, and nothing bulky. He had decided against food and wine, bolts of cloth, casks of olives and jars of honey. Such things could be obtained later at any hacienda. Just now he wished to get portable valuables and hurry back to the coast.

Men were detailed to seize horses and have them in readiness. Certain large houses were to be attacked in force after the smaller ones had been disposed of. The inn was to receive special attention, since it was whispered that the fat landlord had hidden wealth.

Down upon the town they crept, and suddenly they charged into the plaza from either side. Into the inn they poured, cutting and slashing at natives until they fled screeching with terror, stabbng at the fat landlord as he called upon the saints.

They took what the landlord had, and gave their attention to the houses and shops. And now bedlam broke loose as it was realized what was taking place. Doors were smashed, terrified men and women were driven from room to room. Things of value were seized. Jewels were ripped from dainty throats and delicate fingers. Silken shawls were torn from beautiful shoulders.

Here and there a man gave fight, but not for long. The pirates outnumbered the citizens, because they traveled in force and the citizens were scattered. Shrieks and screeches and cries stabbed the air. Raucous oaths and fiendish laughter rang across the plaza. And above the din roared the voice of Barbados, the human fiend, as he ordered his men, commanded them, admonished them, led them to an easy victory.

It was quick work, because the descent had been so unexpected. It might have continued throughout the night, until the town was stripped bare, until not a native's hut was left standing. But Barbados wanted quick loot and a get-away. He wanted to reach the coast during the bright moonlight, get the planks of the ship's deck beneath his feet once more. He trusted Captain Ramón, but he feared that the soldiers might return.

Across the plaza the pirates charged, with Barbados at their head. They broke into the church. They filled the sacred edifice with oaths and ribald jest and raucous laughter. They darted here and there, torches held high above their heads, searching for articles of worth.

From a little room to one side stepped a fray. His hair was silver, his face was calm. Erect and purposeful. he stood, looking across at them. Quick steps forward he took toward the altar, where there were relics he loved.

"What do you here, señores?" he demanded.

His voice seemed soft, yet at the same time there was the ring of steel in it. They stopped, their shouting ceased, there was a moment of silence.

"Who are you?" one shouted.

"I am called Fray Felipe, señores," came the response. "Just now I am in charge of this house of worship. How is it that you so far forget yourselves as to bring your tumult here?"

"Fray?" one shouted. "Fool and fray? Why do we bring our tumult here? For to get loot, gowned one!"

"Loot?" Fray Felipe thundered, taking another step forward. "You would profane this house? You would lay sacriligeous hands on what is to be found here, even as you have voiced sacriligeous tones within these walls? Scum of the earth, begone!"

They surged toward him. "One side, fray!" shouted a foremost one. "Respect the black flag and we respect your gown!"

"Spawn of hell! Sons of the devil!" Fray Felipe thundered. "Back to the door, and out of this holy place!"

He scarcely hoped to stop them. There were rich ornaments on the altar, and in the uncertain light the torches shed he could see the eyes of those nearest glittering. And the gem-studded goblet was there!

Thought of the gem-studded goblet gave new strength to ancient Fray Felipe. It was a relic highly prized. Fray Felipe loved it, and cared for it tenderly. There was a legend connected with it. Once it had been touched by a saint's lips, men had said. To have this scum as much as touch the sacred goblet was too much — to have them steal it would be unthinkable.

Once more they surged forward, and Fray Felipe sprang before the altar and threw up his hands in a gesture of command.

"Back!" he cried. "Would you damn beyond recovery your immortal souls? Would you commit the unpardonable sin?"

"Ha!" shouted a man in the front of the throng. "Worry not about our souls, fray! One side, else you'll have a chance to worry about the state of your own! We have scant time to spend on a fray!"

"What would you?" Fray Felipe asked.

"Loot, fool of a fray!"

"Only over my dead body do you take it! I am not afraid to die to protect holy things! But you — you will fear to die, if you do this thing!"

"Slit his throat!" cried one in the throng.

"Are we here to argue? The work is not done!"

Once more they surged forward. The light of the torches sent rays of fire shooting from the ornaments on the altar. Their lust for loot consumed them.

Fray Felipe braced himself, seized the nearest, raised him half from the floor, and hurled him back against his fellows.

"The fray shows fight!" one cried. "Use your knives, you in the front! A stab between the ribs, and let us go!"

Again they rushed, and Fray Felipe prepared for one more feeble attempt, the one he deemed would be the last. He made the sign of the cross and waited calmly, waited until they were upon him, until he could feel their hot breathing upon his face, until the stench of their perspiration was in his nostrils.

But, even as a man raised a cutlass to strike, there came an interruption. The bellowing voice of Barbados rang out above the din.

"Stop!" he shrieked. There was something terrifying in the sudden and unexpected command. The pirates stopped, fell back. Barbados charged through them and to Fray Felipe's side. The pirate's face showed white in the light of the torches.

"Back!" he commanded. "This fray is not to be harmed! Out, fools and devils! There is one rich house yet to be robbed. Let us not tarry here!"

"There is loot — " one began.

He did not complete the sentence. Barbados whirled, and with, a single blow he stretched him senseless.

"Out!" he commanded. "This fray is not to be touched!"

They backed away from him, rushed back to gather near the door. They did not pretend to understand this, but Barbados was chief, and perhaps he knew what he was doing. They saw him turn, knew that he spoke to the fray, but could not make out his words.

"I had no doing in this," Barbados said. "I assault no fray nor priest! I stopped them in time. Had I not remained outside a moment to watch affairs I would have stopped them before."

"You are not wholly bad," Fray Felipe said.

"I am wholly bad, fray — make no mistake about it! But I keep my hands off frailes and priests!"

He whirled around and rushed to the door, shrieking at his men. Only the soft light of the candles glowed in the church.

Fray Felipe took a step forward and looked after them. He turned back toward the altar, a look of thankfulness in his face.

And suddenly that look changed! Misery took its place. Fray Felipe gave a little cry of mingled surprise and pain, and tottered forward. The precious gem-studded goblet was gone!

He sensed at once how it had happened. When they had charged upon him, before Barbados came, one of the pirates had snatched the goblet away.

Fray Felipe whirled toward the door again, took half a dozen steps, seemed at the point of rushing after them. But he knew they were on the other side of the plaza now, and that an appeal to them would be useless. However, he could try.

He faced the altar again, and the expression of his old countenance was wonderful to see. And then and there Fray Felipe took a vow.

"I go!" he said. "I return with the saintly goblet, or do not return at all!"

CHAPTER 5
Zorro Takes the Trail

BARBADOS had saved the casa of Don Diego Vega for the last. He had kept an eye upon it, however, while his men were looting the town, but had seen nothing to indicate danger from that quarter. And now he remembered Captain Ramón's commands, and it pleased him to carry them out.

Don Diego's was the finest house in the village, and seemed to promise rich loot. Barbados placed four of his men outside to guard against the unexpected return of the soldiers, and led the remainder straight to the front door.

They hesitated there for a moment, gathered closely together, then Barbados gave the word, and they rushed through the door and hurled themselves inside, to go sprawling over the rich rugs and carpets and stop in astonishment and confusion. Barbados swore a great oath as he strove to maintain his balance.

Before them was a wonderful room lavishly furnished. To one side was a wide stairway that led to the upper regions of the house, and priceless tapestries were hanging from a mezzanine. But what engaged the attention of Barbados and his crew the most was the big table in the middle of the room and some score of richly dressed caballeros sitting around it.

Here was the unexpected, which Barbados always feared. He came to a stop, thrust forward his head, and his little eyes began glittering. The soldiers were gone from the town, but here were a score of, young caballeros who were fully as good as soldiers in a fight, and who loved fighting. Barbados had seen such young blades handle swords and rapiers before.

The entrance of the pirates had followed closely upon the announcement of their presence in the town to Don Diego by the servant. And when they tumbled through the door, showing their evil faces in the strong light, the caballeros struggled to get to their feet, reaching for their blades, the smiles swept from their faces and expressions of grim determination showing there instead. But the calm voice of Don Diego quieted them.

"Ha!" Don Diego said. "What have we here? Señores, it is the night before my wedding, and most persons are welcome to partake of my hospitality. But this happens to be a select gathering of my close friends, and I really cannot remember of having sent you invitations — "

"Have done!" Barbados bellowed, his voice ringing with a courage he scarcely felt. "Have done, fashionable fop! We are men who sail under the black flag, terrible alike on land and sea!"

Don Diego Vega threw back his head and laughed lightly.

"Did you hear that, Audre, my friend?" he asked Ruiz. "This fellow says that he and his comrades are terrible alike on land and sea."

Don Audre entered into the spirit of the occasion, as he always did. "Diego, I did not know that you were such a wit," he said. "Have you hired these fellows to come here and give us a fright? Ha! It is a merry jest, one that I'll remember to my last day! For a moment I was ready to draw blade."

"Jest, is it?" Barbados cried, lurching forward almost to the foot of the table. "Twill be considered no jest when we have stripped you of your jewels and plaything swords and this house of what valuables it contains! Back up against that wall, señores, and the man who makes a rash move will not live to make another!"

"I have made a multitude of rash moves, and I still live," Don Audre Ruiz told him. "Diego, it is indeed an excellent jest! I give you my thanks!"

"Pirates!" Don Diego said, laughing again. "In reality, I did not hire them to come here and furnish us with this entertainment. But since they have been so kind, it is no more than right that I pay them!" He sprang to his feet, bent forward with his hands upon the table, and glared down the length of it at Barbados. " You are the chief bull pirate?" he asked.

"I am the king of the crew!" Barbados replied. "Back against that wall, you and your friends!"

Don Diego Vega laughed lightly again. And then the laughter fled his face, and his eyes narrowed and seemed to send forth flakes of steel.

"Si! You must be paid!" he said. "But there are many ways of making payment!"

The sword of Señor Zorro was beneath his hands. And suddenly it was out of its scabbard, and he had sprung upon the table and had dashed down the full length of it, scattering goblets and plates, drink and food.

Off the other end he sprang, and struck the floor a few feet in front of Barbados, who had recoiled and was struggling to get his cutlass out of his belt. The sword of Zorro flashed through the air, describing a gleaming arc.

"Pirate, eh?" Don Diego Vega cried. "You have come to collect riches, have you, Señor Pirate?"

"What is to prevent?" Barbados sneered. "You and your pretty toy of a sword?"

"Ha! You insult a good blade!" Don Diego cried. "The insult shall not go unpunished! Look you here!"

Don Diego Vega whirled suddenly to one side, his sword seemed to flash fire, and its point bit into a panel of the wall once, twice, thrice! Barbados looked on in amazement, his lower jaw sagging. His little eyes bulged, and he looked again. Scratched on the panel of the wall was a Z.

"That mark!" the pirate gasped. "You are Zorro! That mark — the same the commandante wears on his forehead — "

Don Diego had whirled to face him again. "How know you there is such a mark on the forehead of Captain Rasnón?" he demanded. "So! The commandante deals with pirates, does he?"

"That is how it happens that my friend, Sergeant Gonzales, and his soldiers are not here! Ha!"

Barbados blustered forward, his cutlass held ready, striving to regain the mastery of the situation. "Give us loot, or we attack!" he thundered.

"Attack, fool?" Don Diego cried. "Do you imagine that you hold the upper hand here? Up with your blade!"

The last thing Barbados wished to do was to fight a caballero under such circumstances. He had the fear of the mongrel for the thoroughbred. But here was a thing that could not be avoided unless his leadership of the pirates suffer.

The caballeros sprang from their chairs, drawing their swords, shouting in keen anticipation of a break in the deadly monotony of their lives. They rushed to the right and the left, and engaged the pirates as they rushed forward. Don Diego Vega found himself at liberty to engage Barbados only, a thing he relished and which he did with right good will.

Barbados fought like a fiend, mouthing curses, puffing out his cheeks, but he did not understand this style of fighting. Don Diego Vega seemed to be wielding half a dozen blades that sang about his head and threatened to bury themselves in his throat. His cutlass seemed heavy, useless, his strokes went wild.

Back toward the wall went Barbados, while Don Diego grinned at him and taunted him, played with him as a cat does with a mouse.

"Pirate, eh?" Don Diego said. "Terrible on either land or sea? 'Tis a jest, Señor Pirate! A thin jest!"

Barbados sensed that the termination of this combat was not to be to his liking. He got a chance to glance once around the big room. What he saw staggered him. Two of the caballeros were stretched on the floor, blood flowing from their wounds. But, aside from those two, the caballeros were getting much the better of the combat. The pirates were retreating toward the front door. Their heavy cutlasses were of no avail against flaming, darting light swords, especially when the men who handled those swords refused to stand and be cut down, but danced here and there like phantoms.

But Barbados did not have time to contemplate the scene long. Don Diego Vega pressed his attack. Back against the wall went the pirate chief. He crouched, fought his best. But suddenly he felt a twinge of pain in his wrist, and his cutlass left his hand and shot through the air, to fall with a crash in a corner.

Barbados stared stupidly before him and then came alive to his immediate peril. For Don Diego Vega was standing before him, smiling a smile that was not good to see.

"Payment shall be made!" Don Diego said.

His blade darted up and forward, and Barbados gave a little cry of pain and fear and recoiled. On his forehead, it seemed, was a streak of fire. Again the sword of Zorro darted forth, and there was a second streak of fire, and yet a third time. And then Don Diego Vega took a step backward and bowed mockingly.

"You wear my brand," he said. "It is an honor."

Terror had claimed Barbados for the moment. Now he slipped a short distance along the wall, while Diego followed him, and suddenly he shrieked his commands and darted toward the door. Into the plaza tumbled the pirates, with the caballeros at their heels.

Barbados shrieked more commands, and the pirates ran with what speed they had. Those left behind in the plaza gathered the horses they needed and the loot, and those coming from the casa of Don Diego rushed toward the horses now. For the greater part, those horses were fine-blooded stock and belonged to Don Diego's guests, mounts used to traveling at a rapid rate of speed between some hacienda and the town.

Barbados urged his men to haste. Only compact loot could be carried. They, sprang to the backs of the horses and dashed away. The caballeros pursued on foot until the plaza had been crossed. And. then they stopped and gathered around Don Diego.

"There can be no pursuit," Diego said.

"They have made away with your horses, my friends, the soldiers are not here, and the only mounts remaining in town are not fit for caballeros to ride."

"Yet they must be pursued," said a voice at his side.

Don Diego whirled to find ancient Fray Felipe standing there.

"They have stolen the sacred goblet," Fray Felipe said in a calm voice. "I have taken a vow to regain it."

"The goblet!" Diego gasped.

"Don Diego, my friend, you will help me in this?" Fray Felipe asked. "I have known you since you were a babe in arms. I have loved you — "

"Tomorrow I wed," Don Diego said.

"But I shall do everything in my power. We'll get horses as soon as possible and pursue. I'll open my purse, and up and down El Camino Real men will go, seeking where these pirates touch shore again. We'll get the goblet!"

"I have more faith in your sword arm than in your purse, my friend," Fray Felipe said. "But do what you can."

The caballeros had gathered now. Men and women were pouring from the houses, telling of what had befallen them. Barbados and his men had been merciful, for pirates. They had taken wealth, but they had taken few lives.

Don Diego Vega started back across the plaza toward his house, his friends around him.

"For a moment I was Señor Zorro again," he said. "Those drops of blood you mentioned grew hot for a time, Audre, my friend."

"Glorious!" Audre Ruiz breathed. "I would we had horses and could follow them — even a ship to follow them out to sea. Don Diego, my friend, your bachelor supper is a great success."

"Then let us return and conclude it," Don Diego said. "We have a couple of wounded friends in the house. Let us attend them."

"Let us bathe their wounds in wine," Audre suggested.

They hurried into the house. The frightened servants came forward again and began putting things to rights. The two wounded caballeros were in chairs already, and men working to bandage them. Once more Don Diego sat at the head of the table, and the caballeros dropped into their chairs, and the servants made haste to fill the goblets. Don Diego put the sword of Zorro on the table before him and proposed that they toast it again.

There came a sudden commotion at the door, and a man stumbled in. Don Diego was on his feet instantly, for he knew the man. He was a leading workman at the hacienda of Don Carlos Pulido. A horrible fear gripped Don Diego's heart.

The man was exhausted. He staggered forward, and would have fallen had not Diego grasped him and braced him against a corner of the table.

"Señor!" he gasped. "Don Diego — young master!"

"Speak!" Diego commanded.

"Pirates attacked the hacienda more than an hour ago, while others were attacking here — "

"Tell it quickly!"

"Don Carlos is sorely wounded, señor! Many of the buildings are burned. The house was looted!"

"The señorita?" Don Diego questioned.

"Do not strike me when I speak, young master!"

"Speak!"

They carried away the señorita. They, slew six who would have saved her — "

"Carried her away!" Don Diego cried.

"Toward the sea," the man gasped. "I heard one of the pirates shout that she was to be treated gently — that she was to be the prize of some great man."

Don Diego. Vega tossed him aside, and once more the blade of Zorro was in his hand. His friends were upon their feet and crowding forward.

"A rescue!" Don Audre Ruiz cried. "We must save the señorita!"

"They have stolen the bride of Don Diego, the fools!" another shouted.

" 'Worse than that, for them!" Audre screeched. "They have stolen the bride of Señor Zorro!"

Don Diego Vega seemed to recover from the shock.

"You are right, my friends!" he cried.

"This is touch enough, to turn my blood hot again. Don Diego Vega is dead for a time; Señor Zorro takes the trail! Andre, get me the best horse you can! You others, wait!"

He dashed up the stairs as Andre hurried through the front door. The others waited, talking wildly of plans for reaching the shore of the sea. Frightened servants stood about as though speechless.

In a short space of time Don Diego returned to them. But he was Don Diego no longer. Now he wore the costume he had worn when as Señor Zorro he had ridden up and down the length of El Camino Real. And in his face was a light that was not good to see.

Don Audre hurried in. "I've got one good horse," he said.

"I go!" Don Diego cried. "I follow them to the sea. The two forces will meet there."

"We are with you in this!" Don Andre cried. "With you as when you were Zorro before. With you, my friend, until we have the little señorita safe again!"

Their naked blades flashed overhead in token of allegiance.

Don Diego thanked them with a look.

"Then follow me to the sea!" he cried.

"A trading ship is due there in the morning. Mayhap we'll have to take it and trace them, across the waves. I go! Zorro takes the trail"

He dashed to the door, the others following. He sprang into the saddle of the mount Don Andre had procured. He drove home the spurs cruelly, and rode like a demon through the bright moonlight and up the slope, then taking the shortest trail to the sea.

Chapter 6
Zorro Strikes

A T THE hacienda of Don Carlos Pulido the outer door was opened slowly, stealthily. A villainous face showed. Then the door was thrown open wide and half a dozen men stormed into the room. Dona Catalina gave a shriek of fear and sprang backward, and as the little señorita rushed to her, clasped her in her arms. Don Carlos looked up quickly from a garment he had been inspecting and sprang to his feet.

"Pirates!" he roared.

The aged don seemed to renew his youth with, the cry. He darted back against the wall, shrieking for his servants and his men, his hand darting to the blade that happened to be at his side. But the surprise was complete, and there was no hope of a victory over the pirate crew. Servants rushed in loyally, to be cut down. Doña Catalina and Lolita crouched in a corner, the aged don standing protectingly before them.

Sanchez made for him, seeing the girl. The pirate laughed, attacked like a fiend, and Don Caries went down before he could give a wound.

Doña Catalina's shriek rang in his ears.

Then there came another shriek as Señorita Lolita felt herself being torn from her mother's arms. Sanchez whirled her behind him, and another of the pirates clutched her in his arms.

"Easy with the wench!" Sanchez cried. She is to be saved for some great man!"

The little señorita struggled and fought, her gentleness gone in the face of this emergency. Horror claimed her and almost destroyed her reason. She had heard whispered wild tales of what hapemsd to women captured by pirates.

Out of the house she was carried, shrieking in her fear. The pirates poured out, too. Some of the outbuildings were ablaze now, and the shrieking, swearing crew was looting the house for what valuables could be carried easily.

Men of the hacienda came running, to be cut down with a laugh. More huts were set ablaze. Pirates came running from the house, carrying jewels, silks, satins. Señorita Lolita realized dimly that her wedding garments had been ruined by these men.

"Diego!" she moaned. "Diego!"

Horses were procured, her father's blooded stock, and she was lashed to the back of one. The pirates mounted others, and Sanchez urged them on their way toward the distant sea. He had orders to get there before the dawn, and he feared Barbados too much to disobey his orders.

Señorita Lolita glanced back once, to see flames pouring from the doors and windows of the home she had loved. She thought of the father she had seen cut down, of her tender mother. And then she slumped forward in a swoon, and Sanchez steadied her in the saddle.

Two men of the hacienda carried Don Carlos Pulido from his burning home and placed him down at a distance beneath a tree. Doña Catalina knelt beside him, weeping.

"Find a horse!" the aged don commanded one of the men. "Ride like a fiend to the town, and tell Don Diego Vega of this. As you love the señorita, spare neither yourself nor your mount! Ride — do not bother with me!"

And so the man found a horse and rode away toward the town, going like the wind, and so the news came to Don Diego Vega.

The señorita, coming from her swoon, found that the pirates were traveling at a high rate of speed. Mile by mile they cut down the distance to the sea. There was an excellent trail used by traders, and Sanchez followed it swiftly.

It was like a nightmare to the little señorita. Again she wondered at the fate of her father and her mother. Again, mentally, she called upon Don Diego Vega to save her.

But her proud blood had returned to her now. She curled her pretty lips in scorn when Sanchez addressed her, and would make no reply. Her eyes snapped and flashed as she contemplated him. Her tiny chin tilted at an insulting angle. She was a Pulido, and she remembered it. Whatever fate held in store for her, she would be a Pulido to the end.

And finally, after some hours, they rounded a bend of a hill and saw the sea ahead of them, and the mouth of the dark cañon that ran down into it. Sanchez dismounted them beside the curving cliff. The loot was piled on the sand, the horses were turned adrift. Señorita Lolita was forced to dismount. Her wrists were lashed behind her, and she was compelled to sit on the ground with her back to the cliff's wall.

Some of the pirates lighted a fire of driftwood. Sanchez stood looking out to sea, watching for the ship that soon would be due.

And then came Barbados and the pirates from the town.

"Fair loot!" Barbados cried as Sanchez questioned. "But we were outdone. Some devilish caballeros were having a supper, and we stumbled upon them, twice our number. But we have fair loot! And you have the girl!"

"Si! We have the girl!" Sanchez replied.

Barbados walked over to her. "A pretty wench!" he declared. "Small wonder a man wished to have you stolen! Proud, are you? Ha! We'll see what pride you have remaining by the end of the next moon!"

He whirled to look over the camp. "Sanchez," he commanded, "put a sentinel up on top of the cliff. I do not expect pursuit, but it is best to be prepared. I ran across that fiend of a Zorro, and he marked me. But there are not horses enough left in town for himself and his friends, and he would not dare follow alone. Nevertheless, put a sentinel on the cliff."

Sanchez obeyed. A man mounted to the top. On the level stretch of sand, before them they could see his shadow in the moonlight as he paced slowly back and forth. Back and forth he went, while Señorita Lolita sat and watched the shadow and shivered to think of what was to come.

Barbados and Sanchez prepared the loot for the ship's boats when they should come. There was an abundance of wine, and the pirates began drinking it. They shouted and laughed and sang, while the little señorita shuddered and watched the shadow of the sentinel as it went back and forth, back and forth.

And suddenly she bent forward, for there were two shadows now. Hope sang in her breast. One of the shadows was creeping upon the other.

Diego!" she breathed. "If it could only be Diego!"

The moon was dropping, was at the point where the shadows were lengthened, grotesque. And suddenly Sanchez gave a cry and pointed to the stretch of sand. Barbados turned to look. The pirates, stopped drinking and crowded forward.

There on the sandy stretch a picture was being enacted. They saw the silhouettes of two men fighting, thrusting and slashing at each other. From above came the ringing of blades that met with violence.

The pirates sprang back, tried to look up and ascertain what was taking place there. The shadows disappeared from the sand for a time as the combatants reeled back from the edge of the cliff.

"Above, some of you!" Barbados cried.

They started — and stopped. Down the face of the cliff came tumbling the body of the pirate sentinel. It struck the sand, and Barbados and the others crowded forward to see.

"By the saints!" Barbados swore.

His little eyes bulged. On the cheek of the dead pirate sentinel was a freshly carved Z.

"Barbados! Look!" Schez cried.

He pointed to the body. Fastened to the man's belt with a thorn was a scrap of parchment.

Barbados went forward gingerly and plucked it off. On it were words, evidently traced in blood with the point of a blade. Barbados read them swiftly:

Señores! Have you ever seen this one?

CHAPTER 7
Senor Zorro's Daring

T HERE was a moment of horrified silence, during which nothing was heard save the soft lap of the sea against the shore and the labored breathing of the terrified pirates. And then Barbados swore a great oath and looked toward the summit of the cliff once more.

"'Tis that cursed Señor Zorro, the land pirate!" be shrieked. "Spit upon him! After him, dogs! Bring me his heart on the end of a cutlass blade! Or fetch him alive, if you can, that we may have the keen pleasure of killing him slowly."

Some of the pirates already were struggling to get up the narrow path that led to the top of the cliff, slipping and falling back as the soft soil and gravel rolled beneath their feet.

Sanchez started with them, eager for combat. Barbados, however, lingered behind, seeing to the loot and his fair prisoner. He was very busy about it, for he was not eager to join the others and run chances of matching blades with Señor Zorro again.

Barbados remembered well how he had felt during the fight in the house of Don Diego in Reina de Los Angeles, when he bad realized fully that Don Diego was merely playing with him and could have silenced him forever when he willed.

The pirates reached the summit finally, but could see nothing there save a few clumps of brush and a few stunted trees that looked grotesque in the bright light of the moon. They examined the shadows carefully, but located no man. Yet from the near distance came a ringing, a mocking laugh.

They would have pursued, but Barbados hailed them from below, ordering them down to the beach again. The boats were putting in from the ship.

Down to the strand they tumbled, getting ready to store away their loot. They did not bother about the dead pirate, since he was an ordinary fellow who did not count. They guzzled more wine, ran down into the surf to help drag the boats ashore, greeted their fellows, laughed and shouted and jested and cursed in raucous tones.

Barbados turned to where the Señorita Lolita was sitting with her back against the cliff wall, her tiny wrists lashed behind her. She raised her face and looked at him bravely, her black eyes snapping, her lips curled in scorn.

"This Señor Zorro, I have been given to understand, has some concern in you," Barbados said.

"If he has, Señor Pirate, it is time for you to feel afraid," she replied.

"Think you that I fear the fellow? Ha!"

"He is no fellow! He is a caballero with the best of blood flowing in his veins, if you can understand what that means — you, who have the blood of swine in yours!"

"By my naked blade!" Barbados swore. "Were you not to be saved for a great man, I'd punish you well for that remark, proud one! Pride of blood, eh? Ha! 'Tis a thing you will be willing to forget, and eager, within a moon's time. When this man of whom I speak — "

"Is it necessary to speak at all to me?" the little señorita wanted to know.

Barbados snorted his anger and disgust.

For a moment he turned away to issue a volley of commands to the men who were loading the boats. He berated Sanchez for being slow. He glanced up the face of the cliff once more, as though expecting Señor Zorro to come rushing down, deadly sword in hand. Presently he called two of his men to him.

"Take the wench to one of the boats!" he commanded. "Keep her wrists lashed. Make certain that she does not hurl herself into the sea. These high-born wenches have some queer ideas and are not to be trusted at a time such as this.

The two men grasped her roughly and forced her to her feet. The señorita gave a little cry, more because of her injured dignity than from pain or fear. Barbados whirled toward them again, anger in his face.

"Easy with the wench!" he commanded. "She is a proper and valuable share of the loot. If she is delivered in good condition then do we share greater in the other things."

Down to the edge of the hissing surf they went, Señorita Lolita Pulido forced along between them. She still held her head proudly, but the light of the dying fire reflected in her face showed a trace of glistening tears that could not be choked back. Still, she had some hope. Don Diego was near at hand! He already had demonstrated his presence. And he would not entirely desert her while he lived. He could be expected to play Señor Zorro now to the end of the chapter.

They lifted her, carried her between them, and put her down into one of the boats. She sat at one side of a middle seat, a wide thwart. Her bound wrists were over the side, and by turning slightly she could see the tossing water less than two feet below her, for the craft was heavily loaded.

The pirates tumbled into the boat and picked up the oars. One thrust her cruelly against the side. Barbados himself sprang in last of all and ordered his men to give way. The other boats prepared for the start also.

On the summit of the cliff Don Diego Vega crouched and watched them. But he was not the easygoing, fashionable, nonchalant Don Diego now. His eyes were narrowed and piercing. His lips were set in a thin, straight line. Don Diego had vanished, and in his place was Señor Zorro, the Fox, the man who had ridden up and down El Camino Real to avenge the wrongs of frailes and natives. And Señor Zorro would know how to deal with this grievous wrong, which touched him personally.

The pirate craft was anchored close inshore. It would not take long for the boats to reach her. The moon was sinking and soon would be gone. There would be but a brief period of darkness before the dawn came stealing across the land to the sea.

His caballero friends were far behind him, he knew. And they would make for the trading schooner anchored a few miles away, perhaps, instead of coming here. And Señorita Lolita Pulido was in the hands of the pirates, and expected to be rescued.

Señor Zorro realized these things even as he watched the pirates preparing to launch their boats. It did not take him long to make a decision. He crawled backward a short distance, sprang to his feet, and ran to the edge of the cliff in a little cove a few yards away, a spot the pirates could not see from their boats.

He made certain that his sword was fast in its scabbard. He tightened his belt. He went to the edge and glanced down at the hissing sea a score of feet below, where it rolled and eddied in a deep pool close to the rocks.

Back he went again. And suddenly he darted forward, took off at the very edge, and curved gracefully through the moonlight in a perfect dive.

He struck the water and disappeared, but in a moment he was at the surface and swimming away from the treacherous shore. And he found that it was treacherous and the tide an enemy. It pulled at him to drag him down. He fought and struggled against it, and finally won to safety.

The boats were just starting from the land. Señor Zorro, low in the water, swam as though in a contest for a prize, straight toward the nearest of the boats, which was the one in which the señorita was sitting a captive.

Señorita Lolita was struggling now to be brave. The pirates were singing their ribald songs and indulging in questionable jests. They swore as they tugged at the oars, cursed the heavy load of loot, and blasphemed because of the work they were forced to do.

The señorita, remembering her proud blood, had tried to maintain her courage, but now she felt it ebbing swiftly. There seemed to be no hope. She could not believe that Don Diego could come to her rescue in the face of such terrible odds.

Once she gulped and felt herself near to tears. She leaned backward to keep as far as possible from the pirate sitting beside her. The stench of his body and breath was almost more than she could endure.

Now they were halfway to the pirate ship. Lolita had arrived at a decision. She would be no prey for pirates if she could find at hand the means for taking her own life. She remembered what Barbados had said about her being the prize of some great man, and wondered at it a bit. But suppressed terror occupied her mind and kept her from wondering much. Again she leaned backward, and her bound hands almost touched the water over the side.

The pirates, nearing exhaustion, were rowing slowly now, sweeping their long oars in unison but without their usual force. And suddenly the Señorita Lolita flinched, and almost cried aloud, then struggled to overcome the shock she had felt. Her hands had been touched.

At first she thought it was some monster of the sea, and then that a cold wave had washed them. But the touch came again, and she knew it for what it was—the touch of another hand.

Another touch and her cheeks flamed scarlet. The señorita had had her hands kissed before, and she knew a kiss when she felt it.

She turned her head slowly, leaning outward, and glanced down. And. her heart almost stood still.

For Señor Zorro was there, his face showing just at the surface of the water! Don Diego, her husband-to-be, was there, swimming alongside, smiling up at her, within a few feet of the pirates who bent their backs and rowed and never thought to look down.

Fear clutched at the señorita's heart for an instant — fear for him — yet admiration for his daring, too. Her blood seemed suddenly hot instead of cold. The touch of his lips had been enough to do that.

He dared not speak, of course, though the pirates were shouting and singing. But his lips moved and formed voiceless words, and the señorita understood.

"Courage! I'll be near!" he mouthed.

She nodded her head slightly in token that she understood. And Don Diego Vega smiled yet again and sank slowly out of sight beneath the waves.

The boats were almost to the vessel now. The bright moon shipped a last ray across the tumbling sea and sank to rest. On the deck of the pirate craft torches flared suddenly to guide the boats.

They reached the side. Rough hands lifted the señorita and forced her to the deck above. Swearing, sweating men commenced handing up the loot. Barbados howled his commands and curses, Sanchez echoing them. To one side the señorita was held by the two men who had guarded her on the shore, awaiting disposition by the pirate chief.

"With speed, dogs!" Barbados shrieked "We must be away before the dawn!"

The entire crew was working amidships, getting in the plunder and the boats. They, gave no thought to bow or stern.

And up the anchor chain and into the bow crept a dripping figure, with a cry for vengeance in his heart — and the sword of Zorro at his side!

CHAPTER 8
The Goblet

SENORITA Lolito Pulido, after a time, was conducted by Barbados to a tiny cabin below decks. It was no more than eight feet square, and had a bunk along one side of it.

Certainly, it was no place for a delicately-reared lady of gentle blood.

It was far from being clean, in the first instance. Vermin that meant nothing to pirates caused the señorita to shudder and almost scream. Even as she entered, two huge rats scampered through a hole in the cabin floor, rushed down into the bowels of the ship.

"'Tis no palace," Barbados admitted. "I'll leave the torch so you may have light until the day dawns, which will not be long. The torch will keep the rats away. The smoke will drift through that open porthole. You will be safe here. There are no weapons, and even such a small and dainty tender human being as yourself cannot squeeze through that porthole and drop into the open sea!"

He fastened the smoking torch to a wall, went out and slammed the door behind him, and Señorita Lolita heard a heavy bar being dropped into place.

The ship was old, the floor worn and full of holes, and the walls had cracks in them. From one side came a stench, as though supplies had been stored in the space adjoining, and had spoiled. Through the porthole she could see the black night.

She heard a tumult on the deck, a great noise, the sounds of clanking chains, and knew from the feel of the ship that she was under sail. Above her head feet pattered on the deck. The great voice of Barbados and the echoing one of Sanchez came to her as from a long distance. The rushing wind pulled the smoke of the torch through the open porthole.

She closed her eyes for an instant, as though that would shut out the horror of her thoughts, but found that it did not. It seemed to her that she heard a faint hiss, but she supposed that it was the wind or the water.

She opened her eyes again and almost shrieked in alarm. Four inches in front of her face the point of a sword had slipped through a tiny crack in the wall, coming from the space adjoining!

The señorata recoiled a space, but watched the blade as though fascinated by it. Inch by inch it slipped through the wall, until two thirds of its length was inside the cabin. And again she restrained a cry, but this time a cry of joy. On the blade, marked with some black substance, was a big Z!

So Zorro even now was near! He was on the other side of the partition, only a couple of feet from her! She bent her head forward as the blade was slowly withdrawn, put her lips close to the tiny crack in the wall.

"Diego!" she whispered.

"Not Diego, but Zorro, señorita, at your service," came back a low tone.

"Thank the saints!" she breathed. "But, what can you do? You must be careful!"

"Think you I would allow them to carry you away, and not follow?" he asked.

"If they find you — "

"Do you put such small value, señorita, upon my ability to care for myself?"

"Diego! Zorro!" she whispered. "To you I am not backward in confessing it — I am so afraid!"

"Then will I sing for you, beloved!"

"Zorro! Dare not to do it! They may hear!"

"Let them hear a decent song for once in their wicked lives!" Zorro said. "Be of strong heart, señorita! And be not frightened at what you may hear or see. It is in my mind to terrorize these vermin who call themselves men, preparatory to rescuing you!"

"Brave words, Diego!" she said. "But you cannot fight against four score. If, at the end, you could do me one service — "

"And that?" he asked.

"Death is to be preferred to dishonor, Diego!"

"Why speak of dying? Do you forget that you are my affianced bride? You are to live, and I am to live, señorita, and have many happy years. Think always on that, and not on the other! And be of good cheer, for I am near you always!"

She heard a slight movement on the other side of the partition. He did not speak again, nor did she. Her heart was beating like angry waves against a rocky shore. Her face was flushed. It gave her courage just to know that he was near. Zorro, she felt confident, would find a way.

There was silence for a moment, and then she heard the soft hiss again.

"Si?" she questioned.

"This is some sort of a storeroom," he said, "in which Zorro has made a temporary nest. But I do not intend to remain in it forever. It is in my mind to look at you through the porthole before the dawn comes."

"Diego! To dare such a thing — "

"What would not a caballero dare for love?" he asked. "For love of such a one — "

"Diego!"

"Call me Zorro, for, by the saints, that is my role now! I find that I have a dual personality, and the tamer part of me is not working at present. I am Zorro, the daring in love and war!"

"Have a care, for my sake," she begged.

"I have work to do and a game to play, and they may be combined," he answered. "For the moment, Adios!"

Again she heard the little sound, as though he were retreating from the partition and crawling over boxes and bales. There was deep silence for a time, save for the noises on the deck. And then she heard his voice, raised in song, and her heart almost stopped, for she knew that the pirates must hear it, too.

She leaned her head against the wall, that she might hear the better, though she was sorely afraid. She had heard the song often before, from Diego's lips, and when other young caballeros had come to her father's hacienda serenading. But never had she heard the real Zorro sing it before, and never before had it sounded so thrilling and so sweet.

"Atencion! A caballero's near! To guard the one to his heart most dear! To love, to fight, to jest, to drink! To live the life and never shrink! His blade is bright, his honor, too! Atencion!"

The voice grew louder, more ringing. It seemed to the señorita to swell through the ship and across the tossing sea. Her heart beat faster, though she still feared for him. Well she knew his audacity, the reckless courage of her Zorro!

"Zorro!" she breathed. "Man of men! Caballero mine!"

There was silence on the deck above, and then she heard the harsh, loud voice of Barbados, but could not understand his words. Zorro was continuing his song:

"Atencion! I've a thrust in store
For rogues, for foes, an abundance more
To shield my lady from all harm,
To save her from the world's alarm;
A Caballero calls to you Atencion!"

The señorita's eyes closed, her lips parted slightly, her breathing became as the stirring of a leaf in a gentle breeze. The song had lulled her fears.

"Zorro!" she whispered, as the verse was ended. But there came no answer from the other side of the partition.

Up on the deck, however, there was consternation. Barbados, having listened, whirled angrily toward his crew.

"Who dares sing such a song?" he shrieked. "Are there not royally good pirate ditties, that some of you must use the mush-like tunes and words of the high-born?"

"Every man is on deck," wailed Sanchez, who had been superintending the storing of loot. "'Tis a ghost song!" he exclaimed.

"A ghost song!" shrieked some of those nearest him.

Barbados shuddered. "There will be ghosts aplenty if this nonsense does not stop!" he declared, whipping his cutlass out of his belt. "It was no ghost singing. A ghost would have a more perfect voice. If I hear it again — "

He heard it again. It seemed to come from the sails above, from the waves overside, from the cabins below.

Barbados walked to the rail and stood looking down at the dark water, and then toward the land, where the dawn was almost due. Through the darkness and up to him slipped one of the pirate crew.

"Master!" he whispered.

"To your work, hound of hell!"

"A word with you, master!"

"Concerning what?" Barbados demanded.

The man edged closer. "Master, I have a present for you — a goodly piece of loot that is not in the common store."

"How is this?" Barbados said. "You steal from your comrades?"

"Softly, master, else they hear!" the man whispered. "This is something special, and I got it for you."

"In Reina de Los Angeles?"

"Si, master! In Reina de Los Angeles. It was while we were in the church there."

"In the church?" Barbados gasped.

"When the old fray first stood us off, master, and before you came. We had rushed forward, and I was in the van. And when the old fray was hurled backward the first time, I got it."

"A golden goblet, master, studded with precious stones. See — I have it here! I saved it for you, master, and thought perhaps that you might give me promotion — "

Barbados looked at the goblet, struck by the light from the nearest torch. It glowed and glistened like some live thing. The pirate chief recoiled.

"Away with it!" he cried. "I do not want to touch it — do not wish to see it! It is a thing of ill omen, the thing that old fray was trying to protect."

" 'But, master — "

"Ill-luck will follow the man who has it. It is some sort of holy thing! Away with it! Keep it for yourself. Gamble it away, and the sooner you get rid of it the better. You may be struck down for taking it. I had a friend once who robbed a church and struck a priest, and I do not care to remember what happened to him! Are you going to take it away?"

The man gasped, astonished, and put the golden goblet beneath his shirt.

"I may have it all for myself?" he asked.

"Si. I would not touch the thing! I call upon the saints to witness that I never touched it!"

So, through all the ages, have wicked men, in moments of fear, called upon the gods they have pretended to scorn.

CHAPTER 9
Love and Mystery

SEÑOR ZORRO, having concluded his song, crept over boxes and bales to the little door of the storeroom. There he crouched and listened for a time, but heard nothing save the noise from the ship's deck and the wash of the sea and singing of the wind through the rigging.

Presently he opened the door a crack and peered out into a pitch-dark, narrow passage. He slipped through and closed the door after him. Again he stopped to listen, and then he crept forward, reached a ramshackle ladder, and went up it swiftly and silently to a tiny hatch.

Lifting the hatch he crawled out upon the deck near the rail, hidden from the glare of all the torches. He had seen such a ship as this before, and knew her build well. There were no mysteries for him.

Along the rail he went like a shadow, and as silently. He reached a point where he could look amidships. Barbados was back among his men, now, urging them to greater speed, and Sanchez was echoing his commands. The ship was sailing at a fair rate of speed before a freshening breeze.

He slipped on along the rail, now and then peering over. After a time he picked up a line, fastened it to the rail and tossed the other end overboard, tried it with the weight of his body, made a loop in it, and slipped one leg through the loop.

Over the rail and down the side he went, slowly and carefully, the sword of Zorro in its scabbard at his side. And presently he came to a porthole, through which light streamed. He swung around, grasped the edge of it.

Lolita, looking up suddenly, almost shrieked in sudden alarm. But the next instant she was off the bunk and across the tiny cabin, and her face was within a foot of his.

"Zorro!" she said. "You are doing a reckless thing — "

"Would I allow a few score mere pirates to keep us apart?" he asked. "Am I that sort of caballero?"

"But you are in grave danger, from the men above and the sea beneath!"

"Danger is the spice of life, señorita! After we are wedded it will be time enough for me to be tame."

"But that may never be, Diego."

One of her hands was at the porthole's edge. Zorro, clinging to the rope, grasped it in his right hand and carried it to his lips.

"The most beautiful señorita in all the world!" he said.

"Zorro!"

"And for once I have you, señorita, when your duenna is not present to pester us. We are betrothed. We were to have been wed today.

I will have more courage, señorita, if I have felt your lips against mine. the memory of our betrothal kiss still tingles in my veins, but it is a memory that should be refreshed."

"And then you will climb above and take heed for yourself?"

"With a kiss for incentive, I could climb to the summit of the world and reach for heaven!" Zorro declared.

She blushed and then inclined her head. He bent forward, and their lips met in the porthole.

"Go!" she said then. "Go, Zorro, and may the saints guard you!"

"My arm is strengthened," he declared. "And your wishes are to be obeyed. Señorita, adios!"

An instant their eyes met, and then he was gone, climbing up the line hand over hand through the darkness. Lolita tried to watch him, but could not. And so she hurried back to the bunk and curled up on it again, holding one hand to her flaming cheek, moistening with her tongue the lips that the lips of Zorro had pressed.

Zorro reached the deck and disconnected the line, wishing to leave no trace behind him. He glanced toward the land, and realized that soon the dawn would come. Along the rail he slipped, until he came to a spot from where he could watch the pirates.

The majority of the loot had been stored away. No man was aloft. Barbados was cursing at a group near the opposite rail. Zorro looked across at him and wished that he was near. He saw Sanchez, too, knew him for the lieutenant, and it came into his mind that Sanchez had commanded the squad that had abducted the señorita.

And, as he watched, Sanchez started across the deck, around the mast, bore down upon Zorro where he stood in the darkness. Soon he would be in the darkness near the rail. But before he could reach it he would be forced to pass beneath one of the flaring torches, and for an instant the strong light would be in his eyes. Zorro whipped out his blade and crept forward to the edge of the blackness, keeping behind a mass of cordage piled upon the deck.

His eyes were narrowed now, his lips in a straight line, an expression of determination in his face. So he stood and watched Sanchez approach, holding the sword of Zorro ready.

The moment came. The blade darted forward and struck, and its point worked like lightning. Sanchez gave a scream of mingled surprise and pain and fear, and reeled backward, clapping a hand to his forehead.

Barbados whirled to look. Zorro, as silently as a shadow, darted along the rail through the black night, on his way to the little hatch and the storeroom below.

"Fiends of hell!" Barbados was shrieking. "Sanchez, what is it? You screech like a shocked wench!"

Sanchez, still shrieking, staggered back and turned beneath the flaring torch to face them. On his forehead was a freshly cut letter Z.

"The mark of Zorro!" Barbados gasped. "So — "

"A demon struck me!" Sanchez cried. "I saw no man! Something came out of the night and struck me!"

"Fool!" Barbados shrieked. "A blade made those cuts."

"But there was no blade, no man! Out of the dark it came — "

"Think you Zorro is aboard?"

"No man, I say!" Sanchez shrieked. "It was a ghost. There is a ghost aboard. We are doomed — the ship is doomed!"

"By my naked blade!" Barbados swore. "A sword in the hand of a human made that cut! Do I not bear one myself?"

"But how could this Zorro get aboard?" Sanchez wailed. "It was a ghost!"

CHAPTER **10**
A Dead Pirate

B ARBADOS, cursing loudly, strode to the middle of the deck. He drove the men to finish their work, grasped Sanchez roughly by the arm, and led him aside.

"Understand," he said, "either this Zorro is aboard in some mysterious fashion, or else there is a traitor among us playing this Zorro's part."

"A ghost — " Sanchez began.

"Another word of ghosts, and I run you through!" Barbados warned. "The men are silly fools, but you are supposed to have some sense, being second in command. When the day comes we search the ship; and if we find this Zorro in hiding we deal with him in a way he will not relish. He is one man against many!"

Sanchez shivered and raised a trembling hand to his flaming forehead. The blood had streamed down his cheeks from the wound Zorro had put there; and Zorro, on his way to his hiding place, had paused for an instant to watch this comedy. A few minutes later he was safe among his boxes and bales in the storeroom.

He crept across to the tiny crack through which he had whispered to the señorita, but he could not see her where she was sitting on the bunk — could see only straight-ahead.

"Señorita!" he whispered.

"Zorro!"

"Safe again, señorita. The dawn is coming. Have you rested?"

"I could not sleep," she replied. "There were thoughts of you, and of other things."

"But now I guard," he whispered. "Sleep, and I will watch."

She started to make reply, but instead she hissed a warning. Heavy steps had sounded outside the cabin door. She heard the bar being removed. And then the door was opened and one of the pirates stood in it, grinning, a torch in his hand.

"I have brought food," he said "at the chief's command."

He stepped into the little cabin and closed the door behind him. And then she saw that he carried a bottle of wine and half a cold fowl. She gasped as she looked at the wine, for there was a label upon the bottle and it bore the stamp of her father's hacienda.

It returned to her with a rush — memory of her father being struck down, of her home in flames, of her weeping mother crouched over her father's body. She gave a little cry and reeled back against the wall.

"Leave me!" she commanded "Out!"

The man leered and stepped toward her. She darted away from him, horror in her eyes. He put the bottle and fowl down upon the bunk.

"I leave the food and drink, pretty wench," he said. "You may use it or throw it through he porthole into the sea—it is all the same to me."

"Out!" she cried again.

"You do not like me?" he asked, getting closer to her. "Many women have. You are not to be spoiled, being the prize of some great man, but a kiss will not spoil you. Never have I kissed a wench with proud blood in her veins. It will be something to remember and boast about!"

Now she crouched against the wall, her heart pounding at her ribs, her breath coming in little gasps. Her eyes were dilated with terror.

"Out!" she said, though her fear reduced her screech to a mere whisper. "Your master shall know of this!"

That sobered him for a moment, but the picture of her pretty self was before him, tantalizing him, tormenting him. He reached out a hand to clutch her. She could retreat no further. She put up her tiny hands as though to beat him back.

"What is a kiss?" he asked, laughing. "I would not harm you — only a kiss!"

"I would rather die!" she gasped.

"For that I shall take two — a dozen! Proud wench, are you? Ha!"

He grasped her wrist and started pulling her toward him. She lurched backward, fought with what strength she could, felt that she was about to swoon, and realized that she must not. He followed her, reached out the other hand to grasp her better.

And like the darting of a snake's tongue came the sword of Zorro through the crack in the wall. In and out it darted with the swiftness of thought. The señorita, reeling back against the wall, felt herself released, saw the pirate sag before her, to his knees, topple forward, and collapse at her feet.

Terror-stricken, she looked down at him, her eyes bulging wide. Blood flowed from his breast and formed a pool on the floor of the cabin. A hiss from the other side of the partition brought her to her senses. She realized, then, that Zorro's blade had done this thing to save her an indignity.

"Señorita!"

"Si?" she questioned.

"Take the fellow's dagger from his girdle! Dip it in the blood on the floor! Have courage and act quickly! 'Twill appear as though you did it when he offered you insult!"

She realized what he meant, and was quick to obey. She needed the blood of the Pulidos to aid her now. Stooping, she reached out a hand and grasped the hilt of the dagger in the dead man's belt. She drew it out, shuddered, turned her head away for a moment, faint at the sight of the blood.

"Courage!" Zorro's whisper reached her ears. "And make haste, señorita! Some man may come!"

Now came the thing that tested her courage. But she felt that the eyes of Zorro were upon her. Again she bent forward, and she bathed the blade of the dagger in the pool of blood upon the floor. Then she sprang to her feet, holding the dagger in her hand, her face white.

"Open the door," Zorro whispered from beyond the partition, "and shriek!"

She hurried to the door, shuddering as she pulled her skirts away from the dead man. She opened it, and peered out. And the shriek that she gave was no acting, but the sudden outpouring of what she felt.

There was a moment of silence, and she shrieked yet again. And down from the deck tumbled Barbados, rage in his face. He looked at her and at the dagger in her hand. He thrust her aside and stepped into the cabin.

"So!" he said. "What has happened here?"

"A lady of my blood does not suffer insult!" she said.

"Ha! The dog forgot his instructions, did he? 'Tis well that he is done for! You have saved me a task!" Barbados declared. He turned and looked full at her. "A wench of spirit!" he said. "I have half a mind to keep you for my own!"

Back to the door he went, and shouted to those above. Two men came rushing down. Barbados yelled commands at them, and they carried the dead man away. Another brought water in a pail, and dashed it over the floor to wash the blood down the cracks.

Barbados turned and looked at her again.

"You may keep the beast's dagger for a souvenir," he said. "Let me clean it for you."

She surrendered it willingly. Barbados wiped the blade on his trousers, bowed, and handed it back to her.

"Take it!" he urged. "Use it when you will, if there are others who try to disobey my commands. You are to be delivered, unspoiled, to a certain man. Failing that, I claim you for myself. And put out the torch when I have gone. The day is here!"

He went out and closed the door, and once more the heavy bar was dropped into place. Lolita tossed the dagger from her, hurried to the bunk, and collapsed upon it. Her senses seemed to be reeling.

"Señorita," Zorro whispered from behind the partition.

But she made him no reply. The terrors of the night had taken their toll. She had swooned at the dawning of the day.

Chapter 11
Zorro Walks the Plank

THERE was no dawn in the dark, evil-odored storeroom, but Zorro, by peering through the crack and into the little cabin, could tell of the approach of the day. The interior grew gray, and then brighter, and finally a ray of sun penetrated and touched the dingy hole with glory.

The ship was riding easily on the long swells, sailing swiftly toward the south. The señorita slept, and in the dark storeroom Zorro reclined on a pile of sacks and tried to think things out. In an emergency he was quick to think and to act, to take advantage of every opening, but to sit still and analyze a situation was beyond him. He was a man of action, and it was action he craved.

He did not doubt that Don Audre Ruiz and the others had obtained possession of the trading schooner and would follow. But would they follow the correct lane of the sea? And, if they caught up with the pirates, what would follow? The caballeros would be greatly outnumbered. Not that such a thing would cause them to hesitate about an attack, but it would work against them, of course.

For an hour or more Zorro thought on the problem, itching to be in action and knowing that he should remain quiet. The pirates would be searching the ship, he supposed, since he had marked Sanchez the way he had. He would have to remain in hiding, bury himself in the storeroom in such a manner that they could not find him.

Then, after a time, he heard a noise in the little cabin, and quickly made his way to the crack in the wall. He could see that the door had been opened, and then he saw that Sanchez was standing just inside it.

"Senorita!" the pirate lieutenant called. "Sleep not when the chief commands!"

Señorita Lolita came from her slumber and sat up on the bunk with a little cry.

"Do not be afraid," Sanchez told her. "By my naked blade, I will keep my distance! I have no wish for a knife between my ribs, driven there by a high-born damsel who thinks nothing of murder!"

"What is your wish?" she demanded. She was herself again now, scorning him, her chin tilted.

"It is no wish of mine," Sanchez protested. "I but carry the commands of the chief. He orders that you come on deck, and at once."

"I prefer to remain here, Señor Pirate," she replied.

"No doubt. But the commands of Barbados are made to be obeyed, as I learned some years ago. He has said that you are to go on deck, and so you shall, even if I have to carry you."

One step he took toward her, but she sprang from the bunk and crouched against the wall.

"Dare not touch me, foul beast!" she cried. "'Twas you cut my father down! 'Twas you stole me away from my home and fetched me to the coast!"

"I do not want to touch you, little spitfire!" Sanchez informed her. "I have but come to escort you to the deck. What Barbados wants with you I do not know. Perhaps it is to have you get some fresh air, so you will look pretty when you are delivered to the great man. Ha! You are pretty enough now to suit any man who is not too exacting."

He turned back toward the door, offering her no affront. And there he waited, as though with deep respect.

"Are you coming?" he demanded. "Barbados is not the man to be kept waiting."

Once more she curled her lip in scorn, once more her chin was tilted, and she went forward, drawing aside her skirts, and swept past him like a queen leaving an audience chamber. Sanchez grinned and followed her.

Zorro, through the tiny crack had witnessed this scene. He did not believe that Barbados merely wanted her to take the air. He felt sudden fear for her, and once more his eyes narrowed and seemed to send forth flakes of steel. He scrambled over the boxes and bales toward the little door.

Up the rickety ladder he went and to the hatch, and there he listened for a time, hearing nothing alarming. And then he raised the hatch slowly, an inch at a time, blinking his eyes rapidly at the bright light of the day.

None of the pirates were in sight. Zorro slipped out and dropped the hatch covering, whipped out his blade, and crept through the little passage toward the spot from where the deck of the ship could be viewed.

He was in time to see the señorita piloted across the deck to where Barbados was standing alone. The crew were forward, some sleeping sprawled on the deck, others leaning against the rail watching the antics of the flying fish.

Barbados whirled and stood with his arms akimbo, regarding her narrowly. She faced him bravely, her hands clasped behind her back.

"Señorita," the pirate said, "queer things happened during the night. I would question you concerning them."

"Is it necessary?" she asked.

"By my naked blade, it is!" he roared. "I am not to be treated like a dog by you or any of your ilk. This is my ship, and here I am sole master, and it would be well for you to remember it."

"I am quite sure none other would desire the mastery of her," the señorita replied.

"You have a biting tongue," Barbados said. "I would hate to be your husband. Else that tongue were tamed by love, it would be a hot dish to have continually."

She turned away from him and gazed across the sea. He took a step nearer her.

"Is this Señor Zorro aboard?" he demanded suddenly.

"Would I know it, were he?" she countered.

"Possibly. I am asking a question, and desire an answer," Barbados said. "It has been said that a high-born wench such as yourself scorns to utter falsehood. Let us see if that is correct."

She made no reply, and the face of Barbados grew purple with wrath. He closed and unclosed his great hands as though he would have liked to strangle her.

"Tell me all you know about this Zorro!" Barbados commanded. "Did you slay the man in your cabin, or did this Zorro do it? Answer me, wench! Reply here and now, else I teach you a lesson you will remember to your last hour."

He sprang forward suddenly and grasped her arm cruelly, and she cried out because of the indignity and the pain.

Zorro, from his place of watching, flinched as though he had experienced the indignity and pain himself. He wanted to hurl himself forward and to the attack, but he realized that it would not last for long. He could not hope to engage the entire ship's company, though he made a long and running fight of it, and emerge from the combat the victor.

But there came an interruption. From forward was a hail:

"A sail! A sail!"

The pirates sprang to their feet. Those who had been sprawled upon the deck asleep awoke.

Barbados forgot the señorita for a moment and turned to look.

Behind, and bearing down upon them swiftly, came another ship. Zorro knew, as did the pirates, that she had put out from the land before the dawn and far to the south where the pirate ship had been at anchor.

Hope beat suddenly in Zorro's breast. She was a trading schooner, he could tell even at that distance. If only she carried Audre Ruiz and his friends! It was a question what would happen. If she was some honest vessel, perhaps she would fall victim to the pirate craft. She might not be prepared to fight.

Barbados issued a volley of commands. The pirate craft turned for a run farther out to sea, so that she could tack back and catch the oncoming ship between her and the shore.

Lookouts were posted to watch carefully. Sanchez ran here and there, echoing the orders of his chief.

From his hiding place Zorro watched the now-approaching vessel, and now the deck where Lolita was standing against the mast, forgotten for the moment.

Were he quite sure that the ship carried his friends Zorro could go into action. For he flattered himself that he would be able to hold his own until the other ship came up.

It appeared that the other vessel had no intention of running up the coast. She changed her course also, and bore after the pirate craft.

Zorro watched her carefully. He could not make out her flag. At the distance he could see nothing except that she was of the type of trading schooner, and that she had swift heels. For she was gaining rapidly, as though sailed by experts. And the pirate craft was foul of bottom, needing careening and scraping.

Barbados had hurried to the rail and was watching the oncoming ship. Lolita saw it also, but did not seem to realize that it meant hope. Perhaps she feared that the ship was but coming into grave danger, running into conflict that would mean capture and death for her crew.

Zorro glanced at the deck, and then back at the approaching vessel again. He saw that another sail was being sent aloft. It was broken out, snapped into place, the lines tautened. Zorro with difficulty restrained his cheer. On the white expanse of the sail, painted there in haphazard fashion, but easily made out, was a monster Z.

So his friends were on that ship! Zorro felt better now. He glanced once more toward the deck, and realized that Barbados had seen what was on the sail also. For the pirate chief left the rail and stamped back to the señorita's side, determination in his manner and rage in his countenance.

"Now you'll speak the truth, wench!" he shouted. "Is Zorro aboard this ship? If those are his friends coming up, then will we attend to him before we attend to them."

"I do not care to hold conversation with you," she said.

"No? By my naked blade, I am in command here!" he roared. "An answer I intend to have."

He lurched forward and grasped her by the shoulders, shook her as a terrier shakes a rat, held her at arm's length and shook her again. She fought against crying out, but could not win the battle against such cruel odds.

One plaintive little cry drifted across the deck and straight into the heart of Zorro.

He transferred his sword from his right hand to his left. He whipped the dagger from his belt and hurled it. His aim was poor, yet he had come close enough. The dagger was driven, quivering, into the mast between Barbados and the señorita.

Barbados, with a cry, sprang backward, and the señorita slumped to the deck at the foot of the mast. And Zorro realized in that instant that he had stepped forward too far and had been seen. Sanchez gave a cry and started toward him. The pirates whirled from the rail to look. Barbados saw him.

"'Tis Zorro!" Barbados shrieked. "After him! Fetch him to me alive! An extra share of loot to the man who gets him!"

It was the promise of loot that drove them on. They shrieked and rushed forward. Zorro put the blade of his sword between his teeth and darted up into the rigging. And then began a fight the like of which the pirates never had seen before. Zorro seemed scarcely human. Up the rigging he went like a monkey. He sprang from spar to spar.

Down the ratlines he rushed, down the ropes he slid.

Now and then he clashed with one of the pirates, and always the sword of Zorro darted in and out, and a wounded man was left behind.

"Seize him!" Barbados shrieked. "After him, dogs! Is one man to hold you off forever? Do not slay him! An extra share of loot — "

Zorro struck the deck and darted across it. Sanchez retreated before his darting blade. He pierced the breast of a pirate who stepped before him, hurled another aside, sprang to the mast, and recovered his dagger.

He stooped for an instant, and pressed the lips of the señorita to his own, and dashed on.

Now, he was cornered, and now he fought his way to freedom. A dagger whirled past his head and buried itself in the deck beyond. Into the rigging he went again, up the ratlines, out along a spar.

They followed him, and he put his sword into its scabbard and sprang. Far below he caught another spar, ran to the mast, started downward again. One glance he gave at the approaching ship. His friends were gaining, but they still were far away.

Again they had him cornered, and again he escaped them by jumping to the deck below. He dashed around the deck cabin, met and defeated another man with a single clash of blades, and was at the rail.

There was grave danger on the deck, he knew, and so he went aloft once more. Up and up he went, while Barbados and Sanchez shrieked to the others to follow and get him.

"Alive!" I want him alive!" Barbados screeched.

Another spring from spar to spar. Zorro almost missed because of the rolling of the ship. But he caught and clung on, and scrambled to a place of safety. In toward the mast he hurried.

But there was a treacherous spot on the spar, where the mist had struck and clung, a wet spot made to cause a boot to slip. Zorro felt himself reeling suddenly to one side. He grasped wildly — grasped nothing but empty air. His heart seemed to stop beating for an instant.

He felt himself falling through space. To his ears came the terrified cry of the little señorita. The deck rushed up to meet him. He struck it with a crash and the darkness came.

Lolita gave another little cry and covered her face with her hands. Barbados and Sanchez rushed forward, the others at their heels.

Zorro was unconscious for the moment, though the fall had broken no bones.

"Bind him!" Barbados cried, glancing back at the oncoming ship. "We attend to him first, and then to his friends. Water his head well and bring him back to life. Get ready a plank!"

The pirates rushed to do his bidding.

Zorro's wrists were lashed behind his back. One man hurled water into his face, and he groaned and opened his eyes, and tried to sit up on the deck.

"Ha!" Barbados cried. "So it is Zorro, eh? And now we can repay you for this little mark you put on my forehead, señor! Barbados, also, knows how to make payment!"

He gave the signal, and the pirates forced Zorro to his feet. He tried to fight, but they overpowered him. They braced him against the mast, while the senorita crept aside and watched.

"Hold the wench!" Barbados commanded two of the men. "We don't want her throwing herself overboard. And I wish her to witness what is to come."

The two men held her. Zorro, half throttled, was kept against the mast. Barbados made another sign, and some of the men carried forward a heavy bar of iron and lashed it to Zorro's wrists.

"To the rail with him!" Barbados commanded.

They forced him to the rail, and the two men urged the señorita along beside him. Over the rail a long, wide plank had been extended.

Zorro knew what they meant to do to him. And now Lolita realized it, too.

"No, no!" she shrieked. "You must not do this thing!"

"Ha! Revenge is sweet!" Barbados cried. "Zorro, you are about to descend to a watery hell! We'll let you take your sword with you, since you may need it fighting demons. You take the plunge, and then, when yon ship comes up, we attend to your friends! As for the señorita, know that she will be delivered safely to one who has bargained for her."

"Why not give me a chance in a fair fight?" Zorro asked. "Any two of you — any three — "

"Your friends are coming up, and we must prepare for them," Barbados replied, laughing. "You have fought your last fight on earth, señor. See if you can mark the brow of the devil with your cursed Z."

"Diego!" the señorita moaned.

"As a special favor you may kiss the wench," Barbados said. "It will be practice for her. And take with you to the bottom of the sea the knowledge that another will kiss her soon."

The señorita rushed forward and threw her arms around him and kissed him, unashamed.

"Diego! I'll follow you!" she said.

"'Tis a merry end," Zorro declared. "Be brave of heart! Our friends are at hand, señorita! If Don Audre Ruiz is aboard that ship he will know how to save you — and how to avenge me."

Again they kissed, and then the two pirates jerked her roughly backward.

Barbados laughed like a fiend.

"Practice for the other man!" he roared. "When Captain Ramón—"

"So it is Ramón?" Zorro cried.

"Si! And a lot of good the knowledge will do you now."

"This much good — that I shall not die!" Zorro answered.

"If you do not, then indeed are you a man! With a weight on your lashed wrists — Enough!" he exclaimed. "Put him on the plank!"

They lifted him and stood him upon it, facing him toward the sea. They forced him a short distance from the rail.

"Diego!" the señorita cried, agony in her voice.

At her cry the plank was tipped.

And with her cry ringing in his ears Zorro shot downward like a man of metal — shot downward into the tossing sea, and was gone!

CHAPTER 12
To the Rescue

U PON the frantic departure of Don Diego Vega from Reina de Los Angeles, Don Audre Ruiz took command of the situation and the caballeros simultaneously. There was none willing to dispute his leadership. Don Audre always had been a leader when there was an enterprise that called for hard riding and hard fighting in the bright face of danger.

Captain Ramón was not to be found, and Sergeant Gonzales had ridden away with the soldiers. So Don Audre noised it abroad that he and his friends intended pursuing the pirates as speedily as possible, and made a quick search for mounts.

They acquired enough, presently, but the horses were a sorry lot when compared to the caballeros' own, which the pirates had stolen. And without changing their attire, retaining the splendid costumes they had been wearing at Don Diego's bachelor feast and with their jeweled swords at their sides, they rode up the slope and took the trail that would carry them to the sea.

Don Audre decided against following the pirates' tracks. He knew that they would reach the coast long before the caballeros, and would embark. Don Diego would do what he could, which would be little. And Don Audre realized that their only hope was to get to the trading schooner, put out in it, and make an attempt to overtake Barbados and his evil crew.

Hour after hour they rode, urging their jaded horses to their utmost, glad that the moon was bright and that they could make as good progress as in the day. And, when they finally were within a couple of miles of the sea, and also an hour of the dawn, Don Audre suddenly reined in his horse. A native was standing in the middle of the trail.

Don Audre approached him slowly, hand on the hilt of his dagger. There were some natives who were not to be trusted. But when he drew near he recognized the fellow as one who had worked at his father's hacienda.

"What do you here?" Don Audre demanded.

"I saw the señor coming from the distance with his friends," the native answered. "I have news."

"Speak!"

"I was coming across the hills, señor, and saw the pirates."

"Ha! Talk quickly!" Audre Ruiz commanded.

"I went into hiding, lest they slay me. They had good horses and much loot, also a girl — "

'Tell us of that!"

"It was the señorita Don Diego Vega expects to wed," the native said.

"They took her with them to the shore, and presently more pirates came from the Reina de Los Angeles. They went aboard their ship, taking the señorita and the loot with them."

"What else?"

"There was a man appeared, señor, and killed one of the pirates. I got a glimpse of him, Don Audre, and it was Señor Zorro, the one that — "

"Ha! Zorro!" Audre shrieked. "Speak quickly!"

"He ran from them, and they gave up the pursuit. But when the boats started from the land, he dived into the sea and swam after them. And he did not return!"

'Then he is aboard the pirate craft!" Don Audre declared.

"The pirate ship sailed to the south, señor."

"Good!" Audre cried. "Know you anything of the trading

schooner?"

"Si, señor! She is anchored straight ahead, and the men expect to start for Reina de Los Angeles in the morning to trade."

"They will not, though they do not know it," Don Audre said. "Here is gold for you, fellow. Ha! So the pirate ship sailed to the south. That means that the rogues are going to their hidden rendezvous somewhere down the coast. We'll get the trading schooner and pursue! Forward!"

But, as they would have started, Don Audre raised a hand and stopped them again. From the rear had come the beating of a horse's hoofs.

Nearer grew the beating of hoofs, and a horseman appeared, riding frantically through the moonlight down the slope and toward them. The reckless rider was Sergeant Gonzales.

"Ha, señores!" he called. "I have overtaken you finally, it appears."

"And to what end?" Don Audre Ruiz asked, urging his horse forward and glaring at the soldier. "You have news?"

"Not so, señor! I come in search of it. I returned to Reina de Los Angeles with my troopers to learn of the pirates and what they had done. I learned, also, of your departure, so left my men and rode after you. Captain Ramón was not at the presidio. As the next soldier of rank — "

"It is in our minds to get the trading schooner and give pursuit," Ruiz told him.

"That is a worthy idea!" Sergeant Gonzales declared. "Too long have these bloody pirates infested our shores. Meal mush and goat's milk! Let us go forward!"

"Ride you with us!" Don Audre said. "Thus we have the sanction of the soldiery and official approval of our deeds."

"I shall approve anything that has to do with causing the death of pirates!" Sergeant Gonzales declared.

The moon disappeared entirely, and the night was dark. They rode forward slowly, careful not to get off the trail, but they did not have much farther to go. Soon they came to the crest of a hill, and below them they heard the hissing of the sea, and saw the lights of a ship riding at anchor a short distance from the shore.

Down to the surf they urged their mounts. And there they met with another surprise. For a horseman was awaiting them there in the darkness. Don Audre gasped in astonishment when he recognized old Fray Felipe.

"We left you in the town, fray!" he said. "And how is it that we now find you here? Is this some sort of a miracle?"

"I departed the town while you were yet searching for horses," Fray Felipe explained. "I got a mount for myself and came ahead, because I cannot ride like the wind, as do you young caballeros. It was in my mind that you would make for the trading schooner. I heard you say as much."

"But why have you come?" Don Audre wanted to know.

"I have known Don Diego Vega and the little señorita since they were babes in arms, and I was to have married them today," the old fray replied.

"But fighting is not your forte!" Don Audre declared. "You are old, and you wear a gown. Do you remain behind and pray for our success, and let us wield the blades! That were better, fray."

"I am willing to make my prayers. But I have taken a vow," Fray Felipe replied. "I must return the golden goblet the pirates stole from the church."

"Then you would go with us?" Don Audre asked.

"Si! I have already communicated with the captain of the trading schooner, señor. He is coming ashore now in one of his boats. Thus time will be saved."

CHAPTER 13
Tragedy at a Distance

THE CABALLEROS dismounted stiffly and gathered near the water line. In from the distant trading schooner a boat was coming, driven over the choppy water by silent oarsmen. Half a dozen men were in her, and their flaring torches touched the sea with streaks of flame. They approached the shore carefully, and on guard, as though fearing some trap set by thieves, and by the light of torches those on the land could see that the men in the boat were heavily armed.

Don Audre Ruiz and Fray Felipe went forward and met the boat at the water's edge and greeted the schooner's captain as he stepped to land. He was a regular trader who carried goods overland from the sea to Reina de Los Angeles every now and then. He traveled as far as San Diego de Alcala to the south, and as far as San Francisco de Asis to the north—a bold fellow and honest, well and favorably known.

"What is all this tumult?" the captain demanded. "Fray Felipe, are caballeros and men of rank, also! In what way may I be of service to you, señores? Have you ridden out all this long way in the night to have first choice of my stock of goods?"

Don Audre Ruiz told him swiftly. "We want your ship, to pursue a pirate craft!" he said.

"How is this, señor?" the captain cried. "There are pirates in these waters?"

"Si! And possibly within half a dozen miles of you," Don Audre told him. "Early in the night they raided Reina de Los Angeles. They also raided the Pulido hacienda, and carried away the señorita, who was to have wed Don Diego Vega this day."

"By the saints!" the schooner's captain swore. "They stole the bride-to-be of Señor Zorro? Is he here with you?"

"He followed them, going ahead of us, and possibly managed to get aboard their ship," Don Audre explained. "The pirate craft has sailed by this time. They went toward the south. They will beat out to sea for a distance. If we can start soon it may be possible to overhaul them."

"How many rascals in the pirate crew?" the captain of the schooner asked.

"Not more than three score, as nearly as we can judge," Don Audre replied. "And here are a score of caballeros, and we are ready to fight!"

"Señores, I am yours to command!" he said. 'My ship is yours, and her crew. If I can do anything to help rid the seas of such vermin, I am more than willing. My schooner is a swift vessel in light winds such as we find now. I'll signal the other boats and have you aboard as soon as is possible."

"You will not fail to profit by it," Don Audre Ruiz told him.

"I am not doing it with the expectation of profit," the captain declared. "I detest thieves, and I admire honest men! I have many friends in Reina de Los Angeles, some of whom probably have suffered at the hands of these pirates. And, above all, I did admire the exploits of this Señor Zorro, as Don Diego was called. It will be a pleasure, señores, to aid you in this."

He called to his men, and they signaled to the ship with their torches. Out of the darkness and across the tumbling sea came more boats from the schooner. The caballeros turned their horses adrift, knowing that they would be picked up and returned, made certain that they had daggers and swords handy, and got quickly into the boats and put out to the ship.

Soon they came alongside the schooner and mounted to the deck by the light of torches. The boats were swung aboard, and the captain and Don Audre Ruiz held a long conference. Then there came a volley of orders, the anchor came up and the sails filled, and the schooner crept off the shore and away from the land through the black night.

Straight out to sea they went, gathering headway, and in time a faint streak of light showed across the land and the dawn came. Caballeros and crew strained their eyes and swept the sea in every direction. And finally the sharp eyes of one of the men aloft discovered a sail.

The course of the trading schooner was changed, and the chase began. Nearer the quarry they crept as the sun came up and bathed the sea and the land, glistening through the haze. Glasses were leveled at the distant craft.

"She is the pirates!" the schooner's captain declared. "Her flag of iniquity flies from her mast!"

He bellowed another volley of orders to his crew, and they crowded on all sail. They rushed about the schooner, preparing her for the battle. The eager caballeros looked to their blades, the crew to their cutlasses.

"If Zorro is aboard that craft he should know that his friends are near at hand for the rescue," Don Audre said.

And then it was that they got out a sail and painted a gigantic Z upon it, and sent it aloft. It was their banner of battle, a flag of war that betokened their allegiance to a man and a cause.

"Courage and swift work does it!" the schooner's captain told Don Audre. "We are greatly outnumbered. But my crew has had dealings with pirates before, hence each man will fight with the strength of five. And you and your friends, Don Audre, have good reason for fighting like fiends."

"We are prepared to do it," Don Audre replied. "Think you that we can overhaul the pirate?"

"It is but a question of time," the captain declared. "The pirate sails prettily, but her bottom is foul. I can tell that much at this distance.

Pirates are too lazy to keep a ship in perfect shape. And this little schooner of mine is a swift craft and in prime condition."

They gained steadily, and meanwhile they watched the distant pirate ship continually. They saw that there was some sort of a tumult on board. Don Audre Ruiz, standing at the rail near the bow, with a glass glued to his eye, watched carefully.

"It is probable that Zorro is fighting the entire pirate company," he announced. "I can see men running about the rigging. Let us pray that we may be in time."

Don Audre Ruiz gave a gasp and called some of the caballeros to his side.

"Look!" he directed. "They are making some poor devil walk the plank! By the saints, 'tis Zorro!"

"Zorro!" the others cried.

"Look! And the little señorita is standing at the rail, forced to watch!"

There was a moment of horrified silence. The face of Don Audre Ruiz was white as he contemplated the fate of his friend. The caballeros said not a word, but those who had glasses watched, and the others strained their eyes in an effort to see.

And then Don Audre Ruiz gave a low cry of horror and turned quickly away, as though he could endure the sight no longer.

What he had seen had been enough. There were traces of tears in his eyes, and his voice choked.

"He is gone!" Don Audre said. "Don Diego, my friend! We can only avenge him now!"

"Gone!" Sergeant Gonzales cried, sudden tears in his eyes, too. He brushed them away roughly and blinked. "Don Diego gone? Then, by the saints, will my blade be thrust as it never has been thrust before! Now, by the saints — "

His vow ended in a choke of emotion and he turned quickly away. Don Audre, his eyes stinging, his lips set in a thin, straight line, turned to Fray Felipe.

"Say your prayers for him," he directed. "And pray, also, that we will know how to avenge him when we come alongside! Dios! Give strength to my arm!"

Chapter 14
Out of the Depths

S MILING in the face of death, Zorro yet battled to keep from showing his genuine emotions, because of the presence of the señorita. But in that awful moment when he stood upon the plank, looking first at the evil faces of Barbados and Sanchez, and then at the agonized countenance of Señorita Lolita Pulido, he knew what torture meant.

Barbados gave his last mocking laugh, and Zorro felt the plank tipping. He felt himself losing his balance. The heavy weight on his wrists was almost bending him backward. He knew how swiftly it would carry him down into the depths of the sea. Then would come a brief and useless struggle, he supposed, a moment of horror — *and the end!*

His eyes met those of the señorita yet again. And then it seemed that everything gave way beneath him and he shot downward.

There came a splash of water as he struck the surface — he felt its sudden chill — and then the waves closed over his head. He was a famous swimmer, but no man can swim with a heavy bar of metal tied to his wrists, and those wrists lashed behind his back.

Mechanically Zorro protected himself as he struck the water, as though for a deep dive. He drew air into his lungs until it seemed that they would burst. He kicked in vain against the down-pulling power of the heavy weight. Down and down he went into the depths until the light from the surface faded and he found himself in darkness.

Zorro prayed and worked at the same instant. He jerked his wrists from side to side behind his back, trying to force them apart. He expelled a tiny bit of air now and then as he descended, but retained it as much as possible.

Often he had played at remaining as long as possible beneath water, but it is one thing to do so when a man has the knowledge that he can spring to the surface at any time, and quite another when he has reason to believe that he never will reach the surface again at all.

Yet he continued to struggle as he shot downward. Red flashes were before his eyes now, and a multitude of faces and scenes seemed to flit before him.

In that awful instant he relived half his life.

"Dios!" he thought. "If this be death — "

Another tug he gave at his wrists. The man who had lashed the heavy weight there had not done his work well. Perhaps he was too busy watching Barbados and fearing him. Perhaps he had held a sneaking admiration for this Señor Zorro, who had offered battle to an entire ship's company. However, the rope that held the weight gave a trifle.

Zorro, in his agony, realized that. He tugged again, and then pressed his palms close together and drew in his wrists as much as possible. The heavy weight, dragging downward, pulled the loose loop over the wrists and hands. Zorro felt an immediate relief. He realized what had happened. And then he began his battle to reach the surface. The weight was gone, but his wrists were still lashed together behind his back.

He kicked and struggled and shot upward. He expelled more of the precious air his lungs retained. His chest was burning, his ears were ringing, he was almost unconscious because of the pressure of the water he had been forced to endure.

He saw a glimmer of light, but knew that the surface was yet far away. And it occurred to him that even the surface did not mean life. For his wrists were yet bound behind him, and he was miles from the shore.

On he went, up and up, struggling and fighting. He jerked at his wrists until they were raw and bleeding, but to no avail. Those who had lashed his wrists had done better than the one who had fastened the weight to them.

And finally he gave a last struggle, a last kick, and felt the blessed air striking upon his face.

The pirate ship was some distance away, sailing slowly before a gentle breeze. Zorro found himself floating in her wake. He could see men rushing around her deck and up into her rigging, but at the distance could not guess their tasks. Bearing down upon him was the other craft, the one with the gigantic Z upon the sail. Zorro saw that he was directly in her path.

Those on the approaching ship did not see him, for they were watching the pirate craft and preparing for the battle that was to come.

He hailed those on board, but his voice was drowned by the roar of the water against the schooner's bows. He saw that she would strike him, and kicked frantically to work himself to one side of the track she was following. Had he saved himself from the depths, he wondered, to be crushed senseless by the bow of the craft that carried his friends? Then she was upon him. He rose with the crest of a wave and was hurled at the bow.

He saw an anchor chain that was loosely looped and a dragging line. If he could but catch one of those and make his way to the deck, there might be some chance. Once more the sea whirled him and cast him forward. He came against the swinging loop of anchor chain with a crash, grasped it, was lifted and dropped, but held on!

The bow of the ship dipped, and Zorro felt himself soused beneath the water for an instant. He gripped the chain with his hands and his legs and fought to maintain his position. His arms were aching, and the chain had cut through his clothing already and was chafing at his leg. Once more the bow dipped, and Zorro slipped a few feet along the chain, unable to stop his descent.

He gripped with his leg again. His hands came to a stop, and he realized that the rope that bound them had found an obstruction. Zorro worked slowly and carefully with his fingers, even as he held on. One of the links of the chain, he found, was imperfect, had cracked, and presented on one side a jagged edge.

Hope sang in his breast once more. But he knew that he would have to work carefully. He did not dare to release his hold entirely, for a sudden dip of the bow and the quick wash of the water would be enough to sweep him from the chain. But he sawed back and forth as well as he could, pulling the rope across the rough edge of the chain link.

He glanced ahead. The ships were not far apart now, and the schooner swung a bit to starboard, so as to bear down upon the pirate craft from a more advantageous angle. Zorro worked frantically, and after a time he felt the rope give.

He sawed and sawed, and once more he glanced ahead. It would not be long now before the ships clashed. He wanted to be upon the deck, normal breath in his nostrils and the sword of Zorro in his hand, to aid his friends, to fight his way to the deck of the pirate craft, and to the señorita's side.

The rope gave again. Zorro was forced to rest for a moment, leaning back on the chain. A wave swept him to one side, and he thought for an instant that he was gone. But he regained his balance and continued his sawing.

And presently he knew that he was free. The rope dangled from one wrist only. He gave an exclamation of delight and thanks, gripped the chain, and turned over. He regarded his bleeding wrists, hesitated a moment, gathered breath and courage, and commenced the perilous ascent of the chain.

It was a painful and difficult task. Every few feet he was obliged to stop, to gasp for breath and close his eyes for a moment because the pain in his wrist and leg made him weak with nausea.

He came within a short distance of the vessel, slipped back, and forced his way upward again. And finally he grasped with one hand the chain port and held on.

A moment he rested, then forced his way upward again. The schooner was very close to the pirate ship now. On the deck above him Zorro could hear Don Audre Ruiz shrieking instructions to the caballeros and the captain shouting to his crew.

He managed to get up to the butt of the bowsprit, and there, safe from the sea, he rested for a moment again. The two ships would crash together in a minute or so, he saw. He raised his head weakly, and took a deep breath, and then struggled to his feet, ready to spring down to the deck.

His hand went down to whip the sword of Zorro from its scabbard. The schooner yawed suddenly as her helmsman fought to get a position of advantage. The big jib swung back, whipped by the angry wind.

Zorro was looking down at the deck, and he did not see his danger.

Don Audre Ruiz turned at the instant, shrieked and rubbed his eyes. "Zorro!" he cried.

He was seen from the deck of the pirate craft, too.

Barbados and Sanchez caught sight of him. Sanchez crossed himself quickly, and the face of Barbados turned white.

And then the jib cracked against Zorro's body, knocked him from his precarious perch and hurled him once more into the sea!

CHAPTER 15
A Show of Gratitude

THE schooner sailed on, and came against the pirate ship with a crash. But here was a battle unlike the usual one when honest men met pirates. As a usual thing, the pirates could be expected to board and slay without mercy, to loot, and then either to destroy the ill-fated vessel or take it away a prize. And the honest men could be expected only to offer what defense they could. But here was a case where the honest men were more than willing to carry the fight to the pirates. For Don Audre Ruiz and his caballero friends had seen Zorro walk the plank, and also they fought to rescue a lady.

But both forces found themselves disconcerted at the outset. Don Audre Ruiz, glancing toward the bow of the schooner, was sure that he saw Zorro standing there against a background of sky and water, his figure dripping. He rubbed his eyes and looked again — and Zorro was gone!

"'Tis the spirit of Zorro come to aid us!" Don Audre cried. "I saw him for a moment, waving his hand at me and reaching for his blade! The spirit of Zorro fights with us!"

The ships crashed together. But the pirates did not rush as was their custom. For fear had clutched at their superstitious natures, even as it had clutched Barbados and Sanchez, his evil lieutenant. Sanchez had shrieked the news, but Barbados did not heed his intelligence. Barbados himself had seen Zorro standing against the sky. And how may a man do that when he has been sent to the bottom of the sea with a heavy weight fastened to him?

"Fiends of hell!" Barbados screeched. "This Zorro must be a demon!"

"We cannot fight against ghosts!" Sanchez cried. "We are lost before we commence."

Barbados seemed to come to himself and shake off his terror in part. He instantly was eager to win free from the trading schooner. He did not fear the caballeros, who were greatly outnumbered now, But he did fear the supernatural. He forgot the chance for murder and loot, and wanted only to get away.

Barbados shrieked his commands, and the half-stupefied pirates ran to execute them. The pirate craft swung away from the schooner, so that men could not spring from one ship to the other. There were less than half a dozen clashes of blades; less than half a dozen minor wounds.

Slowly the pirate craft fell away. The helmsman of the schooner worked frantically to bring his ship back into the wind. Barbados howled more commands. From the pirate ship came a rain of fire balls, and flaming torches were hurled. It was a favorite pirate trick, and the men knew what their commander wanted. Clouds of pungent smoke rolled across the deck of the schooner.

The caballeros gasped and fought to get clean, pure air. Their nostrils and throats were raw, their eyes stinging.

Through the dense smoke they could see little. The pirate ship gradually was lengthening the distance between her and the trading schooner. The pirates' work had been done.

For the sails of the schooner were wrapped in flames, and bits of them fell burning, to the deck below. Flames licked at the tarred rigging and spread out on the spars.

"She's making away!" Don Audre Ruiz cried. "She's running from us!"

There seemed to be no question about it now. The pirates were hurrying away without giving battle. And the raging caballeros wanted battle, and they remembered that the señorita was yet on the pirate craft.

The captain was howling to his crew, and the men were fighting the raging flames. The caballeros, forgetting their silks and satins and plumes, ran to help. Here was a foe more formidable than pirates of the open sea.

The schooner drifted with the water and the wind in the wake of the pirate ship. The smoke drifted away, and finally the fire was extinguished. Quick inventory was taken of the damage.

It did not amount to so very much, since the rigging had not been burned to a great extent. But the sails were gone, for the greater part, and pursuit for the moment at an end.

Again the captain shouted his commands, and as his men hurried to carry them out he turned to Don Audre.

"I have other sails, señor," he explained. "They will be in place as rapidly as my men can get them there. The craft of ill-omen cannot get far before we are upon her heels again. She, is running out to sea once more. She would lose sight of us before she turns toward the accursed spot where they have their land rendezvous. Their behavior astounds me; they acted as if they had seen a ghost!"

"And so did I!" Don Audre declared. "I'll swear that, for an instant, I saw Zorro standing at the butt of the bowsprit — and then he was gone!"

'By the saints, I saw him myself!" Sergeant Gonzales shouted. "He was here to aid us! Man or spirit, I know not — but he was here! And now he has disappeared!"

The caballeros were busy helping the crew with the new sails. One by one they were sheeted home, and presently the schooner gathered headway once more. On it sailed, in the wake of the pirate craft, vengeance only delayed.

Far behind, Zorro watched her grow smaller and smaller, and the flare of hope that had been in his heart dwindled to a mere spark again.

His unexpected plunge into the sea before he had recovered from the first ordeal had unnerved him for the moment. He had come to the surface to find that the schooner had drifted away. Before he could handle himself to advantage she was at some distance, and the pirate craft was drawing away from the ship of smoke and flame.

There was a strong tide running, and Zorro was too weak to fight against it. Near him there drifted a spar that had been torn away when the ships had crashed together. He struggled through the swirling water and managed to reach it, and drew himself upon it to sprawl there almost breathless, gasping, exhausted. He was too weak to signal his friends, and he doubted whether they would see him did he do so.

He began to take stock of his predicament. Far away he could see a dirty streak on the horizon, and he knew it for the land he would have to reach.

He was in sore condition for the hazardous journey. His wrists were raw and bleeding; his leg pained him. He scarcely could see because of the glare of the sun on the water. Thirst tortured him; hunger added to the torture.

Zorro sat up on the spar and smiled a sorry smile. He made sure that his blade still remained at his side.

"Sword of Zorro, we are in a sorry state!" he declared. "This is an emergency such as never have we faced before. But we must win through!"

A moment he hesitated, and then, as though to give courage to himself, he raised his voice again, this time in his song:

"Atención! A caballero's near — "

But his voice broke, and he told himself that he was a fool to attempt to sing out there in the wild waste of waters, clinging to a spar. Far better to concern himself about getting to the land.

Zorro rested a short time longer, watching the disappearing ships.

And turning, he looked at the distant land.

"Sword of Zorro, we travel toward the east!" he announced. "If ever I touch dry land again, there I remain for some time to come. This seafaring is a sorry business!"

He adjusted himself as well as he could, and started to swim, clinging to the spar. That rendered his progress slow, but he did not dare cast it aside, for he knew that he never would reach the distant land. For a time he swam, and then he floated on the spar and rested, and then urged himself to swim again. On and on through the hours, while the sun traveled across the heavens, he forced the spar through the water.

At times songs rang through his brain, at other times he caught himself mouthing meaningless phrases. And then he thought of the Señorita Lolita, and swam on.

Twilight came. The sun disappeared. There was a period of darkness, and then the surface of the sea was touched with the glory of the moon. Zorro could not see the land now, but he knew in which direction it lay, and swam on, a few minutes at a time.

And thus passed the night. But before the dark space just before the dawn, Zorro was laughing raucously, out of his wits. Some god of good fortune kept him swimming in the proper direction. And when the sun appeared again, it brought a new agony to his eyes, new tortures of thirst. He swallowed salt water and spat it out, and found that it had made him ill. For a time he was stretched across the spar, weak, sick, on the verge of delirium.

He fancied that a myriad of pirate vessels were about him, bearing down upon him. He saw the pretty, laughing face of the Señorita Lolita in the mist that hung above the sea. He laughed back at her, and once again his cracked voice rose in a song:

"Atención! A caballero's near — "

He felt himself grow suddenly weak. It seemed to him that the land was near at last, but he could not be sure. He drew himself upon the spar, sprawling across it.

"Must-rest — " Zorro gasped.

And with the gasp he passed into unconsciousness.

Back to earth he struggled as through a land of hideous dreams. He tossed and groaned and tried to open his eyes, but felt that he could not. There seemed to be a roaring in his ears that was not of the sea. And finally it came to him that it was a human voice, attempting to beat through his unconsciousness and bring him to an understanding of things.

"Señor! Señor — " the voice said.

Zorro struggled yet again, groaned once more, and opened his eyes. But not into the burning glare of the open sea! He was in cool shade, he found, and from a distance came the hissing of the surf. He blinked his eyes rapidly, felt something at his lips, and drank deeply of pure, cold water.

"Señor!" There was the voice again. "For the love of the saints, señor, come back to life!"

Full consciousness returned to him in a breath. He opened his eyes wider and struggled to sit up. Then he saw that he was in some sort of a poor hut, and that a native was beside him, with an arm beneath his shoulders.

"Thank the saints, señor!" the native cried.

Zorro, with the help of the native, sat up. He had been stretched on a sort of couch, he found. He glanced around the interior of the poor hut, through the open door at the sparkling sea.

"What — " he began. "I found you yesterday, señor, far out to sea, riding on a piece of wreckage," the native said. "You had lost your wits. You fought me when I tried to take you into my boat, and tried to draw blade against me. Then you went unconscious, and I had my way with you."

"And — and then?" Zorro gasped.

"Why, señor, I fetched you here!" the native explained. "And throughout the night you raved, and so far today. The sun has but two more hours to live."

"Where is this?" Zorro asked.

"On the coast, señor, far to the south of Reina de Los Angeles. I am but a poor neophyte who eats what fish he can catch. Once I worked on a hacienda, señor, but the governor took all for taxes. And so I got me a boat and came down the coast and built this poor house. And here I live alone and am happy. There are times when I carry fish to the stronghold of the pirates, and trade them for some other things — "

"Ha!" Zorro cried. "The stronghold of the pirates? Where is that?"

"Less than ten miles down the coast, señor, in a little bay. There are huts, and women and children, and every now and then the pirate ship puts in after a raid. They are safe there, señor, though they are within eight miles of the presidio of San Diego de Alcála."

"By the saints!" Zorro swore. "And how does it come that you did not rob me of my sword and the few things of value upon me, and toss me into the sea?"

The native looked at him frankly. "Pardon, señor," he said, "but I never would do such a thing as that. For I knew you instantly, señor. You are Señor Zorro, who rode up and down El Camino Real and avenged the wrongs of the natives and frailes. You once punished a soldier who beat my father. If it is necessary, señor, I am ready to die that you may live."

"There was a pirate ship in the offing, and another," Zorro insinuated.

"Si, señor! The pirate ship ran from the other, going out to sea. But a short time ago I saw her pass, going toward the bay where the pirates have their headquarters. And the other ship passed but a short time ago, pursuing."

"By the saints!" Zorro cried. "I would go to this pirates' den of which you speak, and as speedily as possible."

'The señor must eat first, so that he will have strength," the native said, firmly. "Then I will guide the señor to the spot. It is ten miles, and the señor is a weak man."

"I will eat the food gladly," Zorro replied. "Do you prepare it as speedily as possible. There shall be an ample reward."

"It is reward enough that I have been able to save the señor's life," the native answered, "The friends of Señor Zorro do not forget what he did for them!"

CHAPTER 16
Singing Caballeros

BARBADOS was like a maniac after the pirate craft swung away from the trading schooner. He shrieked at his men to make sail, and they needed but little urging. The fear of the supernatural was upon them, superstition ruled their minds.

Gradually they crept away from the schooner, but Barbados continued to watch her closely. He saw the new sails going aloft, and realized that there would be a pursuit. So he turned out to sea and began running for it.

He did not attempt to explain things to himself. He knew that his men outnumbered those on the schooner, and he felt reasonably sure that, in an engagement, the pirate crew would emerge victorious. Yet something seemed to tell him that the proper thing was to avoid the engagement if possible.

"We will lose that sorry craft in the wide waters," he told Sanchez, "and then we will turn and go to the rendezvous. There we'll unload and apportion the loot, and care for the wench until the man comes to claim her. If we are followed, we can outfight the caballeros on land. The ghost of a man drowned in the sea is powerless on land, I have heard."

"And, if they follow us ashore — " Sanchez questioned.

"Then we fight them, fool," Barbados said. "You are still shaking like a child! A pirate — you? Ha! By my naked blade, you are no better than a woman in this business!"

Throughout the day he gave his attention to the sailing of the ship, but he could not shake off the schooner which followed.

Then came the night, and once more Barbados cursed the bright moon. For, though his craft showed no lights, yet could she be seen from the schooner. Back and forth Barbados sailed, but always failing to shake off the other ship. And when there came the dark hour before dawn he changed his course abruptly, and ran before the breeze.

But when the dawn came there was the schooner, a greater distance away, but still in sight. And so Barbados put off to sea again, for he wished, if it were possible, to go to the land rendezvous without drawing his foes there. Else he slew all of them, news of the pirates' headquarters would leak out, and they would have to move.

He ran before the wind, he tacked, he beat in toward the shore, out to sea, to the north and the south and the west. Now he gained, and now the schooner gained upon him. He cursed and drove his men, but they could accomplish nothing.

And finally he started running down the coast, intent upon reaching the rendezvous. If the men of the schooner dared follow him to land, they would be annihilated, he promised.

Once or twice he felt like turning and forming an attack, but thoughts of the ghost of Zorro deterred him.

"A sea ghost cannot fight on land!" Barbados told himself. "On land I have them at my mercy!"

The day started to die, and the pirate craft rushed down the coast with the schooner in close pursuit. It was almost nightfall when Barbados and his men guided the ship into the little bay. The schooner was some miles behind.

The anchor dropped, the ship swung broadside to the shore. From the land came sounds of a tumult, and down into the surf rushed men and women and children. The pirates' stronghold could be seen back some distance from the water.

There was a wide expanse of beach, a deep open space fringed with stubby trees and brush. Hills landlocked the scene. A score of huts dotted the edge of the flat. Fires were burning on the shore, stock ran wild among the habitations.

Overside went the boats, and the pirates commenced handing down the loot. Shrieks and calls came from the women and children on the shore, from the men who had been left behind as guards.

Barbados went ashore in the first boat, and began issuing his commands. The camp was to be put in a state for defense, he explained. Guards were to be established on the three land sides, and other men would watch the sea. The ship was warped closed to the shore, so that she could be defended easily.

Just as the night descended, the trading schooner sailed across the mouth of the bay, and presently she returned, farther out to sea. Barbados boarded the ship again, and took the señorita from her cabin. Sanchez lashed her wrists behind her.

"You go ashore, wench!" Barbados said. "And there you are to be held until such a time as this Captain Ramón comes to claim you. Why he should want you is more than I can explain to myself. You are a pretty wench, it is true, but too much of a spitfire!"

He watched her closely when she was in the boat. And when they landed, the pirates' women and the ragged children rushed forward to jeer at her as she passed beside the flaming fire. Barbados took her to a large adobe building, the best structure in the camp. He opened the door and thrust her inside.

A woman cooking over an open fire whirled to look at him. She looked at the señorita, too, and her eyes flamed.

"What is this?" she demanded, her fists against her hips. "Is it a younger and prettier woman?"

"It is indeed, Inez," Barbados laughed "She is a share of the loot!"

"Your share, eh? And you dare to fetch her here?"

"Peace!" he cried. "I want none of the wench! She is to be kept a prisoner until claimed. A share of the loot she is, but not my share. She was stolen for a great man!"

"This is the truth?" the woman asked.

"Do I generally speak falsehood?" Barbados thundered. "Enough! Put her in the storeroom, and feed her well. Treat her gently. She must be in prime condition when she is claimed. We were followed by a schooner upon which are caballeros striving to rescue her. She must not be rescued!"

The woman grinned horribly. She opened the door of a room adjoining and motioned for the señorita to enter.

Barbados hurried outside again. The black night had descended, but soon the moon was shining. Guards were sent into the fringe of woods, and a watchman to the summit of a hill in the rear. Men were posted on the ship, men walked around the huts, alert, ready to repel an attack.

But there came no attack during the night. The trading schooner had run down the coast and back, and then anchored two miles north of the bay.

"I know the place," the captain told Don Audre Ruiz. "Once some years ago I ran in there during a storm. Their camp must be in the open, and there will be no advantage in the attack. There can be no surprise, of course."

"What is your good advice?" Don Audre asked.

"That you land here with your caballeros, approach the camp and wait for the dawn. I'll land as many of my crew as can be spared from the ship, and let them circle the camp to attack from the other side.

There must be men enough held here to get the schooner to sea for a run if the pirate craft comes out at us.

"That is agreed!" Don Audre said.

"But it will be a sorry business, Don Audre! You will be outnumbered three to one. And you may be sure that there are men in the camp who were not on the pirate ship. They may have a few pistols they have captured from ships, but it will be hand to hand work with blades. Three to one, at least, Don Audre!"

Don Audre Ruiz drew himself up. "Three beasts to one caballero," he said. "It is an equal affair. There can be no hesitating, señor. Senorita Lolita Pulido is held a captive by these beasts. And I am not forgetting what happened to Don Diego, my friend! There is but one thing to do — attack! At least, we can die!"

There was a short conference, and then the boats began carrying the men to the shore. The caballeros approached to within a mile of the pirate camp and stopped to rest, sending scouts on ahead. The men of the crew circled to the other side.

Some of the caballeros slept, sprawled on the sand. But Don Audre Ruiz sat beside a tiny fire he had kindled, his knees drawn up and nursing them with his hands.

"At least we can die, Diego!" he said, softly. "And we can strive mightily before we do that!"

The black hour came, and then the first finger of the dawn. Don Audre rose and stretched himself, and walked for a time up and down the beach. The caballeros shook off their sleep, bathed their faces at the edge of the sea, exercised their muscles, whipped out their blades and fanned the air.

Don Audre Ruiz led the way along the shore. They crept nearer the camp of the pirates, spread out fan fashion, and approached boldly. They reached the crest of a slope, and saw the camp spread before them in the first rays of the morning sun.

The pirates seemed to be more numerous than even Don Audre Ruiz had expected. It looked to be a hopeless task, this attack. But there was something to urge them on.

They stopped to look at one another. In silks and satins and plumes they were, and their jeweled swords at their sides. And before them the stronghold, with the ragged, dirty pirates there ready to give battle.

"If Zorro were only here to lead us!" Don Audre Ruiz said, with a sigh. "But he is not — and let us remember why he is not — and strike the harder because of our remembrance. If you are ready — "

He whipped out his gleaming blade and waved it above his head, and the caballeros drew blades in turn, and answered him with their cheers.

And so they advanced to the attack — slowly, carefully, in a perfect line. And Don Audre Ruiz, because he wanted to give himself and the others added courage, and because he felt that it was fitting, sang lustily a song of old:

"Singing caballeros, going forth to die!
Laughing in the face of grinning Death!
Facing task that's hopeless, ready yet to try!
Singing with the last of earthly breath!"

The caballeros took up the refrain and sang it through to the end, their voices ringing across the sea and the land. And, the song at an end, they were grim and silent again, intent upon the bloody business before them. The pirates were preparing, they could see. In a very few minutes the clash would come.

And suddenly, from the distance, from the slope between the two attacking forces, came a solitary voice, also raised in song:

"Atención! A caballero's near — "

They glanced up, astounded. Running down the slope toward them came a figure they knew well. Don Audres Ruiz gave a great cry of joy and thankfulness. The caballeros cheered, and wept unashamed. For well they knew the singer and the song.

"Zorro!" they cried. "Zorro!" And so they rushed to the attack!

Chapter 17
A Wild Ride

THE pirates evidently had decided to make the fight at some little distance from their huts and adobe houses, so they rushed forward, shrieking their battle cries, brandishing their weapons, shouting and cursing to give themselves courage. The great voice of Barbados rolled out above the din in a multitude of commands. The shrill voice of Sanchez echoed him.

The caballeros advanced in a perfect line, their shining blades held ready, grim and silent now, their minds intent upon the bloody business confronting them. Zorro, they could see, was making his way down the slope toward them as speedily as possible, shouting that he was coming, still singing bits of his song between his shouts.

The pirates had a few firearms, but little ammunition for them. And they were more used to fighting hand-to-hand with naked blades. Yet they discharged their firearms as the caballeros advanced, and took a bloody toll. The caballeros had nothing but their blades, for they had come from Don Diego Vega's bachelor supper, and they had worn no firearms to that affair.

There was a moment of silence pregnant with dire possibilities, the lull before the storm — and then the two forces met with a crash! Blades clanged together, men gasped and fought and fell.

The line of caballeros was broken almost immediately, and each found himself the particular foe of three or more pirates. Yet they fought like maniacs, silently at times, right merrily at times, feeling that they were doomed, but determined to do what damage they could before the battle went entirely against them.

And then there was a sudden tumult on the opposite side of the pirates' camp, and into it and among the huts charged the crew of the trading schooner, the captain at their head.

But the pirates were so great in numbers that they were disconcerted only for an instant. From the huts and the adobe buildings poured men Barbados had been general enough to hold in reserve. The crew of the trading schooner was overwhelmed. The men of the sea fought valiantly, but they died with their captain.

And now Zorro had reached the bottom of the slope, and, blade in hand, rushed to join his friends. His sword flashed as he entered the light and tried to turn the tide of battle. His shouts rang out above the bedlam.

'Ha!" he cried. "At the scum, caballeros! They cannot stand against proper men!"

'Ha!" roared the great voice of Sergeant Gonzales, as he fought off two of the pirate crew with his long sword. "To me, Zorro! We'll carve a pathway through the swine!"

But Zorro did not hear him. He had seen that his old friend, Don Audre Ruiz, was sorely pressed, and he fought his way quickly to Don Audre's side. His blade seemed to be half a score as it flashed in and out and downed one of Don Audre's opponent's. Like a man possessed, Zorro pressed forward again, straight at the pirates in the foreground.

"Atencion! A caballero's near — "

He sang it as he fought, stopping the song now and then for an instant to grunt as he made an unusually hard thrust. The men before him broke and fled, and Zorro, with Don Audre at his side, seized the minor advantage of the moment. The other caballeros rallied and followed.

"The ghost!" one of the pirates shrieked. "It is the ghost from the sea!"

"Ha!" Zorro cried, and cut down another man. "Ha, scum! So you fear ghosts? Have at you — "

"Pirates, eh?" Sergeant Gonzales was crying, puffing and blowing out his great cheeks as he fought. "Stand, pirates, and fight like men! Is this a fight or a test of speed, dolts and fools? Meal mush and goat's milk!"

"A ghost!" another man shrieked.

Barbados whirled around in time to see Sanchez, a look of terror in his face, about to retreat. He took in the situation at a glance.

"It is no ghost, fiends of hell!" he shrieked at his men. "'Tis this Señor Zorro somebody has saved from the sea! At him! Fetch him to me alive. Does a ghost fight with a blade that runs red? Get the fiend!"

His words carried weight. The pirates gathered their courage and surged forward again. The other men came running from the huts and the adobe buildings, now that the crew of the trading schooner had been handled. The caballeros found their line broken once more, found that they were being scattered.

Still side by side, Zorro and Don Audre Ruiz fought as well as they could. But here in the open they could not get their backs against a wall. However, they did the next best thing — they stood back to back and engaged a circle of foes.

The fight swirled around them. Zorro's face wore an expression of anxiety now. He knew, fully as well as did Don Audre Ruiz, that this wonderful show of courage and blade skill was availing the caballeros nothing. Slowly but surely, the pirates were traveling the road to triumph.

And now there came an added menace. Among the huts there was a ramshackle corral, in which the pirates had put a number of blooded horses stolen from hacienda owners. And now some of the fighting men crashed against the insecure fencing and demolished it, and the animals, frightened at the din of battle, rushed through the broken place and into the open.

The fighting men, the clashing of blades, the shouts and screams seemed to infuriate the beasts. The smell of blood was in their nostrils. The horses charged wildly through the throng, upsetting caballeros and pirates alike. One noble stallion brushed aside the foes of Zorro and Don Audre Ruiz, but separated them also. Their enemies rushed toward them again before they could get together — and they were no longer back to back.

Their case was desperate now. Each was surrounded and overwhelmed. Zorro fought with what skill he could, keeping a wide circle with his flashing blade. He heard the voice of Sergeant Gonzales roaring in the distance. He heard, also, the thunderous voice of Barbados.

"Alive! Take them alive!" the pirate chief was screeching. "There will be rich ransom! Ransom and torture! Take them alive, fiends!"

Here and there in the open spaces a chorus of fiendish shrieks told that a captive had been taken, his sword whipped from his hand. Zorro suddenly found himself hard pressed, but fought free and made an effort to reach the side of Don Audre again. But that was no easy feat, he discovered.

"Get that Señor Zorro!" Barbados was shouting. "A reward to the men who fetch him to me alive! Ha! This time we'll make a ghost of him indeed!"

Zorro knew a touch of despair for a moment, but he fought it off quickly. If he were captured, the Señorita Lolita would have no protector, and would be at the mercy of these fiends and Captain Ramón. Were it not better to escape, to make an effort to return later, than to fight until death at the side of his friend?

"One of us must win free!" Zorro cried. "There is the señorita to be considered!"

"Get away, Don Diego, my friend!" Audre Ruiz shouted. "Save yourself, and the saints bless you"

"I will return!" Zorro shouted the promise. "Let the beasts take you, Audre! Alive, you may be of some service! Dead — you are gone forever!

Zorro did not listen for an answer. He hurled himself forward, stretched one man on the ground and put the other in momentary flight. And then he whirled again, darted swiftly away, fighting to clear a path.

Down toward him rushed the big stallion, still frightened because of the din of battle. Zorro swept another man from before him and sprang at the horse. He went upon the animal's back, lurched sickeningly for an instant, and righted himself. His balance regained, he kicked at the flanks of his mount. It was all that he could do. The horse was without saddle or bridle, without even a halter.

The animal hesitated, and Zorro kicked again with what strength he could. And the horse, suddenly terrified, sprang forward like some supernatural beast. The pirates went down before him and before Zorro's blade.

Up the slope the big stallion started, almost running down Sergeant Gonzales and the pirates who had already taken him prisoner. Past Fray Felipe he sprang, and Zorro saw the aged fray's hand raised in blessing.

Like a wild animal the stallion dashed at a group of the victorious pirates, who shrieked and scattered to either side. Zorro rode erect, his sword flashing and he was laughing wildly, like a man on the verge of hysterics.

"Señores! Have you ever seen this one?" he screeched.

And so Zorro rode on up the slope, and away from the pirate's camp rode his fiery, unmanagable mount straight at the fringe of trees on the top of the hill.

From the distance came Barbados, fiendish cursing, because the man he most wanted to capture had made an escape.

And Zorro answered it, also from a distance, with a burst of song:
"Atención! A caballero's near — "

CHAPTER 18
Hope is Crushed Again

SENORITA LOLITO PULIDO passed into the store room of the adobe building with her head erect and a look of pride in her face. But when the heavy door was closed behind her, and she heard a bar dropped into place, she changed swiftly.

For a moment she leaned against the door, listening to Barbados and Inez, his woman. Then Barbados went away, and the woman also, and the señorita dropped upon a stool that happened to be in one corner of the room, and buried her face in her hands.

It was dark in the store room, but presently the door was opened and the woman, Inez, entered with a small torch made of palm fiber and tallow. She fastened the torch to the wall, went out again, and returned with food.

"Eat, wench!" Inez commanded. "Eat, and drink your fill of the water! A dainty morsel you are, but there be some men who like women of a different sort. Ha! 'Twould do you no good to make merry eyes at my Barbados!"

The señorita got up from the stool suddenly and stepped forward. Her hands were at her sides, her chin was raised, there was pleading in her face.

"You are a woman," she said, softly. "In your heart there must be some sympathy for other women."

"Not much," Inez acknowledged. "Few women have shown sympathy or kindness toward me. I was a poor girl working on a hacienda, and listened to the lies of a handsome traveler. And when my fault was discovered it was the women who turned their backs. A woman of your class, wench, kicked me out!"

"That is the way of the world," Lolita told her. "Still, you must have in your breast some inkling of pity. Would you see the thing happen to me that is going to happen if I cannot avoid it?"

"Ha!" Inez laughed. "What would you?"

"Help me get away!' the señorita begged. "Help me to be free, and in some manner I'll get up El Camino Real in Reina de Los Angeles. I have friends. In time I'll send you more money than Barbados will get from Captain Ramón."

"And Barbados would take the money from me, slit my throat, and find him another woman," Inez replied, laughing coarsely. "I know nothing of his business deals with Captain Ramón or any other. Nor do I care to know them!"

"Have you no pity?"

"I have nothing to do with it," the woman declared. "I have orders to give you water and food and a light, and I have done so. That is the end."

"Before the señorita could speak again the woman had gone out and closed the door. By the light of the torch she inspected her prison room. There was nothing in it except some old casks that once had contained olives and tallow. There was but the one door, and only a single window, and the window was small and had bars of metal across it.

Escape was impossible, the señorita decided. Tired, exhausted by the events of the day, she found sleep descending upon her.

A din awakened her. The torch had burned out and the light of day was pouring through the little window. The little señorita was stiff and uncomfortable. She got up and hurried to the window, and by standing upon one of the empty casks managed to peer out of it.

She could see a portion of the camp. The pirates were arming themselves and rushing here and there like madmen. She could hear the great voice of Barbados as he issued his commands. And then there was a lull, and she heard singing in the distance. Another lull and she heard a single voice raised in song:

"Atención! A caballero's near — "

Her heart almost stopped beating for a moment. But in the next instant she told herself that she had been foolish to hope. It was Zorro's song, but he was dead at the bottom of the sea. And other caballeros knew it. It was some caballero singing in the distance. But that gave her a small measure of hope, for it meant that Don Diego's friends were at hand and would make an effort to rescue her.

There was another time of comparative silence, and then the battle began. The señorita could see none of it at first, for she was on the wrong side of the building. But she could hear the shrieks and cries, the ringing of blades, the screeches of pain and curses of anger.

Down from the cask she dropped. She ran across to the door and pounded upon it with her tiny fists, struck it repeatedly, until her hands were cut and bleeding. After a time it was opened, and the woman, Inez, stood before her, thrust her away and entered.

"A battle is taking place, wench!" the woman declared, bracing her fists against her hips. "Some caballeros came in a ship and saw fit to attack the camp. The caballeros are being cut down, of course. We have them three to one! Some are to be taken prisoners, some held for ransom, others tortured. There will be rare sport if this Señor Zorro is taken prisoner."

"Zorro?" the señorita gasped.

"The same, wench! You were to wed with him, I have been told. Ha! He'll not be ready for his wedding when Barbados has finished with him!"

"Señor Zorro is dead'!"

"I know that he walked the plank. And the fools thought that he was a ghost when he appeared here. But somebody must have saved him from the sea. He's out there now, fighting. They will make a captive of him!"

The señorita's heart beat wildly. Then it had been Zorro she had heard singing in the distance!

But in the next instant she told herself that it could not be. Zorro

had walked the plank with a weight fastened to his wrists. The pirates were mistaken. It was some other caballero who looked like Zorro, who fought as he fought, and acted as he acted.

She threw aside the momentary hope, and crept toward the woman Inez again. If the fight was going against the caballeros, if the pirates were to be victors, she had scant time.

The señorita began acting as she never acted before, and though she was new to the game, her woman's intuition, her terror and her desperate need served her well.

"So the pirates are to win!" she said. "And there will be a lot of ransom money and loot. Is it not peculiar that Barbados took me the night before my wedding?"

"Ha! Can you speak with plain meaning?" the woman asked.

"Did you believe the story of Captain Ramón?" the señorita demanded. "I did, too, at first! And then I thought differently. You are getting old, you see, and fat. It is plain to me what is to happen. Barbados means to have me for himself. There is no escape."

"By the devils of Hades!" the woman swore. "If I thought this to be truth — "

"Can you not see that it is?" the señorita queried. "Captain Ramón may have dealings with Barbados, but it does not follow that Captain Ramón is to have me. That was just a little falsehood to fool you, possibly."

The woman Inez was quiet for a moment, and then: "You are right," she replied.

"Help me to escape," the señorita said. "If I am gone, you are in safe possession of the affections of Barbados. He will not raid again soon, will not soon have a chance to find him another woman. And you can, in the meantime, win back his love again."

"Ha! If I aid you to escape he will kill me!"

"Make it appear that I escaped myself," the señorita replied. "You are strong. You can tear out that window until it is large enough for me to get through. Let him think that there was some tool in the storeroom and that I did the work."

The woman hesitated, searching the señorita's face with her keen glance. Then she grunted and hurried into the other room. But presently Inez returned, and she carried a peculiar strip of iron with one sharp end, a bit of wreckage, perhaps, from some ill-fated ship.

"Watch you at the door, on the inside!" she commanded. "Do not go into the other room. They are still fighting and perhaps there will be time." Inez was tearing out the masonry and adobe around the window. The metal bars already were inside the room and out of the way.

"I must have some old clothes — ragged and dirty clothes," the girl said. "I will leave some of these."

The woman did not reply, but she hurried from the storeroom with a gleam of avarice in her eyes. She was more than willing to trade ragged garments for some of silk and satin.

Back she came, after a time, and the señorita pulled off her gown and put on the ragged one, shuddering as she did so, not because of the rags, but because of the dirt. She streaked her face with dirt from the floor, and washed her hands in it, disarranged her hair, and threw a ragged shawl over her head.

"I am afraid!" the woman said.

"And are you afraid, also, of seeing another woman in your place here?"

The face of Inez grew purple for an instant, and her eyes blazed. Suddenly she strode across to the door, opened it, and looked out upon the fighting. She closed the door again, and turned back to face the señorita.

"The fighting now is at some distance," she said. "There is a chance. Wait!"

She whirled around to bar the door of the storeroom. The little señorita waited, trying to be calm, though her heart was pounding at her ribs. She was to escape at last! She could get up the slope, hurry through the trees —

"You must use speed!" the woman was informing her. "And if you are caught, you must take all the blame. Barbados would kill me if he knew."

"Give me a dagger," the señorita begged. "Then, if I am caught, I'll do that which will render me speechless!"

The woman hesitated a moment, and then reached beneath her ragged shawl and drew a dagger out. The señorita clutched it, and hid it away in her bosom.

For another moment they faced each other. And then the woman lnez lurched across the room toward the door, the señorita trotting along at her heels.

And hope turned to black despair once more in the twinkling of an eye! For the door suddenly was thrown open, and before them stood Captain Ramón!

CHAPTER 19
Double-Faced

THERE was a moment of astonishment for all three of them. Then the Señorita Lolita gave a little cry of mingled fright and despair, and recoiled against the wall. Zorro dead, the pirates winning the battle against the caballeros, and before her the man she loathed and feared! The future seemed very dark, indeed.

"Do not be afraid of me, hag!" he told the woman. "I wear the uniform of the Governor's soldiery, it is true, but I am the good friend of Barbados! I am Captain Ramón, of Reina de Los Angeles!"

"Ha!" the woman gasped. She dropped the bar of iron and stood with arms akimbo. "That must be true, else you would not have lived to get to this building," Inez said. "And why are you here?"

"To see the little lady standing behind you," Ramón said, smiling. "She has been kept safe, I see."

"Ha!" Inez gasped. It flashed through her mind, now, that Barbados really had no personal interest in the señorita, and she believed, also, that she had almost been tricked into aiding an important prisoner to escape. A glance at the señorita's face confirmed her suspicion, for Lolita was not acting now. Inez realized that she would have to speak quickly to save herself.

"You come in good time," she declared to the captain. "The wench has been kept in the storeroom. But an instant ago, hearing no sounds within, I unbarred and opened the door. And she had enlarged the window, and dressed in those rags. She intended escaping, señor! Had it not been for me now she would be gone."

"You have done well," Ramón declared. "That is the door to the storeroom?"

"Si!" Inez answered. She dropped the bar and threw the door open. Captain Ramón peered inside, then turned and smiled again, first at the hag, and then at the señorita.

Captain Ramón bowed in mockery. "If you will be kind enough to glance through the open door, señorita, you will perceive that the fighting is at an end," he replied. "What caballeros are not dead have been taken prisoners. And the women and children are mocking them. Go, hag, and mock with the others! I'll guard the señorita well."

He leered at the woman as he spoke, and she grinned and shuffled from the building. She was eager to get at Barbados and tell him how the señorita had attempted an escape, and how she, the loyal and faithful Inez, had prevented it.

"Into the storeroom, señorita!" Captain Ramón commanded when they were alone. He thrust her before him into the storeroom, and closed the door behind him.

"If you would rid me of your foul presence — " the señorita began.

Captain Ramón whirled toward her. On the long, hot ride from Reina de Los Angeles, which had taken him the better part of two days, and during which he had not spared mounts, he had thought out everything.

He was playing a sort of double game, this Captain Ramón. He wished to reinstate himself in the good graces of better men, he wanted to make the señorita believe that he had rendered her a great service and try to win her regard openly, and he wished to aid his master, the Governor, in acquiring credit in the southland, where he had small credit now.

He had heard, on his way to the pirate camp, that Zorro had walked the plank. He could take the helpless señorita now for his own, but if he did that he would have to become a renegade forever, live like an outcast. And Captain Ramón loved his uniform, and wealth and power.

So why not play the pirates and honest men against each other and make a double winning? He had had ample time to think it out. And so, as he faced the señorita's scorn, he pretended surprise that she did not understand.

"Foul presence, señorita?" he said. "After I have risked so much to be of service to you?"

"Of service to me?" she cried. "When I was abducted by your orders, when my home was burned and my father cut down?"

"Have the beasts told you that?" Ramón asked. "That is because Barbados knew I was infatuated with you. He believed I would thank him for doing such a thing."

"You are allied with pirates!" she accused.

"Señorita, by your gentle blood I ask you to give me your ear! I have but pretended friendship with these pirates, that the soldiers may take them later, and hang them all."

"What monstrous falsehood is this?" she asked.

"I beg your attention, señorita! Some of them may be coming soon. I have pretended to be in league with them. They raided Reina de Los Angeles while I and my soldiers were gone. I have followed swiftly to rescue you. They think that I am a friend. But now, assured of your safety, I can act speedily. Let them continue thinking, for the time being, that I accept you as a prize. I shall ride away to San Diego de Alcála, which is but a few miles, fetch the troopers from there, rescue you, release the caballeros now held as prisoners, and wipe out this pirate brood!"

"But why — " she began.

"It was the only way, señorita. The soldiers are few, and the pirates have been able to strike the coast where there were no troopers handy. It is a trap that we have arranged for them. Perhaps it may not seem a gentle thing to do — but one cannot be gentle with pirates."

'I wish that I could believe you," she said.

"Believe me, señorita! I love you so much — "

'I am betrothed," she said simply.

"But I have grave news for you. I have been told that Don Diego Vega is no more, that those beasts forced him, as Señor Zorro, to walk the plank."

"I was there," she said, her eyes filling with tears. "I saw it. Nevertheless, I am betrothed to him, señor, now and forever, in life and in death!"

"That is because your grief is new," the captain said. "You are young, señorita, you have a life to live. If you would live it with me — "

"Señor!" she warned.

"I can understand why you dislike me a bit," he said. "Perhaps, in the past, I did some things that a gentleman should not do. But it was because of my great love for you, because I was afraid of losing you. I intend rescuing you and the friends these pirates now hold as prisoners. I am risking my life to do it. And, if I succeed, cannot you look upon me with some favor?"

"If I have misjudged you, señor, I am indeed sorry," she replied. "But it is useless to talk of such things. My heart is with Don Diego Vega, in life and in death!"

Captain Ramón's face flushed and his eyes blazed for an instant. But he still had his game to play, the many-sided game that he hoped would result in great fortune.

"If you could only believe me!" he said.

"Perhaps — after you have demonstrated your loyalty."

"Then I go now to talk to Barbados, then to San Diego de Alcála for the troopers. Guard yourself well until my return. I must pretend that I wish you watched, kept from escaping. A false move, señorita, and all of us are lost!"

"I can only do as you say," she said. "I will be guarded in any case."

"Come into the other room. I'll call the hag! And I'll return to you before I ride for San Diego de Alcála, if there are more plans you should know."

Captain Ramón opened the door, bowed low as she passed through it, and looked after her with the corners of his lips curled. Then he hurried toward the front, calling for Inez.

CHAPTER 20
The Unexpected

C APTAIN RAMÒN bade the woman guard the señorita well, and then hurried from the adobe building. Captain Ramón darted to the end of the building, so he would not be seen. It was not in his mind to be suspected at the outset. The game he was playing was one of hazard, and he knew that the slightest mistake would be disastrous.

He had planned with Barbados to conduct the raid, and thereby had gained the pirate chief's confidence. And now he had further plans. He would tell Barbados that he would draw to the camp the troopers at San Diego de Alcála. Barbados and his men could ambush them and wipe them out. Then the pirates could cross the hills and raid and loot rich San Diego de Alcála.

But the captain intended no such thing in reality. Knowing how Barbados would prepare the ambush, he would lead the troopers in such a manner that the pirates would be wiped out to a man. Then the caballeros and the señorita could be rescued, and Captain Ramón would pose as their heroic rescuer. He hoped in this manner to regain the good will of the caballeros and a better standing with them, and to earn the gratitude of the señorita also.

Word of the exploit would run up and down El Camino Real. Men whose hands were now raised against the licentious and unscrupulous Governor would think better of him because the pirates had been wiped out. The Governor, in turn, would be grateful to Captain Ramón. And he would order Don Carlos Pulido, who was not dead of his wound, to give the hand of his daughter, Lolita, to Captain Ramón. Don Carlos scarce could refuse without endangering his fortunes further.

It was a pretty plot, the plot of a master rogue willing to sell friends and foes alike to advance his own interests. Captain Ramón grinned as he thought of it, and twirled his mustache, and marched around the corner of the building and across the open space toward where Barbados was standing and shouting orders concerning the disposition of the corpses.

"Ha!" the pirate cried. "You must have made haste to get here in such season."

"I almost killed two horses," the captain said.

"In such eager haste to see the wench, eh? And have you seen her?"

"She is safe and sound. She made an attempt to escape, but your woman stopped her."

"I wish you joy of the wench. There is too much of the fire of anger in her makeup to suit me," Barbados declared, laughing raucously. "The taming of her will take more than an hour's time, commandante!"

"Leave that to me!" Ramón said. "There are other things to be discussed now."

They walked some distance, to a spot where they would not be overheard.

"You know, certainly, the meaning of all this," Ramón said. "The Governor, who hates this southland, is eager to have it troubled as much as possible, even if he is forced to sacrifice a few of his own men."

"Si!" Barbados said, both in question and in affirmation.

"See that the senorita is guarded well, and, in the meantime, before I think of such things as love, let us attend to more serious business."

"Is there a chance of profit?"

"How would you like to raid rich San Diego de Alcála when there would be small danger?"

The eyes of Barbados glistened. He knew a great deal about San Diego de Alcála. The town was rich, and the mission also. Wealth had been stored there since the earliest days of the missions.

"Attend me!" Ramón commanded. "You have certain caballeros held as prisoners, and the señorita also. I'll go to San Diego de Alcála and spread the news at the presidio. I outrank the commandante there, and my words will be commands."

"I understand, capitan!"

"There are only a few troopers there now, the remainder having been sent to San Juan Capistrano to put down mutinous natives. I'll lead these troopers back to the pirate camp. Do you arrange an ambush at the head of the little cañon. I'll lead the men into it. You and your crew can cut them down. And then the way to San Diego de Alcála will be open to you!"

"By my naked blade — " Barbados swore.

"You must understand this thing, of course — it must look like a mistake. No man ever must think that the Governor had a hand in it, or that I did myself."

"I understand, capitan!"

"I'll have speech with the señorita again, and then ride like the wind. As soon as I have departed, arrange your men in the ambush. I'll return with the troopers before nightfall. You can wipe them out, attack San Diego de Alcála tonight, return, abandon this camp, and sail away and establish another on the coast of Baja California. You'll have wealth, women; your name will be spoken with respect!"

Captain Ramón whirled around and hurried back toward the adobe building. Inez had the señorita in the front room, guarding her well. She had just finished a tirade concerning the attempt of the señorita to engineer an escape through cunning words and implications.

Captain Ramón ordered the woman outside, and urged the señorita to go into the storeroom again.

"It is arranged," he said. "I ride for San Diego immediately. Do you continue to remain a prisoner, señorita, and save yourself from harm. Before the fall of night I'll be back with the troopers, this pirate brood will be wiped out, and you and the caballeros will be liberated. Then you can go up El Cainino Real to your father."

"If you accomplish this thing, you shall have my gratitude," the señorita said.

"Nothing more than gratitude?"

"I have spoken concerning that, señor. There can be nothing but gratitude."

Captain Ramón suddenly whirled toward her. "It is something more than gratitude that I want!" he said. "Is your heart made of ice? Mine is flaming!"

"Señor!"

"What whim is it that makes you cling to the memory of a dead man?" he asked. "You are young, with a life before you."

"Please leave me with my sorrow, señor!"

"Then I may expect better treatment when your sorrow is somewhat dulled by time?"

"I am afraid not, señor."

"I risk my life in the service of you and your friends, and am to have no reward?"

"A man of gentle blood would not think of being rewarded for such a thing," she replied.

The face of Captain Ramón flushed and he took another step toward her. "I am sick of hearing so much of gentle blood," he said. "Mine is gentle enough, but it also can be hot at times. Am I a man to brook such nonsense? You owe me gratitude, and something more! One embrace, at least, here and now!"

"I would rather die than have you touch me!" she cried. "You show your true colors again, commandante!"

"One embrace, and I make you forget this Señor Zorro!"

"If he were here, señor, you would not dare speak so!" she said. "You would cringe in terror, you who wear the mark of Zorro on your brow! It was for an insult to me that he put it there! It is like a coward to attack a helpless girl! If Zorro were here — "

"But he is not here!" Ramón cried, laughing and leering at her. "And so — "

Again he started toward her, and her hand darted to her bosom to snatch out the dagger the woman Inez had given her earlier. But she did not draw out the dagger.

The window behind them was suddenly darkened, and the light shut off. Into the storeroom plunged a man who struggled to get free from the woman's clothes which he wore over his own. As Captain Ramón recoiled and the señorita gave a little cry of fright the intruder's head flew up.

A blade flashed, the señorita found herself hurled to one side gently and Captain Ramón found two eyes blazing into his — the eyes of Zorro!

And, with his left hand, he slapped the commandante of the presidio of Reina de Los Angeles so that his head rocked!

Chapter 21
Face to Face

ZORRO, on the back of the infuriated and unmanageable stallion, had made his escape easily from the pirate camp. There was no question of him being overtaken, but for a time there was a grave question of Zorro stopping the steed he rode.

Over the crest of the slope the animal beneath him plunged down into a ravine and galloped along it. Zorro sheathed his sword and held on to the horse's mane. He bent low to avoid tree branches that promised to sweep him from the animal's back.

Some distance the frightened horse traveled, and then he made a great circle and returned toward the pirate camp. But Zorro had no wish to return there too soon, lest he be captured in the vicinity. And so he waited until the horse, negotiating a slippery incline, slackened pace somewhat, and slipped easily from the animal's back.

He was quite a way from the camp, but he could see it in the distance, see the dead and wounded on the ground, and a crowd of the pirates, with their women and children, in front of the adobe building that was being used as a prison.

Zorro sat down to rest and watch. He knew that he was confronted by a dire emergency and a tremendous task, but he refused to admit it to himself. The señorita was down there, and she was to be rescued. And Don Audre Ruiz and the caballeros were there, to be rescued also.

Zorro, after a breathing spell, got up and walked slowly along the crest of the slope among the stunted and wind-twisted trees, making certain that he could not be observed from the camp. He came a distance nearer, and watched for a time again. And he saw Captain Ramón!

If it had been in the mind of Zorro to await the night before descending into the camp again that idea left his mind now. He hurried forward as speedily as possible, stopping now and then to listen, for fear some of the pirates may have been sent to search for him.

He did not know, could not think, how he was to enter the camp in the broad light of day without escaping discovery. And he could do little single-handed against the victorious pirate crew. Yet the plight of the little señorita called to him for action, and he knew that something should be done at once.

And suddenly he stopped, for he had smelled smoke. Almost silently he crept forward through the brush, and came to a small clearing.

There he saw a hut, from the chimney of which smoke was issuing. Zorro approached the hut carefully, crept around the corner of it, and peered in at the door to find the place empty. He rushed inside and sought frantically for what he desired. There came a chuckle of delight as he found it.

What he desired and found was nothing more than a ragged skirt and a wide, dirty shawl. Zorro put them on quickly, bent his shoulders, and hobbled back among the trees and brush. It was a disguise that would serve for the time being.

Beneath the skirt was the sword of Zorro, ready to be whipped from its scabbard. Zorro felt confident as long as the blade was at his side.

He left the fringe of trees at some distance from the hut, and made his way down the slope.

As he came nearer the camp he was doubly cautious. The pirates, for the greater part, were gathered around the adobe building where the cabbaleros were being held prisoners.

Zorro perceived that he had arrived at an opportune time. Nobody would give any attention to a woman stumbling along toward the scene of excitement. The pirates, undoubtedly, imagined that Zorro had ridden far away, perhaps to San Diego de Alcála for help.

He approached nearer. There were two large adobe buildings, and he supposed that the señorita was held prisoner in one of them, but he did not know which.

Then he stopped suddenly, and bent his shoulders more. For he saw Captain Ramón talking to Barbados, saw the commandante turn and leave the pirate chief and hurry into the nearest adobe building. Zorro guessed that the señorita was there.

He hobbled forward again, alert to keep a certain distance from any of the pirates or women, for he realized that they knew one another well. He reached the corner of the building, and began to circle it, listening intently for the voice he hoped to hear.

He heard it. Pretending to be picking up something from the ground, Zorro bent against the wall and listened. He heard Captain Ramón's statements, heard the señorita reply, listened with a grim expression on his face while the commandante begged for an embrace.

It would be perilous to enter that building now, Zorro knew. Ramón would call the pirates, but perhaps he could be silenced first. However, there could be no hesitation. The señorita was there, being affronted, and was to be spared insult.

Zorro saw the window, and guessed that he could manage to struggle through it. He raised his head and glanced inside. He saw the señorita recoiling, the commandante approaching her.

Zorro hesitated no longer. He sprang up and scrambled through the window. He tore at the woman's clothing that clung to him, got free of it, and whipped out the sword of Zorro. He pressed the señorita to one side out of harm's way, and confronted his enemy.

His open hand cracked against Captain Ramóns head. And then he stepped back, on guard, giving the renegade officer his chance, though he little deserved it.

"Your are alive!" the señorita gasped.

"Ha! Very much alive!" Zorro replied. "Stand back against the wall, señorita, and turn your pretty face away. This is not going to be pleasant for a dainty lady's eyes to watch!"

CHAPTER 22
A Price to be Paid

THE face of Captain Ramón turned livid as he struggled to get his sword from its scabbard. There was a look of fear in his countenance, too.

"Zorro!" he cried. "Señor Zorro, eh?"

"Si! Zorro!" came the answer. "There is not water enough in all the sea to drown me while there remains something to be avenged. We have crossed blades before, señor, and I have marked you. But this time shall be the last. A fatal wound this time, capitan! It is an honor that I do not cut you down without giving you the chance to defend yourself!"

Captain Ramón finally had his sword out, and now he was on guard. But he could not forget that once before in his life he had crossed blades with Señor Zorro, and Zorro had played with him as a cat plays with a mouse, and finally had left him for dead after marking him on the forehead.

And so the captain grew desperately afraid, feeling that he had small chance against the better sword play of the other. He sprang back toward the door to the front room, but found Señor Zorro before him blocking the way.

"Are you a coward and would run?" Zorro taunted. "A pretty soldier, by the saints!"

"Ha! Señor Zorro is here!" the commandante shouted at the top of his lung power. "Zorro is here! To me, pirates!"

He had no time to say more. Señor Zorro's face assumed an expression of grim determination, and he advanced swiftly. But Captain Ramón had found another method of protection for the time being. He sprang back beside the señorita, grasped her roughly and held her before him, shielding his body with hers. And he continued his shouting, hoping to attract the attention of Barbados and his men.

"Poltroon!" Zorro sneered. "Coward and dog!"

"Fly, Diego!" the señorita begged. "The pirates will be here and take you."

"When I have slain this arrant coward and rescued you, and not before!" Señor Zorro declared.

He danced toward Captain Ramón again, but the commandante was back in a corner now, holding the señorita close before him, and Señor Zorro was afraid to attempt a thrust. The señorita made a struggle to get free, but found that she could not.

In the other room the woman Inez had heard the tumult and the words. She had dared to open the door a crack and peer inside, and then she had closed the door again and barred it quickly, and hurried into the open.

"Barbados!" she shrieked. "Sanchez! Fiends of hell! Señor Zorro is here trying to kill the captain! Come and take him!"

Barbados heard and understood her shrieks, as did some of the others near. They rushed across the open space and crowded into the front room of the building. From the storeroom came the sound of Señor Zorro's voice.

"Hide behind a woman, eh, coward? Come out and fight, poltroon! Come out, renegade! Is there no insult strong enough to bring you forth?"

Barbados motioned with one hand. Inez unbarred the door and threw it open. Into the storeroom tumbled the pirates, their blades held ready.

"Take him alive!" Barbados thundered. "Catch me this land pirate unhurt!"

Señor Zorro whirled to confront them. He darted to a corner and threw up his blade. He sprang forward a few steps wounded a man, retreated again.

But he knew that the weight of numbers was against him in such cramped fighting quarters, and he could not get to the window and make an escape. They hurled themselves upon him, buried him beneath their combined weight, disarmed him, and forced him to his feet again.

They lashed his hands behind his back, and Barbados, now that it was a safe thing to do, stalked forward and spat at him.

"So, Señor Zorro, we have you in our hands again!" Barbados said.

"This time it will be fire or steel instead of water since you seem to swim so well! And this time, senor, we make a real ghost out of you!"

Captain Ramón lurched forward, his face purple with wrath. "Do with him as you will," he said to Barbados. "But let me have a hand in it!"

"Ha! You had your chance, capitan, a moment ago, and did not make much of it!" Barbados replied, grinning. "I'll have him put in the other adobe building with the caballeros. Fiends of hell, take him away!"

The senorita made an attempt to get forward, but the pirates thrust her back. They took Señor Zorro away, and the grinning Barbados followed them. The captain turned to face the senorita once more.

"Señorita, you must try to understand," he said. "I could not act or speak in any other manner. The pirates must still think that I am one of them, else I cannot get to San Diego de Alcála and fetch the soldiers."

"There is small need of further pretense, señor," she replied with much scorn in her manner. "I know you for what you are!"

"You are inclined to show bravery, now that you know this Señor Zorro is alive, eh?" he said. "But will he live long, in the hands of these pirates, some of whose friends he has slain? This Barbados loves ransom money, but Don Diego Vega is one man who never will be ransomed. For Barbados loves vengeance, too!"

"I cannot endure your presence longer," she said. "Leave me alone with my sorrows!"

"Nor can I endure your scorn much longer," Captain Ramón replied. "Has it occurred to you that you are in my power completely, if I will it so?"

"Now you show your true colors again, señor. And there is always death!"

"And torture!" Captain Ramón added. "That will befall this Señor Zorro, no doubt!"

"Torture?" she cried. "Ha! Real torture, such as only these beasts of pirates know how to inflict!" he declared. "No man can stand against such a thing for long. He will beg and shriek for the release of death when the pain begins."

"No — no!" she cried. "And you will be forced to watch it, no doubt!" the commandante continued. "Barbados, his men say, is a master hand at torture of all kinds. They'll chip at him with their knives, sear his flesh with white-hot brands — "

"Señor, for the love of the saints — "

"You do not like the picture? Wait until you see the reality, which will be much worse than words could paint!"

"If I could save him — give my life for his — "

The captain looked at her sharply. "Perhaps there may be a way," he said.

"What mean you?"

"I can have speech with this fiend of a Barbados and coax him to delay the torture until he has accounted for the troopers from San Diego de Alcálda. The troopers will account for him and his men instead, of course, and then Señor Zorro and the caballeros will be released."

"And you will do this?" she cried. "Ah, señor, if only you would!"

"I can do it, señorita — at a price!" "And what is the price?" she asked. "You are the price yourself, señorita."

"Beast!"

"Is that a way to save Señor Zorro by calling me a beast?" the captain asked. "All that I ask is an immediate marriage. Would it be an ill thing to wed with one of his excellency's officers?"

"I cannot! My heart is not my own!"

"Can you hesitate?" the captain asked. "One way, you will be my wife, and Señor Zorro will be saved from torture and will be set free. The other way, senorita, he will be tortured until he dies — and you will come to me unwed!"

"Oh!" she gasped. "That a man could be such a fiend — "

"Love drives men to do strange things, señorita."

"Love!" she cried. "You know not the meaning of the word! To love is to be gentle, to cherish and protect!"

"I know the meaning as it appeals to me," the captain declared. "And I have scant time, if you are to agree. Fray Felipe is in the camp, and he can wed us. Barbados is afraid to affront a fray and will not see Felipe harmed. So he lets him roam around, though he is watched."

"I cannot!"

"Very well, señorita. It is for you to make the decision. But I am afraid that the pirates will have their way. And their way will not be a gentle one!"

"Can you not be a proper man?" she cried. "Can you not save him without exacting such a payment? For once in your life, señor, can you not show yourself a caballero?"

"Save him and let him claim you?" Ramón asked. "You are asking far too much!"

"Is there no other way?"

"None!" he replied. "There are certain things that you must do — be my wife, and I will save Señor Zorro by fetching the troopers from San Diego de Alcála. And afterward you must say that I did but trick the pirates, and that you wed me in gratitude for saving you from them."

"Such a falsehood would not come easily from my lips, señor," she said. "And how can I trust you? How do I know that you would fetch the troopers?"

"I am not afraid to make the bargain," he told her. "You need not wed me until after the pirates are defeated and the caballeros are released. "That is fair enough for both, is it not? But how, on the other hand, may I be assured that you will not forget your part of the bargain, once I have done my share?"

'Señor!" she cried, her face flaming. "Would a daughter of the Pulidos break her given word?"

"Then you give it?" he asked.

"Not yet!" she replied firmly. "There are to be certain stipulations, señor."

"And they — " he questioned.

"I must see Señor Zorro alone and speak to him, and explain just what I intend to do. I would tell him the truth — that you will save him and the others if I wed you. I would not have him think that my heart is one that can change so easily."

"Ha! After that you would have to save him against his will. He would not accept the sacrifice."

"Then will I save him despite himself," she declared. "And you need not fear for the future in such case, señor. Once we were wed, Señor Zorro would not raise his hand against you if I asked him not to do so."

"Perhaps it may be arranged," Captain Ramón said.

He was plotting more, even as he spoke. He did not see how he could lose in this game. If he fetched the troopers, and the pirates were wiped out and the caballeros saved, the señorita would keep her word if she had given it. Men might despise him for taking advantage of a situation, yet would he be safe. And perhaps, for a small sum, he could have this Señor Zorro killed yet.

And if the pirates through some fortune of war managed to be victorious over the troopers, the Captain Ramón could do the other thing — simply seize the senorita, give señore Zorro up to torture, and remain a renegade, perhaps even become a pirate chief himself in the future.

"I will speak to no other man, señor — only Zorro," she said, as he seemed to hesitate. "I will not betray your double-dealing to the pirate crew, for that would defeat all our ends and mean death for Señor Zorro and the caballeros, and much worse for me. But I must speak to Señor Zorro a moment before I give you my decision in the matter."

"I will try to arrange it with Barbados," Captain Ramón replied. "Come into the other room and let the woman guard you until I return. You must play the game well if you would be successful. And there is scant time. I should start my ride to San Diego de Alcála as quickly as possible."

CHAPTER 23
The Senorita Plots Also

CAPTAIN RAMÒN, hurrying outside, found Barbados in the open space before the other adobe building. The pirate chief, it is easy to see, had been drinking heavily of rich, stolen wine. Among the pirates slain were some of Barbados's particular friends, and he was trying to drown his sorrow at their untimely taking off.

He turned as the commandante approached and greeted him with a shout.

"Ha!" he cried, lurching drunkenly. "So you have not started for San Diego de Alcâla yet, capitan? You have just come from the little señorita — si? Yet your face does not bear the marks of her nails, which is strange. I would not want the taming of her. By the naked blade, I would not!"

"Attend me!" the captain commanded, grasping the pirate chief by the arm. "Is it your intention to torture this Señor Zorro your men have taken?"

Barbados cursed loudly, breathed heavily, and squinted his eyes until they were only two tiny slits. "I shall make him squirm and squeal!" he declared loudly. "And then I shall turn him into a proper ghost!"

"Death is nothing to a man like that," Captain Ramón told him. "But torture is a different matter."

"Then I'll see to it that he is prettily tortured!" Barbados declared.

"There are two sorts of torture, Barbados — the physical and the mental," said the captain.

"Mental? I do not understand such things!"

"Torture to the mind," the captain explained. "That is the worst kind by far. If you would have some sport with this Señor Zorro, whom we both hate, listen to me. The señorita, who was to have been his bride, is afraid that you will torture and slay him. I have told her that I will save him by fetching the troopers from San Diego de Alcála — if she will wed with me."

"Ha! Is this treason?" Barbados cried.

"Are you a fool?" questioned the captain. "And am I one? There must be no talk of treason between us. Attend! She will go to this Señor Zorro and explain to him what she intends doing. Just think of that, Barbados! There is torture for you! He, who loves her so much, will think that she is to become the bride of another man. Ha!" He will squirm and squeal indeed! A prisoner, and unable to prevent it! Ha!"

"Ha!" Barbados cried, understanding finally, and grinning to show his appreciation.

"And we will taunt him with it," the commandante continued. "We'll watch him squirm!"

"But it appears to me, capitan, that in this affair you are acting the part of an ass," Barbados dared to say. "Why work so hard to get the wench to agree to wed you when you can take her at your pleasure?"

"Because it will hurt this Señor Zorro a great deal more to know that she gives her consent," the captain replied. "We'll taunt him about it, and then I'll ride for the soldiers. And your men will sweep them off the earth and then ride to San Diego de Alcála and loot the place. As for this Señor Zorro — having tortured him mentally, you will proceed to torture him physically when you celebrate your victory."

"It appeals to me!" Barbados declared suddenly. "He slew some of my closest friends. Yet I would not wait too long! Some of these fine enemies must be tortured soon, while I am in the proper mood for it!"

"And there can be more mental torture," the captain said. "Do not touch him until the very last. Make him watch as some of his friends are being tortured. Let him hear their shrieks of pain. Let him see Don

Audre Ruiz, his boon companion, suffer. That will hurt him as much as being tortured himself."

"Ha! By the naked blade, capitan, you should have been born a pirate!" Barbados shrieked.

"Then it is agreed?"

"Si! It is agreed!"

"I will get the señorita and let her tell Señor Zorro what she intends to do."

"There are two rooms in that adobe building," Barbados explained. "This Señor Zorro is alone in the front one, for I thought it best not to put him with the others. The door between has a heavy lock, and I have the key. You can let the señorita go in there, and we'll listen at the window and enjoy his pain when she tells him. Ha! I say it again, capitan — you should be a pirate! You are wasted in the army!"

Captain Ramón hastened back to the señorita, whispered that he had been able to arrange things as she wished, grinned at old Inez, and then conducted the daughter of the Pulidos across the open space and toward the adobe building where Señor Zorro and the caballeros were being held prisoners.

Barbados was waiting. He leered at the girl, then called one of his men to his side, and commanded that he unfasten and open the door. Señor Zorro, his wrists still lashed behind his back, was pacing around the room. From the room adjoining came the voices of the caballeros.

"Señor Zorro, here is a pretty wench who has some words for your ears," Barbados called. "She is not so pretty as she was, having dirtied herself in an attempt to escape, but possibly she will serve. I give you a few minutes in which to hold speech. Do not abuse the privilege."

"Whatever you may do in the future I thank you for this, Señor Pirate!" Zorro said.

Barbados laughed and withdrew, and closed the door behind him. The señorita stepped forward slowly, her hands held at her breast, a look of anguish in her sweet face. Señor Zorro was smiling down at her.

"The saints are good, señorita!" he whispered. "That I may see you again — "

"Diego, my beloved, it is a sad errand!" she interrupted. "Yet I had to come."

His face was grave for an instant, and then he smiled at her once more.

"So they have sent you to tell me that I must die?" he asked. "I could not receive a warrant of death from sweeter hands. My one regret is that I have failed in your rescue. I do not fear the coming of death. It will be only another adventure. It is for you that I fear."

"Fear not for me!" she said, "Nor fear the coming of death, either. It is not a warrant of death that I bring you, Diego. I have come to tell you that you are to go free."

'Free?" Señor Zorro gasped. "Have pirates turned kind? Has old Fray Felipe demonstrated to them the error of their ways? Is the devil going to mass these days? Señorita, you are trying to make the sentence lighter by saying it in a kind manner. Speak out! Don Diego Vega is not afraid to learn the truth, and most certainly Señor Zorro is not."

"I know that you are not afraid, Diego. I dread to tell you this thing, though it means your life."

He stepped closer to her suddenly, and looked down into her eyes. "What are you trying to tell me?" he asked kindly. "Do not be afraid to speak."

"That you are to go free, Diego," she replied, failing to meet his glance.

"And how may that be?" he asked.

"Captain Ramón is to arrange it."

"Put not your trust in Ramón!"

"Ah, Diego, but there is naught else to do!" she said. "He tells me that he is tricking the pirates. He will ride to San Diego de Alcála and return with the troopers from the presidio there. The pirates will be slain or captured, and you and the caballeros will be saved."

"Ramón will do this?" Señor Zorro cried. "Is there some hidden spark of gentlehood in the beast?"

"He will do it, Diego — for a price."

"I might have known it! Well, I can pay the cur! What is the price?"

"Not money, Diego, beloved! The price is that I wed him."

Señor Zorro sucked in his breath sharply and bent quickly over her.

"You wed with him?" he said. "Wed with a snake like Captain Ramón?"

"Only to save you, Diego! Ah, do not think that I am untrue! He but asks my word — the word of a Pulido! And the wedding is not to take place until he returns with the troopers, the pirates are slain, and you are free."

"Señorita — "

"There will be torture and death for you, else," she was quick to add. "And I will remain true, Diego. I shall but promise to wed him, understand. And after the ceremony, before he can claim me as his bride, I — I shall die!"

"And do you think that I would accept such a sacrifice?" Señor Zorro asked. "Could I live and see you the bride of another man? And could I live knowing that you had taken your own life for me? No, señorita!"

"If I do not, they will torture and slay you!"

"Then let them torture and slay!" he said. "You cannot do this thing! You — a daughter of the Pulido blood! Think of the blood in your veins!"

"I could not be his wife, except in name, but I can die!" she said. "Only a thrust of the dagger after the ceremony! The blood of the Pulidos tells me to do that!"

"I command you — entreat you — "

"Can I see you die?" she asked. "And, if I refuse, there will be nothing except death for me as well as for you. For Ramón will try, then, to make me his bride by force."

"Better to die in defense of your honor, señorita, than have your fair name linked with his even for a moment!" Señor Zorro declared. "I demand that you refuse to do this thing! Ah, señorita, all hope is not gone! They have taken my sword, and they have bound my hands, but I am not helpless entirely. The spirit of Zorro still burns in my breast! Given but a little time, and I'll win through!"

"Diego!"

"If we could work for time — " he said.

"Perhaps I can hold him off for an hour," she whispered. "But no longer than that, I am sure. And — there may be a way. I have thought of something!"

"What is it?"

"Whisper," she commanded "I am sure that they are listening outside the window. Pretend that all is agreed between us. Let me embrace you!"

Barbados and Captain Ramón not only were listening, but also they were peering through the window. And they saw her go up close to him, press against him, saw her arms go around him, as though in a last embrace. But her back was toward the window, and they could not see all.

For, as she pressed against him, the little señorita took from her bosom the dagger that the woman Inez had given her when she had attempted to make an escape, and which had been forgotten afterward. And she reached around him even as she buried her head against his breast, and sawed with the sharp dagger at the cords that bound his wrists.

"Careful!" she warned. "Hold the ends of the ropes, so they will not know that you are free!"

"Si!" he breathed. "Never in all the world was there ever a señorita like you! Hope sings within me again!"

"Do not let it show in your face!" she warned.

Her hands crept to the front again, and she slipped the dagger into the sash around his waist. She knew that he felt it, and knew that it was there. And then she stepped back, and raised her voice so that those at the window could hear.

"It is the only way, Diego!" she said. "I must leave you — I cannot endure this scene longer! Take my lips, Diego — for the last time!"

She raised her head, and her eyes closed. He bent forward, their lips touched. And then she gave a little cry as though of pain and rushed back toward the door. And Señor Zorro remained standing against the wall, anguish in his countenance.

Barbados opened the door and let the señorita out of the room, then closed and fastened the door again. Captain Ramón hurried up to her.

"You have decided, señorita?" he asked.

"Almost am I ready to give you my sacred word, but not quite," she replied. "It is a terrible thing for me, señor. Give me but one little hour. Let me go to old Fray Felipe and have him pray with me."

"I am growing tired of waiting!" Captain Ramón said. "I should be on my way already. Why not decide now?"

"You will have ample time to return with the troopers long before nightfall," she whispered quickly, as Barbados turned away to howl an order to some of his men. "Give me only an hour, perhaps less!"

"Very well — an hour!" said the captain. "But no longer! I'll find the fray for you, and put you both in one of the huts under guard until you can make up your mind."

CHAPTER 24
Into the Open

SEÑOR ZORRO fought the battle of his life, after the little señorita had gone and the door had been closed and barred, to keep from showing his elation in his face.

His hands now would be free at any time he wished to drop the ends of the cords that bound his wrists. He had a weapon hidden in the sash about his waist. Given those minor advantages, Señor Zorro felt that he could disconcert his enemies again, else fail to be Zorro.

But the expression in his face did not change as he walked slowly around the room and finally came to a stop before the window and glanced across the clearing and the beach toward the glistening water of the bay. He looked like a man devoid of all hope, expecting the worst.

Not so very far away was a small hut, before the one door of which two of the pirates sat on guard. Señor Zorro was well aware of the fact that the weapons of the captured caballeros, and those of their comrades who had been slain, were in there, and that his own beloved sword was there also, waiting to be claimed by him.

And, as he watched, Sanchez rode wildly into the clearing on a magnificent horse, undoubtedly stolen from some great hacienda. Barbados' lieutenant dismounted and allowed the animal to wander near the hut while he hurried in search of the pirate chief with some report.

These things Señor Zorro saw quickly, and then he hurried back to the door that opened into the other room. It was barred, and locked with a strong lock, and Zorro had no tools with which to open it. He could not unfasten it and release his friends, but he could hold speech with them.

He made certain that nobody was near the window to overhear, and then kicked against the door to attract the attention of the caballeros.

"Audre!" he called, in a guarded voice.

There was silence for a moment, and then he heard a whisper from the other side of the door.

"Si?"

"I have another chance, Audre. The señorita has cut my bonds and given me a dagger. It is a poor weapon, but better than none. It would avail us nothing for me to let you out if I could, for the pirates greatly outnumber us. But I can try to escape and ride to San Diego de Alcála for troopers."

"Good, Diego, my friend!"

"I know not what may happen before I am able to return. Ramón is in the camp and up to some sort of deviltry. But, should you escape, look to the señorita!"

"Be assured of that!" Don Audre replied.

"If I can do so, when I escape I'll take her with me. If not, I'll return with the troopers as swiftly as possible. The saints be with you!"

"And with you!" Don Audre Ruiz returned.

Señor Zorro walked slowly away from the door and approached the window again. The horse Sanchez had been riding was now but a short distance from the adobe building. The two guards were squatted before the hut wherein the captured weapons had been stored, drinking and talking. Other pirates were in the distance, walking around, stretched in the shade of the huts, gambling, shouting, quarreling.

Señor Zorro knew well that it would profit nothing to get those weapons in the hut, for the caballeros could not be liberated quickly, and so the element of surprise in an attack would be lost. Moreover, were they liberated and their swords in their hands, they would only be cut down by the pirate crew after they had taken some toll.

Señor Zorro wanted his own sword, but did not know whether there would be time for him to get possession of it. He would not dare stop to attack the two guards, for the other pirates would rush up and endanger his chance for escape. It would be far better, he decided quickly, to seize the horse and ride with what speed he could toward the distant village of San Diego de Alcála, get help there at the presidio, and return to the work of rescue with an armed force behind him.

Back to the door he hurried.

"Audre!" he called, softly.

"Raise a din in there, create a bedlam of a sort, and 'twill help me vastly. Pretend to be fighting among yourselves."

He did not have very long to wait. He could hear Don Audre Ruiz whispering instructions to the other cabelleros, and almost instantly they began shrieking at one another, pounding on the heavy door, making a bedlam of noise. Señor Zorro hurried across to the outside window and called to the guards before the hut.

"Come here!" he shouted. "The prisoners are fighting and slaying one another!"

But they refused to leave their posts, the Señor Zorro had hoped they would do. Instead, they shrieked the news at Barbados, who was not far away, and he ran toward the adobe building followed by Sanchez and half a dozen of the men. They unbarred the door and burst in upon Señor Zorro, who stood back against the wall gazing at the door of the adjoining room, as though trying to decide what was taking place inside. From the other side of that door came shrieks and cries and sounds of blows.

"Fiends of hell!" Barbados swore. "They will slay one another, and then there will be neither torture nor ransom! Unfasten that door and stand ready to drive them back if they try to make an escape. And two of you guard that outside door also!"

One glance he flung at Señor Zorro to find him standing against the wall as if his attention were concentrated on the other room. But as Barbados turned toward the door again Señor Zorro shifted along the wall for a distance of a few feet, and glanced toward the door through which he would have to go to freedom.

He waited until the other door was about to be thrown open, until the pirates in the room had their attention centered there, and then Señor Zorro dropped the severed cords from his wrists, wriggled his fingers for an instant to restore the circulation of blood, and suddenly brought his hands around in front of him and tore the dagger from his sash, where the little señorita had put it.

Forward he hurled himself, just as the other door was opened. He took the two men before him by surprise. One he hurled aside; the other he was forced to wound slightly to get him out of the way. Past them he dashed, even as they shrieked the intelligence that he was escaping. Out into the open he darted and straight toward the horse that Sanchez had ridden into the clearing. He would have no difficulty in getting to the horse, he saw. But his escape was all that he could negotiate. A glance told him that the señorita was not in sight, and he had no time to search the entire camp for her.

The pirates were rushing toward him from every side, attracted by the tumult. Barbados, behind him, was shrieking commands and foul oaths. The dagger held between his teeth,

Señor Zorro dodged the two men before the hut and vaulted into the saddle, kicked at the animal's flanks, and was away.

Behind him a pistol barked, but the ball flew wild, and he could hear the insane roar of rage that Barbados gave because he had missed the target. It was a flying target now. Señor Zorro bent low over the horse's neck and kicked frantically at the animal's flanks again. Straight across the clearing he guided the animal, toward the trail that ran to the crest of the slope.

Another pistol roared behind him, but he did not even hear the shrill whistling of the flying ball. He wished that he might make a search for the señorita, but he was afraid that capture might result if he tried it.

And were he captured again Barbados would make short work of him. It were better to get away free and return later to rescue.

He was approaching the edge of the camp now. He knew that there were some mounts with saddles and bridles on, and that there might be a pursuit. Once over the crest, he would have a chance. The pirates would not dare follow him too close to San Diego de Alcála, and that was only eight miles away.

And then he saw, just ahead of him, Captain Ramón. The commandante was drinking from a bottle and talking to some women of the camp. He whirled around when he heard the mad pounding of the horse's hoofs, and Señor Zorro saw his face go white as he struggled to get his sword from its scabbard. The commandante had recognized him.

The women shrieked and fled. Captain Ramón, his sword out, stood his ground. Straight toward him Señor Zorro raced his horse, bending forward, his dagger held in his right hand again. Now he wished he had his beloved sword!

But Ramón sprang out of the way just in time and swung his blade in a vicious blow. It missed Señor Zorro and struck the horse on the rump, inflicting a minor cut. It had the effect, however, of frightening the animal more. Up the slope he raced, and Señor Zorro sat straight in the saddle and shrieked at the top of his voice:

"Atención! A caballero's near — "

It was not merely in a spirit of bravado. It was to let the little señorita know, if she did not already, that he was free and riding wildly for help.

CHAPTER 25
At the Presidio

IN THAT instant, as he watched the singing Zorro racing up the slope toward the crest, Captain Ramón realized that his future was hanging by a very thin thread. Were he to protect his own interests he must move swiftly.

He sensed that Señor Zorro would make a mad ride for San Diego de Alcála and pour a story into the ear of the commandante of the presidio there. And it was highly imperative that Captain Ramón tell a far better story — and tell it first.

Ramón managed to return his sword to its scabbard, and then he raced with what speed he could toward Barbados and the others, who were following lurchingly in Señor Zorro's wake. He grasped Barbados by an arm and hurried him aside.

"What happened?" the commandante demanded.

"The fellow tricked us in some fashion!" Barbados declared with an oath. "His hands were untied, and he had a dagger. If that pretty wench we let speak with him — "

"Attend me!' Ramón cried. "The wench is under guard in one of the huts, and is not to be touched. Get me a horse. Be quick about it! The fool is riding to San Diego for troopers!"

"Ha! Let them come!"

"I must get to the presidio before he arrives," Captain Ramón explained. The lieutenant there will take orders from me. Then I'll lead the troopers into your ambush, as we had planned. And this Zorro — "

"Ha! This Zorro!" Barbados cried. "When I have my hands upon him again there'll be no delay."

"I'll have him imprisoned in the presidio," the captain promised. "Then, after you defeat the soldiers, and when you go to loot the town, he will be at your mercy."

"You think of everything!" Barbados declared. "I say it yet once again — you should be a pirate!"

One of the men, understanding more than his fellows, had fetched the captain's own horse, with saddle and bridle on. The captain sprang into the saddle.

"Arrange the ambush at the head of the cañon, as we planned," he told Barbados. Do it without delay. I'll lead the troopers straight into the trap."

Then he touched spurs to the animal he bestrode and dashed up the slope in the wake of Señor Zorro.

Captain Ramón was an excellent horseman, and he rode an excellent mount. Moreover, he had been through every mile of that country with his troopers some time before. He knew the shortest route to the presidio at San Diego de Alcála, and he felt quite sure that Señor Zorro did not.

Reaching the crest of the slope, Captain Ramón stopped his horse beneath the trees and watched and listened for a time. From the distance there came to his ears the drumming of a horse's hoofs. As he had expected, Señor Zorro had ridden along the bottom of the cañon, and Captain Ramón knew that such a course would take him at least two miles out of his way. Once in that cañon, a horseman was forced to follow it until he came to the other end.

Captain Ramón turned his horse's head in another direction and drove home the spurs. He rode around a hill and emerged upon a flat space, across which he raced toward a row of foothills in the distance. Señor Zorro had the start, but he was taking the long way. Aside from an accident, Captain Ramón could reach San Diego de Alcâla and have his story told before Señor Zorro arrived.

The thing had to be done, he told himself. He would use his authority and have Zorro thrown into the guardroom at the presidio. He would go back to the pirate camp at the head of the troopers, see that the pirates were wiped out to a man, release the caballeros and the señorita.

And then there would be other things to do. He would convince the authorities that Señor Zorro had been allied with the pirates and that the caballeros had not known of it, and have Zorro hanged. He would ask his friend, the Governor, to order the senorita to wed with him because he had saved her and wiped out the pirate brood, and the senorita would be forced to obey his excellency's command. And he would see to it that, all men believed he had been true and loyal continually.

If the señorita spoke out the truth Captain Ramón could smile and say she uttered a falsehood because she did not wish to wed with him. He was guarded against every emergency, he felt.

There was a mere possibility, of course, that the pirates might be victorious, and in such case Captain Ramón would pretend that he had been with the rogues always, turn pirate himself, and have the señorita. But he preferred the other way.

He thought of these things as he rode. Around another hill and down a slope he rushed, and when he came to a wide trail that ran toward the distant El Camino Real he knew that he had distanced Señor Zorro. Yet he rode furiously, for he wanted all the time he could have at the presidio before Zorro arrived,

And finally he reached the highway, and tore along it like a mad horseman riding on the wind. The mount beneath him was showing signs of wearying, but the captain urged him on. Now he was flying past natives' huts scattered along the broad highway. Children and chickens and swine hurried from his path. Women came to the doors of the huts to look after him through clouds of dust.

Then he could see, in the distance, the presidio on its little hill, and the group of buildings around it. Captain Ramón urged his horse cruelly. As he approached men turned to watch him. Before the presidio itself troopers sprang to their feet, as men will when there is a feeling of excitement in the air.

Captain Ramón stopped his horse in a cloud of dust before the presidio entrance and was out of the saddle before the nearest trooper could seize the bridle. The men saluted, but Captain Ramón spent no time in answering their salutes. Drawing off his gloves, he strode through the entrance and straight toward the office of the commandante.

He had lied nobly to Barbados. Instead of their being a smaller force of soldiers than usual at San Diego de Alcâla, there was an extra detachment, come to relieve others who were to go toward the north. But only a lieutenant was there by way of officer, the real commandante being on a journey to San Francisco de Asis to explain certain things to the Governor.

Captain Ramón opened the office door and strode inside, gasping his breath, slapping the dust from his uniform. The lieutenant sprang to his feet.

"Ramón!" he cried. "So far from home — "

Captain Ramón stopped him with a gesture.

"Have your trumpeter sound the assembly, and gather your men while we talk!" he commanded. "This is serious — and urgent!"

The lieutenant was a good soldier, and did not question. He sprang to the door and called an order, and almost immediately the commanding notes of a trumpet rang through the place. Then the lieutenant closed the door and hurried back to the long table in the middle of the room, before which Ramón was sitting.

"Pirates within eight miles of you!" Ramón declared. "They have a large camp. Three nights ago they raided Reina de Los Angeles."

"The news has reached us."

"Ha! I followed by land and approached their rendezvous at an early hour this morning. They abducted Señorita Lolita Pulido. Some caballeros pursued them by sea, fought, and were overcome. Many are being held prisoners, for ransom and torture. The señorita is a prisoner also."

"Where?" the lieutenant asked.

"On the coast, a bit north. I lurked about the camp and made some discoveries. Señor Zorro is mixed up with them."

"Zorro?" the lieutenant gasped.

"The same. His wild blood has broken out again. The señorita is of the opinion that he followed to rescue her, when in reality he had her stolen. He was to have married her, but is eager for lawlessness, it appears. This will be the end of the fiend!"

"Ha!" the lieutenant gasped. "If — "

"Attend!" Ramón interrupted. "I overheard a plot. Zorro is to ride here wildly and tell of the senorita and the caballeros being held by the pirates. It is his intention to lead back the troopers and lead them into an ambush."

"By the saints — "

"So the pirates will wipe out your men. And then San Diego de Alcála, unprotected will be before him!"

"The fiend!" the lieutenant gasped.

"Call half a dozen of your trusted men and have them ready. When he enters and begins his story have him seized. Throw him into the guardroom and put him into the maniac's shirt. Then I'll help you lead the troopers. I know how the ambush is planned. We'll attack in the rear, save the caballeros, and rescue the señorita — and gain considerable credit. Promotion will come to you!"

"It is agreed!" the lieutenant said, his face beaming.

"Be quick about it. I'll disappear while Zorro tells his tale. Seize him, throw him into the guardroom, put him into the maniac's shirt, leave two men to guard him. When we return we'll see that he is punished for his perfidy. Caballero or not, he'll be hanged for this."

The lieutenant sprang from his chair to issue the necessary orders. But the door was hurled open — and Señor Zorro rushed into the officer's room!

CHAPTER 26
Helplessness

O N THE OCCASION of this meeting it was Señor Zorro who was properly astonished instead of his foe. Captain Ramón had been the last person he had seen at the pirates' camp; he had ridden at great speed, and yet here was the commandante ahead of him at the presidio in San Diego de Alcála.

But it did not take Señor Zorro long to guess that the captain had taken advantage of some short cut across the county and so had arrived at the presidio first. And, since he was here, Señor Zorro found himself in something of a predicament.

For weapons he had only the short dagger and his courage. The element of surprise upon which he generally depended so much was acting against him instead of for him in this present encounter; but he did not despair.

He took two quick steps forward, and the dagger suddenly was in his right hand. He glanced quickly at the lieutenant, who had picked up his sword from the long table and was drawing it from the scabbard, and then whirled toward Captain Ramón, who already had his sword ready for use.

"So!" Señor Zorro cried. "You got here ahead of me, did you? Renegade and traitor!"

"'Tis you who are the renegade and traitor!" Captain Ramón

declared. "Friend of pirates!"

"Ha! So that is the tale you have told?" Señor Zorro gasped. "Lieutenant, I am Don Diego Vega, of Reina de Los Angeles. Perhaps you have heard the name?"

"The lieutenant also has heard of Señor Zorro, and knows that he and Don Diego Vega are one and the same man," Captain Ramón said before the other officer could reply. Captain Ramón felt some small degree of courage now, since Señor Zorro had no weapon except his short dagger.

"Ha! Who has not heard of Zorro?" came the reply. "And it is not to be expected that one of his excellency's officers would go far out of his regular way to do Señor Zorro a service. Yet an officer will serve his duty, and there are certain things to be considered, lieutenant. In a pirate camp a few miles from this place is a señorita of proper blood and several caballeros who must be rescued before they are tortured. I have ridden here for help, having made an escape."

"Made your escape?" Captain Ramón cried. "You came purposely with the story to lead the soldiers into a trap, you mean. Your story will avail you nothing, Señor Zorro. The lieutenant already is planning to ride to the rescue of his men. But you will remain here, a prisoner in the guardroom, in a maniac's shirt — "

"Ha!" Señor Zorro shrieked. "Lieutenant, make no mistake about it. This Captain Ramón may outrank you, but he is a traitor, and I would have all honest men know it. He is in league with the pirates himself."

"You scarcely can expect me to believe that," the lieutenant replied, smiling.

"It is the truth, by the saints! He is planning to lead your men into an ambush, no doubt!"

"I think that we have had enough of this nonsense, Don Diego!" the lieutenant said, his official manner upon him.

"You believe Captain Ramón in preference to me?"

"I do! You are to consider yourself a prisoner, Don Diego. You'll be held here safe until the rescue has been accomplished, and then there will be an investigation of this entire affair."

"It will not be necessary for you to keep me a prisoner," Señor Zorro replied, his eyes narrowing. "Lead your own soldiers, as you will, and be quick about it, and do not listen to the advice of Captain Ramón. The senorita who is held a captive is my betrothed. Her name is Lolita Pulido. At least allow me to remain free to aid in her rescue."

"I cannot forget that you are Señor Zorro as well as Don Diego Vega, and that the Pulido family does not have the friendship of the Governor," the lieutenant answered. "Captain Ramón has preferred a charge against you also. You remain in the presidio a prisoner."

The lieutenant picked up a silver whistle from the table, and started to put it to his lips to blow a blast that would call his orderly. But Señor Zorro, it appeared, had no intention of being kept a prisoner. He glanced swiftly toward Captain Ramón again, and then darted forward.

The lieutenant's whistle was knocked from his left hand, but Señor Zorro did not succeed in getting possession of the officer's sword as he hurled him aside. He dashed on to the wall, struck it and whirled away, and came back with considerable momentum. Captain Ramón had started toward the door.

But as he put out a hand to pull the door open Señor Zorro grasped a small stool that stood at one end of the long table and hurled it with precise aim. It struck the captain's arm and caused him to recoil with a cry of pain.

The lieutenant was young, and enjoyed the recklessness of his youth. He bellowed his challenge and charged. Señor Zorro caught his sword against the dagger and warded off the blow. But, to do so, he was compelled to give some ground, and so Captain Ramón got to the door and opened it.

"Troopers!" he cried. "Help! This way! Your commandante is attacked!"

Señor Zorro fenced the lieutenant for a moment, but he knew well that he could not do so for long with any great degree of success. And suddenly he dropped to his knees, and the lieutenant, lunging with his blade, tripped over him and sprawled on the floor. Zorro was upon his feet again before Captain Ramón could reach his side. Again he whirled, and Captain Ramón recoiled against the wall, his sword advanced, his left arm stretched out across a wood panel.

Señor Zorro did not dare to encounter the long blade with his dagger; besides, he heard the soldiers coming. His arm flashed, and the dagger flew through the air. Through the sleeve of Captain Ramón's uniform coat went the sharp blade, to be driven almost to the hilt in the wood beyond. The captain was held safely for the moment.

There was one large window in the officer's room, and it was swinging open. Zorro dashed for it, reached it, sprang up as the wondering troopers rushed in through the door. Through the window Señor Zorro plunged, sprawled on the ground for an instant, and then was upon his feet again and running with renewed vigor toward the front of the building.

But disaster waited for him there. The horse he had ridden had been jaded, and a soldier had taken the mount to the rear to rub it down. Zorro found his horse gone, and that of Captain Ramón also. The troopers in front of the presidio were in their saddles. And they surrounded the unmounted horses of those who had rushed inside in answer to the captain's call.

Señor Zorro turned immediately to flee. But the shrieks from inside the presidio told the troopers what was happening. They forced their mounts forward, ran Señor Zorro down, cut off his flight, and surrounded him. For a moment there was a pretty battle; but the troopers did not strike to slay, not understanding, quite, the status of this man who seemed to have run amuck. However, they prevented an escape.

The lieutenant shrieked from the window, demanding an immediate capture. Señor Zorro made one last attempt to escape. He darted beneath the belly of a horse, got outside the circle of troopers and dashed away. He reached the corner of the low building and went up it as a fly goes up a wall, using the rough masonry of the corner as steppingstones.

Across the roof he darted, while the soldiers urged their horses forward again in an effort to surround the building. Down the other side of the roof he ran, skipping across the Spanish tiles until he reached the eaves.

Below him was his horse, and the hostler was wiping one of the animal's forelegs. Señor Zorro did not hesitate. He crouched and sprang, and landed in the saddle. The hostler rolled to one side in fright as the animal lurched forward.

Señor Zorro whirled the beast toward the highway. But he saw at a glance that there was small chance of escape. The mount he bestrode was almost exhausted, and the troopers had fresh mounts. And they were upon him with a rush.

Weaponless, he could do nothing. They charged around him, pulled him down from the saddle, made him prisoner, and then marched him back to the entrance of the presidio, where the lieutenant and Captain Ramón were waiting.

"The maniac's shirt for him!" the lieutenant commanded. "Put him into it and then into the guardroom. Two men will remain behind to see that he does not escape. But I scarcely think that even Señor Zorro can escape the maniac's shirt!"

"Put me in it, and I hold it against you!" Zorro warned.

"I have given my orders," the lieutenant replied loftily.

"One last word for your ear!" Zorro said. "You are making a sad mistake. I tell you here and now, before some of your men, that this Captain Ramón is a renegade and a traitor. Heed not his advice! And ride swiftly, else you'll not accomplish the rescue. I charge you to take the señorita to a place of safety."

"Certainly, senor!"

"You'll not let me ride with you?"

"I have given my orders."

"Lieutenant, I swear by my honor as a caballero that all I have told you is the truth. Does that carry weight with you?"

It seemed to carry weight, for the officer hesitated. A caballero does not pledge his honor lightly. But how could it be possible that an officer like Captain Ramón could be anything but loyal and true. And Captain Ramón himself decided the lieutenant.

"For a caballero to swear by his honor is a great thing," the captain said. "Yet now and then we find a man of caballero blood who forgets the honor that should be his. And we remember that you are Señor Zorro, also."

"Señor — " Zorro began angrily.

But the lieutenant cut him short. "I have decided," he said. "You will be held a prisoner in the maniac's shirt until we return. Take him away!"

The soldiers grasped him roughly, hurried him inside and to the guardroom. There, Señor Zorro tried to fight again, but could accomplish nothing against so many foes. They lashed his ankles and knees and tied his wrists together in front of him. And then one fetched the maniac's shirt. The latter was exactly what it was named, an instrument used on violent maniacs to prevent them harming themselves or anybody else. It was a long bag of leather, constructed so that a man could be slipped into it bound, and the top of the bag then gathered around his neck with a leather thong.

Protesting to the last, Señor Zorro was put inside the leather bag and the neck thong tightened. And then they propped him up on a bench in a corner, and left the room. The door closed; he heard the bar go against it.

The soldiers hurried away. There was a moment of silence. And then Señor Zorro heard the clattering of horses' hoofs as they rode toward the highway. And he was left behind, bound and helpless. in the guardroom of the presidio, in the maniac's shirt, and with two troopers just outside the door.

CHAPTER 27
Fray Felipe Uses His Wit

BARBADOS, who had been drinking heavily of the rich, stolen wine since the culmination of the fight with the caballeros and the crew of the trading schooner, had reached the stage where he was surly, mean, dangerous. The sensational escape of Señor Zorro had been as oil poured upon flames with the pirate chief. He roared and cursed like a fiend after Captain Ramón had ridden away in pursuit, cuffed some of his men out of the way, and then stood with his fists planted against his hips, his feet wide apart, a black look in his face, his tiny eyes glittering ominously as he glanced toward the adobe building wherein the caballero prisoners were quartered.

Sanchez and the others who knew Barbados best had been busy keeping out of his way and so escaping trouble, but now Barbados bellowed loudly for his lieutenant, and Sanchez was forced to disclose himself. He approached his chief warily, ready to turn and run if Barbados was in a belligerent mood; but he saw at a glance that what wrath Barbados was enjoying was not directed toward his second in command.

"Sanchez! Fiend of the fiends!" he shouted. "By my naked blade, it is in my mind that we are growing weary because of the lack of sport."

"Then we must have sport," Sanchez said. "If you've anything to suggest — "

"We have prisoners," Barbados remarked, licking his thick lips, and it is possible that a little torture would not be amiss. Say, roasting at the stake for one of those high-born caballeros whose blood is gentle."

"Ha!" Sanchez grunted. "It is an excellent idea—if we draw out the man's agony."

"The drawing out of his agony can be accomplished without a great deal of trouble," Barbados declared. "We'll make him squirm and squeal."

"But there is an ambush to be prepared for the soldiers," Sanchez suggested.

"There will be ample time for that at a later hour," replied the pirate chief. "It will take some time for those troopers to gallop out here from San Diego de Alcála. We can fight better if we have more wine to drink and some sort of sport to watch before giving battle."

"And which of the caballeros shall be roasted?" Sanchez wanted to know. All of them are valuable men from the standpoint of ransom."

"Ha! One can be spared," said Barbados. "Not a man in that adobe but has very rich relatives. What sum we lose from the one we roast we can fasten on the others. We'll force them to gamble and decide the victim themselves. That is a happy thought. Come with me and fetch half a dozen trusted men along."

Barbados, having arrived at a decision, started straight for the adobe building as Sanchez shouted to some of the men nearest. The pirate chief unfastened the outer door and entered with the others at his heels. Then he unlocked the inner door and threw it open.

The caballeros were sprawled around the room, talking to one another in low tones, and they turned and looked at Barbados as he stood before them, much as men might have looked at an intruder. Scorn was in every face, the pirate chief was quick to notice it.

"So you raised a din and attracted our attention, and thus aided this Señor Zorro to escape!" Barbados accused. "It is in my mind that there must be some punishment for that."

The caballeros turned from him again and began talking to one another once more as though Barbados had not addressed them. He growled a curse low down in his throat and took another step toward them, glaring ferociously.

"I have here a pack of cards properly shuffled," Barbados said, his glare changing to a fendish grin. "I'll put them on this bench, and you prisoners will form into a line, walk past the bench, and each draw a card. The man who draws the first deuce will be the victim."

"Victim of what?" one asked.

"Of torture!" Barbados roared. "The stake! Roasting! My men demand sport, and I am the one to give it to them. It is an even thing for you — the gods of chance will decide."

"And suppose, señor," said Don Audre Ruiz, stepping forward with a great deal of sarcasm and scorn in his manner, "that we do not care to play your game?"

"Ha! The solution of the difficulty is easy if you do not," Barbados assured him. "In such case, since you seem to be the leader here, we'll torture you and thereafter two others picked out at random."

"Death is close behind you, pirate if you do this thing!" Don Audre warned.

"But you will not be here to see it if you are roasted first," the pirate chief reminded him. "Line up, prisoners! Do caballeros shake with fear at such a time?"

Don Audre Ruiz took another step forward and sneered in the face of Barbados. "Caballeros are not aware of the existence of such a thing as fear!" he declared. "If there is no other way, put down your pack of cards. But if you have courage and the spirit of fair play, let me fight it out with any two of your crew of fiends — a dagger against long blades."

"Do I resemble a fool?" Barbados requested to know. "Have I but half a mind? Run a needless chance when we have you powerless already? Ha! A cabellero might do such a fool thing, but I am not a caballero."

"A blind man could see that," Don Audre retorted.

"Ha! More of your insults and I'll roast the lot of you! Line up! Here are the cards."

Barbados put the greasy pack down on the end of the bench and stood back, folding his great arms across his chest. Don Audre Ruiz glanced around at his comrades, and they began forming the line. Sergeant Gonzales, feeling a bit out of place, dropped back to the end. And then the line moved forward, and the first man turned a card and saw that it was a ten and passed on.

One by one they advanced to the bench, picked up a card, showed it to Barbados and moved forward again, playing with death, but with inscrutable faces.

"Ha!" the pirate chief cried. "Fortunate caballeros, eh? But one of you must draw a deuce soon. And then my men will have rare sport. We'll see whether a caballero of gentle blood will squeal and squirm when the hot flames lick at him. We'll let the women torment him first, and the children! Well — Ha!"

Barbados suddenly bent forward, an evil smile upon his face. Don Audre had reached the bench and had turned over his card — the deuce of spades!

Don Audre drew in his breath sharply, but his face gave never a sign of emotion. The others crowded forward.

"Ha!" Barbados shrieked. "It is well done and appropriate! You are their leader, señor, and possibly will set them an example how to die. For you we will make the fire hotter and the torment longer. We'll see how long you can live."

"He'll flinch quick enough!" Sanchez cried, grinning.

Don Audre Ruiz tossed the card away and dusted his hands as though the bit of pasteboard had soiled them. Then he raised his head proudly and looked Barbados straight in the eyes.

"How soon?" Don Audre Ruiz asked.

"How soon, caballero? Now, at once, and immediately! My men crave sport!" Barbados cried. "And while they listen to your shrieks and pleas for mercy they can drink some rich wine we took from Reina de Los Angeles."

"Are you human man enough to let me have speech with Fray Felipe before I die?" Don Audre asked.

"Want to pray with him, do you?" Barbados sneered. "I'll have him at the stake for you. You can pray through the smoke."

There was a sudden jostling in the crowd, and Sergeant Gonzales shouldered his way to the front.

"Foul pirate!" said he. "Murderer and fiend, let me make a deal!"

"What is this?" Barbados asked.

"I am a bigger man than the caballero here, and fatter men roast better. Also, I wear the uniform of the Governor, and you hate such uniforms. I'm twice the coward that Don Ruiz is. I'd squirm and squeal twice as much. Ha! Would it not be better sport to roast me at the stake?"

"You want to die for him?" Barbados asked.

"I offer myself in his place, since your fiends must be amused. I did not get a chance to draw a card, or surely I'd have drawn a deuce."

Don Audre put his hand on the sergeant's arm.

"This is useless, my friend," he said.

"Not so!" Sergeant Gonzales declared. "You are a fine man of parts, Don Audre Ruiz, and really amount to something in the world. And I am but a big pig. There are many better men who can fill my place."

"Whatever your birth and station, you are now, in my estimation, a caballero and a brave man," Don Audre said.

Barbados roared his laughter.

"A hero!" he sneered. "I cannot let you take the caballero's place, fool soldier, but, since you wish to be roasted, your wish is granted. We'll roast you later, when we have need of more sport. These other caballeros will be ransomed, but there is nobody in the world who would ransom you for as much as a bottle of thin wine,"

"That is true, fiend of hell!" Sergeant Gonzales said.

"But it is not true!" Don Audre Ruiz cried, his face lighting. He whirled to confront the other caballeros. "Friends, promise me this last request — have your people make up a purse and ransom this soldier," he said. "He has been the friend of Don Diego Vega for years. We used to smile at that peculiar friendship, but now I can understand. The sergeant, also, is a man of parts, and Don Diego realized it while we were blind. A last handshake, and then — "

They surged toward him, and Barbados and his men stepped back to the door and waited. There was an evil grin on the face of the pirate chief again. The gods of chance were working in his favor, he felt, when they had delivered this caballero into his hands for his evil purposes.

"Come, señor!" he ordered. "It is not gentlemanly to keep my men waiting long for their fun."

Don Audre Ruiz shook the hands of his friends for the last time and turned away. They led him out and closed and barred the door again. They conducted him through the front room and into the open, first binding his hands behind his back.

"If you are a human being, let me see Fray Felipe." Don Audre said.

"I'll have him beside the stake," Barbados promised. "He can mumble over you all he likes."

Some of the pirates were shouting the news of what was to occur. Men came running from every direction, shouting and laughing and waving bottles, determined to see how a caballero could die. Women and children hurried from their huts.

The stake was ready, for it often had been used before, both for prisoners and pirates. It was a favorite method Barbados had of punishing traitors and those he deemed guilty of breaking some of the many laws he laid down. It stood near the sea, a long metal bar upright in the soil, the debris of many fires scattered around it and half buried in the shifting sand.

Already some of the men were hurrying toward the stake with fuel. The women and children were shrieking insults at the condemned man. But Don Audre Ruiz held his head proudly, and his lips were curled in scorn. Only the unusual pallor in his face told that there was a tumult of emotions within his breast.

They lashed him to the stake and made his body fast there with ropes and leather thongs. One chain they wrapped around him to hold him fast after the ropes had been burned away. Women spat at him, children hurled at him small stones and scoops of sand. The pirates danced around him like savages, waving wine bottles and brandishing their cutlasses.

"So you think that you will not squirm and squeal, eh?" Barbados taunted. "In a very few minutes we'll learn the truth concerning that."

"You promised me the fray," Don Audre Ruiz replied. "But I did not think that a pirate could keep his given word."

"Ha! I'll show you that I can play at having gentle blood!" Barbados

laughed. "Matter of honor, eh? The fray! Fetch me the old fray, some of you!

The dancing and drinking was continued, and more fuel was heaped around the stake and its victim. A few feet distant stood a man with a flaming torch. Barbados, his arms folded across his chest, stood waiting to give the word. And after a time old Fray Felipe thrust his way among them and reached the side of the pirate chief.

"What is this that you would do?" he demanded.

"We intend to broil this caballero until he is done properly," Barbados replied. "Being a pious soul, he has need of a priest before he dies. So we have sent for you."

Fray Felipe knew that there was small chance for an argument here. Ordinarily Barbados was exceedingly superstitious where a man of the church was concerned, but now wine had given him a false courage. If Fray Felipe saved Don Audre Ruiz now it would not be through an appeal to the heart of Barbados.

And so Fray Felipe did a peculiar thing — a thing that startled them all, and Don Audre most of all. He threw back his gray head and laughed.

Barbados blinked his eyes rapidly, and Sanchez swore softly beneath his breath. Had the fray gone insane suddenly? Were his wits wondering? It was a horrible thing to see an old fray laugh like that.

"So it is as I suspected," Fray Felipe declared. "I had thought for a moment Barbados, that you were a pirate leader in truth, a general with brains. But you play the boy."

"How is this?" Barbados cried.

"Traitors play with you, and you walk into traps. You and your fiends spend time at such cruel sports as this while your enemies are preparing to annihilate you — "

"Fray, what is your meaning?"

"Are you blind?" Fray Felipe asked. "Are you an utter and simple fool? You have put your confidence and trust in this Captain Ramón. And at this moment he is riding back from San Diego de Alcãla at the head of the troopers, perhaps."

"Ha! I know it, fray. He is leading the soldiers into an ambush!"

"So you are such an easy dupe!" Fray Felipe said. "I know his plans, and so does the little señorita. You will form your ambush at the head of the cañon. And he will lead the troopers around it, attack you in the rear, cut you off from your camp, and annihilate you. By doing that he'll save his face and gain favor with decent men and women and with the Governor. He'll claim that he saved the señorita, and ask her in marriage, get her for a bride without cutting himself off forever from honest men. A man who can be traitor to one cause, Señor Pirate, can be traitor to another."

"Lies!" Barbados thundered.

"They are not lies!" Fray Felipe declared. "And you are playing here when you should be preparing for the battle. Easy victims you'll be for the troopers!"

Barbados seemed to hesitate. There was a quality in the fray's words and bearing that indicated truth. Then there came a woman's screech, and Inez thrust herself forward.

"The old fray speaks the truth!" she declared. "I overheard the commandante talking to the señorita. He told her that he was tricking you."

"By my naked blade!" Barbados swore.

"He is doubly a traitor!" the woman screeched. "I would not trust him. Make ready to fight the soldiers. Do not be caught in a trap. The man at the stake can wait. It will not hurt him to be bound there and meditate for a time."

Barbados suddenly seemed convinced. He began shouting his commands, and Sanchez echoed them as usual.

Men also ran to get horses and weapons.

"Catch me in a trap, eh?" Barbadoes cried. "I can arrange a trap myself, and not in the cañon!"

He rushed away, shrieking more orders. Don Audre Ruiz, fastened to the stake, was forgotten for the moment. Fray Felipe approached him.

"It was the only way, caballero," the gentle fray said. "It would have been far better to have let the traitor wipe out these rogues entirely, but I had to save your life. And the soldiers will triumph when they come. Right is on their side and fights with them. Also Señor Zorro is at liberty!"

"Loose me, fray!"

"I cannot, señor. There is one chain that is too strong for me. But they have forgotten you now. I'll search for some tool with which I can remove the chain. The ropes and the leather thongs will be easy."

Fray Felipe bowed his head and shuffled away. Don Audre Ruiz remained lashed to the stake.

CHAPTER 28
Unexpected Help

L EFT behind helpless in the guardroom of the presidio, Senor
Zorro fought to control his emotions, telling himself that he
could think out no proper line of action while his brain was in
sad tumult.

His case seemed hopeless. He was unable to make an escape, and
Captain Ramón was leading the troopers against the pirates. Señor Zorro
began wondering whether his good fortune had deserted him entirely.
The señorita was in grave peril, and also his friends the caballeros, and
he could do nothing.

But there was a certain outside influence at work regarding which
Señor Zorro knew nothing, an influence caused by his just acts when, as
Zorro, he had ridden up and down El Camino Real righting the wrongs
inflicted on fraile and natives.

The native fisherman had guided him to the vicinity of the pirates'
camp before dawn, and then had disappeared. Señor Zorro did not
wonder at that, since it was commendable in the native to save his own
skin.

The fisherman, however, had continued across the hills to San
Diego de Alcála to pay a visit to relatives and friends. There he waited
impatiently, anticipating news of a fight at the pirate's camp. And,
because he admired uniforms, though they inspired fear in him as well

as admiration, he drifted near the presidio.

He was in time to behold the arrival of Captain Ramón, and later of Señor Zorro. After a time, he saw Señor Zorro's attempt at escape, and watched the troopers gallop away. And then, by loitering near the presidio, he ascertained something of the truth — that Señor Zorro was being held a prisoner in the maniac's shirt and would be dealt with at some future time.

The native wandered around the huts of the village, doing more genuine thinking than ever before in his life. He remembered how Señor Zorro, a long time before, had saved his father. He was a neophyte native, and he remembered, also how Señor Zorro had fought for the frailes when they were being persecuted.

The native fisherman did not have to think long on the subject before arriving at a conclusion. Having done so, he went to the hut of a cousin and begged a bottle of palm wine, potent stuff that could make a man mad.

He took a good drink of the palm wine and slipped away, carrying the bottle. He had a short, sharp knife that he used for the cleaning of fish, and he took this out and inspected it, and then hid it beneath his ragged shirt and in an armpit, fastening it there cleverly with a bit of rag.

Having made these preparations, the native fisherman drank more of the wine and gathered false courage. He spilled some of the liquor on his sorry clothes, so that its well-known odor mingled with that of fish. And then he approached the presidio again.

One of the two troopers remaining was sitting before the main door, and the other supposedly, was in the corridor outside the guardroom, where his duty called him. The native fisherman went close to the man before the door and regarded him evily. He held up the bottle and guzzled more of the palm wine. The trooper looked up and saw him.

"Dog of a savage!" he cried. "Know you not that it is against the laws and wishes of his excellency for natives to drink the stuff?"

The native blinked his eyes at him. "May the devil take the laws," said he, boldly, "and his excellency also!"

"What words are these?" the soldier cried, getting to his feet.

"Every man who wears a uniform is a rascal and a thief!"

"This to me? A dog of a native speaks so to one of the soldiers of the Governor?"

"If the Governor was here," said the native, "I'd throw this drink in his face! And if you trouble me more, I'll throw it in yours!"

"Ha! In that case — "

"For you dare not put me in the guardroom!" the native declarec. "I have too many friends."

The trooper exploded and rushed forward. "Low-born dog!" he shrieked. He caught the native and cuffed him, and instead of taking the blows calmly, the native fought back. It was too much!

"Into the guardroom you go!" the soldier shouted. "And when the commandante returns he probably will order you whipped. And I'll wield the lash! Give me that bottle!"

The trooper took the bottle and sat it down carefully, having noticed that it was half full, then hustled the native inside and along the corridor to the door of the guardroom. The other soldier looked up questioningly.

"This dog has been drinking palm wine and making remarks about his excellency!" the first soldier said. "Throw him into the guardhouse. He is fit company for Señor Zorro!"

The door was opened, the native was hurled inside, and the door was closed and barred again. The two soldiers peered through the small aperture in it. They saw the native pick himself up and look around as though dazed.

"Ha!" one of the troopers cried. "He will wonder what it is all about before morning. That palm wine is dangerous stuff."

"And I took half a bottle of it from the dog before we put him in," the other whispered.

"Let us watch a moment before we sample it."

The native glanced toward the corner where Señor Zorro, in the maniac's shirt was propped up on a bench. He lurched toward him, bent forward, and peered into his face.

"A white man!" he gasped. "In the guardroom the same as me!"

He threw out his chest and strutted around the room, as though a great honor had come to him. The soldiers at the door laughed. The native turned and blinked his eyes at them, mouthed some meaningless phrases, and appeared to be dazed again. Twice he shrieked like a soul in torment. He beat his fists against the wall of the guardroom.

"Si! That wine is strong stuff!" one of the soldiers said.

Still they remained watching. But the native, it seemed, was exhausted. He slipped down to the floor, crawled over against the wall, and let his head topple to one side. Twice he nodded, and then he began to snore. The troopers closed the little door of the aperture. The fun was over.

Though he had recognized the native Señor Zorro had spoken no word. He was not certain whether the man was under the influence of palm wine or shamming. He listened and heard the two soldiers walk down the corridor, then turned his head and glanced at the native again. The native had opened one of his eyes and was watching the door.

"They are drinking your wine," Zorro hissed.

'Si, señor! One moment!"

The native slipped slowly and carefully along the wall until he was within a few feet of Señor Zorro.

"I thought it out, señor," he said. "I know those maniac's shirts, for once they bound me and put me in one. And I have a sharp knife — "

"Careful!" Señor Zorro warned. "If you succeed in this I will make you rich for life!"

"I am not doing it for riches, but because you have been kind to my people and to the frailes," the native said. "I must do my work swiftly."

He had the knife out now, and began working at the tough leather of the shirt. The thong that drew the shirt about the neck was fastened with a metal clasp, and sort of lock, and so the tough leather had to be cut. The native sawed through it, and loosened the thong.

He stopped to slip noiselessly across to the door and crouch and listen there. He hurried back and began peeling the leather sack off SeñorZorro. He worked frantically, guessing what would be in store for him if he happened to be caught.

'If I escape, then must you do so," Señor Zorro said. "And keep away from San Diego de Alcâla for many moons to come."

"I understand, señor. And, if I do not escape, remember, please, that

I did what a poor man could."

"I'll help you, and I can."

"A good horse belonging to one of these soldiers is just in front of the presidio, señor."

"Good!"

"And some daggers are in leather boots near the front door, on the wall."

"Again, good!" Señor Zorro said.

The native slashed the last of the bonds, and Zorro stood and moved his limbs to restore circulation. Then he motioned the native toward the door.

"Stand on that side," Zorro directed. "And shriek as though you were being killed."

The native shrieked. Señor Zorro himself felt shivers run up and down his spine at those bloodcurdling shrieks. The two soldiers listened, and then hurried back toward the guard room. They opened the little aperture in the door. They saw neither of their prisoners, but they did see the empty maniac's shirt in one corner of the room.

And then they did what Señor Zorro had judged they would do — unlock and open the door and rush inside. Zorro hurled himself upon the first and floored him, rolled aside just in time to escape the rush of the second, delivered a blow that laid this second on the floor unconscious, got the dagger from the soldier's belt, and whirled to take the rush of the first, now upon his feet again.

"Fly!" he ordered the native. But the fisherman stood just outside the door, waiting to see the outcome.

Señor Zorro had no quarrel with the soldiery, and he did not want to wound a trooper. But it was demanded of him that he make an escape as quickly as possible, and make certain that he could not be followed for some minutes.

And so he rushed his man with the dagger, and the other gave ground and put himself on guard. But suddenly Señor Zorro whirled and rushed backward instead of attacking, darted through the door, slammed it shut, and shot home the bar. Inside were the two soldiers.

"Señores, adios" Zorro said at the aperture. "I regret that you cannot accompany me and see the fighting."

"For this — " one of the imprisoned troopers began.

"Have you ever seen this one?" Señor Zorro asked. And he slammed shut the door of the aperture, laughed loudly, saw that the native fisherman was free, and ran like the wind down the corridor and through the front door and into the sunshine.

A moment later he was in the saddle and galloping like a madman in the wake of Captain Ramón and the troopers.

CHAPTER 29
The Plight of Ruiz

C APTAIN RAMON, riding with the lieutenant at the head of the soldiery, considered his plans.

The captain had told Barbados how to arrange an ambush at the head of the cañon, and he expected to lead the troopers around the ambush and to the rear, cutting the pirates off from their camp, and either exterminating them at once in the cañon or driving them up into the open, where the troopers could ride them down one by one.

Captain Ramón knew, of course and naturally, that the pirates would be watching the advance. But, just at the mouth of the cañon, Captain Ramón could lead the soldiers swiftly to one side and reach the rear before the pirates could understand the maneuver and hasten back to protect themselves.

He had not the slightest doubt regarding the outcome. The troopers were about equal in numbers to the pirates, and while the latter would fight desperately, knowing that capture meant the hangman's rope for them, the troopers were seasoned men who had been through several native uprisings and knew how to handle themselves in battle.

The soldiers had a few pistols, but they were not to be depended on so much as blades and a hand-to-hand conflict. The pirates had a few firearms also, but they lacked ammunition. It would be swords against cutlasses for the greater part, Captain Ramón knew, and the advantage would be with the troopers' swords.

As to his own part, Ramón realized well that Barbados would recognize his treachery at once. And so there would be no protection for him from the pirates after Barbados had passed the word to get him, and Ramón would have to fight with the soldiers as a loyal officer. But he did not doubt the outcome of the combat, and so felt secure.

They rode swiftly and in perfect military formation along the dusty highway, and presently turned off and galloped across rolling country toward the sea. Now they proceeded with caution, flankers out, but they did not slacken speed. It was mid-afternoon, and they wanted to do their work before nightfall.

They approached the mouth of the cañon, and Captain Ramón shaded his eyes and peered ahead, but could see nothing human. The pirates were under cover, he supposed, waiting for the troopers to ride down into the narrow cañon and so into a trap from which they could not escape. Ramón spoke his plans to the lieutenant again, and the junior officer nodded that he understood the arrangements perfectly.

They came to the cañon's end, but swerved suddenly toward the right and galloped along the rim and up a gentle slope, the last before reaching the sea. Captain Ramón expected to hear roars of rage from the cañon, but he did not. He almost chuckled. Barbados evidently supposed that the commandante was playing some trick, he took it for granted.

They reached the crest of the slope and pulled up among the trees and looked down upon the pirate camp. A few women and children were running about, but they could see no men.

"Down the slope, then turn and gallop back toward the cañon," Captain Ramón instructed. "Thus we take them in the rear and have the rogues at our mercy."

"How do you know that they are in the cañon?" the lieutenant asked with quick suspicion.

"Did I not hear this Señor Zorro make his plans?" Captain Ramón demanded with some show of anger. "Am I not your superior officer? They are now in the cañon, expecting us to gallop into the trap they have planned."

"Then they saw us approach," the lieutenant declared.

"Si! And they are wondering what is happening, no doubt. It is possible that they have seen me at the head of the troopers and have noticed that Señor Zorro is not present. But they have not had time to get back to their camp. Their trap has been turned against them. Forward!"

Down the slope swept the troopers, and women and children screeched and ran into the huts and buildings. In a big circle the soldiers from San Diego de Alcâla swerved and started back toward the cañon's mouth to hem in their foes.

And, in that instant, the commandante found that things were not as he had expected, and that he had been fooled. Reports of firearms came to his ears, bullets whistled among the troopers, and some of them fell from their saddles. And from the huts and buildings of the pirate camp poured the motley crew of Barbados, screeching their battle-cries, eager to wipe out the soldiery that would have tricked and slain them.

Captain Ramón cursed and began shouting commands. The troopers fired their pistols, drew their blades, and prepared for bloody and more intimate work. From behind the largest adobe building dashed a number of mounted pirates, Barbados and Sanchez riding at their head.

"At them!" the commandante shrieked wildly. "Forward! No mercy!"

The lieutenant, who was by far the better field officer, was endeavoring to make himself heard above the din. The pirates and the soldiers clashed, fought like maniacs, the troopers at the outset having much the better of it. But Barbados and his mounted pirates joined the battle and fought like fiends, because they saw visions of the hangman's noose if they failed to achieve a victory complete.

Captain Ramón had one close look at the face of Barbados, and heard the pirate chief shriek "Traitor!" at him. Thereafter he managed to keep well in the rear of the fighting, under pretense of handling the men. His blade was the only one not red.

Ramón had no intention of liberating the caballeros until the fight was over, for he wanted to claim full credit for rescuing them. He wanted another talk with Señorita Lolita, too, before her friends approached her. She had not given him the promise that he had expected, and the necessity for it was over, since Zorro was free of the pirate camp. But

Ramón hoped to get the promise yet, and have an immediate marriage, saying that he was the one man who could give testimony that would save Señor Zorro if he was tried for conspiracy against the Governor.

The battle raged around him. Barbados and his pirate crew were endeavoring to keep between the troopers and the adobe building wherein the caballeros were held prisoners. The caballeros were crowding at the little windows, watching the fight. Don Audre Ruiz was still bound to the stake, for Fray Felipe had been unable to reach him before the fighting began, and now the aged fray was busy with the wounded men.

The señorita was under the close guard of a single pirate appointed to the task by Barbados. She was in one of the buildings, and Captain Ramón did not know where to find her. Convinced of the commandante's treachery, Barbados had no thought of letting him get possession of the seoñrita. She could be held for ransom, the pirate chief decided.

Back and forth across the open space, up and down the sandy beach the fight progressed. Here groups of men were battling like fiends, here one pursued a lone enemy. The women and children were keeping to the huts.

"Fire the place!" Captain Ramón was ordering. "Burn them out!"

Some of the troopers were quick to do his bidding. A pistol flash was enough. The poor huts began burning fiercely, the dry palm fronds with which they were manufactured flaming instantly.

Ramón began to worry some. The battle seemed an even thing. Both sides had lost many men, and the two forces now were about even.

It came to his mind that, unless the soldiers triumphed very soon, he would have to release the caballeros and let them join in the fray.

Back toward the slope the pirates drove the remaining troopers. And there the battle waged at some distance from the burning huts of the pirate camp. The women tried to quench the flames, but could not.

The wind from the sea carried flaming pieces of palm frond and fired more huts.

Don Audre Ruiz had tugged at his bonds until almost exhausted, but had been unable to get free. Once the battle surged near him, and then away again. Clouds of smoke from the burning huts rolled over him, surged around him. Great chunks of flaming material floated past him on the still breeze.

Don Audre wondered whether the pirates were to be victorious, whether, in the end, they would roast him at the stake, as they had started to do. He choked in the dense smoke; his eyes smarted and then pained; he tried to see how the fight was going, but could only get a glimpse now and then.

And then he saw something that caused a thrill of horror to pass through him. One of the burning brands had fallen at the edge of the pile of fuel about the stake. It smoldered, burst into flames again. The fuel caught, and the flames spread.

Don Audre Ruiz, helpless against the stake, watched the flames creep nearer, the fire spread and become more raging.

Once more he struggled hopelessly against the chain and ropes that held him fast. What irony was this that he should burn without human hands firing the fuel?

Already he could feel the heat of the flames. Slowly they were eating their way toward him through the heaps of fuel the pirates had dropped. Soon they would touch him, smoke and fire would engulf him, and later men would find naught but his charred remains.

Chapter 30
Fray Felipe Gets His Goblet

S ENOR ZORRO thanked his saints that the horse he had seized in front of the presidio at San Diego de Alcála was a noble animal of endurance and speed.

He kicked at the mount's flanks and rode like the wind in the wake of the troopers. He knew that he was gaining on them, but they had such an advantage of time that he realized he could not reach the pirate camp before Ramón and his soldiers.

As his horse negotiated the last slope before reaching the sea, Señor Zorro could hear, coming from a distance, the din of battle. He stopped his mount in the fringe of trees and looked down on the scene.

The soldiers and pirates were fighting hotly at some distance from the buildings. The huts were ablaze. Women and children were trying to escape into the brush. These things Señor Zorro saw at a glance, and also that the fight was an even one, with the advantage to neither force.

He ascertained that the caballeros were still prisoners. Only a moment he hesitated, and then kicked his horse's flanks again and raced the animal down the slope. The fight was to one side of him, and so he encountered neither soldier nor pirate. He had a glimpse of Ramón in the distance, and believed that Ramón saw him in turn. He rode wildly among the blazing huts, and so came to the adobe building where the prisoners were housed.

Señor Zorro sprang from his horse and dashed into the building. With a metal bar, he broke the lock of the inner door and shrieked to the caballeros that they were free.

"Follow me to your weapons!" he shouted. "Fight with the troopers against the pirates! Catch me this renegade and traitor of a Ramón! Remember, Ramón is mine!"

They answered him with glad shouts and rushed at his heels out of the building and toward the hut where the captured weapons had been placed, and before which there were no guards now. The roof of the hut already was blazing.

Señor Zorro kicked open the door, dashed inside, and began tossing out swords. The caballeros rushed forward, shouting as they claimed their weapons. Zorro dashed outside again, his own beloved blade in his hand. Already the caballeros were running toward the fight.

"Zorro, by the saints!" It was the bellowing voice of Sergeant Gonzales that hailed him. "What is this talk of my captain being a traitor?"

"He is!" Zorro cried. "He was in league with the pirates, and then turned against them. He is a double traitor! Forward, sergeant! Use your blade well! Ruiz! Where is Ruiz?"

"The devils took him out to roast him at the stake," the sergeant replied. "That was long before the fighting began."

"To roast him — " Señor Zorro gasped.

"Let me at a pirate!" the sergeant bellowed, dashing away. "There are scores to settle!"

Señor Zorro, his heart sinking within him, peered around through the smoke. And then hope flamed within him again, for in the distance he saw Don Audre Ruiz, the flames leaping around him. Señor Zorro ran swiftly through the billows of smoke toward the stake.

Don Audre's clothing already was being scorched. He had turned his head away from the smoke and the heat, fighting to the last to keep from drawing deadly flame down into his lungs, and his eyes were closed.

He did not see the swift approach of Señor Zorro, did not guess that rescue was at hand until he heard Zorro's voice.

"Audre!" he cried. "Audre!" Speak to me! If the fiends have slain you — "

Don Audre Ruiz opened his eyes and smiled, and Señor Zorro smiled in reply. Then he kicked away the burning fuel and leaped toward his friend.

"You are just in time," Don Audre said. "I had given up hope, Diego, my friend."

"A moment, and I'll have you free."

He tore away the ropes and leather thongs, and worked frantically at the heavy chain, which was hot to his touch. He was alert and on guard as he worked, but the fight did not approach him. The caballeros had joined it, he saw, and the pirates were being cut down, and some taken prisoner.

And finally the heavy chain fell away, and Señor Zorro helped Don Audre a short distance from the stake and thrust a sword into his hand.

"Remember, Ramón belongs to me!" Zorro said. "Let us take him alive!"

Afoot, they dashed across the open space toward the edge of the fight. But they looked in vain for the commandante. He was not in his saddle, nor was he dead or wounded and on the ground.

"Find him!" Zorro cried. "He will be trying to get the senorita away!"

They ran toward the adobe buildings to commence their frantic search. They watched the slope, and the beach in either direction, half expecting to see the commandante carrying Señorita Lolita away on his horse.

"Find him! We must find him!" Zorro screeched. "With me, Audre, my friend! She may be in one of the burning huts — "

And so they rushed through the smoke, calling, searching, fear in their hearts.

Sergeant Gonzales was looking for his captain also. The sergeant told himself that he was in a quandary. His commander and his friend, it appeared, were fighting each other, and the sergeant could not be loyal to both.

He bellowed a challenge and engaged a pirate in combat, took his man, and rushed on. He dodged a charging trooper who almost ran him down, darted around one of the blazing huts, and came upon a scene.

Fray Felipe, attending the wounded, had risen from the ground beside one to find a pirate rushing toward him in flight. The man stumbled and fell headlong, and from the sash he wore about his middle there fell something that flashed and glittered in the sun. Fray Felipe gave a cry and rushed forward. He had seen his beloved sacred goblet!

There was no escape for the pirate. When he regained his feet he found the old fray standing before him.

"Beast and fiend!" Fray Felipe said. "Give it me!"

"Ha! Would I not be a fool to do so?" the pirate challenged. "One side, fray! One side — or you die!"

The other raised his cutlass to strike. But Fray Felipe could not be driven back by such means while the sacred goblet was in the possession of the other.

"Give it me!" he commanded.

"One side — "

Fray Felipe took a quick step forward and jerked the goblet from the other's hand. The pirate cursed and darted forward again. Fray Felipe caught the descending arm.

Back and forth they struggled, and the fray dropped the goblet to the ground again. He was a strong man for his age, but the pirate was young and strong. He forced Fray Felipe back against the wall of the burning hut, throttled him, raised the cutlass again.

"I warned you, fray!" the pirate hissed.

And then he hissed again, a hiss of pain and fright. Through his body a blade had been plunged. He dropped the cutlass, threw wide his arms, shrieked once more, and fell with face toward the ground. And Sergeant Gonzales merely glanced down at him, then picked up the goblet, wiped it against his tunic, and bowed before Fray Felipe.

"Allow me," the sergeant said. "It is a fortunate thing that I was near, fray!"

"I thank thee, son!"

"Son?" Gonzales cried. "You call an old sinner like me by such a name?"

"Perhaps you hold more worth than you yourself think," the old fray replied.

Sergeant Gonzales could not endure such talk. He grew redder in the face, blew out his cheeks, gulped and cleared his throat.

"I am a rough soldier!" Sergeant Gonzales declared. "And I belong in the battle, which is almost at an end."

"Go, son, and my blessings go with thee!"

Gonzales bowed his head an instant. Then, as though ashamed of himself, he bellowed at nothing at all and charged away through the smoke.

CHAPTER 31
"Meal Mush and Goat's Milk!"

THE appearance of Señor Zorro at the scene of battle when he was supposed to be behind bars in the presidio at San Diego de Alcála terrified Captain Ramón. He had a sudden feeling that the fates were against him — that his treachery was to be punished. And he found that his plans were ruined again.

He had no faith in a personal encounter with Señor Zorro. Something seemed to tell him that such would result fatally for himself. And he had small faith in proving Zorro a traitor after the fight, and a great fear that Zorro and some of the captured pirates would, on the other hand, prove him to be one.

Captain Ramón felt desperate. He had an idea that the señorita was under pirate guard in one of the buildings. He would make away with the guard and get her, he decided — ride with her away from the camp and scene of battle.

He could say, afterward, that he had believed the pirates were to be victorious, and that he wanted to rescue the señorita while yet there was time. Possibly he could make them believe that he had departed before he saw the caballeros released and the tide of battle turned.

He had no definite plans after that. Perhaps, he thought, he could keep the señorita a prisoner of his own in some out of the way place, and force her to consent to wed him. Any wandering fray could perform the ceremony. Or, else failing, he could turn criminal, play highwayman, force the señorita to do his bidding. In an emergency, a knife thrust in the heart, a secret grave, and Captain Ramón could wander back among men, saying he had seen nothing of her, possibly claiming that a blow on the head during the battle had robbed him of his wits, and that he did not know where he had been or what had happened.

Captain Ramón had a fertile brain when it came to plotting. He watched for his chance, and escaped through the clouds of smoke, urging his horse to its utmost. He galloped around the buildings, so that the smoke screened his movements. Behind an adobe building he dismounted, and then crept along the wall toward the front. He crouched beside a window, lifted himself slowly, and peered inside.

There sat the señorita, her hands to her face, and lounging near the door was one of the pirates on guard.

The commandante drew his blade and crept nearer the door. He waited for a lull in the din of battle and then shouted loudly.

"At you!" he cried. "Die soldier!"

The subterfuge had immediate results. The pirate opened the door, stepped out a couple of feet, and peered into the smoke. Captain Ramón guessed that the fellow thought the battle was drawing near.

A quick thrust, and the pirate was down, coughing out the blood of his life. Captain Ramón dashed into the building, sheathing his red blade.

The señorita sprang to her feet.

"Quick, señorita! There is scant time!" he cried. "The pirates are having the best of it — "

"I am safer with them than with you!" she said with scorn.

He reached out and grasped her cruelly by the wrist.

"There is to be no more nonsense!" he exclaimed. "I am master here! You do as I say, señorita! Come with me!"

"Beast!" she cried.

"Hard words will not stop me now. Am I to be balked by a bit of womankind?"

He jerked her forward, put an arm around her, half lifted her from the floor, and carried her out of the building and through the billowing smoke. Around the corner he hurried, to his horse. Still holding her by the wrist, he vaulted into the saddle, then pulled her up before him.

"Help!" she cried. "Diego! Zorro!"

"Ha! Call to the fiend, but this time he does not come!" Captain Ramón exclaimed.

But Señor Zorro had heard her shriek. And the smoke lifted, and he and Don Audre Ruiz saw the commandante on the horse, the señorita held before him. Captain Ramón saw them, too, and kicked frantically at the animal's ribs. The frightened horse plunged away through the smoke.

Señor Zorro was more maniac than sane man as he dashed forward to follow. The fight swerved toward him. He sprang up and grasped a soldier, pulled him out of the saddle, sprang into the saddle himself, and gave chase.

Out of the clouds of smoke he rode, to see the commandante and his prisoner a short distance to the left. In the smoke Captain Ramón had lost his bearings for a moment.

Señor Zorro shrieked a challenge, whirled his horse, and took after his foe. Ramón found that he could not get up the slope without meeting Zorro and having a clash with him — the thing he most wanted to avoid. Desperate, he whirled his horse and charged back into the smoke again, thinking to outwit his pursuer.

Suddenly he found himself in the thick of the fighting. Again he whirled his horse. The frightened steed refused to answer rein or pressure of knees, refused to spring forward at the cruel touch of spurs. The smoke swirled away on a breath of breeze. And Captain Ramón found himself inside a ring of caballeros, two of whom were holding his horse, another reaching to help the señorita down, others reaching up to seize him.

Señor Zorro came to a stop within a few feet of him, and dismounted swiftly, a grim look on his face.

"Down, renegade!" Zorro commanded.

Captain Ramón, in the face of such an emergency, could appear calm, though he was not. He sneered, lifted his brows as though in wonder, and slowly got from the saddle. Once he looked straight at Zorro, and then around the circle.

The fighting was at an end. What pirates had not been slain were captives. Barbados, himself a captive, stood to one side under guard. The lieutenant and his troopers were coming forward.

Ramón called to the officer. "Here is your Señor Zorro!" he shouted.

"In some strange manner he has escaped the presidio. Seize him and see that he does not escape again!"

The lieutenant gave a quick command, and some of the troopers dismounted and started forward. But they found before them a line of determined caballeros with ready swords.

Don Audre Ruiz bowed before the lieutenant and spoke. "Señor," he said, "I dislike exceedingly to interfere with a man in the proper performance of his duty. But I must ask you and your men to stand back for a time. There is a little matter between Señor Zorro and Captain Ramón that must be settled."

"I am in command here, under Captain Ramón," the lieutenant said. "This Señor Zorro is an escaped prisoner."

"Nevertheless, you must remain quiet until the affair is at an end," Don Audre said. "The caballeros are equal in number to your troopers now. If you care to fight it out — "

"Do you realize that you are taking up arms against the Governor?" the lieutenant demanded.

"As to that, we are not alarmed," Don Audre replied. "This Ramón is a renegade and a traitor!"

"Ha!" That he is!" cried Barbados. "He joined hands with us, planned for us to raid Reina de Los Angeles and steal the girl. Then he turns against us, plans to trap us! Traitor and dog, he is!"

"And I say so, too," Don Audre declared. "Here are a number of gentlemen whose honors and names are unquestioned, señor. If there is a mistake made here this afternoon we will be responsible for it and take the consequences."

The lieutenant looked puzzled. Certainly he did not want to arouse the hostility of those of gentle blood by setting his troopers on the caballeros; and he doubted the outcome of the fight if he did that.

"Arrest the fellow!" Ramón thundered. "Are you to be held back by these meddlers?"

An open palm cracked against his cheek as he finished speaking. Señor Zorro stood before him, blade held ready. Don Audre Ruiz took the señorita by her arm and led her away.

"Ramón, double traitor and plotter against peace!" Senor Zorro addressed him. "Abductor of women! Foul in word and action and thought! On guard, señor!"

Captain Ramón felt like a trapped animal. He saw his sergeant in the ring.

"Gonzales!" he shrieked. "Seize that man! I command it!"

"I do not take commands from traitors!" the sergeant replied.

"I'll have you punished — "

"'Tis you will receive the punishment, when you gather courage enough to lift your blade," Gonzales replied.

Don Audre Ruiz had turned the señorita over to Fray Felipe. The old fray knew better than to make an attempt to prevent the duel. He belonged to the times, and he understood such things.

"On guard, señor!" Zorro warned again. "I do no like to pollute my blade with your blood, yet must it be done! On guard, renegade! Must I cut down a man who will not defend himself?"

Señor Zorro advanced a step. Captain Ramón, his face white, started to raise his sword. He did not believe, could not force himself to believe, that he would be a victor. Yet he could do his best!

The blades touched. And in the next instant Señor Zorro had sprung backward, and a chorus of cries had come from those in the ring.

For Barbados, not watched as carefully as he should have been watched, had taken vengence himself. He thrust one of his guards aside, snatched a dagger from the belt of another. His arm went up, came forward, the dagger whistled through the air. And it lodged in Captain Ramón's back, the point in his heart.

"That for a traitor!" Barbados cried. "Since I must be hanged, let me settle accounts first! Señor Zorro, you are a man! I, who have fought you, say it! Your blade is too true, señor, to be buried in a foul carcass such as that!"

***

The moonlight came again, touching the sea with glory and showing the trading schooner running up the coast before the breeze. Those of the crew who had been left aboard handled her well, and the caballeros gave aid.

Away from the scene of carnage the little ship rushed, the water hissing at her bows. Fray Felipe was polishing his beloved goblet. Don Audre Ruiz and his caballeros were dressing their hurts in the cabin. Big Sergeant Gonzales was wandering on the deck.

The sergeant stopped near the rail, leaned against it, looked Over the sparkling sea toward the dark line that indicated the land.

Voices came to him, the voices of Zorro and the little señorita.

"The sword of Zorro! Let us hope that it has a long rest," the señorita said.

"A long rest!" Señor Zorro echoed. "As soon as we are at Reina de Los Angeles we'll be wed by Fray Felipe."

"Si!" she said softly. "Then years of happiness and peace."

"Si!"

"Yet, I am not sorry for what has happened," said Señor Zorro. "It has brought us closer together. Peril knits hearts, señorita."

"Once — when I thought that you were dead — "

Sergeant Gonzales observed a suspicious silence at this juncture. He raised his head and peered through the gloom around the mast. He could see nothing at all save the inky darkness there, but he heard a sound that needed no translation. It was the sound of a kiss.

"Meal mush and goat's milk!" said the sergeant.

Zorro Deals with Treason

*Were there two Zorros? Yes — but one
was an imposter, and one was to die!*

CHAPTER I

DOWN the canyon and toward the temporary summer village of the Calientes rolled a tattoo of hoofbeats which grew rapidly in volume and echoed from the rocks.

The tribesmen at the fires sprang quickly and silently to their feet, reaching for their weapons, and some darted back out of the revealing moonlight to positions of advantage in the darkness. They knew that it was not a native's pony coming, but the mount of a white man, for the sounds told them clearly that the mount wore shoes.

But the unknown rider was not approaching furtively, like an enemy or a spy. So those about the fires relaxed, though they kept their weapons handy and curiosity remained with them. Down the narrow trail, presently, the rider came.

The horse he bestrode was a huge black, like a shadow in the bright moonlight. The rider wore a long black mask, and there was a blade at his side, moonlight glinting from its polished scabbard.

" 'Tis Señor Zorro!" somebody cried.

"Zorro … Zorro!" Those around the fires took up the cry, greeted him with wild shouts.

At the edge of the circle of amber light cast by the nearest fire, the rider drew rein. The tribesmen hurried toward him, to group and stand silently and respectfully, waiting for him to speak.

Here was Señor Zorro, the mysterious one, and their friend. In many ways, he had demonstrated his friendship. Here was the elusive rider who made fools of the soldiery who tried to catch him, who punished those who mistreated the natives and cheated them, crossing blades willingly with any and all, and leaving a jagged letter Z on the cheeks of those he fought, so marking them forever as men who had been vanquished by him.

"You know me?" he shouted at them.

"Zorro … Zorro!" they cried in answer.

He lifted a hand in a demand for them to be silent, and they gave him instant attention. Then he spoke:

"I have done what little I could to protect and defend such as you. But it is impossible that one man do everything. Also, it is written that a man must help himself as well as take help from others."

They muttered at his words, but none of them made reply. They could not understand to what his remarks were leading.

"You are being abused, cheated, wronged," the masked rider continued, his voice ringing back from the rocks.

"You are treated worse than the flea-bitten dogs of the pueblo. You stand still and mute while the lash is being put across your backs. Are you men?"

They began muttering again, and sounds of rage rumbled from their throats as they remembered certain indignities and wrongs.

"Now, there is a plan afoot to make all of you slaves. Do you wish that?"

"No! No!" they howled.

"Then you must band together, and strike! Spare the few whites who are your friends, and slay the others. Use the torch on their buildings. Take what goods you wish from their homes. Drive your enemies from the land of your birth, and be free and happy again. You must prepare at once. The other tribes are preparing, and the Calientes must get ready also. I shall lead you to victory."

***

THEY cheered wildly when he said that, until the rock walls of the canyon rang with the echoes. The masked rider lifted a hand again in a demand for silence.

"Use care in your planning," he cautioned. "Do not let your enemies know what you do. The attack must be a complete surprise. Tomorrow night, at this same hour, I shall come to you again. That is all."

The shrill voice was still, and the echoes died away. A moment longer he remained there, looking down at them, then the black horse was turned. Hoofs spurned the flinty ground as he galloped back along the canyon trail, up to level country, back toward the little pueblo of Reina de Los Angeles.

Again, the tribesmen gathered around the fires, their heads bent forward. They talked in whispers until the dawn came stealing over the hills.

Señor Zorro would lead them against their enemies! They would use the torch and their knives, and be masters again in the land of their birth!

Wrongs, indignities would be avenged. They could not fail, for Señor Zorro himself would lead them. He would come again the following night to their camp, probably with complete plans for the uprising.

But Señor Zorro – which is to say Don Diego Vega – knew nothing of all this. He was not abroad this night, riding his black horse, with a mask over his face and a blade ready at his side.

He was in his father's house in Reina de Los Angeles, reading the works of a poet, confined to his room, sneezing and sniffling inelegantly because of a cold in his head.

CHAPTER II

DON DIEGO VEGA retained the cold the following afternoon when he went to take the air in the plaza, though his chest had been well greased with tallow, and he had eaten quantities of honey into which some evil-tasting drug had been mixed by good Fray Felipe of the chapel.

Don Diego strolled leisurely toward a mean hut wherein resided a certain Bardoso, a reformed and retired pirate. He could see Bardoso sitting on a bench on the shady side of his hut, the ever-present wine jug beside him.

Bardoso had one good eye, which lighted with interest when he beheld Don Diego's approach. The other eye had been lost during an affray on the high seas some years before, the man who had caused its loss having gone over the side an instant later to be food for sharks, and carrying Bardoso's cutlass with him in his breast.

Bardoso arose from the bench and bowed low, almost upsetting himself, for his legs were none too steady, due to the wine he had taken.

"A good day to you, pirate!" Don Diego said.

"The best day ever to you, Don Diego!" Bardoso replied. And, as he bowed low again, he added cautiously: "A private word with you señor, if you don't mind."

"Do not stand to windward of me," Don Diego ordered, as he brushed a scented lace handkerchief across his nostrils. "I have a bad cold in the head, but there are some odors so penetrating — "

"I trust that I do not offend you with a stench," Bardoso said. He was but jesting. Concerning odors, Bardoso felt secure, for he had taken a bath the last full moon, and there would not be another full moon for two or three days.

"How goes life with you, Bardoso?" Don Diego asked.

"I have some gossip which may amuse you."

"Say on!"

A swift glance around assured Bardoso that nobody was within earshot. "A certain tribesman of the Cocopahs, a neophyte known as José, who had listened to the frailes of the missions and has consented to adopt Christianity and work for them for nothing — "

"Enough!" Don Diego interrupted. "Use fewer words. I know José of the Cocopahs."

"This morning he told me a strange tale, repeating what had been told him by a friendly Caliente. It was that Señor Zorro appeared last night at the Caliente camp, and urged the tribesmen to an uprising."

"Indeed?" Don Diego said, casually.

"As the tale runs, Señor Zorro is to visit the camp again tonight at the same hour, in furtherance of the plan. It is in my mind that the troopers of the presidio may hear of it and lay a trap to catch him."

Don Diego blinked rapidly. Here was news.

"I cannot believe that the man was Zorro," Bardoso continued. "Zorro is not one to urge rebellion. Some rogue must be leading the natives astray."

"Possibly," Don Diego agreed.

"It is putting a stain upon the name of the real Zorro."

"I am wondering," Don Diego said, "who would go to the trouble of staining Zorro's name, and why."

"Ha, that is a thought! It is some deep plot, perhaps."

"No doubt," Don Diego agreed. "Is there more gossip, pirate?"

"It is rumored that the new officer at the presidio, this Captain Marcos Lopez, is great friends with the person calling himself Don Miguel Sebastiano, lately come from San Francisco de Asis."

"I find nothing particularly strange in that." Don Diego remarked.

"As you say, Don Diego, there is nothing strange in it — birds of a breed fly together."

Don Diego chuckled and tossed Bardoso a coin. "Drink you my health, Señor Pirate," he said. And, in a lower voice, he added: "The health of Señor Zorro, also."

"With deep pleasure, Don Diego."

"Your one good eye sees much. But, which is better, you still have two good ears."

Don Diego chuckled again and strode on, glancing across the plaza toward the inn. He was thinking.

So a spurious Señor Zorro was abroad, stirring up the natives and getting the genuine Zorro a reputation for treason. No doubt, it was expected that the genuine Zorro would learn of it, and visit the camp of the Calientes to get at the truth, and there be captured.

Recently, there had been an exchange of officers at the presidia in Reina de Los Angeles, where Capitán Marcos Lopez was now in command. It was said that this Capitán Lopez stood high in the regard of His Excellency, the Governor.

And His Excellency had some suspicion that Don Diego Vega was Señor Zorro, and would like to expose him as such, having an abiding hatred for Don Diego's father, who preferred honesty in affairs of state, and did not hesitate to say so.

Also, there had arrived some days before a certain Don Miguel Sebastiano, supposed to be touring through the country for pleasure. Don Diego knew him for a rogue with blade for sale. He would not be tarrying in Reina de Los Angeles did he not expect profit from the visit. And he was friendly with Capitán Marcos Lopez!

Don Diego's cold was not so bad but what he was able to smell a plot. No doubt, Don Miguel Sebastiano was the counterfeit Zorro. And the genuine Zorro was to be decoyed into a trap and destroyed.

Strolling slowly, Don Diego came presently to the shady side of the plaza and entered the inn. The fat landlord made haste to welcome him bowing low, dusting off a bench, and bring his best wine mug — a ponderous thing studded with semi-precious stones.

There was loud talk in a corner of the room, and Don Diego saw that Don Miguel Sebastiano was there. The fellow affected fine raiment, but carried it as a crow would the feathers of a pheasant.

He observed Don Diego in turn, and his eyes gleamed maliciously. He whispered to his companions of the bowl, and as they watched, he lurched to his feet and reeled toward the table beside which Don Diego was sitting.

"Have I the rare honor of addressing Don Diego Vega?" he asked, smirking.

"As you have remarked, señor, it is an honor," Don Diego replied, his eyes like steel.

"I have been informed," Don Miguel said, with a sneer on his lips, and speaking loudly enough for all in the big room to hear, "that you waste time reading the works of poets."

"Time is not wasted in reading, señor, if one is intelligent enough to understand what one reads."

"And do you also do needlework?" Don Miguel asked, with a broad smile.

"When I do, señor, the needle I use has a sharp point," Don Diego replied.

"How is this — you grow angry? Your blood is hot? Are you not afraid of a stroke?"

"Nor of a thrust, señor!" Don Diego assured him.

"Ha! That remark would be creditable for a fighting man. But sweet love nonsense is more to your liking than fighting, is it not?"

THE frantic landlord was hovering near, fearing for a tragedy in his place, but he could do nothing to prevent this. The others in the room enjoyed seeing the aristocratic Don Diego Vega baited.

"I perceive," Don Diego said to his tormentor, "that you are trying to force a quarrel upon me. You have intimated that I am not a fighting man."

"I have, Don Diego."

"Perhaps, señor, that is why you are trying to pick a quarrel. Would you be so eager, if you thought that I had fighting ability?"

Don Miguel's face turned almost purple with wrath as somebody in the rear of the room laughed.

"Are you making an effort to be insulting, Don Diego?" Don Miguel roared.

"Making an effort? Alas, I thought that I had succeeded," Don Diego replied. "However, I am not adept at giving insults. It is a thing a caballero does not do well."

"Señor! Your words are almost beyond endurance!" Don Miguel cried.

He lurched forward angrily, and probably would have drawn blade, had there not been an interruption. But there entered from the plaza Capitán Marcos Lopez, and the commandante, understanding the scene at once, hastened forward with an arm upflung in warning.

"Señores!" he cried. "Let us have no serious trouble here! Don Miguel Sebastiano, you forget yourself! Perhaps you have taken too much wine."

Don Miguel acted like a man who suddenly remembers something of the utmost importance. He looked at the officer sheepishly, muttered some words that could not be understood, and lurched back to the corner to continue his wining and dining.

"We have troubles enough already, with this confounded Señor Zorro planning an uprising of the natives," Capitán Lopez continued.

"What is this?" the landlord cried. "The natives are to trouble us again?"

"What did you expect? This Zorro pretends to right their wrongs to get a following, then turns renegade. It is always so. He should be hunted down like a mad dog," the capitán said. "But have no fear! My troopers will handle this precious Señor Zorro. For his treason, he shall hang!"

Don Diego Vega politely stifled a yawn with the back of his hand as he arose to leave. "I would not shape the noose, capitán, until I had caught him," he suggested.

"It might be only a waste of your valuable time."

CHAPTER III

A T DUSK that day, Sergeant Pedro Gonzales stood stiffly at attention in the presence of his commanding officer in the latter's quarters at the presidio.

Don Miguel Sebastiano was sitting beside the capitán, having dined with him, and he quaffed wine as he inspected the burly sergeant from hat to boots.

"Understand me well, Sergeant Gonzales, and make no errors," the capitán was saying. "You will take all the troopers except my orderly, and ride at once to the canyon, and go into hiding there, careful that you are not observed by the natives."

"It is an order, capitán."

"Don Miguel, as the bogus Zorro, will visit the camp again and utter treasonable words, which you and your men will remember if called on later to testify."

"Understood, capitán."

"Allow Don Miguel to ride away. The genuine Zorro may visit the camp. If he does, capture him. Then the treasonable words of the false Zorro may be fastened on the real Zorro, and he may be convicted of treason and hung. It will serve better than slaying him in fight, for all will rise against him as a renegade, and it will mean disgrace for his proud family."

"It is understood, capitán," the big sergeant said. His countenance remained inscrutable.

"You know the identity of the man we have under suspicion. His house is being watched. If he departs therefrom, when he returns he will be asked to explain his absence — that is in case you do not capture him."

"It is well, capitán," the sergeant said.

"A simple plot, and effective! He is decoyed to the canyon. Don Miguel utters treason, and you swear that Zorro said the words. You and your men will remember seeing only one Zorro."

"It is all understood, capitán."

"To your duty then!"

Sergeant Pedro Gonzales saluted smartly and hurried to the barracks to issue orders. Capitán Lopez turned to his companion.

"Miguel, you are supposed to be here all evening," he said. "I shall take my orderly and go to the inn, and talk there of Zorro's treason, inflaming men against him. And I shall say, also, that you took too much wine when you dined with me, and are sleeping."

"It is an excellent idea!" Don Miguel said.

"Slip out unseen now, and get into your Zorro garb, and get your black horse from the ravine. Give the troopers ample time to get into position before you appear at the camp of the natives."

Outside the window, crouching close to the adobe wall in the darkness, José of the Cocopahs heard all that. Now he continued to watch for a time, then hurried to the Vega house, and went to a servant's hut in the rear of the patio, as though on an ordinary visit to a friend.

But, a few minutes later, he was inside the house itself, through a secret entrance, explaining the entire affair to Don Diego.

DON DIEGO paced the floor, his head bent and his hands clasped behind his back, evidently thinking of a plan. Presently, he faced José.

"Zorro rides!"

"Sí, señor!" The native's eyes flashed.

"This time, José, I need your help and that of some of your friends. And there is scant time to prepare matters."

"You have but to command, Don Diego."

"Listen carefully, then." Don Diego spoke at length, in hushed tones. "Now, go and prepare everything," he concluded. "And stand ready for me by the big rock on the San Juan Capistrano trail."

"It shall be as you say, Don Diego."

José departed. That the house might be watched by some of Capitán Lopez's spies worried Don Diego not at all, nor did the presence of family and servants. It was supposed that he had retired early because of his cold, and none of the latter would approach the chamber to trouble him.

He slipped silently along a corridor and down a rear stairway, and, unseen by any, came finally to the great cellar with its storerooms for food and drink. Candle in hand, he went to the rear, and got through the wall where there was false masonry at a tunnel's mouth.

He finally emerged in an adobe hut at the rear of the patio. Then, wrapping a black cloak around him, he darted from shadow to shadow until he was some distance from the house.

Half a mile out of town, in a depression not far from the highway, José of the Cocopahs had the black horse waiting. Don Diego changed garments swiftly, put on his mask and buckled on a blade. Then he muttered further instructions to José, and rode slowly away through the night.

For the present, Don Diego Vega did not exist. Señor Zorro was abroad.

Cautiously, he skirted the edge of the town and neared the inn, riding along the bottom of a ravine and keeping in the shadows. He tethered his horse to a clump of brush where it was quite dark.

Then he went forward afoot, continuing along the ravine, but leaving it presently and going toward the long, low building which housed the inn.

José had informed him that the troopers had ridden away with Gonzales at their head, that Don Miguel Sebastiano had left the presidio. Capitán Lopez and his orderly servant should now be at the inn, the former making talk to carry on the plot.

The rear of the building was in darkness, save where a streak of light came through the partially opened door. Getting near, Zorro peered inside and saw the fat landlord dishing up food.

He slipped through the door like a shadow and glided forward.

S UDDENLY the startled landlord found Señor Zorro standing there at his elbow, his manner threatening, his eyes gleaming through the holes in his mask.

"Silence, or you die!" Zorro hissed at him. "Speak only to answer, and then in whispers. Is Capitán Lopez now in the big room?"

"Sí, señor!" the landlord whispered, shaking with fear.

"What others?"

"One soldier with the capitán, and two travelers who have just come off El Camino Real. They are merchants."

"How is it that you have such scant company tonight?" Zorro demanded.

"There is a cock fight at a hacienda out the San Gabriel trail. Everybody has gone there."

"Go forward now, ahead of me, with your hands held high above your head." Zorro ordered.

The trembling landlord obeyed. They passed through the door and into the big room. Capitán Lopez sat at a table near the fireplace, and his orderly was on a bench in a corner. The two travelers were at another table not far away.

Señor Zorro pricked the fat landlord with the tip of his blade so that the landlord gave a squeal of terror, and thrust him aside. Those in the room turned to look. By the light from the reeking torches and tallow dips, they saw Señor Zorro standing not far from the end of the fireplace.

Now he held a pistol in his left hand, as well as the blade in his right. He took a quick step forward, his eyes seeming to blaze through the holes in his mask.

"Against the wall, capitán!" he ordered. "You others remain as you are."

Capitán Lopez sprang to his feet. "What is this?" he cried. He had been caught at a disadvantage. He had removed belt and sword some time before, and loosened his clothing to be comfortable; the weapon was on another table some distance from him. The trooper was not armed at all.

"It is Señor Zorro, as you know well, though you never have had sight of my face."

"And you dare come here and face me — you, an outlaw?" Lopez cried.

"As you see, señor."

"What is it you wish — to surrender and throw yourself on the mercy of His Excellency?"

"I am still in my right mind, señor el capitán. And His Excellency has no mercy."

"You have come here to murder me, perhaps?"

"I am not a murderer, señor, though you would have people think so of me. Sit on the end of that bench against the wall, and lend ear."

Capitán Lopez obeyed the order, moving slowly and with evident reluctance, thinking swiftly the while. His sword was on the table several feet away. He did not have a pistol in his sash, for he had come to the inn merely to drink and talk of Zorro's treason, anticipating no trouble or duty. And here was Zorro facing him — and he was supposed to be in the canyon inciting natives to rebellion.

Badly frightened, the two merchants were watching and listening. The landlord crouched trembling against the wall. The lone trooper made no move, not caring to advance upon Señor Zorro unless his officer so ordered.

"CAPITÁN LOPEZ," Zorro said, "according to the learned doctors, it is impossible for a man to be in two places at the same time. Is that not so?"

"Certainly."

"Señor Zorro is standing here before you, and in the plain eyesight of these others, so it is impossible for him to be elsewhere — say in the canyon toward the sea."

"I fail to make sense of what you say."

"Since Señor Zorro is here with you, the man who is busy stirring the natives to rebellion cannot be Zorro. Hence, if Zorro is accused of treason, you will know that the accusation is false."

"And who says Zorro is here?" Lopez asked.

"Have you not eyes, señor! Can you not see me?"

"You?" Capitán Lopez exclaimed. "Ha! I understand this affair now. Señor Zorro, while at his dark work of treason, has a friend appear here in a duplicate of Zorro's raiment, pretending to be he."

"That would, indeed, be a pretty subterfuge," Zorro admitted. "Your meaning is that I am unable to prove that I am the genuine Zorro?"

"Exactly, señor!"

"Ah! But I shall endeavor to leave behind me absolute proof of my identity, señor el capitán."

"And that?" Lopez questioned.

"Is it not possible for you to guess? Have you no wit? Take up your blade from the table, señor," Zorro ordered. "And you others sit quietly as you are, else this pistol of mine will bark at you. I am about to cross blades with you, señor el capitán."

"You will give me fair fight?" Lopez cried, springing toward the table, hand open to grasp the hilt of his sword and tear it from its scabbard. "I welcome it!"

"I give you fair fight, señor, though I am at a loss to understand why you welcome it. After it is over, His Excellency will be compelled to send yet another officer to the presidio here."

"Ha! You are so certain you will slay me?"

"I have no intention of slaying you, señor. I am only going to leave proof that the real Zorro has been here, that he was not in the canyon preaching rebellion — and that your poor cat's paw was."

Suddenly, Capitán Lopez understood. For an instant, something like fright swept through him. He reeled back against the wall and fought to gain control of himself.

"Zorro always leaves his mark, señor el capitán! Perhaps the bogus one could not do so much."

CHAPTER IV

THERE was nothing to do now but fight, Capitán Lopez knew. He was an officer, and one of his own troopers was in the room, as well as the fat landlord and two strange travelers, to tell the tale afterward. And there was a possibility that Señor Zorro would not win this combat. Capitán Lopez fancied himself as a master of fence.

But, when the blades crossed and clashed and rang, and he got the first feel of Zorro's wrist, he knew that this fight would be no light bout. He was facing a man who knew how to wield a blade. Caution came quickly to replace the rash rage with which he had at first attacked, and he fell back and fought carefully.

With bulging eyes, the others in the room watched the fighting, aware that Señor Zorro glanced their way frequently, and held pistol ready in his left hand as he fought. The merchants were not of fighting stock, nor was the landlord. The trooper made no move; he would not unless his officer called for help.

"Not bad, capitán!" Zorro cried, as he brushed aside a lunge. "A little too low, señor — a" as he parried another. "It is a blade you hold, not a bludgeon."

"You'll not put mark on me!"

" 'Tis scarce a fair time to make a wager, yet I am willing to do so," Zorro said. "If I mark you, let us say, you will leave Reina de Los Angeles, and save the Governor the trouble of recalling you in disgrace."

"I make no wager with an outlaw!"

"Ha!" Señor Zorro's blade suddenly darted forward, and the capitán gave a cry and recoiled. Zorro dropped the point of his blade and stood waiting, laughing a little, scorning to follow up the advantage. " 'Tis only the first cut, señor — the top bar of the Z."

"I shall kill you!"

"It is your rare privilege to try."

Capitán Lopez advanced to the attack again. It was a wild attempt and for a moment Zorro was compelled to retreat, to sidestep, so that a man who did not know fence might have believed he was being hard pressed. But the soldier who sat on the bench in the corner knew that he was only being cautious and waiting for an opportunity.

Presently, it came. The sword of the capitán flashed out of his hand and clattered to the floor. In that same instant, Zorro's blade darted forward again.

"The lower bar of the Z, capitán," he said. "I join the two bars at my leisure. Pick up your blade, señor, and continue. Do your best, I beg of you, and at least make this combat interesting for me."

C APITÁN LOPEZ darted across the room and retrieved his blade from the floor. The flickering light from the nearest torch revealed that his face was ashen, save where blood trickled from his twice-wounded cheek. That Zorro had him at his mercy, he knew well.

But this was a time, Capitán Lopez told himself, when the rules of proper combat need not be observed to the letter. This Zorro was an outlaw, and was not entitled to the treatment one should give a caballero. If he could slay Zorro now, or wound him and take him prisoner, there would be certain rich rewards from the Governor.

"Soldier!" Lopez cried. "Help me take this man! He is an outlaw!"

As he finished his speech, Capitán Lopez charged wildly, his blade a flashing and erratic thing. He confused Zorro for an instant because of his utter disregard of proper method. As Zorro retreated, the trooper sprang.

The pistol Zorro held barked and flamed. A cloud of smoke swirled in the room. The trooper gave a cry and reeled back to the bench, to drop upon it weakly, clutching at a left shoulder that spouted blood.

Then Zorro pressed the fighting angrily.

"Craven!" he cried. "For that — "

"At him, man!" Lopez roared at the wounded trooper. "He has discharged his pistol. That stool — hurl it at him! Bring him down!"

The trooper lurched to his feet as Zorro compelled the capitán to retreat again. He picked up the heavy stool and hurled it, but Zorro sidestepped swiftly, jerked his head aside, and let the stool fly past him.

"The door!" Lopez cried. "Get help!"

Weakened by the effort in throwing the stool, the wounded trooper staggered toward the door. But Zorro was before him. His blade bit lightly into the trooper's other shoulder, and the man reeled back.

"Now, señor el capitán!" Zorro cried.

He pressed forward again, a trace of anger in his manner. His blade was like a live thing, a flashing menace. Lopez could not stand against it. Again the point darted forward, and again the capitán felt a burn on his cheek. And his own blade was torn from his grasp once more, and clattered to the floor.

"Now you bear my mark, señor," Zorro said, as he leaned against the wall. "Sit down at that table. Be glad that I did not run you through!"

"This is not the end!" Lopez cried. "Though you know it not, Señor Zorro, I have you in a trap."

"I fear no traps." Zorro turned to the trembling landlord. "Get materials, and attend to that soldier's wound," he ordered. "Then bring supper for your two guests. I regret, señores that necessity compelled me to interrupt your meal."

He looked again at the capitán, who was trying to stanch the flow from his wounded cheek, and darted swiftly to the kitchen door.

"Señores, a Dios!" he cried.

And then he was gone.

T HROUGH the shadows he went, and reached the ravine where he had left his horse. He recharged his pistol, meanwhile listening for a din at the hostelry. But there came no outcry.

The soldiers were out at the canyon. The majority of the younger townsmen were at the cock fight down San Gabriel way. And Capitán Marcos Lopez, moreover, did not care to hasten the moment when knowledge of his discomfiture would become public.

Through the moon-drenched night Zorro rode again, unseen, and so came to a ravine which ran around the other side of the town. A soft hiss reached his ears. He stopped the horse.

"Señor!" José of the Cocopahs was before him.

"Everything is in readiness, José?"

"Everything, Señor Zorro. We shall do as you have ordered."

"I see nobody but you."

Soft words came from the lips of José. They penetrated the brush. From behind the shrubs and rocks crept men — furtive natives who approached Zorro as though awed.

"You understand fully?" Zorro asked them, speaking in low tones. "This false man would have led you into trouble. You would have been slain by the soldiers. Never would I counsel you to rebellion, for such a thing is wrong. Be prepared to do as José has instructed you."

They growled and muttered, trusting Zorro fully. José had explained the meaning of the affair to them. Now their hatred was against the man who would have used them for this purpose, though it caused the soldiery to slay them and burn their village.

"You have found his garments?" Zorro asked José.

"They are here, señor, where he changed."

"Send a man with them, far back among the rocks, so they cannot be found quickly. And now go into hiding again, and wait for my signal."

They disappeared like so many shadows. Zorro held his head high, listening. From the far distance came the sounds of a horse's hoofs. Guiding his black deftly, Zorro rode back into the shadows.

The hoofbeats came nearer. The rider was making little speed, was moving with caution. Yet he wished speed above all else.

Don Miguel Sebastiano had visited the camp of the Calientes again, and had tried to stir them to war. Then he had ridden away, sure that the waiting troopers in ambush had heard him.

He was eager now to change clothing, turn loose his horse, and get back to the presidio. For, only when he had done that, would he be safe. As long as he was abroad in the garb of Zorro, there was a chance of the masquerade being detected.

Into the ravine Don Miguel rode, piloting his horse to the place where he had left his clothes. He stripped saddle and bridle from the animal and turned him loose, and hid the gear behind some rocks. Then he went to the spot where he had left his garments behind a clump of shrubs. A muttering of profanity came from his lips when he saw the clothes were not there. He began searching frantically behind other clumps of shrubs.

"You seek something, señor?" a soft voice asked.

DON MIGUEL SEBASTIANO sprang backward, his right hand diving toward the pistol he carried in his sash. But out of the darkness came a rope, hissing and coiling like a serpent, and it fell about him in a noose, and was jerked taut, pinning his arms to his sides.

Then an avalanche of men descended upon him out of the brush and from behind the rocks, natives who smothered him with their weight, who lashed his wrists behind his back.

They carried him to his horse, which they had caught. Saddle and bridle were brought from hiding and put on quickly, and Don Miguel was put into the saddle, and his ankles lashed beneath the mount's belly.

His mask had remained in place during all this. Nor did any one attempt to remove it now. Don Miguel cursed and howled, then began pleading and offered rewards for his freedom, but they answered him not at all.

From the darkness by the rocks came another horse, and he saw a replica of himself, as far as garments were concerned. From behind the

A rope, hissing and coiling like
a serpent ... was jerked taut,
pinning his arms to his sides.

mask of this second rider came a chuckle.

"So Señor Zorro has been captured at last! His end will be a pretty one, no doubt. For those who dabble in treason, there is always a rope waiting. There is a fine reward offered by His Excellency for Zorro's capture, too, I believe. These natives may claim it, and be right rich. They will be able to buy fine clothes, in which to dress when they attend your public hanging."

"Whoever you are — " Don Miguel began.

But Señor Zorro waved a hand at the men, and motioned to José of the Cocopahs. Then he turned his horse and rode away through the darkness.

Now the natives put into effect the instructions they had received. Some rushed toward Reina de Los Angeles, shattering the calm night with their cries.

"Zorro is taken! ... Señor Zorro is captured! ... They are taking him to the presidio!"

The din awoke those who slept, and brought out into the plaza men of prominence, and a few ladies also. The mystery of Zorro had intrigued them. They wished to see the man's face.

Two natives rushed to the presidio, where Capitán Marcos Lopez had gone from the inn, to doctor his cut cheek. Their howls brought him forth.

"Zorro is captured — "

"One of you give me details!" he roared.

One stepped forward. "He was riding his black horse, and stopped where some men were talking. They bound him with ropes and are bringing him here. We share in the reward."

"Where was he caught?" Lopez asked.

"As he was leaving the town by the ravine. They are bringing him here."

Capitán Lopez was hoping that the genuine Zorro had been caught as he was riding away from the inn, but he was worried because Don Miguel had not returned. And another thing worried him — that this matter was to be so public.

Up the slopes from the plaza the men of the pueblo were coming. Among them were dons of importance, who had to be handled with velvet gloves. They would see his wounded face, and know that Zorro had bested him.

They gathered in front of the presidio, under the light of the torches which burned at either side of the entrance. Capitán Lopez retired quickly to his quarters. He bathed his face quickly again, but could not hide the wounds. And the swelling was extremely noticeable.

It was no disgrace to be marked by Zorro, however, so he would go out and face them. Zorro's capture offset everything. He would toss the natives a few coins, and take the huge reward to himself.

C APITÁN LOPEZ strolled through the corridor and to the front door when he heard another din at the corner of the plaza. He greeted the important men of the community with professional dignity.

"The rogue has been preaching sedition," he explained. "My troopers rode out tonight to catch him. Undoubtedly he escaped them, only to be caught by others."

He could see a man on a black horse, with natives leaving the mount and others walking on either side. The rider wore a black cloak, black mask. The shouting natives brought him on, screeching in their excitement.

They stopped the horse inside the light cast by the torches. Some of them rushed toward the capitán.

"Pay the reward to José, and he will share with us all," one said. "We are all Cocopahs."

"I thought Zorro was the friend of the Cocopahs," Lopez said, sneering a bit. "So you betray your friend for gold?"

"He planned an uprising and that is bad," José said, as he strode forward. "Many of us would have died. He escaped your soldiers, señor el capitán, but we captured him."

They brought the horse on, and then Capitán Lopez knew the worst. This rider was garbed much as the real Zorro had been at the inn. But there were slight differences which Lopez noticed. They had captured Don Miguel Sebastiano.

Here was a predicament. Lopez must save this man, to save himself. He thought quickly. If he could get Don Miguel into the prison room without his mask being removed, if he could lock him in, and drive all away, then let Don Miguel out and say that Zorro made an escape, all might be well.

"Untie the man!" Lopez ordered. "Take him from the horse. Leave the rope on his wrists. I'll take him to the prison room."

"Take off his mask!" somebody cried.

Lopez pretended not to hear. He began bellowing orders to the natives. He shouted for his orderly to take charge of the affair, and strode forward himself.

"Back, señores!" he cried. "We can take no chances here. The rogue may have friends among you, and there'll be no rescue!"

"Let us see his face!" some man cried again.

They had unfastened Don Miguel's feet and helped him out of the saddle. They started leading him toward the door. Through the crowd, two men of prominence thrust their way.

"Capitán Lopez! We demand that this man's mask be removed. We would know the identity of Zorro."

"Presently."

"Now!" one thundered.

The other reached out and whipped away the mask. "Don Miguel Sebastiano!" he cried.

CHAPTER V

THERE came a chorus of cries as the identity of the prisoner was made known. The crowd surged forward. Capitán Lopez was powerless to do more than bark at them. His one man could not help much, and Sergeant Gonzales and the troopers had not returned from the Caliente village.

"I'll get him into the prison room," Lopez cried. "Stand back, señores! This trooper of mine will help me."

An elderly don, who had some idea of his own regarding Zorro, stepped forward.

"This man is your friend," he accused. "It would be an easy thing for him to escape, under certain conditions."

"Señor, you dare intimate — " Lopez began.

"A few of us will go with you and the prisoner to your own quarters, capitán, and there have an understanding about this affair."

Lopez stormed, but it availed him nothing. They named a committee of men he dared not deny. They brushed aside his protests.

As they went down the corridor to the capitán's room, both Lopez and Don Miguel were trying desperately to think of some way out. The members of the committee kept them apart, so they could not talk.

Lopez had some wild idea of disclaiming knowledge of Don Miguel, other than he had come recommended to him. Not trusting the capitán overmuch, Don Miguel expected that, and was preparing to offset it.

They closed the corridor door, thrust Don Miguel on a bench against the wall. Capitán Lopez sat at his desk, and the men of the committee stood around him.

"There is some mistake," Lopez said.

"How is that, señor el capitán! Here is the man, dressed as Zorro always dresses. He had a mask on his face, and rode a black horse. He fought you in the inn, marked you — "

"Then how could he have been at the canyon talking to the tribesmen?" Lopez asked.

"We do not know. But here we have Zorro, who has done many good things, but who has wiped out them all by trying to create trouble with the natives. He will be guarded carefully, so he cannot escape. We demand, capitán, that you give him immediate military trial, and hang him at the corner of the plaza at sunrise."

"Perhaps it would be better to communicate first with His Excellency."

"His Excellency is in San Francisco de Asis at present, and it would take many, many days for him to be informed. Why bother the Governor with this? You have ample power to prosecute and punish under military law any highwayman or traitor, and this man seems to be both."

"But Don Miguel has but recently come to Reina de Los Angeles," Lopez protested, "and Señor Zorro has been committing his lawless acts hereabouts for more than a year."

"How do we know but what Don Miguel has been in this vicinity for that length of time, perhaps with a hiding place in the hills, or in some native village?"

Capitán Marcos Lopez glanced across the room at Don Miguel, and a look of hopelessness was in the face of each. The capitán decided to fight for time.

"What have you to say for yourself, Don Miguel?" he asked.

Don Miguel's eyes flashed. He had some idea that Capitán Lopez was about to desert him.

"Why not tell them the truth?" he asked. He looked at the committee. "Señores, it is easily explained. The joke is on me — "

"You consider treason a joke, señor?" one barked at him.

"It was a subterfuge, in an attempt to catch Señor Zorro. I was to play at being Zorro, visit the native camp and talk of an uprising. We believed that the real Zorro would hear of it, and go there, and the soldiers catch him. That is all — except that by accident the natives caught me. And the genuine Zorro was there when they did it.

"He was there?" Lopez cried. "Then he knew of our scheme?"

"Evidently," Don Miguel said.

"I see it all now. He fought me at the inn, then hurried out and helped the natives catch you. The thing must be explained to the townsmen. Zorro laughs at us again. I'll take off your bonds, Don Miguel — "

"One moment, señor!" a committeeman protested. "You did not tell this tale at first. Now you are saying there are two Zorros — one false and one real. Let us question the natives who made the capture."

"They will lie," Lopez cried. "They adore this scamp of a Zorro. They will swear Don Miguel's life away."

"We have one Zorro here, and that is enough. If there is another, where is he?"

A voice from the corner answered: "Look this way, señores!"

THERE stood Zorro, blade in hand.

He had ridden back to the presidio, and left his horse behind the building in the darkness. Through an open window he had crawled into the room adjoining the quarters of the capitán, and through an unlocked door he had entered.

"Do not compel me to violence, señores," he said, now. "Stand as you are, please. Keep that pistol from the hands of the capitán!"

Zorro held his own pistol in his left hand, they noticed now, and menaced them with it.

"You have heard the truth," he said. "Don Miguel is not Zorro. He and the capitán were trying to catch me by a trick. That is permissible in the game we play. But to try to make me out a renegade — ah, señores, that is too much!"

"You — " Lopez began.

"Silence, señor el capitán!" Zorro cried. "I have helped the natives at times, have punished those who mistreated them. But never have I counseled them to an uprising. I love them too much for that. They are but simple children, easy victims for unscrupulous men."

"You admit you are Zorro?" Lopez cried.

"Seize him, you men!"

"Be warned!" Zorro cried in return, sweeping the pistol around in front of him. "Señores, this Don Miguel is not Zorro, and cannot be blamed for Zorro's acts. But the fact remains that he uttered treasonable words and tried to stir up the natives. So he is guilty of treason. And should he not be punished for that?"

"That is true," one of the committee said. "And this capitán, who abetted the plot — we shall see that the Governor recalls him."

"Are you all in league with this highwayman, this outlaw?" Lopez screeched. "You are lawbreakers yourselves if you do not aid me now in his capture."

"I am holding a pistol on them," Zorro observed. "And I have a task here. Don Miguel Sebastiano, we must have a settlement. A man cannot impersonate me and have me called renegade without being called on to account for it."

"You have pistol and blade, and I am unarmed," Don Miguel said.

"I give you fair fight, señor. I ask these señores to see that all is fair. Guard you the capitán, that he does not interfere. Unbind the man's wrists, and give him a blade. At the end of it, you may decide what is to be done with me."

The protests of Capitán Lopez were as nothing. Those of the committee liked the idea. There were some who had suspicion of Zorro's real identity. None liked Don Miguel and his tactics. Here was a chance, moreover, to see swordplay.

So Don Miguel was unbound and given a blade and the draft of wine for which he asked. Capitán Lopez was thrust into a corner and held there. More candles were lit, that the room would be bright with light.

DON MIGUEL's eyes gleamed strangely, and his tongue moistened his lips as though they suddenly had become parched. It was in his mind to slash at Zorro's mask and reveal the face of the man. It also was in his mind to run Zorro through, thus wiping out this stain and earning the reward of His Excellency.

Capitán Lopez could have told Don Miguel something of the way Zorro handled a blade, but he had no opportunity. Steel rang, and the fighting began.

They felt each other out cautiously. Don Miguel had considerable skill, and Señor Zorro was a man who never made the mistake of underestimating an antagonist. But caution soon gave way to speed, spirited attack and defense.

Don Miguel found himself out-generaled in an instant. Zorro's blade scratched his cheek. From the corner, Capitán Lopez gave a cry of warning:

"He's trying to carve his mark on you, Miguel!"

"The upper bar of the Z," Zorro said. "And here is the lower bar, señor!"

Don Miguel gave a great cry of rage, as he felt the tip of the blade bite again. Zorro was prolonging the agony, as he had in the case of the capitán. Usually, that jagged Z was made by one stroke, by the tip of the blade playing over the cheek in a series of quick twists.

"And now, señor — " Zorro said.

But Don Miguel seemed to go insane. He rushed out, cut and slashed and lunged, like a man who knew nothing of fence, trying to overpower his enemy and bear him down. For a moment, Zorro was compelled to fight fiercely to save himself. His footwork accomplished this. Then Don Miguel, winded, his burst of passion spent, was off-guard a moment, and again Zorro's blade bit.

"You wear the Z, señor!" he said; and disarmed his man.

The blade clattered to the floor. Panting, Don Miguel reeled against the wall, waiting for the end. A swift advance, a quick thrust, and it would be over.

But Zorro did not give the thrust. He stepped back, and motioned with the weapon he held.

"Pick up your blade, señor," he said.

Stepping away from the wall, Don Miguel Sebastiano went across the room and retrieved his sword. Again he faced Zorro, the point of his blade down.

"I have marked you, señor," Zorro said. "That is for daring to oppose me. Now, I shall deal with you for your treason, for having me thought renegade, for arousing the poor natives and almost getting them into serious trouble — and for some other things. You fight for life now, Don Miguel Sebastiano!"

Capitán Lopez made a last effort to stop this. He sprang off the bench and started forward.

"Enough!" he cried. "Señores, I call upon you to help me take this man!"

But they tossed him back upon the bench, and warned him to remain there, and turned to watch the fighting.

P ERSPIRATION stood out in great globules on the face of Don Miguel. He called upon all the science he knew. But there came to him the realization that he was no match for Zorro.

Every attempt he made was blocked. For every trick, Zorro had defense. Señor Zorro was but playing with him, wearing him down. Through the holes in his black mask, the eyes of Zorro glittered like those of a deadly serpent. Then came a furious onslaught, and Don Miguel gave ground. His lower jaw was sagging and a great fear was in his face. He brought up against the wall, called upon his remaining strength.

Another clash of steel, and Zorro's blade was thrust in the fatal stroke. Don Miguel dropped his sword and gave a sigh. He collapsed slowly to the floor.

Señor Zorro darted forward and bent over him.

"Needlework, señor!" he said, just loud enough for Don Miguel to hear.

"So!" Don Miguel was dying as he spoke. "Capitán!…Señores! This…this man…is — "

But Don Miguel did not speak the word.

Zorro faced the others. "Señores, my work here is done," he said. "Pardon me, if I now make my escape. Remember, señores, I still hold my pistol."

He backed to the door, watching them closely.

From somebody outside came a peculiar cry that made Zorro straighten slightly. And there was a sudden thunder of hoofbeats. Sergeant Gonzales and his troopers had returned from the canyon.

Capitán Marcos Lopez gave a glad cry and sprang off the bench again. He shouted orders for his orderly out in the corridor to hear.

"Warn Gonzales! Zorro is here! Make a capture!"

Señor Zorro darted into the adjoining room and closed and barred the door. He was through the window an instant later, and running to the rear of the presidio building, where he had left his horse.

"José!"

"Señor?"

"Into the saddle. Wait a moment, then ride. Decoy them for me."

"Sí, señor!"

THERE was a tumult in front of the presidio. Gonzales was howling to know what had happened. Capitán Lopez got past those of the committee and to the door, rushed into the corridor, and to the front.

"Zorro … here … escaping," he cried. "Gonzales! Leave half your force, pursue with the others!"

At the rear of the building was a sudden clatter as a horse jumped into action. A black streak passed through the moonlight.

"There he goes!"

Capitán Lopez was fairly dancing with excitement and anger as he urged his men after the swift, dark shadow that had already vanished.

Troopers started in pursuit. But it was José of the Cocopahs in the saddle, though they knew it not, and José feared not at all that any of the troopers could overtake the big black. He would out-race them, get to hiding — and Zorro would disappear again.

As for Señor Zorro, he was traveling cautiously from shadow to shadow, skirting the town, and coming down the slope toward his father's house. He got into the hut at the rear of the patio, through the tunnel, and into the house. Working swiftly, he hid his Zorro garb and blade, put on a dressing gown, and threw himself upon his elegant couch.

Completely at ease now, he picked up a volume of poems.

He was soon engrossed.

Back at the presidio, the townsmen scattered. Capitán Marcos Lopez called to him the troopers left behind.

"We surround the Vega casa immediately," he said. "Any one who seeks to enter must be stopped. Perhaps we yet shall catch the fox, if Gonzales fails in the chase."

The commandante had lost much this night, and he was determined not to fail in this final opportunity. So he swiftly ordered his troopers to their horses, his voice breathless and strident.

They galloped across the plaza and took station, some in front, some in rear, and some on either side. In the moonlight, their movements were seen clearly. Word flashed through Reina de Los Angeles that the Vega house was being watched by the soldiery.

Capitán Marcos Lopez himself remained in front, watching and waiting. But he did not have long to wait. The big front door of the house was opened. Two servants appeared holding huge candelabra. And then, through the open door, came Don Diego's proud, white-haired father, and Don Diego himself was a step behind him.

"Capitán Lopez!" the head of the Vega house called. "Do me the kindness to take your soldiers away. They are disturbing my household. We do not need their protection."

"Protection?" Lopez gasped.

This was too much.

"Could they possibly be here for any other reason?" Don Diego's father demanded. "If so, be good enough to state that reason!"

He stood there erect and magnificently cool, his eyes fixed on the commandante; and his son behind him was properly grave. Quite obviously these gentlemen were not to be crossed.

Lopez hesitated only an instant. "They shall be removed, señor."

He was outwitted in some manner, he knew. There was Don Diego standing in the doorway. No use to guard the house to catch him entering it, when he was inside already.

And now Don Diego brushed his nostrils with a scented handkerchief, and sneezed a bit, and spoke:

"It appears, señor el capitán, that something has happened to your face. You have been playing roughly, perhaps, and got it scratched. But those who play roughly may expect to be hurt. That is the way of life. *Buenas noches, capitán!*"

The Mysterious Don Miguel

The keen blade and rapier wit of Señor Zorro were legend in
Spanish California—and there was dire need for them now!

CHAPTER I
Don Nameless

THE hourglass had run its course several times since the twinkling
candles had ceased casting their erratic beams through the windows
of the houses. The reeking torches had been extinguished in the adobe
huts of the natives. The night watch had given his eerie call so often that
now it was half stifled by a yawn, and, instead of the stentorian call of
the early evening, was a thing with no ring of authority in it.

A bright moon streaked the tumbling waters of the bay. In from the
distant sea wandered a soft breeze to stir the fronds of the palms around
the little plaza in San Diego de Alcála, and to be welcomed by the weary
troopers who stood their shift of guard at the presidio.

Before the hourglass had run its course twice more, the pink dawn
would come stealing in from the east and the business of another day
would begin.

Droves of stock — cattle and horses and sheep — would be driven
in for trading. Hides and tallow, jars of honey and preserved fruits would
be brought in for barter. Heavy carts would come into the town along
the dusty trails from many a hacienda.

At the mission up the valley, robed Franciscan brothers would be up and busy at their eternal work of changing gentile natives into neophytes, and of building up the mission empire their own Junipero Serra had founded. But, in the large main room of the inn at the corner of the plaza, were some who did not seem to realize that the night was far spent already.

They had neglected to eat the food the fat landlord had prepared for them long before. Their fine garments were damp with perspiration induced by excitement and the rich wine they had taken, and their flushed faces wore strained expressions as they watched closely over a long table which had a huge candelabra at either end.

Pedro Pico, the professional gambler, was playing for high stakes again. He was also winning heavily and steadily, and certain of the young caballeros who demeaned themselves by dicing with him were seeking to catch him in some act of clever crookedness, but could not.

Pedro Pico's lean and swarthy face was inscrutable as he played. His eyes were small and black and glittering. His white hands and tapering fingers were no less than things of beauty, adorned with precious jewels which scintillated in the light, as he manipulated either dice or the cards, as the others requested, but both to his own material advantage.

A BOUT a score of men were in the big, dimly lighted main room of the inn. Some were young caballeros who had ridden in from their fathers' estates for a night of sport in the town. Others were but common folk of San Diego de Alcála. And there were several of uncertain standing, who had lately come off El Camino Real, the King's Highway which connected the missions in a chain, and who looked like rogues, and probably were.

"By the saints — !"

One dressed in fine raiment spoke as another cast of the dice went to his disadvantage, and retreated from the gaming table to wipe the perspiration from his face with a square of silk edged with lace.

"The saints, señor, have nothing to do with it," another whispered into his ear. "It is my private opinion that the Evil One has forsaken his usual abode and is with us here tonight in this land of California."

"Ha! It is impossible for one to slay the Devil, it is said, and yet — "

"Do not stain your blade by allowing it to drink foul blood," his friends advised quickly. "There is no law that one must play with the man."

"Yet one must play with somebody, and at times one likes to have dealings with a professional rogue, for the sake of the experience."

"Any robed Franciscan at the mission will tell you that a man must pay dearly for experience."

"And have I not paid dearly? Ha! A full purse of gold gone this night, and one the night before! At this rate I soon shall be beggared. It is beyond belief that one man can have so much good fortune, yet, if it is more than mere luck, we cannot probe his artifice."

The gaming continued. The fat landlord and his two native servants kept the wine mugs filled. Some of the men dozed on the benches. Others grew maudlin and spoke meaningless phrases. But Pedro Pico always remained sober and alert. The young caballeros continued losing to him, and in return got nothing but his flashing smile, and no man could tell whether that was of friendliness or derision.

There were no troopers from the presidio present at the inn tonight, for they were being held closely in barracks against a sudden alarm, as they had been for several nights past. There had been whisperings of an incipient Indian uprising, fomented by a certain and somewhat mysterious Don Miguel Mendez, regarding whom no man seemed to know much.

The torches spluttered in their niches in the walls, and cast their streaks of uncertain light across the broad room, but the gaming table was well lighted by the two huge candelabra. Those in the place who were not too intoxicated had gathered to watch the high play. Among them was a certain Valentino Vargas, a person of evil visage and uncouth manners, who appeared to be the gambler's bosom friend.

Their interest was centered on the dicing. Hence, they did not observe it when, in out of the moon-drenched night, slipped a man who surveyed the scene and chuckled a bit, and then crept slowly and with much caution along the wall and through the shadows, until he was

standing beneath the wall torch nearest the gambler's table. For a time
he watched the game, and then:

"Attention, señores!"

His voice suddenly rang out, so that the echoes of it bounded back
from the adobe walls and sounded up and down the big, low-ceilinged
room.

THE gambling ceased abruptly. All in the room whirled to face him.
Before them, standing against the wall with his arms folded across
his breast, was a man who wore neither hat nor cloak. His blouse of
black silk was open at the throat. He had a blade at his side, and a dagger
in his girdle, and even a pistol in his sash. Over his face was a closely
fitting mask of black, which concealed his features effectually.

"What — ?" Pedro Pico began.

The gambler's lower jaw sagged and his eyes bulged in an expression
of astonishment. His first thought was that here was some highwayman
come to take what gold he might find on the gambling table.

"Your pardon, señores," the masked visitor begged. "It is my wish to
try a cast or two of the dice, and also my wish that my identity be concealed from you all. Have I your permission to advance to the table?"

Pedro Pico's eyes glittered evilly as he watched the masked man.
This was not to be an affair of robbery, then. The gambler gathered his
wits and made a grand gesture.

"All are welcome to play here, if they have the gold with which to
play," he said.

"As to that, you need have no worry," the masked man replied.

The others fell back toward the lower end of the table. The masked
man strode forward into the brighter light, moving with the natural grace
of the cougar, and stopped directly across the table from Pedro Pico.

Valentino Vargas, the gambler's friend, lurched to his feet from the
bench whereupon he had been sitting, a sneer on his lips as he swaggered
forward.

"Ha! So here we have a man who fears to reveal his face," Valentino
Vargas said.

"Some faces are better masked," the visitor replied. "Why do you not mask yours, señor, and spare the good people the sight of your evil countenance?"

Some of the men in the room laughed, and the evil countenance of which the masked man had spoken took on a tinge of purple as wrath surged through Valentino Vargas.

"How is this?" Vargas cried, enraged, as he allowed his hand to drop to the hilt of the blade he wore. "You seek to insult me, señor?"

"Peace, Valentino! You courted that rebuke," Pedro Pico barked at him quickly. " 'Tis not a time for fighting." He made a sign that Vargas was to be quiet.

For this masked man was a mystery Pedro Pico certainly wished to solve. Perhaps this unusual visitor who had come out of the night was some man of high degree with an itch for dice and the cards, yet did not wish it known that he played with a common gambler in a public place. Pedro Pico had encountered many such in his career. A man of that ilk might have much gold which could be taken easily.

The young caballeros had backed away from the table, and were observing the masked man askance, holding themselves haughtily aloof. Now he turned and saluted them in a respectful manner.

"No man here need turn his back or depart because of my presence," he assured them. "Without speaking my name, I give you honorable oath that my blood is as good as that of any man here. Now, Señor Gambler, we begin."

H E TOSSED a fat pouch-purse down upon the table. He opened it and drew forth and threw out some pieces of gold, revealing that there were plenty more such in the purse. Pedro Pico's eyes glittered yet more at this frank display of wealth. He prepared to make the first cast of the dice at the masked man's gesture for him to do so.

Pedro Pico made his cast, and the masked stranger stepped closer to the table and picked up the box. Then he took the dice from Pedro Pico's hand, for the gambler had picked them up and offered them.

But, with the box held aloft, the masked man paused. He dropped the dice to the table without shaking and began a close inspection of the cubes. Those around the table bent forward, breathlessly and silently, to watch, sensing that something unusual was about to occur.

"Some queer things happen at times," the masked stranger said. "These dice are not those with which you made your cast, Señor Gambler."

"What is this?" Pedro Pico cried.

"The dice you cast — one had a tiny nick on a corner, which did not escape my eye. No doubt you have those dice cleverly concealed about your person now, having exchanged them for these. I do not doubt that you have been winning heavily during the night, señor, from those foolish enough to play with you."

Pedro Pico sprang to his feet. He bent across the table, his eyes aflame and his face suffused with rage. He was well aware of the dire necessity of making a swift defense against this charge of cheating.

"You dare insinuate — ?" he began.

"I insinuate nothing!" the masked man interrupted, speaking in stern voice. "I merely state facts. You are nothing more than a common cheat! I knew it when you made your cast. You are not even a clever cheat. I have heard rumors of your heavy winnings here in San Diego de Alcála, and came to learn the reason for them. The reason is now apparent."

"I'll slay you for this!" Pedro Pico cried.

The gambler had a sword with a jeweled hilt, in an engraved scabbard, which he always kept on the bench beside him while he was playing. Now he grasped the scabbard and whipped out the blade, and sprang aside and into the well-lighted space at the end of the table.

"I lower myself exceedingly to cross blades with such as you," the masked man declared. "But my features are hidden, and I shall call myself Don Nameless, so my shame shall not be so great. I warn you, Señor Gambler, that I am expert with a blade. You still desire to fight with me? On guard, then, señor!"

CHAPTER II
A Mark Left Behind

AT THE end of the table they clashed. The caballeros stood back gleefully, bending forward to watch with keen eyes this display of swordsmanship. The others got back against the adobe wall out of the way. A dishonest gambler was about to be sorely punished, they hoped.

That this mysterious Don Nameless was expert with a blade, as he had stated, could be told in an instant. He pressed Pedro Pico back until the gambler was in the shadows. He compelled him to retreat continually, played with him until big globules of perspiration popped out on Pedro Pico's swarthy face and the fear of immediate death shook him.

They circled toward the end of the table again, while the others retreated to give them room. Don Nameless was laughing lightly as he fought, like a man teasing a boy. Pedro Pico made a last desperate attempt to save his life, suddenly forcing the swordplay in a wild attack which had nothing in it of fencing science. But this man who called himself Don Nameless only laughed behind his mask again, and parried and fell back an instant. Then he began forcing the fighting furiously himself.

Back toward the adobe wall he drove Pedro Pico, having his way with the man. The gambler knew that he was lost. Each instant he expected the thrust which would let the life out of his body. His face became drawn and white, and his lips trembled.

Suddenly their hilts were locked. Their arms were held aloft as their breasts crashed together. So they stood face to face, breathing heavily, and each straining to gain the advantage.

"I'll slay you — slay you!" Pedro Pico cried wildly.

The answer of Don Nameless came in a whisper which nobody but Pedro Pico could hear:

"If you do, it may grieve Don Miguel."

Pedro Pico seemed to lose all strength suddenly. His eyes grew wide, but the masked man kept the hilts of their swords locked, and pretended to be exerting his strength, so the others in the room were misled.

"You — you are Don Miguel?" Pedro Pico whispered, as their faces were close together.

"Let us say a trusted man of his."

"Then, why did you expose me?"

"To give you a good excuse for quitting San Diego de Alcála immediately and in a natural manner. There is to be a meeting in the Canyon of the Cocopahs, near Reina de Los Angeles, the night of the full moon. Pass the word to others of whom you are sure, and see to it yourself."

None of the others in the room had heard this whispered conversation of the two men against the wall. They were watching for the deadlock to be broken, and wondering whether a quick thrust by this Don Nameless would end the duel when the break finally came. And now the duelists sprang apart and were back in the bright circle of light at the end of the table. But Pedro Pico suddenly threw up his left arm and lowered the point of his blade.

"Enough, señor!" he cried. "The right of this affair is with you. I am lost if I continue."

It was the speech of a craven. Expressions of disgust came from those in the room, caballeros and common folk alike. Pedro Pico, his head hanging as though in shame, walked slowly back toward his table.

Men drew aside to let him pass, as though touch with him might contaminate them. Pedro Pico was hoping that he could gather the money from the table and depart, and get away without being set upon and beaten.

S OME men did start toward him angrily and threateningly, rumblings of rage coming from their throats as they thought of the money of which they had been robbed. But Don Nameless lifted a hand and called a halt.

"Allow the rogue to depart and take his stench with him," he ordered. "You knew that he was a professional gambler, hence played with him at your own peril. It is enough that he is now unmasked, and must leave San Diego de Alcalá forever."

But Valentino Vargas sprang off the stool upon which he dropped in consternation at Pedro Pico's show of cowardice. That bogus struggle against the wall had misled him. He thought this Don Nameless a man of little strength, since even Pedro Pico had held the hilt of his blade locked for so long. Here was a chance, he thought, to avenge his friend and also acquire a reputation for himself.

Valentino Vargas was a heavy man, with a florid face and a huge black mustache, strong in his shoulders and arms. Beside this Don

Nameless, who was small and agile, he looked like a human mountain.

"So you quit him, Pedro Pico?" he cried. " 'Tis a pity. But I'll take up your quarrel. I am not craven. This pretty fellow who wears a mas — the shape of his body distresses me. I'll carve it more to my liking."

"I have no quarrel with you, fellow," Don Nameless said.

"Ha! No doubt you prefer not to have one, nevertheless one is now on your hands," Valentino Vargas replied. "Face a real man for once, señor! On guard!"

"As you will," Don Nameless replied. "Some men go about the earth seeking trouble."

Those in the room promptly forgot Pedro Pico now. They turned to watch this fresh quarrel, which gave promise of being something better than the last. The gambler quickly gathered up his property and crept around the walls and into the patio, to go to his own quarters in the inn.

Valentino Vargas strutted out into the light space at the end of the table. He whipped out his blade and ponderously set himself for combat. Don Nameless darted forward immediately, and they engaged.

Valentino Vargas was a much better swordsman than Pedro Pico by far, having more skill and also weight and strength. It occurred to those who watched that Don Nameless estimated him correctly as such, and was not rash in his attack.

But, having felt out his man, Don Nameless suddenly began to force the fighting, as though eager to finish it and be gone from the scene. The blades crashed and rang. The duelists swerved and danced, advanced and retreated, now out in the streak of bright light, and now back in the flickering shadows near the adobe wall.

"Fight, rogue!" Don Nameless taunted, as he pressed his adversary cruelly. "I had no quarrel with you … you brought this upon yourself, rogue … I could slay you easily … but perhaps I'll spare your life."

H E SPOKE all this haltingly, as they fought. He punctuated his phrases with swift and violent attacks. Valentino Vargas began tiring from the speed of the bout. This small and agile man was all around him, like a dozen adversaries. There was a strong rally on the part of Valentino Vargas for a moment, a retreat on the part of Don

Nameless and an equally swift recovery.

Then something happened so swiftly that the caballeros watching were unable to tell afterward just how it had occurred. But the blade of Valentino Vargas was torn from his hand and whipped in a flashing arc through the air, to fall and clatter on the hard-beaten earth of the floor.

Don Nameless lunged, and the point of his blade darted forward like the tongue of a snake. Then he bounced backward like a rubber hall, and Valentino Vargas reeled against the wall, holding his left hand to his left cheek, from which blood was streaming.

The watchers marveled that Don Nameless had not slain, a thing he could have done easily. But he only gave a swift glance at the others in the room, as though to see whether they would make a move against him. None did, so he darted to the table, and grasped his purse and stowed it away.

He laughed a little, returned his blade to its scabbard, and retreated swiftly along the wall through the shadows, as those in the room surged toward him.

At the door he lifted a hand in salute.

"Señores, á Dios!" he cried.

Through the open door he hurried, to be swallowed by the moon-drenched night. The others in the place rushed out after him, except a few who remained with the wounded man. They heard the rapid drum-fire of a horse's hoofs as Don Nameless swiftly rode away. Back to their ears on the night breeze came a taunting laugh.

Inside the inn, some men gathered around the wounded Valentino Vargas, who was cursing both Don Nameless and his wound. The young caballeros stood aloof and laughed at the man. The fat landlord came hurrying in with a basin filled with heated and scented water, and some soft cloths, and bathed Valentino Vargas' left cheek, where the tip of Don Nameless' sword had cut deeply enough to make a wound which surely would leave a scar.

One of the caballeros gave a cry of surprise and darted forward, and bent over to look.

His exclamation brought the others to his side.

"Dios!" he cried. "We have been blind! Look at this fellow's wound.

Do you not see, and understand? It is in the form of a ragged letter Z, is it not? 'Tis the mark of Zorro! This Don Nameless, as he called himself — he was Señor Zorro! We have seen a master of fence at work — and have seen him leave his mark behind!"

CHAPTER III
Don Diego Arrives

IN PEDRO PICO'S room at the inn, as dawn was breaking, the gambler sat on the side of his couch, while Valentino Vargas strode back and forth before him.

"I cannot understand it," Vargas was saying. "You say he spoke of Don Miguel?"

"He intimated he was Don Miguel's trusted man, and said there was to be a meeting — "

"You have said that before. He exposes you, fights with you, makes it easy for you to get out of the town —"

"Which I must do at once, before they have a mind to set upon me," Pedro Pico said, betraying nervousness.

"Then when I pick a fight with him, he makes this mark of Zorro on my cheek. Why did he not mention Don Miguel to me?"

"Perhaps you had angered him," Pedro Pico said. "And it is possible he did not have a chance, for you were fighting fiercely. He may have thought I would pass the word to you. Or, he may not have known you are in this affair."

"I have yet to meet a man who has seen this Don Miguel," Vargas said. "How this started, none seems to know. A few whisperings to adventurers of our kind, and the thing spread."

"Don Miguel Mendez — whoever he is — is fomenting an uprising. There will be loot for all white men he picks to help handle the Indians — "

"We were sought out," Pico interrupted.

"By a man sought out by somebody else, who had been sought out in turn. This Don Miguel certainly keeps to cover."

"Until everything is prepared, perhaps. He may be some man of high degree, irked by politics, who does not wish his identity known until it is time to strike. No doubt he will be at the meeting in the Canyon of the Cocopahs."

"And this Zorro — ?" Vargas questioned.

"It is true you do not know of him, since you but lately arrived by ship from Mexico. This Señor Zorro made his appearance some time ago, and worked his will with the soldiery. He punished those who mistreated natives and monks — "

"Ah, I have heard, but did not know the name! So it was this Señor Zorro who mentioned Don Miguel to you, and also put his mark on me?"

" 'Tis a way he has — marking the letter Z on the cheeks of men with whom he fights but does not wish to slay."

"This Señor Zorro, it then appears, is in league with Don Miguel?"

"And why not, señor, my friend? Has he not always aided the natives? He may even be Don Miguel himself–who knows? And what difference does it make?"

"I have cast my lot with this Don Miguel," Vargas replied. "But this Señor Zorro is another matter. He has put his mark on me, and for that I shall surely kill him at our next meeting."

"You have tasted his blade once, as have I. What chance would you have in combat?"

"A pistol ball from behind a rock," Vargas suggested. "It is in my mind that I shall have no rest until I slay the man. Now, what is it you intend to do?"

"I must get from the town," Pedro Pico declared. "I'll pack my valuable things and get my horse and ride, leaving my other property here. I'll make for Reina de Los Angeles, so as to be at the meeting the night of the full moon."

"We have other business," Vargas reminded him. "How about this Don Felipe Ramón and his daughter, newly come by ship from Spain?"

DESPITE the situation, Pedro Pico laughed a bit.
     Don Felipe Ramón, a grandee if ever there was one, had lately arrived with his fair daughter, Carmelita, and an old duenna, Señora

Vallejo.

They were to journey to Reina de Los Angeles, to be the guests of Don Diego Vega and his father. It was whispered that Don Diego was to wed the fair Carmelita, if they took a fancy to each other.

But Don Felipe Ramón, carrying much wealth with him, feared highwaymen and bandits. He was waiting in the guest house at the mission up the valley, until Don Diego arrived. This Don Diego Vega, his father being at odds with those in political power, could not obtain an escort of troopers for his friends.

So some gentry of the road, of whom Valentino Vargas was one, waited now like hawks to pounce upon their prey.

If Don Felipe Ramón journeyed to Reina de Los Angeles without escort, somewhere along the way his entourage would be set upon, and he would be robbed gleefully.

"Don Diego Vega is expected soon," Pedro Pico said, "according to rumor. Perhaps he will bring an army of servants with him."

"Natives will run at the first discharge of a pistol," Vargas declared. "We fear only the soldiery, and they will not protect Don Diego or any of his friends. It will be rich picking, my friend. Go your way out of the town, and I'll remain and watch. Our four friends, in this enterprise with us, are watching also. Don Felipe Ramón cannot slip away, by day or by night. When he moves, we have his gold and jewels."

"If the native uprising comes — "

"All the better. It will be a cover for what we do. The natives will be blamed for it."

"You'll be at the meeting the night of the full moon?"

Valentino Vargas swore a great oath. "You may depend upon it. I desire to meet this Señor Zorro again."

" 'Tis in my mind that you'd best avoid him."

" 'Tis in my mind to slay him before I'm done, and that I'll do," Valentino Vargas declared.

"When I have at him again, he has marked his last man. I'll carve a letter V, not on his cheek, but in the heart of him! I'll make a mark of my own! I'll — "

He ceased speaking abruptly. There was a slight commotion in front of the inn.

Natives were yelping like so many curs, and the shrill voice of the fat landlord could be heard.

Pedro Pico sprang to his feet, his face livid, and reached for the pistol he had ready on a stool near by.

"They are coming for me," he mouthed. "I'll sell my life dearly."

"Peace, fool! It is but somebody arriving," Valentino Vargas said. "Somebody of quality, no doubt, with all that fuss being made. Let us see."

"I must get from the town."

"In due time. There is no need for haste. The caballeros you fleeced are sleeping off their wine, and the common louts will not bother you. Let us see."

They left the room and hurried across the patio, and to a doorway through which they could peer across the big main room and out the front door.

A splendid carriage had been brought to a stop in front of the inn. Cringing natives surrounded it, and a native servant was standing in the front of the carriage and threatening them with a whip. The vehicle was drawn by four splendid black horses. Two native outriders accompanied it.

The servile landlord struck natives aside and got to the step of the carriage, and bowed low. Then the occupant came from beneath the hood, and Pedro Pico and Valentino Vargas caught sight of him.

"What a fop!" Vargas said. "He acts as though he scarcely can hold himself together."

"Look at the coat of arms on the carriage," Pedro Pico whispered.

"I know it not."

"I do know it. This is Don Diego Vega arrived."

"That — that — is the scion of the house of Vega?" Valentino Vargas asked, gasping. "By the saints! So this is an example of noble blood! The fellow acts as though about to swoon. The sight of blood would sicken him. A needle such as the women use for embroidery would be more at home in his hand than a blade."

Don Diego Vega was conducted by the landlord from the carriage and into the inn, and the door was slammed in the face of the rabble of natives, all seeking alms.

Don Diego Vega brushed his nostrils with a scented handkerchief, and gave a little sigh. He sat upon the nearest bench, and one of the servants made haste to bring a mug of the best wine. As the landlord hovered near, rubbing his hands and giving his poor smile, Don Diego Vega drank sippingly, and sighed again.

"These be turbulent times," he said, in a thin voice.

"Sí, señor!"

"I rested at the hacienda of a friend, and came on before the dawn. It has been a long and tiresome journey from Reina de Los Angeles. But it was necessary. I have another carriage following, an empty one, but it is to go to the mission direct."

"Sí, señor!" the landlord agreed, not knowing what else to say, but feeling the need of saying something.

"I have come to meet Don Felipe Ramón and his daughter, as perhaps you know. They await me at the guest house at the mission. They, too, have had a long journey — all the way from Spain by ship, to make their new home here in California."

"Sí, señor!"

"You will fetch me some honey and such poor bread as you have in your inn."

"No meat, Don Diego?"

"A bit of bread and honey — that is enough. I seldom eat meat. Such food is for men of turbulent manners, men who brawl and try feats of strength and skill. I tend more to philosophy and the poets."

"Sí, señor!" the landlord agreed. "At once, Don Diego!"

The landlord clapped his hands and hissed at his servants, and hurried to his kitchen.

The servants quickly spread one of the tables with a fine cloth, and put several fine dishes upon it, and a bowl of fruit, and bowed low when Don Diego Vega went to the table and sat down.

One brought a basin filled with warm, scented water, and a cloth, and bathed Don Diego's white hands, as though he had been a helpless infant, and dried them. Then Don Diego sighed again and relaxed, and awaited his bread and honey.

"By the saints!" Valentino Vargas muttered in the doorway. "So this is the man who has come to escort Don Felipe Ramón to Reina de Los Angeles! This man and a few native servants — not more than three or four at the most! The task we have set ourselves seems no task at all. What gold and jewels this Don Felipe Ramón carries belongs to us already."

CHAPTER IV
Concerning A Nut

HAVING refreshed himself with bread and honey and wine, Don Diego Vega tossed the fat landlord a coin and arose to depart. He held his scented kerchief to his nostrils as he walked slowly and languidly through the lane the landlord made for him in the midst of the natives waiting outside, and got into his carriage. He relaxed, and sighed.

The carriage had no driver, but two natives rode the horses of the lead team. Two outriders followed behind, natives whose arrogant manner demonstrated that they knew whom they served. In a cloud of dust the vehicle swept around the plaza and took the trail which ran up the valley to the mission.

While Don Diego Vega had been inside the inn, the second carriage had passed, swathed in dust cloths and empty, and it had two outriders also. This was to convey Don Felipe Ramón and his daughter and her duenna from San Diego de Alcála to Reina de Los Angeles, where the Vegas had a splendid casa.

The carriage slowed as the horses were brought down to a walk to ascend a sharp slope, and Don Diego extended a hand outside, and one of the outriders galloped up beside him.

"Bernardo," Don Diego said, "you will keep your eyes and ears open after the mission is reached. You will have my black horse ready always, and you will be watching closely for any signal from me. It is understood?"

Don Diego glanced up, and the man Bernardo nodded that it was understood. He could not speak, for he was dumb. He was the faithful servant of Don Diego Vega, and knew many secrets, yet could tell none. Nor would he have done so had he a tongue, but would have allowed that tongue to be cut out of his mouth first.

Bernardo retired to his regular position at Don Diego's gesture for him to do so, and the carriage reached the top of the hill, and the horses went forward at a gallop. So they came to the mission which Junipero Serra had founded, with its splendid adobe buildings, its chapel and patio and guest house and storehouses, and servants hurried forward to catch the bridles of the horses and help to hold them still.

Don Diego Vega descended from his carriage, his manner as languid as usual, to be met by a gray-haired old monk, who gave him an immediate blessing.

"I am Brother Marcus, my son. Let me make you welcome to San Diego de Alcála. Your friends await you in the guest house, and I'll conduct you there. Your horses will have careful attention."

Don Diego followed him across the patio and beneath the arches to the guest house. This Don Felipe Ramón was an old friend of his father's, a boyhood friend in Spain, and Don Diego never had seen him.

A T HIS entrance, a dignified nobleman arose and stepped forward to meet him. Behind him a beautiful señorita sat on a bench, busy with her embroidery frame, a grim-faced duenna beside her. The glance of Don Diego strayed there an instant, and the little señorita blushed and bent lower over her embroidery, though that did not prevent her lifting her eyes.

"Don Dicgo, I would have known you for the son of my old friend anywhere," Don Felipe Ramón declared. "You are exactly like he was at your age."

"I thank you, Don Felipe. My father sends his regards, and directs me to escort you and the others to Reina de Los Angeles."

Let me present my daughter, Carmelita, then we may talk."

Señorita Carmelita Ramón acknowledged the introduction with a smile and a blush, though she seemed perturbed because Don Diego made no great show of gallantry. At a sign from her father, she then retired with her duenna to another chamber, and Don Diego and Don

Felipe sat on a bench in a corner of the room.

"This journey to Reina de Los Angeles — how far is it?" Don Felipe asked.

"About four or five days, señor."

"Through rough country, no doubt?"

"We make stop each evening at some hacienda, where you will be a welcome guest. It has been arranged."

"But as we travel during the day — they tell me bandits are abroad in this land."

"There are always such blackguards abroad," said Don Diego, "but I pray you be not alarmed because of them. I shall protect you, Don Felipe."

Don Felipe glanced at him, and the expression in his face seemed to say that he doubted it exceedingly. This Don Diego Vega was of good blood, but did not seem the sort to be able to protect anybody.

"You have armed servants?" Don Felipe asked.

"Two carriages, señor, with two riders and two outriders to each. The outriders carry pistols, but are afraid to use them because of the noise and flame they make. They probably would run if highwaymen descended upon us."

"By the saints, Don Diego! I carry gold and jewels with me," Don Felipe said, lowering his voice.

"I judged as much, señor. No doubt some of the highwaymen have judged likewise."

"An escort of soldiery, perhaps — ?"

Don Diego smiled. "I am afraid not, but I shall try. My father is the outspoken foe of the present Governor, and His Excellency's soldiers would grin if we were robbed."

"What are we to do, Don Diego? Frankly, you did not seem to realize the peril. My gold, my jewels — my daughter! Are all to be subjected to danger?"

"Perhaps," said Don Diego, "there are influences working in our behalf. Be not alarmed, I pray you, Don Felipe. Let us be prepared to start tomorrow at dawn. I have been up most of the night, and require some rest. Do you and the señorita get good rest today also. This evening we shall meet to dine."

"If we reach your father's house in Reina de Los Angeles without having our throats cut, it will surprise me," Don Felipe said. "Why was I not content to remain in Spain?"

"Before we reach my father's house you will love this new land, Don Felipe."

"If I am not first sent to that land from which none returns," Don Felipe replied. "We meet, then, for the evening meal."

B ROTHER MARCOS appeared, and conducted Don Diego to a room assigned for his use, and made him comfortable, and retired. But Don Diego Vega did not sleep. He had sent one of his men to the presidio with a note as they had approached the town, and now was awaiting a reply to it.

The reply came. A rider galloped up to the mission. In a stentorian voice he bade a native care for his horse. He strode into the patio with his head held high, spurs jingling and sword clanking, and addressed a monk who bowed before him.

"Where is this Don Diego Vega? I want speech with him."

"He has retired, capitán."

"Show me his resting place."

Don Diego opened the door of his room and stepped out beneath one of the arches.

"I am here, capitán," he called.

The officer strode toward him, scowling. He was a young man for the rank, and plainly aware of his station and importance. He saluted Don Diego in haphazard fashion, and entered the room.

"I received your message, and I am here," he said. "Though I fail to see why I should come running at your nod. I am Capitán Carlos Gonzales, at present stationed in San Diego de Alcála. But I have just received my transfer to Reina de Los Angeles, and may leave for my new post at any time."

"You know of the presence here of Don Felipe Ramón and his party?" Don Diego asked.

"I do."

"It is known to you also that I have come to conduct them to Reina de Los Angeles?"

"It is."

"These be turbulent times," said Don Diego. "There is continual danger of robbery on the highway. Don Felipe has gold and jewels, and a daughter. I request a suitable military escort, capitán, to insure the safety of the party."

"I regret, Don Diego, that such an escort cannot be furnished. The men are being held in barracks. There are rumors of another uprising of the natives. Some renegade whites, headed by a certain Don Miguel — "

"All the more reason for giving us protection," Don Diego interrupted. "I'm afraid, capitán, that I must insist."

"Insist?" Capitán Carlos Gonzales roared. "I say you cannot have an escort. If you object to my decision, take it up with His Excellency the Governor at Monterey."

Don Diego smiled faintly.

"It would be difficult for a Vega to get the Governor's ear. Since you are transferring to Reina de Los Angeles, at least we may have the pleasure of your companionship on the journey, may we not? A brave officer like yourself would be the equal of a dozen troopers in an emergency."

CAPITÁN GONZALES sensed the sarcasm, but held his temper in check. He arose and bowed. "I regret that I cannot accompany you," he said. "I have not decided on the moment of my departure. When I go, I shall ride swiftly, with only an orderly. Señor, á Díos!"

"One moment," Don Diego begged. "I have asked for protection, and you have refused it. You can have no objection, then, if I take measures to protect myself and those I escort."

Now, Capitán Carlos Gonzales smiled.

"Protect yourself, by all means," he replied. "That is the right of every man."

"By all means, señor?"

"In any way you please. If highwaymen attack you, slay them. Use blade or pistol, Don Diego. Read poetry to them. Tell them philosophy. Scare them off with big words. Wave your perfumed handkerchief at them, perhaps."

"It is an item of philosophy," Don Diego said, "that one cannot tell from the external appearance of a nut just what sort of a kernel is within. And I use a perfumed handkerchief, señor, because at times I find my nostrils offended with a stench."

"Señor!" Capitán Gonzales cried, angrily.

"I thank you for coming here in answer to my note. I regret your inability to furnish me a proper escort. And I thank you for your kind permission for me to protect myself by all means. When you are stationed in Reina de Los Angeles, capitán, call at the Vega casa."

Surprise flashed into the capitán's face at this unexpected invitation.

"I thank you, Don Diego," he said.

"We keep a loaf and a jug of wine always ready for wayfarers. Just ask at the servants' quarters."

"This passes endurance!" the capitán cried. "You presume on your weakness, Don Diego. For me to challenge and fight you for your words — it would be plain murder. I doubt if you know how to hold a blade."

"As you ride back to the presidio," Don Diego suggested, "remember the item of philosophy about the nut."

CHAPTER V
At the Presidio

D ON DIEGO bathed in perfumed water and dressed in fine raiment that evening, Bernardo assisting him, and went to the big room where the dinner table was ready. He had some speech with Bernardo before leaving his room, and the native's eyes flashed when the speech was over, and he nodded that he understood.

The little señorita was very lovely, and Señora Vallejo, her duenna, very grim, and Don Felipe looked worried and concerned about the forthcoming journey. But Don Diego might have been at home in his father's house, according to his conduct.

Señorita Carmelita could not complain about his lack of gallantry now, and the blushes played continually over her face. Yet she found herself wishing that this Don Diego seemed more of a strong man at times, and less the fop.

He made light of the journey they were facing, and of its dangers, and Don Felipe judged it was to reassure the ladies. But, when they were finally alone, Don Diego talked the same.

"Do you not understand that we may face peril?" Don Felipe asked. "Do you expect us to travel for four or five days through rough country, packing along a fortune, and not be attacked by rogues? You say an escort is denied you. How, then, are we to be protected?"

"Do not, I pray, concern yourself," Don Diego said. "I feel sure we'll reach Reina de Los Angeles safely, and bring through your gold and jewels safely also."

Don Felipe was shaking his head when Don Diego departed for his own room. The lights were being extinguished around the mission. The monks had sought their humble cots, and only a few natives were wandering about the patio and the buildings.

Don Diego Vega closed his window and dropped the tapestry over it, and stripped off his fine raiment. He dressed simply in dark clothing, extinguished the candle, and for a time stood at the door, his ears attuned to catch sounds outside.

Presently, he slipped out. Keeping in the deep shadows, and moving almost as silently as a shadow himself, he went along the patio wall, around the corner of a storehouse, and was outside.

Two hundred yards away, in a little gully, Bernardo was waiting with a big black horse. Don Diego Vega worked swiftly at a change of garments. He buckled on a sword, put dagger in his girdle and pistol in his sash, and finally put a black mask over his face.

Don Diego Vega was gone for the time being. Señor Zorro was there in the gully with Bernardo and the black horse.

"Wait here, Bernardo, for my return."

He mounted and rode slowly away from the mission, and down the valley toward the town, keeping some distance from the main road but paralleling it. Over the brow of a hill, he approached the presidio.

Lights were gleaming in the barracks room, and he could hear some of the troopers roaring a drunken song. He dismounted in a dark depression a short distance behind the building and went on afoot, cautious and alert. From the shape of the building, he guessed the location of the officers' quarters. Soon he was crouching in the darkness beneath an open window.

Capitán Carlos Gonzales was talking to a certain Sergeant Juan Ruiz, he made out, and their conversation interested him.

"Such is the report, capitán," the sergeant was saying. "The masked man cut a letter Z on the cheek of this rogue of a Valentino Vargas, a fellow it may be well to watch. Hence, some of the caballeros are certain that the masked man was Señor Zorro."

"Zorro!" Gonzales cried. "If the fellow is really in our district, we must be alert. His Excellency would be more pleased at capture of him than at anything else I may name."

"One thing I may say, if the capitán will allow it. There was a time when it was suspicioned that Zorro and this Don Diego Vega were the same. Zorro appears at the inn, and a few hours later Don Diego comes in his carriage — a — "

THE wild laughter of the capitán stopped him. Gonzales gave vent to a gale of merriment, and finally was able to speak again.

"I have heard of that," he said. "But — I have met and talked with Don Diego Vega. Zorro — he? It is a jest! That weak, puny caballero who reads poetry and talks of philosophy? The sight of blood would turn him ill. Think you he could do the deeds this Zorro has done? If Don Diego and Zorro are in this neighborhood at the same time, it is a coincidence, and nothing more."

"It is as the capitán says," Sergeant Juan Ruiz replied.

"If Zorro really is here, and we can capture him — ! Keep your eyes open, sergeant, and your ears. Watch the natives, and have some of the men who play with the bronze wenches question them. This Zorro befriends natives, and no doubt they are concealing him."

"It is understood, capitán."

"What a country! Zorro — and this mysterious Don Miguel with his infernal scheme for a native uprising! I shall be glad to get me to Reina de Los Angeles."

"When does the capitán depart?" the sergeant asked.

"My relieving officer should be here by dawn. Then, I may leave at any time."

"And your escort, capitán?"

"I am taking you with me, Sergeant Ruiz, and nobody else. You are a good man, and have served me well. In Reina de Los Angeles, there will be better advantages for you."

"I thank the capitán."

"We'll take one good pack horse along. See to it, sergeant. Now, I'll make inspection, and then retire."

Crouching in the darkness outside the window, Señor Zorro heard them leave the room, heard the heavy door slam and their boots ringing on the stone floor as they strode away, and also the sergeant's stentorian bellow calling the men to attention for inspection.

Señor Zorro waited a moment, then vaulted through the open window, and found himself in the capitán's quarters. It was a spacious room, lavishly furnished. Señor Zorro made a hasty inspection of it, then sat on a bench in a corner, and drew his pistol from his sash and held it ready.

He could hear orders being barked in the barracks room, and weapons clashing, and the snappy voice of the officer and the harsh one of Sergeant Juan Ruiz as they made the inspection. Then came the thump of boot heels on the stone flooring of the corridor, and Señor Zorro got to his feet and stood against the wall, ready and waiting.

Capitán Gonzales opened the door and entered, closed the door and dropped the heavy bar into place quickly, without observing that he had a visitor. As he turned from the door, Señor Zorro stepped out from the corner, pistol leveled.

"Make a sound, and you die!" he said. "Put your hands to your shoulders, capitán!"

Capitán Gonzales was startled, but made no outcry. He saw the masked man there in the shadows, and caught sight of the pistol, and put the tips of his fingers on his shoulders, as he had been ordered to do.

"Sit down at your table, and place your palms upon it," Zorro ordered.

THE capitán complied, but his eyes were flashing angrily. He swept those eyes over Señor Zorro as the latter stepped out into the bright light and advanced to the table swiftly and noiselessly, to sit down across it from the capitán, still holding the pistol in a menacing position.

"Who are you, and what do you want here?" Gonzales asked, in a low voice.

"I am Zorro!"

"You have courage to come to the presidio."

"There is little danger, capitán." The voice in which he spoke was not that of Don Diego Vega, but was deeper. "I desired to talk to you."

"About what?"

"Perhaps to make a little deal."

"You wish to surrender and throw yourself on the mercy of His Excellency?" the capitán asked. "I cannot accept such a surrender. Word has been sent to catch Señor Zorro and hang him, and there can be no mercy shown, though you walk in and deliver yourself."

"I have no intention of surrendering," Zorro said. "Nor do I intend being captured. It is not of myself I wish to speak. You are about to transfer to Reina de Los Angeles, I understand. I would put you in the way of promotion."

"In what manner — and why?"

"Have you not heard rumors of the uprising being fomented by Don Miguel? Suppose I tell you, capitán, where and when you and your troopers may capture, at one swoop, all those white renegades who have taken service under this Don Miguel."

Capitán Gonzales betrayed a lively interest. He bent forward, and his eyes glowed.

"You can do that, and will? Why? Ah, I see! Rogues have fallen out. You and this mysterious Don Miguel have quarreled, and you would betray him."

"I am not in league with him. But I do not care to see white renegades lead natives to the slaughter. I am the friend of the natives, as you know. I would stop this uprising before it can get a good beginning."

"What have you to tell me?" Gonzales asked.

"You know the Canyon of the Cocopahs, near Reina de Los Angeles?

Very well! There is to be a meeting of the conspirators in the canyon, the night of the full moon. I know it for a certainty. Is that enough?"

"It is ample, if true," Gonzales said.

"What motive could I have in telling an untruth about it? I have explained my motive for telling you this much. I do not wish to see ignorant natives stirred to revolt, to be slain and punished as a result."

"And what reward do you ask for this information?" Gonzales wished to know.

"It shall be my reward when you capture the white renegades, or frighten and disperse them. And, would you catch some big fish in the net, as well as small fry?"

"How is this?"

SEÑOR Zorro bent forward a little and lowered his voice yet more. "Don Diego Vega is at the mission here. He is to escort to Reina de Los Angeles this Don Felipe Ramón and his party. No doubt, highwaymen may attack them, unless they are protected."

"I have been obliged to deny them escort."

"Indeed? It may be to your interest, capitán, to see that they reach Reina de Los Angeles safely. They should arrive a couple of nights before the full moon. Don Diego and his family do not have the love of the Governor, I understand. If, when you capture the big fish — But I need not explain everything to a man of your understanding."

"What?" Gonzales cried. "You mean to intimate that — ? If this be true, I am a made man. If any of the Vegas are concerned in this affair, and can be caught at it — "

"And if a rich friend newly come from Spain brings gold with which to further the enterprise — " Zorro hinted.

"By the saints! I almost have a friendly feeling toward you, if this is true."

"Why should I tell you false? Where would be the profit? I am not asking that, as a reward, my own misdeeds be forgiven. Take me, capitán, if you can. I am but protecting natives who have not the wit to protect themselves."

"If I furnished an escort, and nothing comes of this, the Governor would demote me."

"Why furnish an escort, capitán? You are riding to Reina de Los Angeles, are you not? Alone?"

"My sergeant will be with me."

"The two of you would be escort enough," Señor Zorro pointed out. "I know your sergeant — a burly fighter. You are not without courage yourself. The party undoubtedly will spend each night at some hacienda. Surely, you and your sergeant can repel any attack by two or three highwaymen in the daytime."

"It is an idea!" Gonzales declared.

"We'll ride with the party. I thank you, Señor Zorro! But I'll capture you the next minute, if I can, and see you hanged, for that is orders."

Señor Zorro arose and bowed but still held the pistol ready. He backed across the room slowly, going toward the open window.

"Do me the favor of standing, capitán, with the tips of your fingers on your shoulders again," he ordered.

The capitán complied once more.

"I have done you a favor," Zorro said, "and even now you are wishing you could get to pistol or blade and try to take me. You are ungrateful, Señor. Ingratitude is a thing often punished, so beware!"

"We'll meet again, Zorro!"

"Undoubtedly — but you may not know me when we do," Señor Zorro replied.

He had reached the window, and now he chuckled a bit behind his mask as the capitán took a step toward him. He got one leg over the window sill, laughed again, and vaulted through.

Behind him, he heard the capitán's roar for the sergeant and troopers. Bending low, Señor Zorro raced along the adobe wall through the shadows, making for the dark depression in which he had left his horse. A pistol exploded behind him, as Gonzales fired through the window, but the ball sped wild. Señor Zorro laughed again, and ran on.

CHAPTER VI
The Crime That Failed

SHORTLY after dawn, Capitán Carlos Gonzales appeared at the mission, mounted for a journey, and behind him rode Sergeant Juan Ruiz. Because they intended accompanying Don Diego and his party, they had left the pack horse behind, the capitán leaving behind also orders for his property to be forwarded as soon as possible.

He was a most resplendent capitán as he dismounted and strode into the patio, drawing off his riding gauntlets. Don Diego's two carriages were prepared, and his natives ready for the trip. Don Felipe's baggage had been loaded into a cart to make the journey slowly, but a strongbox was in one of the carriages, being closely guarded by Bernardo and another man.

The party came from the guest house, old Brother Marcos leading them. The señorita clung to Señora Vallejo's arm, and Don Diego walked on her other side, chatting and smiling at her, and gesturing with his scented handkerchief.

Capitán Gonzales confronted them.

"Don Diego Vega, I have made a reconsideration," he announced. "Though I cannot furnish you an escort — since the troopers are being held in readiness if the natives start an uprising — yet I will escort you and your party myself, and have a sergeant with me."

"It is, indeed, a change of heart, and I thank you," Don Diego said.

He presented Don Felipe and Don Felipe presented his daughter and her duenna and the capitán bowed gallantly to the señorita and claimed her hand for a kiss. Don Diego used his handkerchief again, but this time to hide a smile.

"We are indeed glad of your assistance, señor," Don Felipe said.

"There are many rogues abroad," Don Diego added. "These hints of a native uprising disturb me. Then, there are highwaymen and bandits. And, so I am told, that notorious Señor Zorro has been seen in the vicinity."

Capitán Gonzales reddened. It is said he has been near," he admitted. "The troopers will have him soon, and make short work of him. There is a rope waiting."

Don Diego, it seemed, had made rather peculiar arrangements for the journey. Don Felipe and his daughter and Señora Vallejo were to ride in the first big carriage. The two riders would direct the four horses, and the two outriders would ride behind. Not content with that, Don Diego sent the two outriders belonging to his own carriage to ride ahead of the cavalcade, in the manner of scouts.

He would ride alone in the second carriage, and follow the first, he said, having with him only the two riders to direct the double team. It was Don Felipe and his valuables that must be protected. Don Diego, he declared, had no fear of being set upon as he rode behind. Moreover, it were the part of a gentleman for him to take the dust, instead of letting the others take it.

Down the valley they went, and to the town. Capitán Gonzales rode close to the first carriage, as Don Diego imagined he would do, trying to catch the señorita's eye, and the sergeant rode a few feet behind him.

They passed through the town and followed El Camino Real up into the hills. The sun grew high and the fog lifted, and it began growing hot. The carriages stopped at intervals, for their occupants to see the view, or to get out and walk a bit and stretch their cramped limbs.

E ARLY that morning, word of the departure had been given to some at the inn, and Valentino Vargas had called for his horse, had made ready for the trail and had ridden forth along the dusty highway. A few miles from the town, he met three more men, who were waiting for him.

They galloped far ahead and took position among some rocks beside the trail, and there lay in wait. But, when the carriages approached, Vargas swore mightily.

"Soldiers are with them," he said. "The capitán and a sergeant. Juan Ruiz is the equal of us all in combat, and his superior is no weakling, I have heard. They will be well armed. We cannot attack here."

They left the rocks and rode ahead again, gaining rapidly on the carriages.

"They will stop at the Pulido hacienda for the night," Valentino

Vargas judged. "Pedro Pico will be waiting there, according to our plan. Perhaps we can strike during the night, or when the backs of these two soldiers are turned."

So they rode on, toward the Pulido hacienda, a place which extended hospitality to any who asked for it. At times, they stopped on some crest and looked behind, watching the lifting dust clouds which told where the carriages traveled.

It was almost sunset when they came to the hacienda and asked permission to spend the night. Pedro Pico already was there, eating and drinking wine. The news of his infamy had not reached the hacienda, else he would have been denied food and drink.

Valentino Vargas and the three were shown to a long, low adobe building, which was a sort of guest house for inferiors, and made themselves at home. Pedro Pico came to them as they ate.

"The carriages are arriving," he whispered. "A score of native servants are rushing out to care for the guests. One of the outriders galloped forward with news of their coming."

"Let us see that these native servants of Don Diego have ample wine," Vargas suggested. "It will be well if their brains are addled tomorrow, in case we do not commit our fault tonight."

The master of the Pulido estate met his guests and conducted them into the big house, and soon candles were gleaming through all the windows, and the great table was set, with fine linen and crystal glass and gleaming silver, and heaped high with food.

Leaving the others in the guest house, Valentino Vargas and Pedro Pico passed slowly under the palms in the gloom, and neared a window through which they could peer into the big room of the house and watch the scene.

"If we can learn where the strongbox is kept for the night, perhaps we can obtain it," Vargas whispered. "We can have our horses in readiness, and hurry into the hills as soon as we have the gold and jewels. We can be gone before any can saddle and overtake us."

"How about the soldiers?" Pedro Pico asked.

"The capitán will spend the night inside the casa, and the big sergeant possibly will be in the guest house. We must beware the sergeant, for he is no fool. But he will be tired, and eager to get to sleep. As soon as he snores, we will get busy. Counting you, we are five."

H IDING in the shadows, they watched closely. Lights burned suddenly in the window of a room on the second floor, and they saw two of Don Diego's servants enter it, carrying something which they put down against the wall.

"Dios! It is the strong box," Vargas said. "That window will be easy of access. That strong vine which runs up the wall — a man can climb it. What could be better, Pedro Pico? One man can climb the vine and get the box and toss it out — then we'll be away, and divide the loot."

"Why divide it so many ways?" Pedro Pico asked.

"How is this?"

"Why not the two of us do this thing ourselves, and divide the loot in halves? I can get our horses ready and hide them under the trees. You can throw the others off guard, saying you are slipping out to reconnoiter while they watch the sergean — "

"And I can go up the vine and get the box," Vargas finished for him, "and toss it down to you. And, if you try to make away with it alone — "

"You may trust me, my friend," Pedro Pico said.

"If you played me false, I'd find you, if it took me a lifetime," Vargas hissed. "So be it! The thing is done."

They wandered back to the guest house. The sergeant had gone there, but was outside eating his evening meal, and Vargas called the other three men to him.

"Pedro Pico will go about his business, seeming to have no interest in us," he whispered. "I'll slip out and see what I can learn, and you three remain here and act in a manner natural until the big sergeant is snoring."

He slipped out again with Pedro Pico, and the latter went to get their horses and make them ready for the trail. Valentino Vargas crouched in the shadows and watched the window. The candles were still gleaming in the room. He caught sight of old Don Felipe Ramón once, and then nobody came near the window.

In time, the candles were extinguished. Pedro Pico came slipping to him through the shadows, saying that the horses were tethered a short distance away. Stretched on the ground, they waited until the big house was dark, until travelers weary from a journey should be wrapped in sleep.

"Now!" Valentino Vargas said.

They crept to the wall of the house, and Vargas tested the vine, which bore his weight. With Pedro waiting below, he began the ascent, going slowly and testing the vine repeatedly. He came presently to the open window, and was quiet a moment, listening, clinging to the vine until his arms ached. He could hear low snores.

Through the window he went, and stood panting against the wall. The couch, he made out, was on the opposite side of the room. A streak of moonlight came through, and revealed a bundle of bedclothing,

"I anticipated this visit, señor," said Zorro.

beneath which was a sleeper, Valentino Vargas thought.

He could not see the box in the moonlight, nor could he find it as he felt along the wall. It would be necessary, he decided, to use stern measures, to make a light, arouse the sleeper, threaten him and get the box, which possibly might be under the couch.

In a corner, Valentino Vargas took a bit of candle from a pocket of his jacket, drew out flint and steel, and struck. Soon, the wick caught, and the tiny flame sprang up. Shielding the flame with a hand, Valentino Vargas started toward the couch.

"Stand!" a voice warned, softly.

Vargas stood as though stricken. The voice had come from behind him.

"Turn slowly, and do not let the candle go out, unless you wish to die!"

Valentino Vargas turned, his heart hammering at his ribs, trying to think how he could make his escape through the window and down the vine. Some man had been left there as guard, he supposed.

The light of the candle penetrated to the corner, and Valentino Vargas's eyes bulged. Standing there with leveled pistol was Señor Zorro.

CHAPTER VII
Futile Search

"You, señor?" Vargas mouthed, almost dropping the candle in his astonishment.

"Speak in low tones," Señor Zorro advised. "What are you doing here? Why did you climb up the vine and get through the window?"

"As to that, what do you here yourself?" Vargas countered. "Are you, perhaps, a welcome guest in the house of the Pulidos?"

"You came to steal," Zorro accused. "Did you not?"

"And I presume you yourself came just to pass the time of day? It appears, Señor Zorro, that we are on the same errand."

"Perhaps not, my burly friend. I did not come to steal the gold and jewels belonging to Don Felipe Ramón, and I am quite sure you did. I anticipated this visit, Señor, though I did not know what man would make it."

"Is it that I must halve the takings with you?" Vargas asked. If he could decoy this Zorro to the ground, where Pedro Pico could give aid, he might be outwitted, Vargas thought.

"There will be no takings," Zorro told him. "The strongbox of Don Felipe is not to be touched."

"How is this? When did Señor Zorro become so considerate of other people's property?"

"You are slightly in error," Zorro told him. "I am not a thief. I never have stolen. I defend the oppressed and sometimes punish dishonest men and boasters — such as yourself."

Vargas remembered the mark on his left cheek. Despite the menace of the pistol, he hissed a threat.

"I'll kill you for what you did to me, Zorro! When I get the opportunity — "

"As to that, the future will tell us," Zorro interrupted. "Just now, I have something to say to you, and you may pass the word to any others who have eyes on Don Felipe's gold and jewels. They are not to be touched. Don Miguel would not like it."

"Don Miguel? What has he to do with this Don Felipe?"

"You may learn that at the meeting in the Canyon of the Cocopahs. Don Felipe is under the protection of Don Miguel, and all interested will do well to remember it. The gold and jewels are destined for a purpose."

Valentino Vargas had retreated to the window, but Zorro followed him, keeping the distance the same.

"Are you not afraid of being caught?" Vargas asked. "Who is sleeping on the couch?"

"Nobody, señor. 'Tis but a roll of bedding shaped to resemble a human body. I, myself, did the snoring when I saw you climbing the vine. Do you descend the vine now, and be gone."

"We'll meet again, Zorro."

"Undoubtedly," Zorro said. "Remember, señor, I have eyes in the back of my head, and I am as good with a pistol as I am with a blade."

"For the mark you made on my cheek, I intend to kill you!"

"A man's intentions are many, but not always does he carry them out," Zorro observed. "Begone!"

He stepped forward and pressed Valentino Vargas back into the moonlight. Vargas extinguished the candle and got through the window, and made a rapid descent. He met Pedro Pico in the darkness.

"He is in that room — Zorro," he whispered. "He confronted me. He said Don Felipe Ramón's property must not be touched, that it is an order from Don Miguel."

"What is the meaning of that?"

"I know not. Don Miguel or no Don Miguel, we try to get the gold and jewels," Vargas declared. "It is a swifter way to wealth than participating in an uprising for the sake of loot. As for this Zorro, come with me. I'll inform the sergeant, and he will be captured."

"If we inform, and he is caught, there may be a reward."

"Precisely," Vargas replied. "Also, I shall have the pleasure of seeing the fellow's face, and of watching it turn black when they hang him. Let us make haste."

T HEY left the horses where they were, and hurried to the guest house, and Valentino Vargas shook Sergeant Juan Ruiz until he came awake, cursing because his sleep had been broken.

"Señor Sergeant, awake!" Vargas whispered. "Zorro is here! My friend and I watched him climb up a vine and enter the house through a window. He can be taken, if you make haste."

Sergeant Juan Ruiz sprang off the cot and reached for the clothing he had discarded.

"You are sure, fellow?" he demanded, as he struggled into his boots.

"Did not the rogue mark my face at the inn?" Vargas demanded. "Did he not gamble with Pico here, and denounce him for a cheat? We know him, my sergeant. He went up the vine and into an open window — "

"Enough!" The sergeant buckled on his blade and reached for his pistol. He aroused the others in the guest house and bade them dress and arm quickly. He darted to the adobe huts and aroused some of the field servants, and ordered them to surround the house.

Then, Sergeant Juan Ruiz pounded on the big front door of the casa, bellowing for everybody to awake. Valentino Vargas and Pedro Pico kept back in the shadows, ready to escape if anything went wrong, yet eager to be present if Señor Zorro was led from the house a captive.

Inside, lights gleamed, and the big front door was opened. Sergeant Ruiz darted inside, howling for his capitán. He aroused the entire household. Frightened servants, half clad, came tumbling down the stairs and into the big room from their quarters in the rear. The master of the house appeared, and Don Felipe Ramón, and Capitán Gonzales with blade in one hand and pistol in the other.

"Sergeant, what is this uproar?" the capitán demanded.

"Zorro is in the house! He was seen climbing a vine and getting through a window. There can be no mistake. I have the house surrounded, capitán."

Capitán Gonzales had faith in his subordinate, and he knew what capture of Zorro would mean for him personally. He strengthened the cordon around the house, then began a search of the interior. By this time, the ladies of the household were awake, and badly frightened, and Señor Pulido was doing his best to quiet their fears.

More candles were lit, and the search began, a methodical search which started on the lower floor and soon spread to the upper. Not a spot was missed. Pistols held ready, the capitán and the sergeant led the others.

B UT no Zorro was found. So, at last, they came to the room through which he was supposed to have entered the house, and pounded on the door.

"Is this room occupied?" Capitán Gonzales asked.

"Don Diego Vega sleeps there," Señor Pulido replied. "He has with him his mute servant, Bernardo."

The capitán pounded on the door again, and they heard the heavy bar being withdrawn, and the door was opened. The giant native, Bernardo, stood there, a bludgeon in his hand and an expression of ferocity in his face. Behind him, wrapped in a silk dressing gown, yawning and rubbing the sleep from his eyes, was Don Diego Vega.

"Has the native uprising begun?" Don Diego asked, in a voice seemingly half choked with sleep.

"Lights!" Gonzales roared. "Search the room!"

"For what?" Don Diego demanded.

"Señor Zorro was seen climbing the vine and entering your window," Gonzales said.

"Nonsense! Bernardo would have heard him. Moreover, my throat is not cut. And Don Felipe's strongbox, which I undertook to guard, is safe there at the end of the couch. Somebody has been dreaming, capitán."

Gonzales' face grew red. The others were commencing to regard him with reproach. Señor Pulido was muttering something about dumb officers.

"Sergeant Ruiz!" Gonzales thundered. "What mean you by this false alarm? You have aroused everybody. You have made a fool of me!"

"Two men in the guest house told me they had seen the rogue climb the vine and enter the window."

"Find them, and hold them until morning, and I'll deal with them," Gonzales thundered. "My friends, I regret this occurrence. My sergeant has been overzealous. He shall be properly punished, I assure you."

Sergeant Juan Ruiz had not waited to hear that. He had dashed down the wide stairs and out the front door, and was howling for Valentino Vargas and Pedro Pico. But that pair had heard of the futile search, and knew what the outcome would he as far as they were concerned. They did not tarry to face the sergeant's wrath. There was a clatter of hoofbeats, and they were away, galloping up El Camino Real.

The din subsided, and Don Diego Vega closed and barred the door. In the candlelight, he looked at Bernardo, and grinned, and Bernardo grinned in reply, knowing there would be no rebuke to him for doing so.

"It is well they did not search beneath the couch," Don Diego said, softly.

For the costume of Señor Zorro was beneath the couch, and Zorro's weapons and mask also, and now Bernardo swiftly made them all into a bundle, to be carried away at dawn.

And it had been no bedclothing in the shape of a human on the couch when Valentino Vargas had been in the room, but Bernardo himself, and all the time he had held a pistol trained on that same Valentino Vargas, for use in case the unbelievable happened and Señor Zorro had been caught at a disadvantage.

CHAPTER VIII
A Brawl On The Beach

THEY were away at dawn, traveling as before, Don Felipe's carriage leading and that of Don Diego following a short distance behind.

That evening they stopped at another hacienda, where they were honored guests, and a fiesta was given in their honor, and natives danced and ate and drank and sang their queer songs. Sitting beneath the arches in the patio, the guests watched, and Don Diego saw Señorita Carmelita's face flushed and eyes sparkling.

"You like our land?" he asked.

"I love it already, señor."

"Give not all your love to the country," he whispered, as he bent toward her. "Save some for perhaps another purpose."

She flashed him a quick look, and dimpled and blushed, then turned her head swiftly and pretended to be watching the dancers again. Señora Vallejo pretended to be deaf and blind, for she had been informed by Don Felipe that it would be better so.

"Another day of journeying, and still another, and we shall be at San Juan Capistrano," Don Diego said. "There is a mission! It is an estate, no less. My good friend, Brother Luis, will be there. If ever I wed, I wish him to perform the ceremony."

"You are thinking of marriage?" Carmelita asked.

"I did not think much of it until recently," he replied boldly. "Not until I made this trip to San Diego de Alcála."

He was leaning back in his seat, brushing his nostrils with the scented handkerchief, still very much the fop. He had been reciting poetry to her earlier in the evening.

Carmelita wished that this noble scion of the Vegas were more a man. She knew well that it was hoped she would wed with him. His family was all that could be desired, and they were wealthy in this new land of California. There was no question about that. But Señorita Carmelita had some romantic dreams, and she wished for lover and husband a man of spirit, at whom she could look up with pride.

She sighed, and he bent closer to her still, and she caught the perfume from his silken handkerchief.

"Shall we take a stroll in the moonlight?" Don Diego asked.

"Señora Vallejo gets a pain in her leg when she goes out in the mist or dew."

"Can we not stroll where she can see us from here?"

"Perhaps some other evening, Don Diego."

"You do not like me," he accused.

"How could it be otherwise, señor? You are courtesy itself. And our fathers are lifelong friends."

"You would have me some different, perhaps?"

"Well — perhaps," she admitted. "A girl has dreams."

"I understand, señorita. You would like me better if I rode spirited steeds, and drank and gambled and fought each time I fancied myself insulted. You would have me play a guitar beneath your window — "

"I would have you be a caballero in fact as well as in blood," she interrupted boldly, getting to her feet and motioning to Señora Vallejo. "You will kindly excuse me now, Don Diego? I must have some rest."

H IS eyes were twinkling as he bowed to her and stood aside to let her pass and enter the house. Don Felipe observed it, and sat down beside him when Don Diego resumed his seat.

"It would please me, Don Diego, and I am sure it would please your father also, if you and Carmelita liked each other," Don Felipe said.

"She would have me more a man, I think."

"It surprises me, Don Diego — not that I desire to criticize, understand — that you are not of a more turbulent spirit. Your own father, when he was your age — ah, what a man! What an adventurous spirit! It led him to this new land with his bride."

"Allow me to repeat to you, Don Felipe, an item of philosophy," Don Diego said. "It is an item I love. It is impossible to tell, by the exterior appearance of a nut, what sort of a kernel is inside."

Don Felipe Ramón glanced at him furtively, cleared his throat, and arose.

"I think," said he, "that I shall retire. We have another day of dusty journeying before us."

Don Diego arose and bowed, and his eyes were twinkling again as Don Felipe departed.

The following evening they made another stop at a hacienda, where another fiesta had been prepared for them, and the little señorita, though polite and courteous, kept slightly aloof. And on the next day they got an early start for San Juan Capistrano, where they intended to make a stop. There had been no attack along the way. Capitán Gonzales and a chastened Sergeant Juan Ruiz had ridden beside the Ramón carriage, and fondly believed it was their presence that kept highwaymen at a distance.

Capitán Gonzales made the most of his opportunities. He sensed that all was not well between Don Diego Vega and the señorita. This Carmelita Ramón appealed to him, and, also, her father had brought wealth from Spain.

Capitán Gonzales, a handsome sort of fellow about whom the women had flocked in San Francisco de Asis and Monterey, believed that he had a way with women. What if he could win the heart and hand of Carmelita Ramón and marry into family and money?

So he paid what court he could and fancied he was making some headway, though it was evident that Señora Vallejo did not fancy him, and Don Felipe was only coldly polite.

Now they were traveling within a short distance of the tumbling sea, and the rushing wind cooled them and blew the dust aside. Over a hill they went, and around a curve in the highway, and saw the mission of San Juan Capistrano before them, with its groups of adobe buildings surrounding it, and crowds of natives going about their work.

Brother Luis welcomed them cordially, but beamed upon Don Diego Vega. The natives, too, crowded around him, not for alms, but as though greeting a benefactor. Don Diego Vega was getting to territory where he was known, not only as himself but also as that Señor Zorro who rode to right wrongs, though this secret was well locked within their breasts.

THEY were ushered into the guest house and given quarters, and a meal was spread for them. The horses were taken away to receive proper care.

Don Diego cleansed himself, Bernardo fetching warm water and perfuming it for him.

"Señor Zorro has been called the Curse of Capistrano," Don Diego said, speaking softly. "This is supposed to be his home. It would not surprise me if he made an appearance here."

Bernardo grinned and bobbed his head.

"At any rate, it would be well that, should he so desire it, he find his horse ready, and his clothing also, in the arroyo behind the huts of the natives any time tonight."

Bernardo bobbed his head again.

"I go now to stroll in the patio, and possibly down to the ocean's shore to take the breeze. You need not attend me."

Don Diego had taken some time with his toilet. When he emerged, he found that others had entertained the idea of a stroll on the beach. Don Felipe Ramón had gone there with his daughter and her duenna, and they were walking back and forth, looking out at the sea.

Capitán Gonzales was in the patio, and approached.

"You are perhaps thinking of a stroll, Don Diego?" he asked.

"Perhaps—alone."

Gonzales' face flamed.

"There are times, Don Diego, when you speak in a tone almost insulting. Perhaps you do not fancy the soldiery. Perhaps you do not favor a reign of law and order."

"The present Governor and his soldiery are not exponents of law and order."

"Is this treason?" Gonzales demanded. "I am one of His Excellency's officers, and cannot endure such talk."

"You are at liberty, Señor, to take your ears where they cannot hear it."

"Those who deal in treason may flourish for a time, but, in the end, they stretch a rope. This mysterious Don Miguel, and this Señor Zorro, for instance — their end soon will come."

"It does not interest me," Don Diego complained.

"If you are thinking of taking a stroll on the beach with the little señorita, spare yourself the trouble. I asked to stroll with the party, and she said she wished to be alone."

"Perhaps you do not have a way with the ladies," Don Diego told him.

"Have I not? More of a way with them, I dare say, than a poet and philosopher. The little señorita is not the sort, I think, to prefer one who is not a man of red blood as well as blue."

"One of blue blood," Don Diego informed him, "does not discuss a lady so frankly."

He left Gonzales fuming and fumbling at the hilt of his sword, and walked on. Down toward the tumbling water he went, where the rollers were breaking on the rocks. Don Felipe and his daughter and Señora Vallejo were just starting to pass around the huge rocks to continue along the beach.

As he started to follow them around the rocks, he heard the señorita scream.

Don Diego ran forward as swiftly as he could through the heavy sand. He rounded the rocks, and came upon a scene.

VALENTINO VARGAS and his friends had been waiting at San Juan Capistrano for the party to arrive. They were hiding in native huts, paying their way handsomely. It was the intention of Valentino Vargas to make a last attempt here to get the gold and jewels of Don Felipe Ramón, regardless of what Zorro had told him of Don Miguel's wish that Don Felipe go unmolested.

Vargas and Pedro Pico were in a hut at that moment, but their three friends were not. They had observed the party walking on the beach, and had crept down through the rocks to intercept them.

Señorita Carmelita wore jewels on her fingers and around her pretty throat, and Don Felipe himself had heavy rings studded with diamonds, and a scarf buckle heavy with precious stones. The three rogues decided to get what they could, and flee to the Canyon of the Cocopahs, for the night of the full moon was only two nights away.

Down from the rocks they had dashed, one holding a pistol and the other two with naked blades in their hands. And when Don Diego rounded the point of the rocks he beheld Don Felipe being forced backward at the point of a blade, and another rogue keeping Señora Vallejo at a distance, while the third had grasped the señorita and was trying to get her jewels.

Though his raiment was that of Don Diego Vega, the spirit became that of Señor Zorro now. His eyes aflame at this indignity, Don Diego whipped out his blade as he ran forward. He gave a cry of rage and made for the nearest man.

The three turned to confront him, and one laughed.

"It is the weakling!" he cried. "Let us muss up his silks and laces."

They set about it, while Señorita Carmelita clung to Señora Vallejo's arm, and Don Felipe lurched forward, though unarmed, expecting to see Don Diego instantly slain by these ruffians.

But Don Diego Vegas appeared fully capable of caring for himself. He disarmed the first man and ran him through the shoulder neatly. The second discharged his pistol, and the ball whistled past Don Diego's ear, and the burning powder scorched the lace of his collar.

"Scum!" Don Diego cried.

His blade flashed, and came back red, and the man coughed as he collapsed to the sand, twitched, and was still.

THE third came rushing forward, howling curses, blade up and ready. Don Diego retreated a few paces before his wild rush, stumbled in the sand, and almost went down, but recovered in time to meet the attack.

This third man knew something of fencing, but not enough. In an instant, as soon as Don Diego got the feel of him, he knew he was undone. He retreated step by step, until he was on firm ground at the end of the mass of rocks. And suddenly he darted aside, turned his back, and ran.

"Scum!" Don Diego howled after him.

Don Felipe's cries had attracted the attention of some at the mission, and they came hurrying to ascertain the trouble, Capitán Gonzales among them. They saw a wounded man and a dead one, and one running away, and beheld Don Diego Vega cleaning his blade in the sand.

"Who says he is not a man?" Don Felipe Ramón was thundering.

*The bullet missed;
the blade did not.*

"Three against him, and he did not falter. What manner of country is this, where rogues may attack persons within a stone's throw of the mission? No doubt it has inferior soldiery."

"Pardon, Don Felipe, but I offered to accompany you on your walk," Capitán Gonzales said. "I feared something like this might occur."

"We had no need of the soldiery," Don Felipe told him. "Gentlemen know how to defend their ladies."

Señora Vallejo had dropped upon the sand, and was sitting there moaning and fanning herself. The señorita left her and stepped to Don Diego's side, and timidly touched his arm.

"Forgive me, Señor, for some thoughts I have held concerning you," she begged, her eyes shining as she looked up at him. "They were wrong thoughts."

He smiled down at her.

"It distresses me that you saw me in a moment of uncontrolled passion," he replied. "But there are things which make a man grow turbulent and cause him to resort to violence. Do you care to take a stroll with me along the beach? I have thought of another poem."

She clung to his arm.

"I'll be delighted to hear it, Don Diego," she said.

CHAPTER IX
Rogues At Liberty

SECLUDED in the native hut, Valentino Vargas and Pedro Pico heard the tumult and wondered what had occurred to cause it. They crept forth and joined the throng of natives and workmen hurrying down to the shore.

Before they reached the scene, they heard rumors of what had happened — that three ruffians had set upon Don Felipe and his party, and that Don Diego Vega, of all people, had turned red-blooded for a moment and had driven them off.

Valentino Vargas and Pedro Pico glanced swiftly at each other, guessing it was their three companions who had done this thing.

"Ha! They tried to steal a march on us, and have been punished for it," Vargas whispered. "Now we shall proceed as we have planned, and really cut the loot only two ways. Nevertheless, they were our friends, and were to join the enterprise of Don Miguel. So it is in my mind to punish this Don Diego at the first opportunity. He is on my list, Pedro Pico, along with Señor Zorro."

"You would slay half the men in the land," Pedro Pico said.

They came to the scene, to find one of their friends dead, and another wounded and held in custody, and the third flown. Capitán Gonzales was shouting loudly, taking charge of the situation, and Sergeant Juan Ruiz was rushing about carrying out his superior's orders.

The sergeant turned and caught sight of them, gave a hoarse bellow, and charged through the crowd, and had them by their collars before they could escape.

"Ho, capitán!" he cried. "Here are the rogues who claim they saw Señor Zorro climbing the vine at the Pulido hacienda, and caused us to arouse the household."

Gonzales strode over to them and stood with his fists planted against his hips, glaring at them.

"We did see somebody climbing the vine, and he wore a mask," Vargas declared. "We thought we were doing our duty in telling the sergeant — "

"Who are you?" Gonzales demanded.

"Valentino Vargas, a trader, going now to Reina de Los Angeles. This Zorro fought with me and cut my cheek, and I certainly know the rogue. I saw him climbing the vine. If you did not catch him when you searched, that is no fault of mine."

"And you?" Gonzales asked Pedro Pico.

"I am a gambler, Señor Capitán, and this Zorro claimed that I cheated, and drove me out of San Diego de Alcála. I travel to Reina de Los Angeles also."

"Two rogues, no doubt," Gonzales declared. "Ruiz, you will place them in custody at the mission, until I have opportunity to dispose of the case."

They howled their demands for release, but Sergeant Juan Ruiz prodded them with the tip of his blade, and threatened them with his pistol, and marched them up from the beach and to a small adobe building set aside from the others, with a heavy door and metal bars across the windows.

Sergeant Ruiz opened the door and thrust them inside, not being gentle about it, for the affair at the Pulido hacienda had earned him a stem rebuke from the capitán.

"There, rogues!" he said, and closed the door and dropped the heavy bar into place on the outside. "No doubt thc capitán will order you a hundred lashes each, when he gets around to it."

I NSIDE the cuartel, Valentino Vargas paced around the little room and howled curses, while Pedro Pico sat on a bench and held his head in his hands. Some natives came to the windows to look in and taunt them, and Vargas cursed at them also. Finally, they tired of their sport, and went to see the dead ruffian buried on the hillside, where there was a burial place for such vermin, and they were left alone.

Came, then, another native, who peered in at them, and then glanced furtively around outside, to make sure nobody else was near.

"You have gold, señores!" he asked. "You would pay a man who told you how to escape your prison?"

"Would pay him generously," Vargas said, stepping to the window.

"Some moons ago, a friend of mine was confined, and I and some others aided him in an escape," the native said. "I can aid you in similar manner?"

"And how is that?"

"First, I must have gold."

"Rogue! I give you gold, and you'll laugh and run away, and tell us nothing," Vargas said.

"I promise, by the saints! Three pieces of gold — "

"One!" Vargas said.

"Three, señor, else you remain as you are, to be taken out and have your back lashed in front of all. Take your choice."

Vargas swore again, brought forth three pieces of gold, and gave them to the native through the bars.

"That bench in the corner, señor," the man at the window whispered. "Shift it, and lift the big flat stone upon which the bench now rests. You will find a tunnel which runs outside the patio wall and opens there in a clump of bushes."

Then the man darted away.

"Not yet!" Vargas warned, as Pedro Pico promptly started to move the bench. "It is the broad light of day, and everybody is rushing around in a state of excitement. Wait until their blood has cooled and they have gone about their business."

"But they may come to get us and whip us."

"Such things are always done in the cool of the evening, when all are at leisure and may watch, as you should know. We have nothing to fear now."

"When we get out, what shall we do?" Pedro Pico asked. "Get our horses and ride for the Canyon of the Cocopahs?"

"There are things to be done here, dolt. I still have my mind on the gold and jewels of Don Felipe Ramón. We know in which room they lodged him, and we saw the strongbox carried there. And there are other things, also. I desire to square accounts with this Don Diego Vega, because of the way he handled our friends, and also with this Señor Zorro, does he put in an appearance here. Not only did he denounce you and mark me, but also he is responsible for the plight in which we now find ourselves."

THEY sweltered in the cuartel during the midday, waiting for the siesta hour. The drowsy mid-afternoon found the mission slumbering. Natives slept in the shade of the walls, and even the friars of the mission had retired for rest.

"Now is the time," Vargas said.

They shifted the bench and lifted the flat stone, and the mouth of a small tunnel yawned before them.

"Go first," Vargas directed Pedro Pico. "I'll put the bench against the wall, and, after I enter the tunnel, will try to drop the flat stone into place. This is a secret which should be well kept, if possible."

Pedro Pico crawled down into the tunnel, sending back a cloud of fine dust. Valentino Vargas waited a moment, then dropped the flat stone into place and followed. It was a small tunnel, and there were places where Vargas feared he could not wriggle through.

He could hear Pedro Pico grunting and panting ahead of him. It was dark, stifling, dusty.

He heard Pico's exclamation of relief, finally, and crawled on and saw the light of day and got a whiff of fresh air. Pedro Pico was at the tunnel's outer mouth, holding back some brush so Valentino Vargas could crawl through.

They found themselves on the bank of a small arroyo, where they were hidden from the mission and the village. Crawling forth, they hurried up the gulch, away from danger.

"We'll hide until the nightfall," Vargas said. "Then we'll return, get our horses ready for the trail, hide them, do what we will, and escape. We'll make for the Canyon of the Cocopahs, and there await the meeting Don Miguel has called."

"You would rob Don Felipe Ramón, after being warned by Señor Zorro that Don Miguel would not like it?"

"I have told you my decision before, Pedro Pico. With the gold and jewels of Don Felipe in our possession, we need not concern ourselves with this affair of Don Miguel's. We'll make for the north and live like princes in Monterey."

A mile up the arroyo they went into hiding in a shady spot where the erratic breeze reached them at times, and stretched themselves out to sleep. When they awoke, the scarlet and gold of the sinking sun were streaking the distant sea and the breeze was coming in strongly.

"It will be dusk before we come to the mission," Valentino Vargas said. "Let us go. Perhaps we can find some native who will give us food for gold, and hide us until the time comes to strike."

CHAPTER X
Blades And Pistols

IN THE room assigned him in the guest house, Don Diego Vega made his toilet for the evening meal. Bernardo assisted him, his eyes glowing as he served his master.

"Zorro may ride tonight, and he may not," Don Diego whispered to him. "However, does he desire to do so, he will expect to find his horse and costume in the arroyo."

Bernardo made a guttural sound and nodded that he understood and would obey.

"This is a merry business," Don Diego observed, smiling slightly. "I go me to San Diego de Alcála to escort Don Felipe and the others. I am denied military escort, and highwaymen are prepared to pounce upon us. By a subterfuge, I get the escort, though I like it not. And by whispering that Don Miguel might not like it, were Don Felipe to be robbed, I hold off some of the bandits. Moreover, I arrange for the troopers to catch the white renegades who would upset the natives and lead them to certain slaughter and punishment."

Bernardo bobbed his head furiously, to show that he understood and approved.

Don Diego went then to the big room where the table had been spread, to find the others already there. Capitán Gonzales was endeavoring to pay court to Señorita Carmelita, and she was holding herself aloof with cold courtesy.

But when Don Diego entered the room her face brightened and she flashed him a smile, and Don Felipe, seeing it, and also the answering smile with which Don Diego greeted her, smiled slightly himself, for he was well pleased.

Friar Luis presided at the table, and native servants served. There were fruits, both fresh and preserved, and roast beef and roast mutton, pots of strained honey, olives, dishes of salads, and vegetables. Rich wines were served with the repast, for the mission had rare wines in its cellars, made from grapes grown near the mission of San Gabriel, and for which San Juan Capistrano had traded other wares.

Then, the meal at an end, they strolled in the moonlight in the patio, Don Diego with the little señorita, while Capitán Gonzales fumed, Señora Vallejo always watching, and Don Felipe talking with Friar Luis, who already had received from the grandee a gift of gold for the mission.

"We start in the early morning for Reina de Los Angeles," Don Diego said, when they were all sitting beneath the arches again. "We shall make it by nightfall, for the highway is firm and well traveled."

"I am surprised we have come this far without having our throats cut," Don Felipe declared. "That affair on the beach reveals there are desperate characters in this country."

"Such vermin are encountered now and then," Don Diego said, loftily, "and needs must be disposed of."

"They were disposed of properly. It will please me, Don Diego, to tell your father of your proper conduct in the affair."

Don Diego smiled slightly. The news of his fight would not exactly startle his father, who knew that his son was Señor Zorro at times.

Capitán Gonzales bade the company good night, and retired to his own room, convinced that he could make no headway with the señorita as long as Don Diego Vega was basking in the bright light of hero worship. The ladies left also, and Don Diego sat for a time talking to Friar Luis and Don Felipe, then went to his own room, after giving his servants orders to be prepared for an early start.

BERNARDO was waiting, and Don Diego gestured for him to be gone. He slipped out through the patio, and hurried away to get the black horse in readiness. Don Diego stripped off his gorgeous raiment and dressed in plain clothing again, extinguished the candle, and presently crawled through the open window and made for the arroyo, keeping to the shadows.

Again he donned the habiliments of Señor Zorro, buckled on his blade, and put on his mask.

"Remain here and have the horse in readiness," he instructed Bernardo. "I may have need of him, and may not. Only the future can tell."

Back through the shadows he went to the patio wall, and there crouched for a time, listening. Some natives were singing around the huts, and a few fires were gleaming in the open air, and odors of cooking meat came to him.

He entered the patio cautiously, slipped along in the darkness beneath the arches, and came to the open window of Capitán Gonzales' room. A gentle snoring came from within.

Señor Zorro crept cautiously through the window. He gently dropped the tapestry down over the opening, while the capitán snored on. Through another window the moonlight streamed, but this window was on the outside, and high in the wall, so nobody on the exterior could see into the room.

Zorro drew his pistol from his girdle and stepped to the couch. He stood beside it, in the bright streak of moonlight, and prodded Capitán Gonzales gently in his ribs.

"Awake, soldier!" Zorro said.

Gonzales rolled over, grunting, trying to kick aside the bed covering and sit up. His wits were befuddled with sleep, and he was sitting on the edge of the couch before he realized what was happening. He opened his eyes, and saw the masked Zorro in the moonlight.

"You?" he cried.

"Keep your voice down, capitán, if you care to live. It is necessary for me to speak to you again."

"What now, rogue? I swear that one day I'll catch you and string you up!"

"Catch me first," Zorro suggested.

I wish to remind you of the meeting in the Canyon of the Cocopahs, night after the next. Do not fail to be there with the troopers from Reina de Los Angeles."

"We shall be there and catch the rogues, if they are present," Gonzales declared. "I think this is but a trick."

"There will be several present. You can tell at a glance, capitán, what men would turn renegade and follow this Don Miguel. And another thing, my capitán — a mistake has been made."

"Regarding what?" Gonzales asked.

"I did intimate to you, at San Diego de Alcála, that possibly this Don Diego Vega and Don Felipe Ramón had something to do with the uprising. I spoke of catching big fish as well as small fry — remember?"

"I remember well, rogue."

"New intelligence has come to me. Of a certainty, neither has anything to do with this affair of Don Miguel. Neither is concerned in the planned uprising of the natives. I regret, my capitán, that my former words caused you to furnish military escort to persons to whom you did not wish to give it."

"Is this a trick?" Gonzales demanded. "You have made a fool of me! I have protected this party, with my sergeant, when undoubtedly it would have pleased the Governor to see them robbed, if not murdered. Who are you, fellow, who know so much?"

"I am Zorro!"

"AND who is Zorro, eh? It was whispered once that Don Diego Vega is Zorro, and I laughed at the idea. But, after what Don Diego did on the beach — perhaps the man has us all fooled. I shall look into this matter at once. If Don Diego Vega is Zorro — if you, señor, are Don Diego Vega — I shall ascertain it, and see you properly punished."

"The moonlight," Zorro said, "makes you rave."

Capitán Gonzales started to speak again. But a sudden tumult stopped him. They heard a woman scream. They heard blades clash an instant. They heard the stentorian voice of Don Felipe Ramón howling for aid.

"Something's amiss," Zorro said. "This may be your business, capitán."

He jerked aside the tapestry and sprang through the window. Candles were gleaming in some of the rooms. The natives were coming at a run.

Zorro darted along the wall and got outside the patio, in time to see two men running toward the edge of the arroyo. From a window a pistol barked. Don Felipe Ramón, in his night clothing, crawled through and into the moonlight.

"Robbers! Thieves!" he cried. "There they go! They have my gold and jewels!"

Señor Zorro took after them, running swiftly over the rough dry ground, stumbling and staggering, but gaining on the two ahead, who were carrying the heavy box between them. A pistol barked as one of the two fired, but the ball went wild.

Señor Zorro fired his own weapon, stopping an instant to do so; they raced on.

His shot had missed. The two ahead dropped over the edge of the arroyo, and Zorro went on after them and dropped over also. Two saddled horses were there, and one man was trying frantically to lash the box behind one of the saddles. The other turned to fight.

He was Valentino Vargas.

"So, rogue!" Zorro cried.

"It is you, eh? The man who marked me! Now, señor, we shall have an accounting!"

Blades flashed in the bright light of the moon. The ground was uneven and rough, and delicate fencing was a perilous thing. Valentino Vargas, therefore, made a desperate attack, depending more on aggressiveness and strength than on fencing science.

"I marked you before, but I shall end you now," Señor Zorro cried. "Then I shall attend to your companion."

They fought desperately, for Zorro knew he had no time to lose. Men were rushing toward the arroyo from the mission. And he was not fighting now as Don Diego Vega, but as Señor Zorro, a so-called highwayman with a price upon his head, and at whom any man had liberty to fire pistol or present blade. Moreover, Capitán Gonzales would be coming, and his stout sergeant, Juan Ruiz, who was a man to be taken into consideration.

THE tip of Valentino Vargas' blade ripped Zorro's sleeve as the latter stumbled over a rock, and Vargas lunged forward to complete his work, thinking he had his adversary at a disadvantage, a cry of delight ringing from his lips. It was his last cry. He found the point of Zorro's blade at his breast, and Zorro promptly ran him through.

Zorro whirled, then, toward the other man, who had continued his work of fastening the strongbox behind his saddle. Now he was getting into the saddle. Men were arriving on the rim of the arroyo, starting to work their way down to the bottom. Zorro could hear Capitán Gonzales barking orders, could hear the strong voice of Sergeant Juan Ruiz answering him.

Pedro Pico kicked his mount in the flanks and started. But Señor Zorro was at his side instantly, reached up and grasped him, jerked him from the saddle and hurled him to the ground. Pedro Pico struck at him with a dagger, and Zorro had his sleeve ripped again.

"Scum!" he cried, and struck with his own dagger, using his left hand. Pedro Pico gave a cry and fell back. The wound was not mortal, but it put the man out of the fighting.

"It is Zorro!" Pedro Pico cried. "He escapes with the gold and jewels! I tried to stop him — he has stabbed me — "

Pistols barked. Sergeant Ruiz had reached the bottom of the arroyo, and came charging like a mad bull, blade out and ready.

"Hold, fellow!" he cried.

Zorro did not have time to get into the saddle, which was his purpose. He whirled, and his blade clashed with that of the sergeant. There was no time for proper fencing now. The others were rushing forward, and Señor Zorro found himself in danger of capture.

It flashed through his mind what capture would mean — the triumph of the Governor, death by the rope, shame and disgrace for the Vegas. The thought made him a madman. He attacked fiercely, knocked the sergeant's blade aside, ran him through the shoulder and saw him fall back, dropping his sword.

Into the saddle of Pedro Pico's horse, Zorro vaulted. He bent low and urged the animal down the arroyo through the heavy sand. More pistols barked behind him, but he rode unscathed through the semi-darkness. Around a bend, and he was safe for the moment.

Bernardo was waiting there with the black horse, and Zorro quickly sprang from the steed he rode, and mounted his own.

"Leave this horse here. Get out and away," he ordered Bernardo. "You must not be found here. I'll leave the black horse at the upper end of the arroyo, behind the storehouse."

He compelled his mount to ascend the slope, and for a moment revealed himself in the moonlight at the top, so that those behind saw him. He sent a wild laugh ringing down the wind, then rode madly.

First, he made for the highway, and clattered along it with as much noise as possible. But soon he turned aside, riding with extreme caution, and cut back around the mission, hearing other riders going past in futile pursuit. He left the black where he had told Bernardo, for the servant had not yet arrived at the spot. He stripped off the habiliments of Señor Zorro, and hurried through the shadows back toward the mission.

CLOSE behind the storehouse he crept. The patio was alive with men. The voice of Capitán Gonzales came to him:

"Where is Don Diego Vega, then? Out riding, as this Señor Zorro! It has been suspected for some time."

"You are mad," Don Felipe Ramón replied.

"We shall see as to that. Every other man had returned to the patio. Where is Don Diego Vega?"

"Perhaps the robbers hurt him when he pursued them," Don Felipe defended. "He may be out there somewhere now, wounded. We must search for him."

"We do not know he pursued the robbers. He shall have some questions to answer when next we meet. He is under suspicion. I shall make it my business to investigate well."

"This Zorro slew one thief and wounded another," Don Felipe pointed out. "He left the horse, with my strongbox on him, down the arroyo and went away on his own. I cannot find it in my heart to blame the man much. I understand he has done naught but befriend the helpless — though that did not always please the Governor."

"Being a friend of the Vegas, it is expected you would talk treason," Capitán Gonzales said, angrily. "Perhaps it would not be amiss if I investigated you, also, señor."

Don Felipe Ramón sputtered his rage at the insult, and turned away.

"But this Don Diego Vega comes first," Gonzales roared. "He has questions to answer. Where is he?"

"I am here, Señor Capitán," said the voice of Don Diego close behind him.

CHAPTER XI
In The Canyon

GONZALES whirled to face him. Don Diego Vega stood there, only partially clad, brushing his scented handkerchief across his nostrils. He looked at Gonzales, and yawned.

"What is all this tumult?" Don Diego asked.

"He accuses you of being Señor Zorro," Don Felipe replied.

"Indeed?" Don Diego said. "I am flattered, Capitán Gonzales. This Zorro seems to be quite a man."

"Where have you been?" Gonzales demanded. "Give an accounting of where you have spent your time!"

Don Diego Vega lifted his head, and his eyes flashed. "I do not relish the tone of your voice," he said. "There is something of disrespect in it."

"As an officer of His Excellency, I demand that you make reply,"

Gonzales said.

"I was awakened by the tumult, Señor. I rushed around as did everybody else, trying to discover the reason for all the turmoil. Then I returned to my room."

"You were not there when I searched for you."

"Possibly not. You may have searched before my return. It appears to me, Capitán Gonzales, that you and your sergeant are not proper soldiers. During the day I was compelled to fight off rogues who attacked Don Felipe and his daughter, and during the night Señor Zorro had to fight off thieves. Everybody does the fighting, it seems, except the soldiery."

"Beware, señor, lest you try my temper too far!' Gonzales cried.

"Do not bluster so much," Don Diego begged. "Surely, there has been enough tumult for one night. And we must start on early in the morning. Are we to have the pleasure of your escort again, capitán?"

"Beware!" Gonzales roared again. I am not a novice with a blade."

"Are you, by any chance, challenging me to a duel by the light of the moon?" Don Diego asked. He beckoned to one of his native servants standing near. "Go to my room, and bring me my sword," he directed.

But Don Felipe Ramón hurried forward to prevent this.

"You forget yourselves, señores," he said. "Both of you have better things to do than fight each other. Drop this for the present, I beg of you. The accusation of Capitán Gonzales is absurd unless he has better facts upon which to base it, and it is beneath the dignity of Don Diego Vega to notice it when it is made."

Friar Luis came forward, speaking in his gentle voice, and urged them to remember that they were at the mission, and that there had been enough violence and blood-letting for one day, so they turned away, each to go to his own room.

At dawn, the carriages were made ready and loaded, and they began the last part of the journey to Reina de Los Angeles. The highway was firm, and there were few hills, and the horses kept up a good pace.

At midday, they stopped at a rancho where Don Diego was known, to eat and rest for a time, sitting in the cool patio where a fountain splashed and scarlet blossoms ran riot over the adobe walls.

" 'Tis but a few miles more," Don Diego said to the señorita and her father. "There are some splendid houses in Reina de Los Angeles, and people of the best. But my father's hacienda — there is the place! Only a few miles from the town, a place of calm retreat. I spend many days at a time there."

S EÑORITA Carmelita seemed to be dreaming. There was a faraway look in her eyes and she was smiling faintly. Don Diego glanced at her, and her father saw the glance, and dreamed also that his wishes would be fulfilled, and his family be linked with that of Vega through marriage.

When the siesta hour was over, they went on. Capitán Gonzales rode beside the first carriage again, and held speech with Señorita Carmelita whenever the horses slowed, but knew he was making scant headway.

This irked him, and built in his breast rancor against Don Diego Vega greater than had been there before. He was thinking, however, of what Señor Zorro had told him regarding the meeting in the Canyon of the Cocopahs. If he had not been misled, soon the air would ring with his plaudits, and he would be the hero of the hour for preventing an uprising of natives, and then, perhaps, Señorita Carmelita would give ear to him.

Through the late afternoon they traveled briskly, until the dying sun stained the tumbling waves of the sea again. They came to a range of small, rounded hills, and followed the highway over them, and at dusk topped the last, and saw the pueblo of Reina de Los Angeles below them, lights already commencing to gleam in the houses and torches in the huts.

Down the slope they rushed with the carriage horses at a gallop, to come to the corner of the plaza, where the Vega casa stood. One of the outriders had gone ahead, and they were expected.

The door flew open, and gray-haired Alejandro Vega, Don Diego's august father, stood there with his arms outstretched in welcome. With two natives carrying torches on either side of him, he advanced to the first carriage, out of which Don Felipe got quickly to embrace him.

"My old friend! My old friend!" Don Felipe said, his eyes growing misty.

Welcome to my poor home!" Don Alejandro replied. "Did my son conduct you in care and safety?"

"He got us through, and my property also, though there were divers and sundry tumults," Don Felipe said. "He conducted himself in those as a caballero should."

Capitán Gonzales paid his respects and galloped across the plaza and toward the soldiers' barracks, with Sergeant Juan Ruiz close behind him. The capitán at once went into conference with the present commandante, whose office he was to take, and spoke of what Señor Zorro had told him.

"We'll catch the rogues!" Gonzales thundered. "We'll take every man, save a couple left to guard."

"It is a small box canyon, and we have to bottle up the mouth, and we have them," the commandante replied. "Tomorrow night is the night of the full moon — that is the time. I, too, have heard some rumblings concerning this Don Miguel. His identity is a question."

"Perhaps, when we take him, we shall be astonished," Gonzales said.

BUT, in the great casa of the Vegas, there was no talk of war and violence. The Ramóns were made at home, and Don Diego went to his own quarters on the upper floor, and dressed in his very best. And when he descended the wide, winding staircase to the great living room, where the table was spread, there was an odor of perfume about him, and he held a book of poetry, and to look at him one would think he did not know how to handle a blade.

On the morrow he played host, for the blooded ladies of the town came to pay their respects to the Señorita Carmelita Ramón, and many of the young caballeros also. Then came the siesta hour, and they rested, and in the evening was a feast of welcome.

There were many guests, so that a man became lost among them, which was as Don Diego desired it. They filled the house and strolled in the patio, and it was difficult for one person to find another.

Don Diego slipped up the stairs to his own room, where Bernardo was waiting.

"The horse is ready?" he asked. Bernardo nodded assent.

"Get to him at once, and I'll follow. Then do you await my return. Have any of the troopers left the barracks?"

Bernardo, who had been watching, nodded assent again, and opened and closed his hands twice.

"Twenty?" Don Diego asked; and once again Bernardo nodded.

"Fair odds!" Don Diego said, chuckling as he stripped off his rich garments, and left them so he could don them quickly again.

He got into his plain clothing, slipped along the hall, went to an open window, and descended to the ground by means of a clinging vine. Through the shadows he went swiftly, like a shadow himself, until he was behind the natives' huts. Bernardo was waiting there with the horse behind some rocks.

Working swiftly, he put on the costume of Zorro again, and the mask, and his weapons. Then he gave Bernardo a pat on his shoulder, and mounted the big black. He rode away through the night, going slowly so there were no resounding hoofbeats.

He did not follow one of the trails, but cut across the open country, traveling with caution, careful not to get against the skyline where he might be observed against the moon. The Canyon of the Cocopahs was but five miles from the town, but by the route Don Diego followed it was seven.

For he did not go directly to the canyon's mouth, judging that the troopers would be on guard and watching there. He judged, also, that Capitán Gonzales would allow any who wished to enter, but bottle up the canyon so they could not escape.

Señor Zorro, however, knew another route into the canyon, down one side through the tangle of brush which covered the jutting rocks. He made for the canyon's rim, going slowly over the rough ground.

Down the slippery slope he urged the horse, pausing every few feet to watch and listen and let the animal have a breathing spell. Half way down, he came to a tiny clearing, and there he stopped again, and looked below.

Two tiny fires were gleaming, and men were around them, and horses were tethered to trees a short distance from the fires. Down the canyon rode two more men, to dismount at the nearest fire and tie their mounts and speak to the others.

Señor Zorro rode on down the slope, slowly and cautiously. Reaching the bottom, he stopped behind some high brush, where he could not be seen.

He was wondering how soon the troopers would advance from the mouth of the canyon. Capitán Gonzales would be eager to be at the kill, he supposed. He listened intently, and on the slight breeze which came in from the canyon's mouth he heard the snort of a horse and the rattling of accouterments.

They were coming, then. They would easily catch these white renegades who were ready to follow Don Miguel in an uprising. It would mean fire and theft for a time, much loot for the white men. Then the soldiers and local natives would get organized, and the malcontents be hunted down like wild beasts, and slain or punished.

Señor Zorro waited a moment longer. Down the canyon, he caught sight of a blade reflecting the light of the moon. He rode out into the open, between the fires and the advancing soldiery.

"Ho, Señores!" he cried.

CHAPTER XII
Fight, And Flight

THOSE at the fires whirled to look toward him. They could see him plainly in the bright moonlight, sitting his black horse, the mask concealing his features, his naked blade held high over his head.

"It is Señor Zorro!" some native cried.

"Where is Don Miguel?" Zorro shouted at them.

"None of us know, señor," one cried back at him. "We were told to meet him here tonight. Perhaps he will come later. Are you one of us?"

Zorro had been watching toward the mouth of the canyon, and from where he sat his horse he could tell that Capitán Gonzales had spread his troopers in a thin line across the canyon's floor, and that now he had stopped them, wanting to listen to what was said.

"No, I am not one of you!" Zorro cried in answer to the question.

"What do you here, then? Why do you ask for Don Miguel?"

Señor Zorro's wild laugh rang among the rocks.

"Fools!" he cried. "There is no Don Miguel! He is but a figure of my imagination. Some time ago I started these rumors of an uprising, and contacted cleverly a few men, who passed the news on to other rogues. The thing grew and grew, without aid from me."

"How is this?" somebody shouted.

"All of you who answered the call — it shows what you would do, were there really a Don Miguel. Renegades! Ready to lead the stupid natives in a revolt, to certain slaughter, for the sake of what loot you may gain! Every man of you stands guilty of treason and conspiracy — and you are without a leader!"

They were grumbling now, and some of them started toward their horses.

"You are entrapped!" Zorro shouted at them. "Even now the troopers from Reina de Los Angeles are creeping upon you from the canyon's mouth. You will stretch rope — "

They howled at that, panic claiming them, and rushed for their mounts, jerking the reins free, springing into their saddles. The horses, frightened at the tumult, plunged and kicked and disconcerted them.

Down the canyon, Capitán Gonzales barked a command. The troopers swept forward, jumping their horses over brush and rocks and making toward the fires.

Zorro swung his horse aside. Pistols began barking over behind the fires, and the soldiers answered the fire. But this was close business, where there was scant time in which to reload, so it was a time for steel rather than pistol ball.

Some of the renegades rode madly straight at the soldiers, in an effort to break through the line and get away, and they clashed in the moonlight. Others tried to get up the slopes of the canyon, and turned back because their horses could not make it.

Back in the shadows, Zorro moved his horse forward a short distance, then waited to watch.

"At them!" Capitán Gonzales was shouting above the din. "Capture or kill every one! Catch me this Señor Zorro, too!"

It was time, Zorro judged, to get away from the scene. He had finished his work. He had decoyed the rogues to the canyon, and the soldiers could do the rest. He turned his horse and started up the winding slippery trail to the top.

B UT he came to a quick stop. No doubt he had been seen riding along the canyon's rim, and followed by some trooper. For now a rider was coming down from the top, following the narrow, slippery trail.

Zorro knew he would be at a disadvantage if he fought there. The other would be above him, and there was not room for two horses to pass. And the fighting would be heard from below, and some would ride up and take him.

He turned his horse and retreated to the floor of the canyon. There was desperate fighting in the clearing now. Two of the renegades broke through, and the troopers gave immediate pursuit. Others were making a stand, though they knew it was futile, preferring to die on a soldier's blade than be captured and strung up by the neck.

Zorro waited in the shadows a moment, watching the scene, waiting for an opportunity to ride through the line. But that line was broken now, as the troopers fought the renegades.

Suddenly, he bent low over his horse's neck, drove home the big spurs he wore, and dashed out from his place of concealment. He was seen instantly, and a cry arose. Between him and the mouth of the canyon were several mounted troopers, and some on the ground, and Capitán Gonzales was there, also.

Zorro got past the first few without taking a sword cut or giving one, merely by superb horsemanship. But he found his way barred by Capitán Gonzales, arrogant in this moment of victory.

"This man is mine!" Gonzales howled. "Attend to the others."

As he spoke, his horse swerved and crashed against that of Zorro. They circled, and their blades clashed.

"I'll wound you, see your face," Gonzales shouted, as they fought. "I think I know the countenance behind that mask."

"Beware your own face!" Zorro cried. "Best call some of your men to help."

"I need no aid!"

He said it bravely enough, but, even as he said it, Capitán Gonzales was worrying a bit. He had heard tales of Zorro's swordsmanship, and now he had the feel of Zorro's blade, and knew the tales were true. The perspiration popped out on his forehead as the horses circled in the moonlight, and they continued fighting.

From the corner of his eye, Señor Zorro saw one of the dismounted troopers drawing near, holding a sword ready. His left hand brought his pistol from his girdle, and as his horse wheeled, he fired. The trooper gave a screech and fell.

"I am fighting an army," Zorro said.

"Stand back! This man is mine!" Capitán Gonzales howled.

He started to press the fighting, while some watched the mounted combat from the distance, and others were too busy fighting themselves to care what happened to their capitán. Zorro's big black was forced backward a distance, and they turned, and Zorro forced the fighting in turn.

"I did not like your manner when last we met," he said. "I cannot change that, but I can make of you a thing the ladies will despise."

"Fight, rogue!" Gonzales howled.

"I have no wish to kill you, capitán. To disgrace you will be enough."

H E PRESSED the fighting again, and suddenly the capitán's blade flew from his hand to strike the ground a short distance away. The capitán, mad with rage, dropped a hand to get his pistol. Zorro had discharged his, and it was empty.

"You would fight unfairly?" Zorro cried at him. "This must be your punishment, then."

His blade darted forward. Capitán Gonzales felt scorching fire on his cheek. A cry of rage escaped him, for he knew what had been done to him. He would bear that jagged letter Z, the mark of Zorro, to the grave with him.

Then Zorro was bending from the saddle, clasping him and tearing the pistol away, to hurl it to the ground. He tossed Capitán Gonzales out of his saddle and to the ground also, gave a wild laugh, wheeled his horse, bent low, and raced down the canyon.

"After him! Shoot him down! Do not let him escape!" Capitán Gonzales was screeching, as he struggled to get back into the saddle again.

Madly, Zorro rode, the big black horse hurdling rocks and clumps of brush. Behind him, pistols barked, and bullets flew near him, but none struck home. He approached another and larger clearing, and saw trouble ahead.

Not all the force of troopers had been led deeply into the canyon by the capitán. Here were a few kept in reserve, to capture any trying to flee.

Señor Zorro saw four men before him, all mounted, and now they began riding forward, converging upon him. His pistol was empty, he had only his blade. He rode straight toward them, but pulled rein slightly and slackened speed.

"One side, señores!" he called.

But they came on at him, and behind him Capitán Gonzales and some of the others broke from the brush in pursuit. Señor Zorro was between two fires.

He dug in with his spurs again, and swerved to the left, and the troopers in front swerved in that direction also.

With a quick pressure of knees and touch of the rein, Zorro swung his horse abruptly back to the right.

He bent low and dashed at them, past them, a pistol exploding almost in his face as he rode. A blade flicked out at him and ripped the collar of his blouse. His horse staggered as another bumped against him, but kept his feet and raced on.

More pistols exploded behind him. One bullet whistled past his ear. There was a drum-fire of hoofbeats as the pursuit began. Capitán Gonzales was howling commands:

"Drop everything else and catch this rogue! He is worth all the others!"

Rage gave the capitán strength in that pursuit. He knew that his handsome face had been marked forever, that the fair ladies would turn from him in scorn, not that he bore a scar as a result of sword fighting, but because that scar was a mark this Señor Zorro gave to men he did not deem worthy of slaying.

Capitán Gonzales howled his orders, and the pursuit settled into a race, with Zorro's wild black horse leading and gaining slowly. But there were good horses in the troop, too, that of Capitán Gonzales especially, and the pursuit hung on.

Zorro was racing across rough land to get to the highway, where the going would be better. His horse was laboring in the soft ground.

And suddenly he stumbled and fell, and Señor Zorro went over his head to land in the dirt.

CHAPTER XIII
Swift Pursuit

HE SPRANG up instantly. His horse was struggling to his feet, and Zorro called softly to him, and hurried toward him. The frightened animal drew back at first, and Zorro lost precious time coaxing him near enough so the reins could be grasped. He got up into the saddle again.

The pursuit had gained during all this, and was too close for comfort now. Another pistol was fired, and the ball came so near that Zorro caught himself flinching. He judged that would be all of the shooting. Those behind could not reload while they rode so madly after him.

He bent low over his mount's neck again, and raked with the spurs, and the big black responded with a wild burst of speed. Señor Zorro had in mind what he had to do, and now it seemed difficult of accomplishment, unless he could gain on them more.

He reached the highway and turned down it, and gained swiftly for a time, until those behind reached it also and could make better speed. He was riding toward Reina de Los Angeles, particularly the spot where Bernardo would be waiting.

As he neared it, he began shouting phrases which none but Bernardo would understand. Madly he raced around a curve, glancing back just before doing so and estimating the distance between him and his foe.

As he neared a jumble of rocks, somebody sprang out into the highway and waved his arms. Bernardo had heard him, and had obeyed.

Señor Zorro skidded the horse to a stop and sprang from the saddle.

"Mount! Ride on, furiously! Make your escape!" he ordered the native.

Bernardo sprang into the saddle, grasped the reins and kicked with his bare heels. The big black plunged onward. Zorro dropped behind the rocks.

Around the curve swept the pursuit, led by Capitán Gonzales. They raced past Señor Zorro's hiding place and continued after the black Bernardo was riding. Zorro darted across the highway and traveled swiftly through the shadows.

He came, in time, to the cluster of huts behind his father's casa, and went through the darkness along a wall and to the vine by which he had descended from the house. Grasping it, he began the ascent.

Half exhausted, panting, perspiring freely, he got to the window and pulled himself through. There had been no time for him to change from the habiliments of Zorro, and the mask was still concealing his face.

He reeled back against the wall, steadied himself, and began hurrying to his own quarters. From below came strains of music, ringing voices, feminine laughter. Possibly he had not been missed.

TEARING the mask from his face, he hurried along the corridor and let himself into his own room. A basin of water was waiting, and soft towels. He stripped off the clothing he wore, and hid it in a closet, deep beneath a heap of other things, and the weapons of Zorro with it.

Washing face and hands in the perfumed water, he dried them quickly, and swiftly dressed as he had been when the reception had started. His breathing had returned to normal now. He grasped a silk handkerchief, slipped quietly out of the room, went along the mezzanine, and descended the stairs.

Don Alejandro met him at the bottom.

"Where have you absented yourself, my son?" he rebuked. "Some have been looking for you."

Their eyes met, and Don Diego smiled faintly.

"I have been about. Perhaps they did not look in the right place," he said.

"They are dancing again in the patio. Perhaps you will find the Señorita Carmelita disengaged."

Don Diego Vega smiled again, and went out into the patio, where the Señorita Carmelita was waiting.

"I wait to see you dance El Sombrero," she told him.

"You'll honor me by dancing it with me?" he asked.

"If you like."

The music changed, and they danced. When it was over, and they had bowed in acknowledgment of the applause, Don Diego led her along the side of the patio toward a bench packed with cushions.

"For quite a time, I did not see you," the señorita said.

"It pleases me that you looked, and that I was missed."

"And then, quite suddenly, I saw you again," she went on, her voice lower and softer. "But you were not dressed as you are now, and you were taking a black mask from your face. But do not be disturbed, Don Diego. I am quite sure that I understand. The things Señor Zorro has done I approve of them. But he should not always court so much danger."

"Perhaps he would court it less, did he have heavy responsibilities, such as, say, the head of a family," Don Diego said, boldly.

There was a sudden tumult at the front of the casa, natives shouting in fright, men calling to one another, horses stomping. There came a thundering demand for entrance at the door. The guests, startled, ceased their merrymaking. Servants rushed to the big front door, but waited for the command of Don Alejandro to open it.

Don Alejandro took up a commanding position in front of it, gestured, and two natives pulled the massive door open slowly. Capitán Gonzales stood there, gripping Bernardo by the arm, and behind him was Sergeant Juan Ruiz and some of the troopers.

"What means this intrusion, Señor Capitán?" Don Alejandro demanded. "I am giving a reception here this evening, and you have startled my guests. You are the new officer in Reina de Los Angeles, are you not?"

"Is this fellow a servant of yours?" Gonzales demanded.

"He is body servant to my son, Don Diego."

"Ah, ha! So he is! Señor Zorro was abroad tonight, señor. We were chasing him. He was riding a big black horse. At a certain spot during the chase, he was obscured a moment. We continued chasing the horse, and caught him, and riding him was this man."

DON DIEGO drifted forward, brushing his nostrils significantly with his scented handkerchief.

"Pardon me, capitán," he said. "That horse, if it is the big black, is a spirited animal. I often have Bernardo exercise him in the cool of the evening, out on the highway."

"And where have you been all this night?"

Don Diego drew himself up stiffly. "Am I accountable to such as you for my comings and goings, señor?" he barked. "You affronted me at San Juan Capistrano, saying you had suspicion that I might be this Señor Zorro. Do not so affront me now, or I'll forget my station and do you the honor of matching blades with you. But it appears you have matched blades with somebody already. There are a series of cuts on your face, my capitán. Been playing in the briers, mayhap?"

"This fellow of yours would not answer questions I put to him."

Don Diego smiled. "For good reason. He is a dumb mute, and all in the town know it. He could not answer did he desire to do so."

"A convenient sort of servant to have sometimes," Gonzales hinted.

"I find him so. Pardon me, Capitán Gonzales, but it would please my father, I am sure, if you would take your uniformed ruffians elsewhere. I am quite sure that they, and you, have no business here."

Gonzales' eyes flashed. "Sooner or later, Don Diego Vega, we cross blades," he said. "I have a feeling that it is to be — or has been."

"If it has been," Don Diego observed, "you will not want to cross blades with me again. A cut on the face is bad enough, my capitán, however you received it. But a cut in the heart — ah, that is the finishing touch! Good night, capitán!"

"Good night!" Gonzales growled the words, and motioned for Ruiz and the men to retire. At the door, the capitán turned. "I grant you that this Señor Zorro is clever. But if he rides on, he will ride into trouble, and a rope."

"If I ever see him," Don Diego observed, "I'll tell him as much. No doubt you are correct. But from all accounts, he is a stubborn fellow — and something whispers to me that he will ride on, as long as there is need!"

Then Don Diego turned his back, and the big front door was closed, and Don Alejandro motioned for the musicians to resume their playing. Don Diego took the hand of Señorita Carmelita and tucked it inside his arm, and led her across the big room.

"There is a pleasant nook in the corner," he observed. "Señora Vallejo may watch us — from a distance. There has been so much turmoil tonight. Let us rest for a time in this cozy nook. I have just bethought me of another poem."

She looked up at him from a radiant face. "I shall be glad to hear it, Don Diego," she said.

"This poem is of my own poor manufacture, *señorita*. It has to do with a mysterious Don Miguel, who never existed, yet had his uses, nevertheless."

About the author

Johnston McCulley

The creator of Zorro, Johnston McCulley (1883-1958) was born in Ottowa, Illinois, and raised in the neighboring town of Chilicothe. He began his writing career as a police reporter and became a prolific fiction author, filling thousands of pages of popular pulp magazines. Southern California became a frequent backdrop for his fiction. His most notable use of the locale was in his adventures of Zorro, the masked highwayman who defended a pueblo's citizens from an oppressive government.

He contributed to popular magazines of the day like *Argosy*, *Western Story Magazine*, *Blue Book*, *Detective Story Magazine*, and *Rodeo Romances*. Many of his novels were published in hardcover and paperback. Eventually he branched out into film and television screenplays.

His stable of series characters included The Crimson Clown, Thubway Tham, The Green Ghost, and The Thunderbolt. Zorro proved to be his most popular and enduring character, becoming the subject of numerous television programs, motion pictures, comic books, and cartoon programs.

In the 1950s, McCulley assigned all Zorro rights agent to Mitchell Gertz. After retiring to Los Angeles, he died in 1958.

MORE ADVENTURE
AND ROMANCE IN VOLUME 3

The Complete PULP ADVENTURES by Johnston McCulley, Vol. 3

ZORRO

BOLD VENTURE
boldventuepress.com

On Sale September 2016!
The further adventures of the original
swashbuckling hero in his
original adventures!

ZORRO IS ACTION!
ZORRO IS ROMANCE!

The original swashbuckling hero in his original adventures by Johnston McCulley! Volume One is available now!

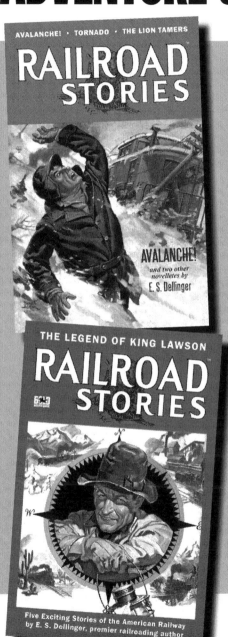

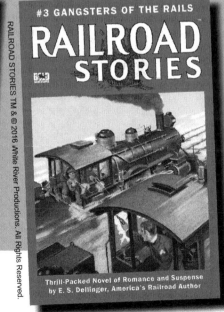

Made in the USA
Columbia, SC
20 August 2023